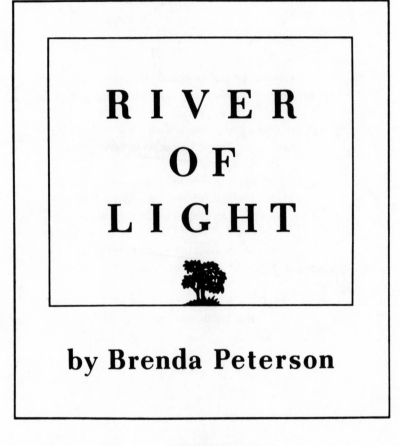

RIVER
OF
LIGHT

by Brenda Peterson

GRAYWOLF
PRESS

First published by Alfred A. Knopf, Inc., 1978.
First Graywolf paperback edition, 1986.

Grateful acknowledgment is due to the editor of the
Sewanee Review in which Chapter 1 was first published
under the title, "Days Pass Away Like Smoke."

ISBN 0-915308-89-4
Library of Congress Catalog Card Number 86-081783

Published by GRAYWOLF PRESS
Post Office Box 75006
Saint Paul, Minnesota 55175

To my Grandmothers Pauline, Virgie, Elsie,
Grandfathers Ralph, Harold –
who tell the stories
to Susan Efird and Susan Pelzer –
who helped me listen
for my parents, and for Pooh, Mosby, Dana Mark –
sisters, brother, my small tribe.

"Light I beheld which as a river flowed"
—Dante, Canto XXX, *Paradisio*

I would like to gratefully acknowledge
the help and kindness of Rachel MacKenzie,
my former teacher Diane Johnson, and
my editor Judith Jones.

CONTENTS

PART I

PROLOGUE

Lloyd Sloan had the sympathy of his family in the matter of his wife's barrenness, though his father, a dirt farmer, warned him off Nettie Mason. Lloyd's Scotch-Irish ancestors had single-mindedly settled this lush piedmont of north Georgia, calling it Jordan County and populating as if "Be fruitful, multiply and replenish the earth" were a personal commandment rather than an instinct for survival. But of the three Sloan children, Lloyd was the only son to share the fifty acres of rolling pasture, loblolly pines and white-oak woods, all bordering on the Yellow River bottom land that once grew cotton like sun weeds; his father fully expected grandsons so they would have enough hands to pay off the mortgage in his lifetime. He gave Lloyd the land but refused him a father's blessings on his marriage. "It's no good your hitchin up with that Mason lot. They ain't natural farmers and their land's the sorriest around. Look where the boll weevil lit down first, and look how long her brother, Ralph, spent pickin squares off his cotton whilst weevils ruint his crop. Now he's rentin his little sons out over Bailey's place.

No, they's beggarly, son, and ifn ye gang up with a Mason, she's gonna eat a hole right through you like them weevils."

"But Nettie's bettered herself!" Lloyd protested, "She keeps that family goin."

Nettie May Mason was a sturdy blonde who had finished two years in a women's college on a religious scholarship. For the past year she taught grades one through six in the schoolhouse down the road from her elder brother's house, where she and her younger sister and brother had been raised. Lloyd saw her almost every day of his life, from his field watching the eager schoolgirl who ran barefoot down the muddy back road, red feet slapping mud against her legs; and later Lloyd watched for her as he chided the mule to finish a row of cotton so he would be near the road and could pause, take off his hat, squint against the sun, and appear to wipe his brow, not court her, as the schoolteacher in long, wide skirts walked by hurriedly, her leather shoes tapping against the tar road like the cadence of a well-shod mare. "Never did see a woman so well fixed as Nettie," Lloyd kept after his father, "hipbones slung low and easy like a cradle. When she walks she's jist rockin along . . . rockin right along."

"Sure, she looks strong enough, but you got to want a woman for more than jist lingerin tween her legs, son. She ain't much in your fields; she's more a bookish gal, always had her sights set higher than correspondin with a Sloan."

"May be . . . ," Lloyd answered with a smile.

He and Nettie had not met in school, but in church; during the long Sunday afternoons they walked off a little way from the potluck supper tables to talk quietly. The town knew Nettie Mason as a good schoolteacher, if a little nervous and short-tempered with the older, truant boys. Outside the schoolroom she was silent. This to her family passed for a sign of wisdom and an even temper. But when Lloyd could find her alone, he saw Nettie laugh heartily, repeating to him the inaccurate and coarse stories she overheard from her sixth-graders; or in more somber moments, she read to him from the Bible and in a bemused, low voice confided her childhood desire to be a missionary to dark places. Lloyd spoke of his plans for bettering the two-mule farm: first, he would build his wife a small cabin on the land his father divided with him; then Lloyd would help pay off the mortgage while borrowing on his future crops to buy more fertilizer, plows, and a neighbor's used tractor. From the beginning Lloyd saw that the missionary part of his wife would not mind picking in the fields alongside her husband and a handful of Negroes working halves on Sloan land. And he would give Nettie enough sons and daughters to fill up her own house; she would not have to go to school to be with children.

Lloyd could not speak of his love for her without speaking of the land. "I never touch a woman mean" was his marriage proposal. "No more than I'd lay anythin but clean, strong hands on God's land; it all gives me back good."

Nettie listened closely, as if he were one of her gawky pupils reciting a lesson. Her eyes went first to his hands and then to her own. She studied her hands for a long time, thinking this man did not read half so well as her sixth-graders and his stocky body would not have the lithe feel of that lover she conjured up from books, the presence that lay beside her at night when she gathered the quilts and hard pillows against her belly and breasts, timid hands clasped instinctively between her legs, as she waited for sleep.

"You got your sights set on that Sloan feller," Nettie's little sister teased her one night. She and Nettie shared a double bed, bunching the quilts between them for a boundary. "Jist try and say it ain't so!"

"It's so," Nettie sat up and looked at her sister, not smiling, but slyly pursing her lips and reaching for a cigarette.

The sister wriggled her small nose and giggled. "Ohh, but he's red and short like an Injun and his beard's like scrub brush. Run your hand along that jaw and you git briars!"

Nettie ignored her, snuffing the cigarette out on the window sill.

"Yes'm," her sister tugged at the bedclothes and squealed with laughter. "I seen you wallerin round in his eyes, Nettie. . . ."

"Hush up, you gals!" the youngest brother in the next bed scolded.

"Nettie's fixin to join up with that Lloyd feller!"

"That so," he muttered and soon his rasping snore was the only sound in the room.

"It's so," Nettie whispered fiercely to his steady breathing as she settled into the gullies of the soft bed. "Never a man spoke so kindly or took such pains," and she moved far over on her side of the bed, leaving her little sister the familiar body of the comforter. The next morning the Mason sisters began piecing the bride's quilts and blue cotton dress that, along with one heifer, a complete set of Shakespeare and cast-iron skillets, the family Bible and a mail-order blue silk dress, was all the dowry she brought Lloyd.

Ten years later when the Depression forced Lloyd to take a second mortgage on his house, on his own land and the other half of the farm his father willed him, saying on his deathbed, "Son, lay down the tractor, cows, and next year's crop as collateral, but don't never look to raise anythin off Nettie Mason"; when cotton was bringing only five cents a pound and the river-bottom land was twice flooded by the Yellow River's spring moods; when the Negroes working halves left in droves for factories up North; when Nettie had suffered several miscarriages and stillbirths and could only perform the chore of milking the two surviving cows—the third cow that came as her dowry had been found dead three days before, her legs poking up from her swollen belly like four fence posts; when Lloyd fended off his kinfolks in town who worried over his marriage, Nettie gave birth to her first son, Ira.

"Got yourself a boy, Lloyd," the midwife hollered out to him as he stood in the kitchen, eyes fixed on the tea kettle's steam whistle. Wiping his hands on the back of his overalls, he bit off a fresh, bitter tobacco plug. First covering his mouth, Lloyd hesitantly entered the bedroom, but he kept his eyes on the floor. "Lloyd, quit! Quit lookin so croupy and come git hold your chile." He took the wrinkled, squalling baby in his wide arms. Jaw clenched, his mouth slack as if to speak, Lloyd suddenly grinned but his lips seemed stretched simply to rest his face from its constant, hard chaw. "Spit out that vile tobaccy, and don't dribble over this chile, he's slippery enough. Care now! Don't dare tetch his belly-band with them dirty fingers; you'll turn him black as tarbaby!"

Lloyd fumbled as the tiny legs kicked up at him, long wails coming in breathless spasms. "He'll rupture hisself sure, if he don't quit bawlin," Lloyd said, and the granny woman shook her head in exasperation.

"Shush him some, Lloyd Sloan. I got no time to fiddle with ye now," she leaned over the bed, her narrow back obscuring Nettie's face. Lloyd saw only a starched white mountain of sheets rising up from the bed, and he remembered this granny woman brought her own sheets with her to every birth. Anyone driving past her house knew she was a midwife by the three long clotheslines, all hung with sheets she had washed in alcohol and a homemade disinfectant that could be smelled brewing for miles away. Anyone who called on the midwife left feeling dizzy and breathless as if drunk off the fumes of her medicinal wash.

But when Lloyd looked up again from his snuffling child, he saw the snowdrift on his bed was fallen into the valley between his wife's raised knees, a pool of bright blood staining the sheets. Lloyd turned away. "There's no more where you come from, punkin," he hushed his child. The midwife looked up sharply, her fingers greased with a yellow salve. Lloyd saw his wife's breasts and sunken belly were covered with this same yellow ointment.

"Right smart of ye to notice, Lloyd," the midwife snapped. "You can see plain as day that somethin ain't good here. I seen it first when her labor stopped. Lawsy! Thought I'd never git her contraptions started in agin. I said, 'Nettie, nothun is born unless there's sufferin,' but she wouldn't budge none. I jist had to do half her natural work myself, reachin way up inside her, spreadin them bones, and practically dragged that chile out by his ears!"

"What's wrong?" Lloyd came near the bed, shifting the baby's weight to his shoulders and leaning over his wife. Nettie lay quietly, her eyes open, glancing past him to the window. "She's subject to die," Lloyd said and suddenly turned away.

"Don't be buryin her along with them rags and innards. She ain't goin nowhere but to sleep," the midwife gathered the bloody sheets in one arm and shook her head. "But she ain't stout, neither."

"Ain't been for a long time now. We spected trouble."

"Not so much birthin trouble . . ." The midwife pursed her lips and fell quiet for a moment. Finally she sighed, shrugging, "Reckon your woman's a bleeder, pure and simple; she bleeds like a stuck pig. Ifn I were supstitious, I'd git me a knife to put under her pillow and fix your axe under the bed,

blade lookin up at her. It do cut the hemorrhage consider-
able."

"You granny women always full of them pitiful supersti-
tions."

"Mebbe, Lloyd Sloan, but it don't take no conjurin to see
you'll need God's good luck. You'll have to mammy this chile
till Nettie mends."

"No ma'am," Lloyd said, "I'll git me a mammy proper ifn I
has to pluck her from my fields."

"Suit yourself, Lloyd. But do it quick, cause her spirit ain't
willin. And didn't nobody figure on no fever or meanness. I
got me a notion. . . ." She laid a finger to the side of her nose
and sniffed. "Mebbe she done catched that milksick."

"What you got is no good sense, Lizzie!" Lloyd snapped.
"That's them niggers you been messin with. They filled you
full of devilment!"

"No sir, I ain't been messin with no Devil. I'm workin for
the Lord!" She sniffed again. "And you better be glad, else
I'd charge you five dollars for this trip."

"Well, I'm glad to know the Lord gots money to pay ye,
Lizzie," Lloyd smiled briefly.

The midwife bristled and went out to fetch her satchel
and coat; she said, "This ain't no laughin matter, Lloyd. And
I sholy hope ifn ye don't got money, then you got some
whiskey hid cause Doc Varnon, he don't work for charity."

"Now, Lizzie," Lloyd protested, "you know damn well
ever time Nettie misfired . . ."

"Miscurried."

"Ever time my wife done missed and lost her chile, you
and Doc Varnon both been here and weren't nothun to do,
he says, but let her git shut of that bad baby by bleedin.
You'uns jist stood around till she dried up and then that Doc
charges me ten dollars more than I got to give."

"You got your chile, Lloyd Sloan," the midwife said quietly, "but you ain't got much left of your wife."

Lloyd looked down at the floor for a moment, then said, "Git that drunkard over here, Lizzie."

"I can fetch him back here before nighttime. Now, you give that chile some black-snakeroot-and-rattleweed tea. I brung my own mix to break the hives out. And keep dosin Nettie with castor oil. I'll be back before dark with Doc Varnon."

"What bout the feedin?"

"I'm fixin to stop by Mammy Nelda's and git her to come nurse. She's got more milk than a cow's teats and it's sweet. You'll have to go some to find a better mammy for nursin two chiles . . . one a growed woman." The midwife took Ira from his father and swaddled him in some old quilts, then laid the child on the bed near his mother. Nettie made no move. Lizzie gathered her things into the clean bag and went to the door. "Best bury them bloody sheets, Lloyd, but way out back where you don't never want to grow nothun."

"Now, wait . . ." Lloyd followed her to the wagon where her mule waited, its ears cocked for the old woman's voice. Lloyd studied the mule, then the ground, and when he finally looked at her, it was with a pale recognition. "You know somethin, don't ye? You know what's ailin Nettie!"

The midwife considered a moment. "We best bide our time and wait on Doc Varnon."

"But you know somethin!"

"Now, Lloyd, all I seen was somethin not right with her mind." She paused, opened her mouth, then thought better of it. She looked at Lloyd closely, pursing her lips and nodding to herself.

Lloyd reached for the mule's harness and held the animal in check. "What? Did she talk on foolish? Nettie always spoke strange; why, that ain't nothun!" He let go of the mule and turned away, but at the door he paused and said very quietly, "She went on bout me, didn't she? I never laid a hand on that woman, no more than I lay a mean hand . . ."

"Come up," the midwife said and her mule's ears trembled, then lay flat back as it refused to budge.

"Say what, Lizzie?"

"I was talkin here to my mule," the midwife spoke resignedly, "but ifn I was to talk to ye like I do to a creature ain't got no sense, I'd say that woman in there figures she's as good as dead; it liked to kilt her but she did her chore by us all."

"Did she say that?" Lloyd demanded. "Did she call down my name that way?"

"No, Lloyd," Lizzie's voice was hushed, "she didn't say nothun a'tall that would make sense to this mule."

"You know, I never . . . ," Lloyd began.

"I know. It were only the sickness talkin," the midwife sucked her cheeks in and let out a clucking sound like the noise women make in pity or exasperation. "Come up, now. Come up, Mattie mule!" and to Lloyd, "She'll have the bloody flux for the comin day; I'll send Mammy soon. And, Lloyd . . . don't lissen to nary a word from Nettie. Ifn I were supstitious, I'd burned them bloody sheets myself, what for all the cussin, and it weren't jist when the labor tetched her, neither. Come up, durn your hide!" The mule bolted away so fast Lloyd was surprised that the frail woman still had hold of her reins.

All that night Lloyd spent by his wife's bedside, listening and praying, longing for her punishing voice or God's wrathful tongue, so lacerating one could not bear understanding though it came from the most primitive depths of his own memory: that moment of birth when he felt his own burning breath for the first time and screamed out against the light, shouting for the lost silence where sound had been a heart's

muffled rhythm and now all was tainted with the meaningless exaltation of strangers and his own instinctive crying.
But neither God nor the woman lying with her eyes half
open against the dark spoke to Lloyd, moved him or explained the vengeance against his family and land. In the
early morning came his son's hungry screeching. Lloyd let
him wail on until the roosters crowed and he heard the
mammy enter the house, waiting for him in the kitchen.

"Mornin, Mr. Sloan."

"I'll be out the pasture," Lloyd said as he went past her,
"where you should be, too. I need all the hands I can lay
eyes on."

In her bedroom Nettie lay awake, her face pale and heavy,
feverish eyes watching the mammy who sat now rocking in
one corner of the room, mumbling and singing absent-
mindedly to the baby at her breast.

"I can nurse my child," Nettie said quietly.

"Nevemine," Nelda said to the child as she rocked. The
mammy was a frail yellow woman, thinner than Nettie, and
her eyes were vigilant, even when she looked at the child.
"You rest up and be strong soon."

"No," Nettie whispered fiercely, "No!"

Nelda gingerly put Ira down in one drawer of the chest
where Nettie had long ago laid quilts and some felt pieces
for want of a cradle. The two women eyed one another a
moment, then the mammy took up a basin and lactating cup.
She drew back the comforter and gently fixed the cup to
Nettie's nipple. The white fullness heaved and fell back flat-
ter each time Nelda pressed the suction cup; she kept up a
steady rhythm, watching carefully as the thin milk splattered into the cold porcelain bowl. Only once or twice did
the mammy look at Nettie, but when she did she saw the
woman's face relaxing, eyes closed as the tears fell easily
down her sharp cheeks.

"Shhh, now, shhhh . . ." The mammy's voice was diffident. "It feels good."

"Shhhh," the yellow woman's voice was suddenly gentle, "course it do, honey; it's good, sweet milk."

"There's sickness in it!" Nettie shifted violently and the suction cup slipped off her breast. Glaring, she pulled the quilt up to her chin. With a certain severe gentleness common to midwives, Nelda drew down the covers and fixed the lactating cup on a bit tighter and pressed. Nettie turned her head, staring out the window as her milk flowed from her fallen teats.

She did not seem to notice when the doctor came into her bedroom. After a few moments with his stethoscope, tongue depresser, gold watch, and his curious, rapping fingers, he banished everyone from the room. A long while later Doc Varnon came into the kitchen and joined Lloyd in a drink.

"Must be the typhoid fever, Lloyd. That's all I can figure," he took three long swallows and frowned. "That's what made her pregnancy so hard. Well, I'll do what I can."

"Meanin you wait like the rest of us fools!" Lloyd spat. This past month of watching for Nettie's delivery Lloyd had let his chores go, and his land had taken on the parched, furtive look of his face.

"Which means I'll wait, yes," Doc said. "Like Nettie's waitin."

II

Every dawn Nettie Sloan now lifted her great, swollen weight from bed, as resignedly as the sun hoisted itself from heavy clouds. In the dark in-between light she moved, slower than a blind woman, groping for the bureau, banging her shins against the credenza, its shelves shuddering, chipped glass bric-a-bric tinkling in the delicate quiet of her farmhouse. In the parlor she rested on a round, sunken hassock. It was as if she had spent her whole life simply moving from chair to chair, never seeming to walk, only to ease her way, lumbering along, her whole body feeling, sidling up to shapes into which she might settle. Often she wedged her wide hips between a sofa and chair to keep upright. To see her making her way to the kitchen was to watch time itself.

In the kitchen Nettie would take a large, dented milk pail and trudge out to the barn. Behind her the screen door always slammed twice; this sharp sound woke her husband every morning; he tossed about to free his legs from the knotted, humid bedsheets, hollering, "Rise and shine, son! Them chores don't git done lyin down." In the next room Ira pulled on his boots and stumbled around, stark naked, looking for a shirt less dirty than the others.

"I'll rise," he called back through the thin wall, always delighted with their ritual, "but I won't shine!" When Lloyd and his son had fed the pigs, fetched well water, and made strong coffee, Nettie was just finishing milking their sole surviving cow. She carried the milk pail into the house, handle chafing her skin raw; then she put the morning milk through a separator and made a fresh batch of biscuits, before retiring to her chair by the window. By the time Ira and Lloyd spread thick, sweet sorghum on their homemade biscuits, Nettie had rolled her own cigarettes for the day, and when her husband and son finished their breakfast, Nettie had smoked ten of the short, gum-sealed cylinders, one hand moving in an even rhythm to light another cigarette from the one already in her mouth. Then that hand would fly back to the bunched-cloth hollow of her lap. She flicked the ashes into one palm, then sifted the fine dust through her fingers.

A delicate skein of thin white air spread over her contempla-tive face, like the veil of a Sunday church hat. Swirling, the gray smoke settled like fog in her deep-set eyes. She listened with these eyes as if against the dark; she saw signs and revelations in the silences. During her meditations she might start up from her chair, startled by some inner vision. But when she straightened, her head jolting above smoke clouds, this illumination was replaced by the view from her win-dow—the macadam road's dark mosaic of broken stones and smooth tar, the gambrel barn and broken spikes of ma-chinery slouched against it; Lloyd's Leghorns flapping in the dirt yard. Beyond this were acres of undulant red mud that the day's heat shimmered over.

Nettie's face had a loose hold on its features; flesh and cheekbones sank inward, like land sliding into its own faults, burying skin in a striated softness that gave her jowls and neck the yielding contours of early age. Her body was gen-erous and sculpted and her legs sturdy, straight as the wood chair's across which the bulk of her body was slung, sagging like old bedding.

Lloyd Sloan said he remembered: Nettie's fingers were brittle, broken at the wrinkles in her knuckles. These tiny white cracks caught cow juices and ragged slits of tobacco. Ira Sloan remembered: His mother smelled of hot, pungent milk and sweet smoke. But no one knew what Nettie re-membered.

That barn always smelled of her deepest privacies, the bitter stench of rumination and the humid memories that come back to her here as she squats in the dried dung, in the damp, scratching hay-strewn crib, her head resting against the warm, shuddering hide as the cow lows, wide nostrils blowing, tail swishing idly as if this woman's hair against her flanks were a horsefly or a bird's wing. "Sooooo now . . . sook-

sook-sook-sooky . . . ," Nettie sings, and the beast's breath comes back, a humid smell like clabbered milk. The cow's great jaws work sideways, cracking feed between rotted teeth—the honeyed smell of oats and raw corn, the ferment of hog swill and much-swallowed silage as the cow buries her smooth muzzle in the bucket and comes up, mouth dribbling a frothy spittle. A deep, troubled bellow and the Guernsey cow lifts her hooves urgently. Familiarly Nettie feels for the udder, fingers drawing down the warm, swelling teats. Inside the cow's belly Nettie hears a rumbling in the second stomach, as if the moon's gravity is moving her milk back and forth, a murmuring sea of white foam; hissing, this sea spews out against the cool inside of the tin bucket, a thin milky-yellow pooling in the bottom, rising with the strong, soothing pull of Nettie's hands. "Soooo . . . sook-sook-sook-sook-sooky-sooooo . . . ," she comforts her, "Shh, we can nurse our child," and the Guernsey's fawn-colored hide shudders against her cheek. Nettie milks to the tempo of a song, saved from her own childhood, but she has never sung it to her son. Singing in a pure, high pitch, keening,

> Lu La Lu La Lu La Lu La Lu Lu
> Underneath the silver, southern moon
> Rockabye, hushabye Mammy's little baby
> Mammy's little Alabama coon

The cow's ears lie back, twitching, her muzzle lifted once or twice from the feed as Nettie's long fingers pull the song from deep inside her memory as if the cow were a bellows, a wind-filled bag instrument that makes this woman's voice.

> This your little Alabama coon
> Ain't been born a very long

They's a gonna christen him very soon
His name's gonna be Henry Long
Someday he'll wear a yellow gown
And have pickaninnies of his own
This rockabye, moaner on my bosom
He'll sing my song,
He'll coooooooo

As the sun poured through cracks in the hayloft Nettie would feel fever in her thighs and temples; she struggled for breath against the sharp, knotted pain in her belly. Only by habit would she remember there was a chore to finish. She lumbered through the barn and back across the pasture, pausing every three steps to get a better grip on the razor-edged pail handle that bit into her fingers.

Crossing the field, she might suddenly begin to hurry, thinking she was late for another chore. The milk sloshed as she ran, spilling over her bare toes, and Nettie remembered: It was years since she'd taught school.

The children in her one-room schoolhouse had faces like hers, soft and white, dazed by the heat. Their eyes asked the same mute questions. Why do we have chores? Why must we milk the mammy cow? Why does she holler in pain when we come near? And Nettie told them a story: The Lord God made earth to bring forth cattle and creeping things. Then there were no chores. The cow was milked by her children, just as the sky nursed the earth with rain and dew. But when God made man and woman they forgot themselves, having no memories of how things were before them. They made myths: The cow was once a beautiful woman whose love was stolen away by a god. For fear that his wife would see his betrayal, the god caused a misting night to fall over the earth and transformed the woman into a beautiful cream-colored cow. The cow could not speak her sorrow, except to make a moaning moo and to move her great, sideways mouth, chewing over the words; no one, not even her father or lover, recognized her lament. Wandering the ends of the world, bellowing, she never again trusted sleep, never lay down when the sky turned dark and cool. And now to look in her singed black eyes, you saw she had only the dimmest memory of a beautiful woman she had swallowed along with her sorrows.

It was a child's first duty to milk the cow, for only a child still believed the woman's past; and when you laid your ear against her belly it was to hear that dumb, ceaseless sea of sorrow moving inside. Her eyes reflected your own mute expectation as you listened with your fingers, drawing out her stories from the hot, rich misery that every child nursed on.

Nettie Sloan remembered the birth of the heifer's calf more clearly than the birth of her own child. It was August, a night as searing and quiet as her own deep fever. Outside, the men waited behind shrubs that divided the cow pasture. When she woke suddenly and looked out her window, she could see shadows running across the field, their lanterns swinging like falling stars. Soon she was running, too, out of the house, her hands locked underneath her belly, cradling the kicking burden. She could not tell who was laughing the loudest, herself from deep inside or the child that waited there, rocking with each step as she made her way to the pasture. All the stars had gathered in the center of the field, and the men were yelling. But she did not go to them. Far away from the lights, Nettie made out a shape standing very still, tail lifted up, swishing. She found her cow by following the sound of her panting breaths. "Soooo . . . sook-sook-sook-sook-soooo," Nettie began, but stopped when she came close.

The cow's flanks were covered in a dark froth, hind-quarters stiff with dried blood, the tail still held straight up in the air as if lashed to an invisible pole. But there was another tail, this one hanging down to the ground—a slime thick and knotted, half transparent in the moonlight. This afterbirth sloughed out of her like a slow-clotting, endless waterfall of blood until Nettie thought she would lose her innards. The men were swearing from across the field, their meaningless curses rising and falling like the stars they swung from their hands, as Nettie reached for her cow, burying her face in the damp, matted neck. Clinging, shushing her cow with wordless song, she did not hear the men yelling as they jammed their knives back into the sheaves. Many eager hands lifted the newborn calf from its muddy sack, holding it up on frail, wobbling legs. Someone called out, "Got a heifer calf, Lloyd."

"Lord, I thought her stillbore; oh, my good Lord," Lloyd laughed and gently slapped the wet flanks.

It was only then that one of them swung his lantern toward the cow across the field, illuminating a woman, her eyes glazed over. All stars fell on her suddenly—these same stars on which she had wished for a son—blinding her in a circle of voices.

"God in heaven! Lloyd, this cow's dead . . . deader than a plank of wood, and still standin!"

Lloyd ran to the cow, pulling his wife away. "Git her in the house!" Someone half dragged Nettie, hands under her armpits so that she rested in the air on her back, watching behind her as the men pushed and shoved against the cow; it fell over on its back, legs straight in the air. They buried her heifer in its own muddy black afterbirth.

Several days later Nettie woke with blunt, tearing pains in her belly. She did not remember the hours of labor, the soft hushing of the midwife, or the moment when her screams became those thin, mewing sounds of her son. She remembered only the fever and the chilling blackness; it lingered still in the corners of her eyes. At first Lloyd had thought Nettie's continuing weakness after Ira's birth was natural, the woman's sorrow that sloughed out of her like an afterbirth. But when the doctor arrived and Nettie was still feverish, lost in delirium, Lloyd knew she had left him for good. Doc Varnon diagnosed typhoid and set Mammy Nelda to steal Nettie's milk—this milk that was meant to nourish her child in her mysteries, to lend him the memory of her wanderings.

Just as Nettie's milk was taken from her, so the rearing of her son was given over, first to the mammy, who stayed on as cook and housekeeper, then to the church women; they formed a missionary circle and set about the task of tidying and converting Nettie's son as if he were the most unregenerate, far-flung pagan. Nettie had never recovered from her fever. She never spoke to anyone enough to tell whether her mind was singed or just ruined in certain places like a burned house whose attic and basement are untouched while the stories inside are all unsettled, creaking and hanging on a single unsure rafter. Nettie seemed a child now, with only a child's chore—to milk the cow before retiring to her window for the day.

During the past five years Lloyd fought off his wife's illness with a grief more tender and consuming than his first love for her. But as she drew farther and farther away from him, becoming alien and fanciful in a way that the schoolteacher in her would have dismissed as stubborn and truant, Lloyd felt his heart harden. This was an intruder who haunted the body of his wife. He was vigilant against Nettie's new personality and struggled to remember a time when he embraced her without doubt. After four years Lloyd watched Nettie with the same stricken but expectant look that he wore staring out across his weary, new-ploughed land.

But Ira saw his mother differently, through a child's charms and conjures. The fever had left Nettie with a new-born's wonder. Her son, suddenly coming upon her in his wanderings, found in his mother a mysterious plaything, endlessly intriguing. Her solitude to him was a curious and mute complicity in his own make-believe. Sometimes he brought her wildflowers and weeds; they sat on her bed, making matted necklaces for the animals. From the corners of her room, her son caught ants and spiders which he dissected carefully with an earnest, startled look that marked all his play. Together they heaped up piles of dust and made their breath the North Wind, scattering tiny hurricanes into the air. His mother did not seem to mind when he found trinkets and wrapped them around her wrists and ankles with twine. Certain days of the year Ira and Nettie declared holidays and made one another gifts that they exchanged with great ceremony—lighting homemade candles, eating a fruit pie apiece, chanting blessings in a made-up language of hoots, horrays, hisses, and punctuated with bird calls Ira invented: the swallow, mockingbird, and crow. They rigged up a string bass with a tub and catgut strung to a broomstick and Ira played metallic runs up and down the washboard, brass bolts fit over his knuckles. Then came the exchange of gifts: Ira presented his mother with a spit-shined bronze bell that she wore on a cowhide string around her neck, hanging over her heart. Every morning Ira woke to her bell's rhythmic clanging as she moved through the house. Nettie gave her son a brown, wrinkled photograph that smelled of tobacco and stale lavender sachet from the drawer where she had hidden it. Here the camera had caught a young girl, only slightly older than he was now, striding up a dirt path, her plaid skirts catching on blackberry briars. On a splintered poke she was toting blues and catfish; her arms, long hair, and blouse were covered with wet fish scales. They glistened, translucent in the sunlight like a hundred silver eyes, watching and winking as she called out for someone to come fishing with her. The photo was too old and creased for Ira to make out her expression, but he thought his mother smiled vaguely.

As Ira Sloan grew older he put aside his treasures and playthings, forgetting what days were his mother's special holidays as he roamed outside farther and farther away, digging in the dirt and watching the tireless birds. He returned to the house only out of hunger, to be fed the morning's leftovers by a church-woman neighbor. By the time he was five years old Ira had acquired a certain patience with his mother, born of habit and the hope that one day she might discover she was healed. But she showed no signs or stirrings of new life.

At last Lloyd came to see his wife's implacable solitude as a deep negligence that perhaps every woman was born with, but which most fought off as if taking a broom to spider webs. Lloyd knew that most women swept earthen floors until the dirt was clean; they scrubbed clothes as if each stain were a bad memory they must protect a child from wearing on his back; they cooked and sang loudly but off-key in the choir and gathered together to piece quilts from ragged clothing that was soiled with memories. No one knew their solitude until one day an old woman would look around her with a certain awe and spy the invisible spider webs gathering around her head, razor-sharp silk cutting wrinkles in her face; she would stand her broom in the cor-

ner and take to bed, shrouding herself in many quilted
memories, saying she was tired and must rest now, undisturbed. Nettie was like this, Lloyd reasoned, only she had
begun to prepare for her old age ever since she did her child-
birthing chore by him.

After Nettie's second bout with typhoid fever, she was so
deep in her make-believe even her small son could not follow.
For Ira she existed only to milk her cow and make biscuits;
but still he woke to her shuffle in the mornings, listening as
she moved through the house; the clinging smell of her
smoke reached his room and he would turn over, furiously
beating a nest in the feather mattress so he might sleep again.

Suddenly Nettie's last chore ended. Ira woke one morning
to the startling absence of sound—no shuffling feet, no
clanging milk pails, no creaking protest of sofa springs, nothing but the sparrows squabbling against the darkness. Ira
waited, listening with his eyes closed. When he opened them
again, the sun was on his face. Never had he been in bed
squinting against the daylight unless he were sick. For a
moment he wondered if he were ailing; but as soon as he
threw off the heavy comforter his fever was gone. He heard
men's voices coming from the far pasture. Running across
the rutted ground, the child drew up short when he heard
his father calling, "Iry, Iry . . . get on back to the house!" and
one of the men said, "Reckon, he's come this far, Lloyd."

"Here, son," Lloyd called out, his arms open. He held Ira's
head against his belly. Ira fixed his eyes on the shiny tin
buttons that hung on his father's shirt, catching glints from
the sun. "Now look ye good."

In one of her languid, rambling talks Ira had learned from
his mother that you named things by numbers. Now, as he
looked on the other side of the long, deep trench, he tried to
count; but he did not have enough names for the many cows

grazing at the edge. Some cows lifted their heads, but most kept nibbling the short grass. The men raised their rifles, took deep sighs, and fired. Ira lost his ears to the choking noise, his eyes to gunsmoke. The hoarse braying and bawling ceased as suddenly as the gunfire as cows toppled over one another into the trench, their glazed eyes alive with buzzing horseflies. They had that same amazed look that Ira had always seen in his mother when she sat by her window. She, too, gave off smoke and a singed smell like the rifles and stiff cows. She, too, lay around with her eyes open, even when she slept, which is what his father told him the cows were doing now. Sleeping and grazing on the good, high grasses of heaven.

Ira was not frightened nor did he weep as his father did, leaning on another man's shoulders. After a while Lloyd picked up a shovel and heaved dirt over the stench that rose out of the grave as thick as if the heat were cow spirits rising into the sky to form clouds. That summer Ira Sloan began believing that the sky was simply an underbelly belonging to a great cow. She bellowed that fright and thunder, wailing to let go all her white rain like good milk from clouds, these soft, hanging udders. This was the smell he remembered, that humid urgency of the sky. It followed you everywhere and there was nothing to do but wait on God; it was He who now milked His sky, did His chores by her. Only He knew the timing and what earth needed her warm white rain.

Ira's father explained it to him differently. He said that the cow's milk was full of poisons and if a child drank it he took the fever, too, like the cow, like his mother. It had taken Doc Varnon all four years since Ira's birth, since the death of not only Lloyd's three cows but every other cow for thirty miles around, to figure out what ailed Nettie Sloan. At first it seemed coincidence, but as more cows died of bovine abortion and more women came down with the same fever he had diagnosed as typhoid in Nettie, Doc Varnon called in a county health official. They tested Lloyd's and his neighbors' cows and finally Nettie Sloan herself. Doc Varnon's worst suspicions were confirmed: undulant fever. The brucellosis was still thick in Nettie's bloodstream. Doc Varnon sent away for the proper medicines and vaccines, and all recovered except Nettie. "It's jist triggered what sorrow she's always carried in her, Lloyd," the doctor explained. "She's sacrificed herself over to this sickness somethin fierce." Even when he could find no traces of the undulant fever in her blood, Nettie Sloan did not get well.

THE LAND

By 1935 Lloyd could no longer keep up mortgage payments on the part of his father's land willed him shortly before Ira's birth, and he lost this acreage, half of all he owned, to the town's bank. They could not extend him more credit, they said, when Lloyd came to sign the foreclosure papers; Lloyd was a bad risk in bad times.

These years since Nettie's fever, he had staggered under the weight of his family's debts, and without proper supplies and field labor, the farm was failing. "Lord, my Lord!" Lloyd swore each summer as he surveyed rows of corn, stunted and weedy for lack of good guano and rainfall, or as he bent over his spindly vegetables, using his jagged thumbnail to slit open a pea pod, scooping the dried green pebbles out with his front teeth, chewing them, then spitting the peas on the ground, wiping his lips of their sour, chalk taste. "That blight on Nettie might as well be the boll weevil over me! She ruint this Sloan land, sure as I see it go raggedy and rooty. My soil's so poor it like to grunt sproutin peanuts!"

Now the bank was demanding full payment on the mortgage for the other half of his land, due this coming spring.

Mebbe it don't matter no more, Lloyd sometimes thought. *That damn bank can come fetch every fistful of stingy mud and ifn they care to—let them take this wore-out patch of misery straight to the Devil hisself!* Let the bank hoard it all. Let the monkey-suited moneylenders strip it for copper; let the factory bosses witch around for wells and then dig deeper pits, those red earthen cellars that passed for company shacks; let them violate it, scar its rude and thirsty face until his land was punished beyond recognition. Then, as now, when Lloyd walked the land he had lost, it would be like staring at the estranged face of a dead aunt and hating her; her death sealed off a part of himself Lloyd had never known—his beginnings.

As a child, before he recognized himself as separate from other shapes of land or flesh, Lloyd was rooted in the memories of these aged womenfolk. The land, like the women, was an earthen storehouse for Lloyd's stories; he lived off them until the women grew so near the unknown spaciousness of death that they could no longer separate stories of Lloyd's beginnings from their own. The women and land withdrew from Lloyd, were dirt and story-poor. At last he buried the ungiving women in the stingy, plowed earth. But the child in Lloyd survived—the now rootless and unknown part of himself wandered. Every time he worked his land or loved a woman Lloyd plundered his own past, desperate for the part of himself hidden there.

"It do give me back good," Lloyd always said, though the sun singed his crops or the river flooded his fields. "Dammit, it'll give me back the good I give it!" Abandoning his anger, Lloyd walked back through his straggling fields, kicking up dirt clods with his boot; when he reached his cabin he al-

ways added, "God willin," because Lloyd realized now that
he didn't own his land. If the bank men stole it, the land
would not belong to them, either. It was the other way
around. Lloyd swore he would explain this to the bank, putting it not in dirt-farmer's words but in words any man, even
one who covets money, might understand. Losing your land
is like losing a woman, he would tell them; but no, Lloyd
finally admitted, it was worse—a man who lost his land lost
his memory.

"I'll swear to git that mortgage cash come spring," Lloyd
told his friend at the farm-supply store when he came for an
advance loan on his next crop. "I already asked them bank
bastards, but they don't understand my proposition like ye
do. Why, hell, you seen Sloan land give! Remember when
my pa hauled in so much cotton to the gin, he made half the
big farmers in the county wait all day?"

"You ain't your father, Lloyd. Cotton's worth nothun ifn
the factories close down."

"I ain't beggin, Sherl, but . . ."

"You know I'm bound to say no, this year leastways."

"I'm gone to hell and back before I beg agin!" Lloyd spat
and strode out to his truck.

"Here now, Lloyd! Take a few sacks of guano ifn . . ."

"Ifn I don't got my land, might as well dump that shit on
ye!"

Finally, Lloyd gave up trying to borrow and took a winter
job as a knitter in one of the few mills around that still did
business. He hoped to work in the hoisery mill until spring
when he could quit, pay off the bank, and, with the leftover
factory earnings, hire or persuade Mammy Nelda's sons and
cousins on the neighboring shares to help him break new
ground for sowing. He dared not think there might be no
spring planting, just as he dared not look at the men around

him in the mill—men who had never owned land or, if they once did, had now forgotten its hold. *These lintheads,* Lloyd thought, when he finally brought himself to stare at their faces; their work was as meaningless and futile as trying to hang mid-air. *They act like spiders,* Lloyd thought, *spiders spinnin their own webs. But they's really like flies goin by and gettin caught up, eaten alive.* The lintheads didn't seem to feel as smothered as Lloyd did when bent over the machines, eyes clicking in time to the jumping, barbed needles; he felt the silken, fine mesh stretch around under and above him, stealthily cutting his skin like that airy angel hair children hung from pine trees at Christmas. Jumping up, he waved his hands wildly as if to fend off the cloying cobweb woven around his face, and he closed his eyes, catching the fine mesh in his lashes, his mouth and nose. Soon Lloyd began hating these lintheads who were proud to be dangling from the sheerest, most fragile threads of life, caught in this silken web that they spun from their own sweat and spittle. Lloyd might have endured the mill's monotony, its deafening lull and almost hallucinatory dimness, if not for the noise that was not mechanical—those steady, urgent shouts from the foreman and the bitter silence of the workers. It was a silence that grew heavier and louder until Lloyd knew someone must break its hold. But it was never broken at the mill, only at night, when the men gathered in open fields. Then Lloyd heard what during the work day all eyes and hands had whispered.

"There's a great, undiscussable change comin!" one of the union organizers promised at the first meeting in mid-February. He had worked in the mill almost as long as he had been alive. That night he passed around union cards. A few men made their marks quickly and proudly while others looked around, waiting for their wives and children to take the cards; then, hopelessly, these men shook their heads and gruffly demanded a card. Without signing they called their families home for a council. Lloyd left this secret meeting early and without signing, but a familiar voice caught him as he stepped out of the circle of quiet men.

"Where ye gone so fast?"

Lloyd swung around to find Ralph Mason, Nettie's younger brother, watching him uneasily. He knew his wife's kin had forsaken farming for mill work but he didn't realize they worked the same factory. *How'd I miss this critter?* Lloyd wondered and then decided it was because all the men, himself and his in-laws included, must have taken on the same sullen, faceless look in their assembly lines. Sometimes when he saw his own image reflected in the machine's metal mirror, he hadn't recognized himself; it was like staring in a grotesque funhouse mirror, the kind they rigged up in county fairs.

"I'm gone home," Lloyd said dryly and walked farther away from the gathering. Ralph followed. Lloyd took note of the expression in his brother-in-law's eyes, the "wildcat-strike fever" folks called it; but to Lloyd those eyes—the ashen-gray iris within whose circle danced orange flecks like sparks thrown from a dying fire—did not reflect the excitement of the union battle so much as the mad eyes of his wife at the exact moment before Nettie's fevers broke. "Where *you* should be, Brother Ralph," Lloyd added more gently, seeing his woman's eyes go out, as if doused by tears.

Ralph stared in that dull, driven way of all lintheads, especially all Masons. "You ain't joinin?"

"What's a farmer doin gittin heavy with linthead unions? Do I need a blame card to work my land?"

"Hell, you bout lost that sorry farm, and we need ye to come."

"I say, got crops and family need me more!" Lloyd spat on the ground and wiped his face with the back of his sleeve. "One of them neediest is that sister of yourn. Might as well signed away my life's blood when I hitched up with her." Silently, Ralph looked down. "And I don't right recollect you and your brother runnin over to join *my* union when Nettie's bills come hard on me. I don't remember you payin no dues then!"

"Ain't Nettie lost your farm."

"Ain't it?" Lloyd demanded hotly.

"Oh, now, Lloyd . . . you jist like us. We ain't farmers neither, we . . ."

"I ain't got a drop of blood in my body resembles ye or your kind! And ifn I did I'd open me a vein so wide and let her bleed so long, when they buried me a body'd think I give the dirt her bloody color!"

Ralph was quiet for a moment, then asked, "How is she? . . . How is my sister?"

"Tolerable, for the time bein," Lloyd shrugged and shook his head. "Ifn I'm not with ye in this mill union, it's cause I got to have money soon, you see?"

Ralph stared at him, then grudgingly nodded.

"Good. Now you want a ride home?"

"Reckon not."

Lloyd walked away, but behind him heard Ralph kicking at the rocks and gravel. Lloyd imagined those gray eyes burning holes in his back the size of bullets—Mason eyes, the color of gunmetal. Like all Masons, Ralph had a violent temper; several years ago he almost killed a man, a bill collector. *Nettie's jist as dangerous in her own way*, Lloyd thought, and kept walking.

"Just don't do nothun agin us, Lloyd Sloan!" Ralph yelled after him.

"Who's us?" Lloyd demanded. "You talkin bout lintheads, kinfolk, or union? Mebbe you talkin bout Masons? Well, son, it ain't me sinned agin Masons." Before the boy answered, Lloyd swung up into his truck and was gone.

The next month was March, the deadline for Lloyd's mortgage payment; but he had saved barely half the money. In desperation Lloyd let Mammy Nelda go, needing her desperately in his fields. Nettie was still able to do a few chores around the cabin—milking the cow and light cooking—but caring for Ira was too much. Some of the church women, hearing of their needs, organized a babysitting and quilting-bee circle out at the Sloans' farm. Now every morning before the mill opened, Lloyd, Nelda, and her two boys worked to break up new ground for planting; Lloyd rode the tractor, Nelda guided the scraper hitched to a borrowed mule, and the two boys worked behind her, hacking the frozen ground with hoes they bought themselves.

One morning a little past dawn Lloyd began his plow work, but when it came the usual time for him to quit, wash up, and drive over to his mill job, he made no motions to go. Instead, he ordered his hands across the road and down a few miles to the old land that had lain fallow since he lost it to the bank last winter. Except for a neighbor's compost heap, a half-acre of stumps left from the bank's selling the pine for timber, and lush kudzu as intimate and deadly as any stranglehold, Lloyd's rolling land was just as he remembered it last season.

"When my cousin's boys come to work here they ain't gonna know we's workin your old field," Nelda began, then stopped in her tracks on the dirt road. "Sides, Lloyd Sloan . . . this ain't your land no more, no how! And you gonna be late for the mill!"

"Dammit, Nelda! You git your ass and that mule over here

to plow where I say or I'll beat the cow-walkin hell out . . . !"

"Bank men gonna hear bout this."

"Who's tellin them?"

"Reckon they got eyes in their heads!"

"That's a heap sight more than I'm gonna have ifn I stay in that damn mill!" Lloyd got down from his tractor seat and came over to stand near her. Raising his fist, he stopped chewing his tobacco, "I swear I ain't never beat a woman before, but I'm aimin to commence ifn . . ."

"Hear Nettie mouthin, why . . . you jist mis- and half-treated her!" Nelda clucked to her mule and moved off down the field.

"Hell, you know my wife's crazy!" Lloyd grabbed Nelda's wrist and swung her around to face him. For a long while he stared at her, his jaw slack. Finally he let go and the two moved down the rutted field, each with a hand on the plow. "Nelda, she's jist been revengin herself on me. She's dis-recognized me since the day my son was born. And I don't know what's gonna come of the chile."

"Fractious as the Devil, Mr. Lloyd," Nelda paused, "You want me back up the house with him?"

"No, reckon church women got to bring him up like his own kind," Lloyd looked away, frowning. "I need ye for plowin."

"And what you gonna do bout mill work, Lloyd Sloan?" she demanded, giving the mule its head and moving off down the field.

Lloyd spat on the ground and shook his head, heaving a long sigh, "Them fools called a strike startin this mornin. All yesterday they give me mean looks, sayin secrets to each other bout me bein agin them. Hell, I ain't agin them! Sorry beggars gonna git their sly heads bashed in today. And I'm damned ifn I cross their picket lines. Now that don't mean

I'm with them, neither. It means I'm gittin shut from this sorry mess. My son ain't raised to be no linthead."

"Well, ifn you ain't workin the mill today, them bosses see it same as you on strike. They don't figure you hung out for plowing thisyere borryed field! So you done lost your knitting job sholy. Now what you gonna do?" Before he could answer she swung her mule around to plow up another furrow. Lloyd stood, his jaw working furiously as he watched the thin yellow woman almost running behind the mule; the keen-edged scraper, that she strapped as sharply as any man, cut into the hard soil and threw it up against her bare, dark legs. He leaned into the cool metal tractor side and surveyed his fallow land, the worn-out soil that his father's father had tilled. Lloyd was the only man left among his kinfolk who still owned and worked the land. His sisters had married and moved north to cities where their husbands found work in automobile factories, and his uncles had long ago settled in town. Uncle Matt Sloan, the sheriff, refused to stake his nephew as long as Lloyd insisted on farming, though he had offered him jobs as handyman and carpenter around town. Though Matt Sloan was a stern and successful sheriff, making good money with commissions from busted stills and making powerful friends from breaking up the many brawls in the factories and fields, Lloyd knew he would not put his job before his kin. If Lloyd could just get his cotton and tobacco crop laid in this lost ground soon enough, without notice, then it would be late spring before the bank men came calling for their money and by then the crops would be too far along for any man in his right mind to plow under. Lloyd figured, *How can my uncle arrest me for working the land he hisself was born and bred on? What will he do—put a farmer in jail for farmin? No, sir,* Lloyd gambled, *he might even settle for a percentage of my crops and let me keep my mortgage till next spring. He might sign the bank note for me.*

"You gonna lay round all day? We got thisyere field to break up!" Nelda's voice came to him from the length of the property. Lloyd waved and clambered up into his tractor seat, but from behind him he heard shouts as Nelda's cousins, two young black boys only a little shorter than himself, excitedly ran down the dirt road. Gracefully they carried their hoes high in the air like trembling feelers. At the edge of the field the cousins greeted Mammy Nelda's sons, and Lloyd smiled, eyes counting his five field hands with gratitude and a surge of—no, he would not call it love, but it was a kindred feeling, one he usually reserved for the land. He chewed hard on the tobacco, sucking the juice down into his throat, then coughing it up again to spit.

"We's late, Mr. Lloyd . . . ," one of the cousins began breathlessly.

"You didn't know I was workin this far out."

"We's late cause our daddy done got hisself shot up crossin that line over the mill this mornin!"

Lloyd's face darkened, "He hurt bad?"

"It were only buckshot in the leg, but he'll be laid up. . . ."

Suddenly his brother interrupted, "What we doin here? This ain't our ground."

"You boys jist keep still bout this, and mebbe I can see my way to lendin your daddy some part of my extry crops come summer."

They both stood very still, considering, then the oldest shrugged, running off to follow Nelda.

"I aim to see some fast hoein!" Lloyd waved the other away and started up his tractor.

The cantankerous spits and chokes of the tractor's rusted gears startled Lloyd as the machine's noise always did when

he was alone in the middle of a field so early that the star-
lings had just begun their morning cackle. When he first
broke new ground with this tractor bought from a shrewd
neighbor the first year of his marriage, Lloyd felt himself
inside the belly of a grumbling animal as he drove it cautiously, not admitting that he feared to fall off the broken,
scooped seat. But after a day's work, the tractor lumbering
along over gulches, the thick mud sucked into its deep tire
treads and spat out behind him, Lloyd felt a child-like joy
over his power. Since that first day with his tractor Lloyd
had not been behind a mule, or been dragged by a plow.

"Like playin with screws on my coffin!" Lloyd now swore
and moved his tractor downfield, the wheels thrashing down
a year's growth of kudzu and crabgrass. "Ain't gonna catch
me back with them lintheads, not for no union, no kin, no
nothun!"

Ahead of him through a wispy cloud of gnats and dandelion puffs thrown up by the tractor's wheels, he saw Nelda
and her boys breaking up the rich red earth. This field had
rested a year and would yield good, heavy crops if only he
worked it right. *Nothun else matters but this land. Not my
wants, not Nettie's, not my son's.* Nothing human mattered;
for now Lloyd knew with certainty that he was kin only to
the land. Wasn't it red with his blood and wasn't it what
rooted him, pulling him down into its depths and mysteries
when no woman did? When no man had use for him,
wouldn't it still want him, opening up its humble grave, closing around him like the firm embrace of a brother?

At the end of that day, half the field was broken, waiting
for him, naked and familiar as before he lost it. He gave
Nelda and her boys his last two silver dollars, and when she
balked, shaming him with her pity, Lloyd had meant to
shake her silly but instead he gave her a great, awkward
hug.

"You a fool," Mammy Nelda said with some embarrassment and disengaged herself, shooing the boys home ahead of her. "Chillun, quit gawkin! You got your mouths cut crossways!" and she shook her head at Lloyd. "My uncle's done been shot up at the mill strike, you gonna get shot up over this stolen land, and my mule bout to burst her eyes out workin this hard ground!" She wiped her pale, sweating face, "Mules of this earth, Lloyd Sloan, that's what we is. Yes, you, too! When it comes to bustin heads and backs, it don't matter ifn they's black or white. You hear me talkin?"

Lloyd laughed and shooed her away with a swat that missed her bottom and hit her back. "I hear ye talkin, woman." For a moment they glared at one another, then slowly, though he struggled against it, Lloyd's lips stretched wide and they both gave way to short, deep belly laughs. "Tomorrow, Nelda."

That night the church women were startled from their quilting bee when Lloyd came in, not squinting and cross, but sunburnt and grinning. "Lloyd, you home mighty early," one of the women eyed him. Ignoring her, he hung his hat on a nail and reached for his son, who sat idly under the kitchen table, covered from head to foot in gaily colored quilt patches and random threads. Lloyd picked up Ira, swung him over his head and onto his shoulders. Wide-eyed, Ira screamed and gulped air, desperately hanging on to his father's cowlick.

Lloyd dismissed the ladies with a polite nod. "Much obliged, but I'll be tendin to my son. He can foller me in the fields now. And Mammy Nelda's there to keep an eye out, too." The women shook their heads and hastily left. Lloyd fried some side meat and potatoes and talked quietly to his son. As he watched Ira eat, he drank from the quart jar he kept hidden in the pantry. The liquor was warm, stinging. Soon Lloyd nodded off, eyes half-lidded. Sometime later he woke with a start to see his wife, one arm propping herself up as she leaned against the cupboard. Quickly, Lloyd looked to the high chair, but Ira was gone.

"You put him to bed?" Lloyd asked, chagrined.

"He knows to go to his room when it gets dark." Nettie shifted her weight from foot to foot, nervously looking around the room. Every time her eyes alighted on her husband she gave an involuntary start as if surprised to see him. Then her eyes fell on the liquor and she frowned. She opened her mouth, then abruptly closed it, her face falling into a look of perplexed concentration. Lloyd was up quickly to get her a chair and he held her arm as she lowered herself into it with a grimace. He heard the bones crack in her knees and her shallow breathing. When finally she spoke her voice was flat, hesitant, but her eyes had that feverish, questioning look that Lloyd feared. "You weren't at the mill today."

"And I won't nary be at that mill agin, Nettie," he declared, then added in a lower voice, "leastways, not ifn ye can git shut of that sickness." He looked at her and his face closed in on itself, but not before it registered a certain startled pain. She had never seemed so peaceful. For all her recent weight, there was a frailty that made him remember how unassuming she had once been in that way large women had of making themselves at once delicate and arousing. This surprised and disturbed Lloyd; for so long he had remembered only her fearsome and oppressive weight as if with each pound gained in her sickness it was that much more money Lloyd must sacrifice. But now she looked at him again, that earnest and dazed expectation in her eyes, and Lloyd felt a rush of shame that bordered on elation. Perhaps now he would do right by her again. "Nettie! Nettie, honey, you're lookin fine. Almost well now, I reckon. I forgit to tell ye how good you look cause we ain't got no time

together," he reached for the liquor, "but that's all changed!
I'm bein near ye from now on." He took her hands and
patted them awkwardly, then poured a drink. "Here now,
honey, it'll cool that fever." Nettie looked at the glass and
slowly took it in her hands. But she did not drink. "No, it
ain't medicine. It's good, go on!" She drank and looked at
him, her eyes more quiet now, almost lucid. She watched
him for a long while, taking small sips from the liquor.

"I heard there's something going on over at the mill."

"How you know that!"

"My brothers were by this afternoon, asking for you. Oh,
my Ralph was beaten up something shameful."

"When it rains it sholy pours," Lloyd said. "What them
rascals want me for now?"

"They got . . ." she made a vague gesture in the air.

"Behinds full of buckshot!"

"Your Sheriff Matt brought them by here, but they took
off again soon as your uncle left them alone. They were
asking after you, Lloyd."

"And what *you* askin for, Nettie?" His voice was harsh as
he put the liquor back on the table. "Take another sip, it'll
ease your pain." For a moment she was still, then she took
the bottle, raising it to her lips. She drank greedily now and
as Lloyd watched her his eyes grew tired, lips stretching
until his whole face was tight. "What you want from me,
honey?"

She said nothing. When he looked up at her she stared at
him and, whether it was the liquor or some moment of lucidity, Lloyd could have sworn that there was an intelligence, a
malevolent and mocking insight in her eyes as they flared up
at him, before dying down to their usual idle and unfocused
grayness. "Let's git on back to bed now. . . ." Lloyd stopped
her hand as it sought the liquor jar. In one motion he lifted

her to her feet and led her back to her room, tucked her body under the quilts. "Sleep now."

She nodded but did not close her eyes. "I been trying to remember . . ." She put a hand over her forehead. "Yes, it was something your Uncle Matt told me." Lloyd waited, taking a seat near the window. Her eyes, dull and troubled, seemed to get whiter with the effort of each thought. *She used to teach chillun to think*, Lloyd thought sadly, *now a simple chile can outwit her*. He waited for her to speak but began to feel impatient. When finally she spoke her voice was stern and direct. "What you aiming to do, Lloyd?"

"Don't rightly know."

"There's a meeting tonight in Bailey's back woods."

Lloyd looked at her sharply. *She's no more crazy or confused than me!* "You know exactly what you say, don't ye, Nettie?" He stood up and scowled. "You want me to be there for your brothers, even though you know I'm damn done with that mill and them pitiful union folk!"

"No, Lloyd," her voice was even, clear, and unhurried, "I want you to go before they . . ."

"Before they what?"

"Before they tell everyone about you getting back that land you lost from the bank."

"But I didn't get that land back . . . ," Lloyd began, then stopped. "What do these scoundrels think? They think I made a deal?" He went to her bedside. "Who beat your brother Ralph up? Tell me!"

"I can't rightly remember. . . ." Nettie closed her eyes.

"You said somethin bout my Uncle Matt. Was the sheriff by today for some reason other'n bringin your brothers here in that sorry shape? Is he the one beat Ralph so bad?"

"Yes," Nettie sat up on her elbow, her eyes suddenly wide, "Sheriff Matt said for me to tell you . . ."

"I'll be damned ifn yourn and my kin gonna be feudin all over creation over somethun so fool ornery as that union!"

"Sheriff Matt said . . ."

"No matter now," Lloyd pursed his lips and nodded. "Them brothers of yourn probably got all riled up and went searching for me. When they seen me in that field I done lost, they must figure I was spyin for my uncle, that's how come he knows who's organizin their strike." Lloyd laughed harshly. "So now they gonna do some spyin on their own, that right? That jist don't make good sense! Ifn I was workin sly for my uncle, do they think I'd be fool enough to start in plowin that lost field the very same day them lintheads go out on strike? Hell, no stool pigeon is that stupid!" Lloyd went out of the room, but called back from the kitchen, "You Masons . . . always was a spiteful and crazy lot. Pa, he first seen it."

When he came back to sit down heavily in the chair beside her bed, Lloyd had another flask of whiskey and one glass.

"They thought you were with them." Nettie's voice was quiet as she watched him pour a large drink. "But you're not with anyone." She saw her husband flinch slightly and push away the whiskey as he moved to sit beside her on the bed.

"Don't you be goin agin me, too, Nettie," hesitantly Lloyd lay his head on her bosom, though she shifted her weight toward him off. He straightened again and she handed him the whiskey. "No, you drink it," he said.

Nettie drank deeply, not only Lloyd's portion, but several of her own until the bottle was drained and she lay against the pillow; her mouth glistened with a moist amber spittle. Lloyd thought she slept, even with her eyes open, for often his wife was lost to him in what he could only imagine was a sleeper's dream; but she raised a hand to catch his sleeve and pulled him against her. Lloyd smelled the sweet dribble of liquor running over her chin, her neck, down his cheek like a tear.

"It's all gone."

"No, honey, I've got another bottle in the cellar." Lloyd rose to fetch it but she held him back.

"It's not me gone against you, Lloyd. I didn't take it away. It's lost, but *we* didn't lose it."

Lloyd eyed his wife tenderly, covering her lips with his hand. "Nothun's gone. I'm workin my rightful land now and a good crop's to come. I've got my son and . . ." he smiled suddenly . . . "and sometimes you come back, Nettie."

She shook her head vehemently as if he were slapping her face back and forth. "No!" she cried. "You've got nothing . . . nothing left now."

Lloyd stopped the wide, trembling shape of her words with his mouth; covering her lips, he took her breaths into his lungs as if they were his own for air. She was a woman beneath him only in contour and smell, for he did not enter her but lay against her body as if fitting himself into the ground's hard and smooth places—careful not to sleep with bone against a knobby root, with belly or breast bruised by a stone. Her breaths rocked him and the deep quiet between her breasts kept her words from him as if his ears were clasped by soft, swollen hands.

She spoke of coming loss and separation, of a new life in which one would not know his own reflection, of a darkness none other than one's deepest self; but if Lloyd listened at all, he heard her words as one endures another apocalyptic sermon—with frailty and a saving sense of distance. Soon he could not separate Nettie's heartbeat from her murmuring voice as she rocked him, her breaths even and musical.

"Lu La Lu La Lu . . ." she sang the words over and over

again, until she felt his body unclench and abandon itself to sleep. "La Lu, Lloyd . . . La Lu La Lu Lu, my Lloyd."

She did not sleep. All night Nettie bore him up until she heard the first knocks at their door. Gently she woke Lloyd by pulling his hair, so that he started up with a grimace. He was startled to see his wife beneath him, and for a moment looked in bewilderment at the empty whiskey bottles on the bedstand. Though the knocks at the door grew more insistent, Lloyd still wondered a moment longer, then asked sheepishly, "I wasn't drunk last night?"

"No."

"Were ye, honey?" He reached for her cheek, but she nodded toward the door.

"Best see who it is," her voice came sluggishly and struck him as tinged with indifference.

"You feel bad? Hungover?"

"I wasn't drunk, Lloyd," she reached for him and pulled him against her almost angrily, clapping him hard on the back as if he were choking. Lloyd heard her heart beating so fast he imagined it a clanging bell. Roughly she pushed him away, "See to that damn door." After Lloyd left, Nettie pulled herself from bed and began dumping the contents of her drawers on the floor, cursing softly.

After much loud quarreling, Lloyd appeared in the doorway to her room; a large man bearing a striking resemblance to Lloyd hovered behind him. "What gave you the right to mortgage all our goods?" Lloyd demanded of his wife, holding on to the door jamb as if to brace himself. "Dammit, woman, answer me!"

"Same notion that let you mortgage this house out from under her, Lloyd!" the man behind him said in a tired voice. "That confounded love of this stingy land. Household goods, this shack, tractor, cows—between your and Nettie's mortgaging to keep this farm, the little left ain't enough to weight a body down or keep him from flying off this earth like a blessed bird."

"The Masons be the ruin of Sloans!" Lloyd stormed out of her room as Nettie continued dumping everything she owned on the earthen floor, moving from bureau to drawer, from closet to bookcase as if she were doing the simplest of tidying-up chores.

Both men watched Nettie, their eyes resting on her graceful movements from one chest to the other; the moment before she emptied a drawer on the dirt floor, she paused, musing over a twisted bobby pin, a cow bell, perhaps a smudged book of matches from one of Lloyd's many roadhouse stops. Then, as if she felt each of these objects was finally complete without her, Nettie gripped the wooden drawer, turned it upside down, and let the rest of the contents spill out. The room resounded with chill, metallic sounds as tin buttons and small change clinked together, spinning on the floor, before the wafting flight of underclothes and chenille flattened all into dense silence.

When the last drawer was empty, Nettie straightened and turned to the man near Lloyd. "Sheriff Matt," she said quietly. "Yesterday when I remembered what you told me, it was too late to tell Lloyd. He didn't know."

"Does now," Sheriff Matt straightened and took her by the arm. "Go on out the wagon with Sallie. She's with the boy waitin to take ye to town. We got a place fixed up. Lloyd and me, we'll see to what's left here."

Nettie nodded and allowed him to lead her to the wagon where his wife and her son were waiting. Nettie took little notice of Ira or Lloyd's aunt. Inside the cabin the women could hear Lloyd and Sheriff Matt haggling. "Banks got a right to land out from under ye, Lloyd. What you figurin when you plowed up that land you lost to the bank? You think they gonna let you squat on it for nothun?"

"Plantin crops ain't squattin! And ifn that damn bank is so broke, why not let farmers keep plantin their land? Mebbe we'll be the ones who feed the bankers now they got no sad soul to loan."

"Don't worry none bout bankers starvin," Sheriff Matt said tersely. "Be worryin bout that son and woman sittin out there waitin to move to town. Fret for somethin else sides that sorry land. This land, it's the only ruin of ye, boy!"

"I ain't gonna be no deputy to ye . . . and I wish I weren't no kin!" Lloyd shouted. "Nettie, the boy, and me . . . we'll live with ye one night, then I'm goin back to the mill, move us into the factory shacks." Lloyd saw his uncle's face fall.

"No sir."

"You don't have no say in this."

"Mills closin down soon, too," Sheriff Matt began, then dropped his head wearily. For a few moments he scuffed his boot heel against the dirt floor. "Lloyd, I told Nettie some hard things yesterday. But tellin her the bank's foreclosin on this farm ain't like tellin her . . ." He stopped and shook his head vehemently.

"Say what?"

"Lloyd, you know I brought them riled-up, unionizin brothers of Nettie's by, all beat up by Bailey's boys. Now you tell me . . . why didn't they stay put here, safe? Why'd they hightail it back to squeal to the bank bout you trespassin on your old land? When the bank men come to me, was all I could do to keep them from takin your hide along with this farm."

"Them fool Masons!" Lloyd began, but again saw his uncle's face fall flat. "I can't be your deputy, because the first thing I'm goin to do this mornin is shoot Ralph Mason!"

"Reckon that ain't possible."

"Ain't got room in that jail for me?"

"Lloyd, Ralph's already dead. I'm not sayin he didn't deserve killin twice. I was so glad you wasn't at that union organizin meetin back of Hap Bailey's woods last night. Ever man that went down I thought was ye."

"You killed him?"

"No, I got there after Bailey's boys. Reckon it was Bailey's way of closin down his mill and gittin shut of that union all at once."

"But you weren't protectin nobody," Lloyd said flatly and turned around to pack his guns.

"No," Sheriff Matt finally said. "Was Bailey's orders to come late."

"You think I'm gonna be your deputy?" Lloyd spat on the floor and strode past his uncle.

"Yes," Sheriff Matt said under his breath and wearily watched his nephew hoist himself up into the waiting wagon.

II

In the late winter of 1937, after serving two years as assistant deputy and living in the second story of the red brick jailhouse that backed off the Yellow River, Lloyd Sloan took over his uncle's job. Sheriff Matt Sloan had died with sunstroke while he was out supervising a gang of prisoners doing public road work. Lloyd accepted his inherited job as he had accepted these past years of living in town, of spying and locking up people who seemed a lot like himself, and as he had accepted the sight of his wife and son watching him with pity and perhaps shame. What he had never accepted was the fact that he might not return to his farm. Ever since the bank had gotten back on its feet through government aid, Lloyd had been dickering with them over terms for a loan on his land. If the bank would relent, let him work the fields, giving them the main percentage of profit from crops, he might again believe that he was more than the man he had come to be—a man almost forty whose back had been ruined not by farming but by stooping, and then at last by a bullet in the backbone, a wound from breaking up a union's picket lines.

But if he could just farm again, Lloyd reasoned, all he had lost in human terms would be granted him in spirit; for surely he would teach his son to farm and would then die, knowing he lived on in the land. His son would sow seeds and stories of his father's spirit, and every generation afterward would thank Lloyd for the harvest. Lloyd's vision was not shared by the bank; but perhaps it was his pestering that finally moved them to sell the troublesome land to Hap Bailey, the onetime mill owner who now profited off his new, if somewhat scoffed-at, chicken business. For the past few months Lloyd had been summoning courage to ask Hap Bailey to let him farm his old land. The land having lain fallow for two years, Lloyd could assure Bailey of decent profits.

One evening Lloyd returned from his visit to Hap Bailey with a bright yellow tractor hitched on a trailer behind his car. When he pulled in front of the jailhouse, he found his son Ira perched on the stairs that led to their second-story home. Pensively the boy studied his schoolbooks.

"Son, I got somethin special for ye," Lloyd said, hitching up one leg on the wooden steps and smiling, but his face was tense. Obediently Ira set his books down on the stairs and followed his father into the back lot. "Over here, boy," Lloyd beckoned from the woods. Ira saw a monstrous shape, like the dinosaurs he was studying in school; but this one was perched on huge, saw-toothed wheels as if the beast's great eggs were hatching, and in the dim moonlight he saw only the hungry teeth of the giant baby birds whose names he had labored to pronounce in school, though they sounded like the nonsense words and frightening gibberish he had often heard from his mother when she took her fits. He knew that this terror in the woods that his father now called him toward was a dinosaur bird, because at one end giant tail-feathers stuck up almost to the sky and at the other was a flat beak with long, spiked tongue poised, ready to swallow the earth.

"Daddy! Daddy! Git away, she'll eat you sure!" Ira yelled as he ran back to the safety of the jail's cellar door. Lloyd could see black faces behind the bars, their eyes lit up like moons and their shiny teeth set in jeers as they stared at Bailey's yellow tractor.

"Ira!" Lloyd called out angrily, but his son would not come closer. Finally Lloyd walked toward him and, in a voice so full of wonder, yet sad, the way his son had sometimes heard him speak to his wife, he said, "You ain't never seen a tractor." He took Ira's hand, half dragging and half pushing him to the woods. When they reached the beast, Lloyd swung his son up into the wide seat and Ira peered out, terrified, as if his father had abandoned him to a cruel, high nest.

"I won't never talk with the niggers agin, Daddy, I promise. . . ," Ira wailed.

Lloyd grimaced and climbed up into the seat, placing his son's hands on the great, spoked steering wheel.

"I ain't punishin ye. I'm gonna learn ye to farm," Lloyd went on, saying strange things about digging in the dirt and

pulling up weeds and plants. Ira was rigid, allowing his father to keep hold of him for fear of falling down into the
sharp teeth that waited below. Finally his father was quiet;
his grip relaxed as he rocked his son back and forth on his
lap. Ira could feel his father's jaw knocking against the top
of his own head as he chewed his tobacco.

"Don't be afeared, little one. I don't never mean to make
you do nothun wrong." For a moment the boy thought of
leaping down and running away, though the bird now surely
had his scent and would hunt him down. But suddenly Ira
felt an opening in his throat and he was sobbing wildly, his
father crushing him against his chest, the rough shirt buttons snagging his hair and the smell of tobacco making each
breath he sucked in burn and tear his eyes.

After a while his father wiped Ira's face with the back of
his hand and lifted him down from the tractor seat. "Best git
on. See bout your mother and help her wash up for supper.
I'll be along directly. And don't stay up late, you got that
school tomorrow," Lloyd's voice was stern, and as soon as he
let go, his son ran to the stairs and was up them two at a
time. Lloyd walked over slowly, bent and picked up his son's
schoolbooks from where he had left them on the steps. Suddenly Lloyd turned to catch the blacks, their faces watching
him, eyes white and narrow. "Quit gawkin! You'uns git your
turns on my tractor soon enough." He started up the steps
and added, "But only them that best behaves. The rest of
you'uns git mules and a plow!"

There was a muttering, a confused laugh, and then one
man spit through the bars.

"Tunney!" Lloyd suddenly yelled.

"Yessir," a voice came from inside the jail office.

"Git some of the men and call Doc Varnon to come over.
Meet me in the pickup."

"But we ain't had supper, Lloyd," his deputy protested.

"We gonna grow our own, boy!" Lloyd laughed and set down Ira's books on the last step. "I'm gone," he called out to his wife and son upstairs. "Don't wait up."

Fourteen prisoners piled into the truck that night with Lloyd, his deputies, and Dr. Varnon. Most of the prisoners had been arrested on small charges from vagrancy to failure to pay mortgages to drunkenness or petty theft. Lloyd knew most of them, and in that wary intimacy of the jail cells the sheriff had learned he could trust them. He could trust them with the task they were about to perform—ridding Hap Bailey of the migrant workers he had hired to pick his fields. The migrants had arrived to find Bailey's crop plowed under because the government now paid farmers to let their land lie fallow, a rest after the depletion of the one-crop decades. Lloyd knew his prisoners would not balk at scattering the migrants, no more than his prisoners had protested over Lloyd's and Bailey's plan to work Sloan land again with a public work gang and Bailey's new tractor. The prisoners—many of them farmers or mill workers who, during these hard times, had ended in jail rather than face a wife and starving kids—figured it was better to spend this jail sentence planting crops than paving country roads; at least when they were paroled they could count on returning home knowing they had helped feed someone, if not their families. Lloyd Sloan trusted his prisoners; he trusted Doc Varnon less, but brought him along every time a fight was anticipated. Though a drunkard, Varnon was good enough to fix folks who might never see another doctor.

Only the deputies had guns; the prisoners were given whiskey. Lloyd was driving. He took his time, letting the men in the back of his truck enjoy the freedom of lying on their backs, passing around whiskey and staring up at the dark skies. Hanging just above your eyes, the stars were so close and fixed it was dizzying, as if you were dreaming, hurtling through the heavens, before falling back to earth, gathering speed as the world's gravity reached up greedily to pull you down, your head hitting the flat truck bed, bouncing up and down with every gully and hole in the hard asphalt road. The countryside rushed past you like a fierce wind, luminous trees coming closer together like those tall black bars you looked through all day, but here, when you reached out, there was nothing to stop you but the wind, pushing your hair back from your forehead like a strong, comforting hand. Then you lost all will to fight the blurred wind, the falling stars, the earth's hold, or the liquor's numb weightlessness. And by the time you got to wherever you were going, nothing stood still, because you were so used to moving, the rhythm of this road was in your bloodstream along with that sweet, giddy whiskey; it made the wind hot, then so cold that you were grateful for the other prisoners, their bodies falling against yours every time the truck hit the shoulder, one wheel throwing back dust and pebbles; and you did not ever want to stop this rocking, shut-eye ride, for here was your greatest freedom.

Lloyd didn't drink, but he drove more recklessly than a drunkard until he came close to Bailey's shacks. As he passed the factory shanties Lloyd jammed down the accelerator, traveling the muddy two miles to the creek so fast the men in the back were splattered black. Suddenly Lloyd cut the engine about five hundred feet from the migrant shanties. After giving orders that the men stay hidden in the truck, he and Doc Varnon approached the migrant camp. Doc Varnon, who had been drinking heavily during the long drive, was barely able to distinguish the trees from the tall migrants—both were vertical shapes leaning as if against the wind. Though the doctor was too intoxicated to make much sense of Lloyd's words, he did know something ailed the man.

Perhaps, the doctor guessed, it was downheartedness on Lloyd's part, but not because of the slanted shacks, some with doors torn off and carefully set aside, leaning against the front of the cabin, some with floor and roof slats laid lengthwise over gaping holes, some porches looking as if one end were kneeling so a child might slide from the high hole that was the cabin's entrance down the porch to the muddy ground, if he didn't mind splinters. No, Doc Varnon thought, it was not the shanties built helter-skelter for mill families and now gutted, wooden frames with whole sides missing like hapless lean-to shelters. Because Lloyd had seen that too many times before; and hadn't he seen it first-hand, too? His old cabin, the one he built for Nettie on his father's land, was now ruined and slanted after two years of living in town. No, Doc Varnon knew it was not even the fact that these migrant shacks now stood abandoned, moonlight streaming through the roofs to illuminate bare dirt floors. The downheartedness was in Lloyd before he even got to the migrants; for the sheriff had fallen into a helpless pity, as if his despair were a reflexive shudder at the sight of every man, woman, and child already packed up and ready to move on. Most sat in their crew boss's sagging truck. They were so quick to oblige that Lloyd could only stand and stare. Sullen-eyed, they moved effortlessly from shack to truck, never carrying anything in their arms; a few women and children ran back and forth to peer inside, eyes dead but taking in every nook of the cabin to fix it in their minds so that they never left.

"Doc, they was promised this land to work and now they walkin off it, without even a word, no meanness, jist movin like they never even was here. That ain't human," Lloyd

strode over to speak with a migrant. After a short talk the
man signaled the other migrants back to their shacks and
Lloyd came over to Doc Varnon. "They got a woman bout to
give birth here," Lloyd said. "I give them till mornin. Now
you best see to that woman's pains."

Doc Varnon made his way over to the back of the pickup
where they had laid the pregnant Arkansas woman. Swathed
in some old bedding, she was naked from the waist down.
He laid his hand on her high belly. "You know, ifn ye keep
this belly naked to where the moonlight can shine on it,
you're gonna have a son sure!"

"I don't want my chile born in no jail!" the woman cried.

Taken aback, Doc Varnon shook his head and began
climbing into the pickup.

"Let her be," a tall woman who sat next to the pregnant
migrant, swathing her forehead with cold rags, stopped him.
"You got a complaint, mister, give it to me. I'm not flat on
my back." The woman nodded to her sons who stood next to
the pickup, two as tall as she and one only a child, but his
face just as vigilant as his brothers'. The woman's sons who
looked very much like her moved as a body toward Doc
Varnon. "I reckon I can midwife my own," she said.

Without another word, Doc Varnon retreated. He found
Lloyd nearby the truck. "That woman says she's a midwife,
Lloyd, and her sons look mean. Let's . . ."

"Ifn them is her sons, reckon she knows how to give birth,"
Lloyd said.

"Hell, she's jist a backwoods granny woman! And I
brought somethin for the pain! You come with me and tell
them fools . . ."

Doc Varnon lurched off toward the pickup, but before he
took three steps Lloyd grabbed him and roughly sat him on
the ground. Even in the dark Doc Varnon could see Lloyd's
face was grim.

"Was a backwoods granny got my son through Nettie's labor. She did it with no help from you, Doc, or from Nettie . . . and she did it when she wasn't drunk!"

The doctor struggled to his feet, "But, Lloyd, I brought somethin for her pain!"

"Let's take a good dose of it, then," Lloyd pushed Doc Varnon back down, then sat beside him. They began drinking and waiting.

Lloyd kept his eyes on the three solemn, dingy shadows leaning against the back of the pickup, their heads bent and sagging as if they guarded a shabby funeral procession, their beloved laid in the back of a truck bound not for glory land that most settled folks envisioned, but simply moving down a long blacktop highway that ended in eternity. Lloyd had seen such caravans, the migrants in their trucks moving, carrying their dead with them like their only possessions, stopping but being moved on until they found night's shelter and could pause stealthily by the side of the back road to bury a father, mother, or that baby the Lord mercifully saw fit to spare a vagabond existence, then moving away, knowing they would never visit or see the burial ground whose only marker was a memory.

Once an indignant farmer summoned Lloyd to inspect a roadside grave, where the migrant dead was at last a successful squatter. "You got to dig it out of my land, Sheriff. Mebbe it's murder, and that's your bidness."

"You afeared he'll take root and grow?" Lloyd said, staring at the flat, sunken earth so poorly concealed beneath gathered leaves and branches. Lloyd imagined a son, a father begging pardon of the body beneath his feet as he stamped down the ceremonial mounding that was to give shape to the spirit rising up from the grave. But a properly marked grave meant a migrant would wander more; if the authorities didn't dig him up, the animals would, so the migrant was laid too deep, the soil's shape of his spirit was flattened with the back of a shovel, dead brush ornamented his grave, and his folks stared down in shame that there was no difference in death—the land still looked as if the migrants had never been here.

Lloyd thought of his own land, now fallow, free of him and his family. In the humid dark he drank deeply from the whiskey and anticipated the feel of his land again, the way he would work it, with a firm and chaste gratitude. Lloyd looked over to the pickup where the midwife's bobbing head was silhouetted in the moonlight as she stretched herself straight and then plummeted back into the truck bed to work with the writhing pregnant woman.

"Don't hold back, honey!" the midwife pleaded. "You've got to give . . . shhhh, now . . . yes, yes! Here comes that chile!"

Suddenly Lloyd laid a hand on the doctor's shoulder and pulled himself up from his tireless squat.

"Yank me up, too, Lloyd." Doc Varnon grabbed his arm, but Lloyd shrugged him off and the doctor's head hit the hard, bright clay. Lloyd saw the doctor's unconscious body folding around itself so that he lay, legs tucked up under his chin, in childish sleep. Lloyd spit and smiled, then weaved over to the truck, but as he came closer the three shadows straightened up, scowling.

"Ma done tole your friend to leave her do the midwifin," the oldest boy said firmly.

"Don't mind, boys," Lloyd said and peered over the wide flat of the truck where the woman lay, legs askew and kicking. When she caught sight of the sheriff the swell-bellied woman went rigid, her eyes rolling backward; the midwife stood up, a tall apparition, hair matted against her forehead.

"Shooo, git on with ye!" she said, "We'll git gone soon enough." Again her sons, their faces not menacing but tight, advanced. But when they came within a few inches of the sheriff, they stopped, arms hanging at their sides.

"I won't bother none," Lloyd said and reached into his pocket. He passed the flask of whiskey first to the boys and then, his chaw going furiously, he spit and took a deep swallow. Finally he reached up and offered the liquor to the pregnant woman, who turned her head to the side and pressed her legs together, a groan escaping through gritted teeth. The midwife took Lloyd's bottle and gestured him away. Greedily, she drank, her eyes closed, her Adam's apple bobbing up and down, straining against the skin. She gave it back to Lloyd, who emptied it, tossing the bottle to the ground. He shook his head and opened his eyes to clear the aching darkness gathered in the corners of his vision. The moon was full but clouded and the sweet promise of rain hung in the dark air. Rapt, Lloyd watched as the pregnant woman flung herself on her back; legs hiked up, bracing them against the side of the truck bed, she pushed and heaved, her wet skin squeaking against the metal as she slid up and down, crying.

"Here, honey, don't be kickin now. Ease up . . . ease . . ." The midwife caught the woman's legs in mid-air, each knee cupped in one hand like stirrups so that the midwife rocked back and forth with every shove, the truck beneath the woman singing on its wheel springs. To Lloyd it looked like a primitive dance, except one partner was flat out and crawling in the air like a daddy-longlegs spider. Then suddenly came the shouting, soothing words. "Work it through, sister! Let go, yess, yesss . . . ," the midwife yelled, her voice joining the pained woman's in a wild soprano that rose up, broke, and began again as a low buzzing in the throat.

Thin blood pooled in the metal grooves of the truck's bed, running over the midwife's bare toes and dripping onto the ground near Lloyd's feet. He stepped forward, mouth hanging open. A small, dented head appeared between the suddenly suspended legs as the midwife hunched over, her large hands pulling and wheedling the quiet baby from its mother's dark cavity. The baby was free suddenly, held by the midwife and by its wet, snaking tether to the mother's insides.

"Cut him loose!" Lloyd yelled, and unsheathed the knife at his belt. He handed it to the midwife, noticing the baby was still. "Cut that naple string! Slap that breath out of him! He's too still!" He jumped up in the truck and leaned over the woman, his knife coming down in a wide arc against the coiled umbilical cord. But the midwife grabbed his wrist, laughing and howling in his ear.

"Fool!" she said and kept hold of his arm. "Now look ye here . . ." Lloyd stared down at the dazed, almost grinning woman. A tiny, blood-sopped creature, eyes pasted shut like a kitten's, lay moving slowly on her flat, sagging belly. "No need to slap a chile born. Let her breathe her mammy's insides a yet longer before we commence scarin it silly," the midwife smiled and waited a long while, staring up at the sky and smoking slowly a cigarette her son had rolled for her. Then she nodded and flicked the cigarette against the dirt. She washed her hands in some homemade disinfectant and took her own clean knife from her belt. With one sure cut she split the cord. Not once did the baby cry, though Lloyd now plainly saw that small stomach rising up and down in her first, shallow breaths. "Now, hand me that tub." The midwife waited for Lloyd to lift up the wide basin of well water that her sons had boiled and let cool until lukewarm. The woman took the pot from the sheriff and gently laid the child in it, up to her chin. "Jist like baptizing," she laughed, washing the blood and the whitish-blue ooze off the new, wrinkled skin. Mewing sweetly, the baby dribbled tiny bubbles down its chin. "See," the midwife said, "you best born at night; it's like you ain't never out of your mammy's belly till come day, and by then you got your breath regular from layin against her breasts where you hear her pumpin heart sayin, 'You ain't gone far away from me, you jist come outside to play where it ain't all cramped like a possum in a pouch.'"

"I'll be . . . ," Lloyd said quietly. "I thought that chile was stillbore like . . ." He stopped and looked down at the baby, still shaking his head in wonder.

"She got to move and hightail so fast the rest of her days, no need slappin and yankin up roots the moment she come in." Suddenly the midwife's voice was cool. She covered the woman's flat, naked belly with a clean quilt and laid the baby in the crook of her mother's shoulder. "Now, go away some, Sheriff. I got to git them settled down before we oblige ye by goin. We don't need no ruptures on the road."

Lloyd said nothing. Unsteadily, he clambered over the bloody rags and belongings that surrounded the spent mother. When he jumped down to the ground Lloyd teetered a moment, watching the midwife cut a piece of string and tie it to the baby's umbilical cord. Lloyd watched intently, knowing that by the time the cord came off, by the time the cloth rotted away from the small, thin-skinned belly, this child would have crossed more country than Lloyd had seen in his entire life.

"What you gonna name her?" Lloyd asked and felt his head spin.

"Never ye mind, Sheriff."

"I got to know," Lloyd steadied himself against the truck.

"You figure to register her in some big courthouse book,

give this chile a birth certificate . . . then unsettle her before she's drawed five breaths?"

Lloyd's mouth dropped open, "No . . . why, no! I ain't makin no record of this," Lloyd wiped his forehead and spat on the ground, then he fixed the midwife. "God in heaven, woman! You think I was borned a sheriff, first opened my eyes to spy on folks, and took my first step to overrun some poor feller who jist happens to be limpin along? Migrants ain't the only creatures this land done wore down and let go. Jist look around, woman! We's all moving agin ourselves."

Wearily the woman straightened up, both hands pressing the small of her back. "What's *your* name?"

"Sloan . . . Lloyd's the first name."

"Sloan. Well, that ain't pretty enough for a girl chile," she paused a moment. When she turned to him her face was drawn, but he only noticed her smile. "How bout you name this chile after some woman, some kin to ye?"

Wide-eyed, Lloyd looked up at her, "No'm, that ain't for me to say."

The woman kept smiling and fussed with the blankets in the back of the truck. She leaned close to the half-sleeping mother and whispered, "You got a name in mind?"

The mother nodded and spoke very low. The midwife's smile widened and she leaned over to Lloyd, "Woman's waitin on ye, too."

Lloyd pondered for a long while. His first thought was to name the girl Nettie, but it pained him to think this namesake would soon desert him as had his wife. *No,* Lloyd thought, *I'll name her after my Aunt Stella, that name I had chose for Iry ifn he'd been a girl.* But the thought of this child wandering all over the world as his aunt now wandered in afterlife made Lloyd feel even more abandoned. Names of first loves, cousins, women in town he'd watched with longing, even names that had no associations other than their sounds ran through his mind like lyrics, until Lloyd was so dizzy he leaned over the truck bed and saw the baby's miniature body, lost in clean rags. His possessiveness now gave way to a pure rush of pity, a desire to protect and give this newborn all the charity he had ever stinted anyone. Then the midwife reached down to modestly cover the mother's breast, to cup the child's dented head in her palm, and Lloyd felt all this yearning within him, the unchanneled compassion of the past years, now center on this stooped, unstinting midwife.

"Ma'am?" He was afraid to reach out and touch her arm. "What be your name? First name."

"Jessie," she said. "Jessie Walsh."

"Name the chile after ye," Lloyd at last smiled.

"That's the name I done give her," it was the mother's voice from the truck.

Quietly Jessie nodded. "I thank ye both." She smiled down at the mother and then let her eyes linger on Lloyd. He noticed her gentle underbite, the way it shivered as if her jaw was unhinged. "Well, now we best be goin on." Jessie called out to her sons, who stood apart, the two oldest idly smoking and the youngest, Nate, facing Lloyd, his eyes bright, unsmiling. "You, Virgil and Leon! Git our things together fore it's too hot to move," then her voice dropped in register and became more gentle. "And you, Nate Walsh! Quit gawkin and go help your brothers."

Her sons obeyed, but Nate held back a little so that Jessie had to stamp her foot and nod toward the cabin before he would move away. Jessie turned to Lloyd. "That youngest son's always been contrary," she said, but her voice was wondering. "I always wanted a girl chile to help me corral them boys. Now I got a namesake might work jist as good."

Lloyd watched her intently. "You ain't . . . you ain't got no husband?"

"I got sons."

"Them sons gonna leave, too, someday." Lloyd's voice was soft, but still he saw Jessie flinch. "Please . . ." he held out his hand to her, "please come down and talk jist a little."

Jessie held back a moment, then jumped down from the truck without his help.

"Lissen," Lloyd walked with her toward a stand of pine trees. Laying his hand against the ragged bark, he spoke for a very long time, his voice urgent as if running after itself, sometimes catching on a word and trailing off into a bleak silence, during which he and Jessie looked away from one another and gazed at the changing sky; the rain misted down, washing the darkness from the night. Finally he was finished speaking, as if he knew not another word in all the world he had not already given her.

Jessie's black eyes were dull and furtive from lost sleep. Her frizzing, nappy hair was the leaden color of those eyes and, when still, her swarthy face seemed flat, barren. But when she began to speak, Lloyd saw all her emotion was expressed in movement; her hands swerved up gently to catch the air, never lighting on anything, and her stooped posture now seemed poised, swaying in rhythm to her words.

"And my sons," Jessie was saying. "They'll settle here, too."

"Yes'm."

"I don't have to watch 'em much now they's almost growed," Jessie stared at the ground. "Except my boy Nate. He needs some care."

"Settle him here."

Jessie's head swung up and for a moment she fixed Lloyd with a grimace. Then she considered and concluded to herself, "No, this time I'll be near Nate." To Lloyd she said, "My little boy was settled once, knows his numbers and writin."

"He ain't so little and he don't need to know more than workin the land for me. Them older boys good hands, too?"

"Sholy."

"Well, I got an offer from a man name of Bailey. He wants me to farm my old land back . . . me and the boys I got in my jail." Lloyd watched her for signs of objection, but she only nodded wearily.

"Well, we been worked like prison gangs all along. After a while you don't much make no difference who you work for."

"But this will be different!" Lloyd protested. "It's my old land they be workin back."

Jessie smiled a little, "Why, that ain't no change."

Lloyd took her by the elbow, "Ifn you work land, it's yourn."

"Ain't never been that way," Jessie gently disengaged herself from him and bent to trace patterns in the dirt, her forefinger drawing circles.

"Ifn your sons and ye settle in my old place, work my land back with me . . ." Lloyd drew a deep breath, "then . . . well, then it's yourn, too."

"No, it ain't," Jessie ruefully shook her head, "but we'll work it anyway. We know how to do that."

"Dammit, woman! I'm saying you can settle here."

"We don't know how!" Jessie burst out. But suddenly she stood up and called her sons. They were quickly by her side. "We gonna settle here," she began speaking to them quietly; her hands groped for their stooped shoulders and lay lightly on their heads as if in leave-taking.

Together the Walshes followed Sheriff Lloyd to his truck, where Jessie settled them in the back. Lloyd started the engine, but let it idle while Jessie went to speak with the other migrants. The whole camp was in movement. As the migrants unloaded their belongings from Jessie's truck there was no weeping or long embraces, simply strong handshakes from women and men alike.

"You woulda left sometime," the mother of the newborn said and Jessie nodded.

"Sheriff says you can stay on awhile ifn ye need. He won't be chasin nobody on."

"No, we best be up North. Heard tell there's apple-pickin in Virginia," the woman looked around. "And there ain't nothun here."

Jessie suddenly said, "We may be follerin fast on your heels."

"No, honey, you jist dig in here deep. We'll be back by."

Jessie reached down to tousle the woman's hair, then let her hand rest on her namesake. "Mebbe it's not such a fine name."

"No'm!" the mother's voice was full. "It's fittin. She's jist beginnin, too."

When Jessie came back to Lloyd's truck, he asked her to climb in the front with him and let her sons drive her pickup. "No, thank ye," she said. "I'll foller ye." As she drove behind Lloyd Sloan, Jessie watched her sons jounced up and down. She found herself grinning at her oldest sons' determinedly blank faces, though she saw their eyes squint into smile lines against the rushing wind. But she did not laugh when she watched Nate. His face was rapt, as if listening.

III

In town Lloyd pulled up in front of a diner and called out to Jessie, "I got an idea. Come on in with me."

"What's this?" Jessie asked.

"You cook good?"

"Tolerable," Jessie said, then added, "People don't come back for no fourth and fifth servings, but they don't complain neither."

Lloyd thought a minute. "You like to work a place like this? Like that better'n diggin in the dirt?"

"Reckon I've had enough pickin to last me."

"All right. Now, don't say nothun in there," Lloyd said, "even if you don't like what you hear."

Jessie hesitated, "What you gonna . . ."

"And you boys stay put, hear?" Lloyd rushed on. "When I give the sign, you can saunter in and eat your fill just like . . ." Lloyd stopped, embarrassed, "well, jist like regular folks."

They went inside the diner. When Lloyd took off his hat and sat down, Jessie remained standing. Lloyd did not gesture her to join him at the counter. "Got any coffee ain't weaker'n well water?" Lloyd asked the manager waiting on him.

"Sheriff, we got the same coffee you guzzled last night."

"O.K., Jake, I'll finish the pot and try my luck with that pie's been takin up room in your cupboard since last month."

Jake swatted the counter with a rag and smiled, then he noticed Jessie. The man's eyebrows arched and he looked at Lloyd, who said nothing, waiting for his food.

"Here, Sheriff. That's on the county, I reckon?"

"Long as my jail don't got no proper cook, them taxes can damn well pay my bill."

"I don't hear no prisoner's thrown hunger strikes over my cookin," Jake grinned.

"They's too weak to say much these days," Lloyd said. "That's what malnutrition does to a body."

"They be no trouble on ye, then."

"And no help, neither," Lloyd said, then leaned over the counter and confided, "You heard bout that farm-work project Hap Bailey set up? Why should we jist keep feedin prisoners? Why not let 'em feed us?"

"I ain't heard bout this at all."

"But I bet you seen that new tractor parked back of the jail!" Lloyd laughed. "I seen you oglin it last night when I drove her home."

"Didn't think much of it."

"No?" Lloyd slapped the counter with the flat of his hand. "I bet you been over every inch of that machine like any good farmer!"

Jake's face changed, fell open, and he laughed out loud. "I ain't seen nothun so good since my wife died!"

"You remember how to work a tractor?"

Jake said nothing, but watched Lloyd eat his pie. "Sheriff, you offerin her to me?"

Lloyd shrugged and picked up the pie crust with his fingers, using it as a crumbling wedge to scoop up the dark berry filling. He grimaced. "Who ever said you was a cook?"

"Bank men and three hungry kids, that's who! Same folks said you was a sheriff. Looks like they got no taste no ways!" It was the first time Lloyd had seen Jake spit since he'd taken over his wife's job in the diner. Now Lloyd saw him wipe up the saliva with a slap of his shammy rag.

"Jake, now don't git riled. I was jist seein if you still had the hankerin in ye . . . that's what makes the difference between a farmer and a hired hand." Lloyd stood up, wiping his mouth on his sleeve. "It's settled, then. You help me run the work gang and . . ."

Jake suddenly slammed his fist on the counter. "Lord Almighty! What about this place? How do I feed my kids whilst I'm off plowin up land's too wore out to keep Sloans? Sheriff, you bout took me for as big a fool as ye!"

Lloyd clenched and unclenched his jaw, then spit on the linoleum floor. He glared at Jake and then surprised him by turning to the tall, raw-boned woman who had quietly stood waiting just inside the door. "My land ain't ungivin like some folks. It didn't never fail me like my own people," Lloyd beseeched her.

Jessie nodded. "We can work it back."

"This woman one of your hired hands?" Jake asked harshly, his eyes taking in her stooped body, her knobby, ruined hands. "You suddenly such a big farmer, Lloyd, you bringin in migrants to pick crops ain't even sowed?"

"She ain't none of that kind," Lloyd said. "She's a fine cook. I found her special to take over here for ye. . . ."

"She ain't fit for decent folk," Jake said, but his voice was a whisper and he dropped his eyes. "She'll lose my bidness."

"I been runnin tractors ever since I was a chile," Jessie spoke only to Lloyd. "I know the land better'n I do the inside of this pretty little kitchen the man gots here."

Surprised, Lloyd was about to silence her when Jake spoke up. "No! I got to farm agin, Lloyd." Jake came around the counter. "Let's go look at that machine." Jake untied his apron and flung it on the stool near Jessie. "You gonna have to fix this woman up before she waits on decent folks," Jake said and went out the diner door.

"You want I should clean and gut her like a catfish?" Lloyd demanded and spit again on the floor.

"One thing . . . ," Jessie said, eyeing both the men. "Anytime I don't like this diner man, don't take to his cookin work, and don't want no customer's wisecracks—anytime I got a right to leave. I'll come work your fields or I'll jist move on. Won't be no hardship for me to go away from here."

Slowly Jake nodded and gestured for Lloyd to follow him, but Lloyd hung back. "Reckon we'll jist let the county pay her like they always done ye, Jake."

For a moment Jake balked, then threw up his hands, "Dammit, Lloyd Sloan! Are you gonna come help me fix this broke-down brand-new tractor?"

"She ain't broke," Lloyd moved to follow him.

"Yessir, I seen some trouble last night," Jake laughed and the two men walked across the street to the jailhouse.

Only then did Jessie move to the counter and run her palm across the callused Formica, flicking away bits of salt and pie crumbs. She tasted the cold coffee and made a face. "Well," she looked around the small eating room, taking in the walls and splattering grill where crinkled bits of black, unrecognizable food still sizzled. "I think I'd might ruther pick apples." Jessie called her sons inside and sat them down at the counter.

"Ma, what we doin here?" they asked.

"What'll it be, Mister Walsh?" Jessie grinned at Nate, who sat gingerly on the stool as if any moment it might spin down through the floor with him on it. "This be on the house."

"Ma," Nate asked, his smile screwed tight on his face. "We stayin here long?"

Jessie's smile wavered but she tried to keep it in place. "You folks jist passin through these parts? She turned to her oldest sons, who stared around at the abundance of food.

"Oh, we don't aim to stay in this one-horse town too long," Virgil said. "Might jist die bored."

"Yessir, sholy would be nice to travel," Jessie agreed. "See all them far-off places. Us settled folks jist git tired of diggin in so deep."

"Ma," Nate insisted, "we settlin here?"

Jessie's face lost its shape and her hands fell slack at her side. "I don't know, son. Please don't keep after me, cause I jist don't know." She turned around and looked for the coffee cups. She served her boys coffee, pinto beans, all the cold cornbread she could find, mustard greens, and biscuits. Then she fixed a plate for herself and stood up to eat, her eyes on the bobbing heads of her three boys.

"You eat out the place?" Lloyd asked when he and Jake came back inside the diner. Subdued, the boys nodded.

"I notice you ain't got many customers," Jessie eyed Jake.

"Slow time of day."

"Suppertime?" Jessie asked and unknotted her apron. "I'll jist be along now. Mebbe I'll see you tomorrow mornin."

Jake looked at Lloyd and shook his head. "Where'd you dig up this woman? Ifn I was superstitious I'd say you done robbed my wife's grave. Women like this sure can haunt a man."

Nervously, Lloyd fiddled with his hat, waiting for Jessie to gather up some leftover biscuits for breakfast. When she was ready she herded her sons out the door and climbed in the truck to follow Lloyd. But he suddenly swung down from his cab and asked Virgil to drive his truck while he came toward her and swung himself up beside her. His smile was wide and admiring. "You a safe driver, Jessie?"

Jessie said nothing, but started the engine and jolted him back in his seat as she drove out of town, watching her sons in the rear-view mirror as they gleefully drove Lloyd's truck over every pothole in the road.

Lloyd directed her down a winding country road that seemed more a dry wash than a planned thoroughfare. At last they came to a clearing and Lloyd told her sons to wait for them in the truck. Jessie and Lloyd walked the rest of the way in to a meadow overgrown with kudzu and dandelion.

"I've got a place for ye," Lloyd said, somewhat abashed. "It used to be real fixed up. These last years it's all . . . well, there she is."

Suddenly Lloyd stood very still, knuckles pressed against his temples to quiet a stiff, throbbing pain that misted his eyes so that when he looked at the rotted cabin he had built for his new wife almost twenty years ago, the image shimmered like a heat mirage. A blackened brick chimney poked up through a hole in the tarpaper roof; the porch was askew and balanced at right angles to the back of the house, where the tattered plastic flapped off window frames, making a sound like dove wings. The leaning structure sat on its haunches like a mule, too stubborn and too worn to fall down any farther.

"It's a mighty good house," Jessie said, moving around the two rooms, eyes blinking as if to scatter the dust, her long lashes dark and thick like straw on a broom that's been used to sweep ashes.

"It's yourn and them sons'," Lloyd said earnestly and took her arm. "For as long as ye need stay." And he had wanted to say *my sons, my son* . . . but instead he said, "My son, name's Iry, this was where he was born. I built it for him, for him and for my wife. He growed up different, jist like his mother. But I done tole you that story last night . . . my wife and son, they won't have none of this place."

"He old enough to work it, your Iry? My sons could help him." Jessie walked into the middle of the cabin, peeking into the extra room that had been Nettie's.

"No, I got me hands now," Lloyd said softly so she would not hear. "My son, he won't have nothun of me. I got your sons now . . ." and as Jessie disappeared inside Nettie's old bedroom Lloyd wanted to cry out, *But it's my son should be here! My sons . . . You'll git me sons, won't ye, Nettie?* Lloyd watched the woman moving in the eerie light of the bedroom. *You'll give me hands? You so well fixed, never did see a woman so . . . When you walk you jist rockin along, bones like a natural cradle to rock my sons inside. Nettie, all them sons you stillbore me, lookin quiet, curled up, perfect, dead little bodies, sullin down and bleedin at the nose like a possum. Sons jist playin possum to the new world, playin dead . . .* Lloyd came into the room beside Jessie, his eyes burning as they roamed over the odd bits of furniture his wife had left behind—a rotted bureau drawer, boxes of mildewed books, their spines broken by the wind or rats; in the corner lay the abandoned bedsprings rusted the color of mud red. *How they used to screech out, them springs, like singing when we lay down and Nettie winded herself around me and smiled, and my roots inside with her dark blood, wet and yielding as loamsoil, my sons sproutin like sun weeds; and she pulls me so deep inside I feel my roots take hold and never let her go. She won't never let me go.*

"It'll do us fine for now," the woman said, and Lloyd slipped his arm around her strong waist, letting his finger follow the straight hipbone. He had meant to pinch her, to crush her against his pulsing body. But his hands were quiet as he cupped Jessie's small bottom and he felt somehow awed as if he held the whole of her in his hand.

And from then on, every morning at first light Lloyd rounded up his grudging work gang—three white men who had been farmers and were forever getting into scrapes at the mill; a dozen Negroes, either sharecroppers who'd lost their leases from Hap Bailey or had been fined for some mischief by the judge; and one or two truant schoolboys, too old to be in school. First thing, Lloyd went into the diner and picked up the canteens of coffee and biscuits Jessie had prepared for him. After a few idle instructions Jake left his place to Jessie and rode the tractor behind Lloyd, both raising dust all along the dirt streets. They stopped along the road for the day's liquor, tools, and guano.

Under Lloyd's direction and his prisoners' care, the fields flourished. Every afternoon Lloyd drove back into town to pick up Jessie's hot lunches, and every evening, after lockup and supper, Lloyd tarried a little before going upstairs to bring three hot plates, each covered with used, crinkled tinfoil, to Nettie and Ira.

Ira could not recall a time when he did not peel this thin metal away from his supper plate, but the diner had lately been serving much better food. Different potato pies and meats cooked as if someone stood guard over the fire, plus salads and fresh bread—the feasts seemed endless.

"How come we're even gittin desserts now?" Ira asked when his father hesitantly set before them a large, brown-crusted pie, still spluttering; hot and sweet, the red, lush filling made sounds like tiny geysers.

"Diner's got a new cook, son," his father answered, glancing sidelong at his wife, who smiled, a private arch to her brow. "Jessie Walsh."

"What is it?" Ira held back with his fork and stared at his helping of pie.

"Strawberry-rhubarb, son. It's good. Go on, it's . . ."

"Tart!" his mother suddenly exploded in laughter, her wide knees shaking the whole table. In wonder, her son and husband turned to her.

"Nettie," Lloyd burst out. But she kept on laughing—rich, hearty swallows of air that welled up from inside her own world. Her laughter was somehow a comfort, cooing and low like a dove. Soon Lloyd was smiling. He watched his wife, his countenance light and incautious of her blessing. Laughing louder and louder, Nettie nodded to him, slapping her thigh as she wiped a hand across her forehead.

"Lord, now, Lloyd Sloan," she roared, "that woman's too

shy! And shame! In front of the boy!" She went on laughing her low, throaty bellow.

Lloyd said, half earnestly, half embarrassed, his hand on the back of her chair, "No . . . no, it's not . . ." Then he turned on Ira. His small son blithely ate his dessert, only looking up to assure himself of his parents' good joke and then, smiling himself, he went back to his strange, new pie. "Well . . ." Lloyd shrugged helplessly and guffawed then, louder than his wife. But all the while he sought Nettie's eyes with hunger and gratitude.

"Well, ain't that woman shy?" Nettie crowed, slapping his thigh.

"Yes ma'am," he answered, standing nearer her. "Yes." Trembling, they held on to their laughter with high, desperate voices.

The next morning Nettie Sloan was gone.

PART II

MIGRANTS

When Lloyd Sloan asked Jessie to stay in his old cabin, she consented gravely, knowing it was her only chance to settle down. She did not mind Lloyd, just as she had not minded other men as forsaken as he during the many years she had been without a husband. Jessie felt little for Lloyd except gratitude and a certain watchfulness born of habit and fatigue. Though she had lovers in that urgent and familial way of her migrant days, Jessie had only had one lover in her mind, and he was the father of her three sons. After him, she expected no other.

Twenty years ago, at age fifteen, Jessie married a cousin from the gang. Luke had picked silently alongside her for three years before he finally stood up, wiped the sweat from his hands, and took the water bucket away from the carrier. Crossing the row of sweet peas in one long stride, he doused her bent head and the small of her back with several ladles of cool well water before she could straighten. "Ifn I wasn't crew boss, you'd be!" He held the ladle to her lips and she drank deeply. "Ain't never seen man nor woman work so hard. I got the Devil pickin longside me!"

"I was tryin to keep up with ye!" Jessie laughed.

"We'll have to find us a judge."

"No one here gonna go against ye, Cousin Luke."

"Why, we'll make us a judge . . ." Luke broke off, eyeing her. Slowly he ladled cold water over her shoulders, dribbling it down in the hollow of her bosom where the cotton halter was just beginning to swell with her maturity. Winking, he gently lifted the ladle to cup her breast. "Ifn our judge drinks deep from this, you'll win sure," he whispered and quickly ducked his head to kiss her firm brown nipple.

"Luke, quit!" Jessie laughed and pushed him away.

"Well, do we git us a judge or not?" Luke watched her almost harshly, embarrassed by her frank and open stare. It was not curiosity, but as if she had him side by side some imagined rival. Finally she met his eyes, hers traveled over him indolently, almost pleasurably; but her voice was sharp as she whispered, perhaps outwitting that invisible rival who stood next to Luke:

"Yes, but I won't be able to pick as fast," and she was off down the row, hands working in rhythm, back bobbing up and down. Dumbfounded, Luke lost time admiring her lithe, spare body and small hips as she picked, never looking back, so sure that he would follow.

She was waiting for him in the woods at the end of her row, leaning against her swell-bellied gunny sack full of sweet peas.

"It's not quittin time," he smiled, swinging his bag onto the ground near her.

"You the crew boss?"

"We jist ain't decided that yet," he took off his jeans but still seemed clothed in a whiter shade of skin, like a tree stripped of its rough bark to reveal pale, stringent-smelling flesh. Jessie was not frightened, only filled with a sudden fear for him. How frail his legs looked without their stiff, broad pants skin, how abruptly his pelvic bones jutted out to pull his belly tight; and though he was hard and swelling, how fragile and lonely he seemed outside of her. So that when she reached out to cover his hardness with her wide hands, it was as a farmer gathers the roots of a tiny, up-rooted tree, with infinite care and sympathy folding her hands around him and looking about for a more giving, deep piece of earth to nourish him—until the moment she understands it is she who must open. She is not the earth, though she has worked it all her life so that it is in her to take roots. With each thrust she rises up to tear Luke away from her, but she falls back against the ground. She does not even feel the pain low in her belly, her thighs, cramping and tearing her pelvic muscles, because her outrage is both body and soul, the blind fighting force of a survivor.

"You wrassle like the Devil, too!" Luke said, breathlessly rolling off her to lie on his back, his belly and root streaked with blood. Coiled around herself, Jessie watched his penis rise and fall futilely, poking high in the air. Luke's eyes were closed, one arm thrown across them protectively. She fought off her sorrow for him, feeling her own pain throbbing between her thighs. "Thank ye, Jessie," Luke spoke slowly, not looking at her. She watched him shrivel so small his root seemed gnarled and dead. Reaching for the bucket, she ladled water over her thighs, washing the blood from between them.

At the end of every day after that, Jessie waited for him at the end of her row, before walking with him into the woods. "You pick so fast, must be hurryin to git to them woods!" he teased her, but carefully watched her face for some sign of pleasure. He had begun wondering if she were too young, if her small hips would ever hold a full-term baby, if she were too good a picker to lose to childbirth. But one day he came to the woods to find her already undressed, the swath of dark skin across her breasts looking as though she were still clothed, until he saw her nipples standing out, small pricks of skin like goosebumps. When Jessie wrapped herself around him, Luke was not ready for the urgency of her caresses and felt himself withdraw, though he wanted to move into her more deeply than ever before. But she embraced him, her legs like scissors that cut into his sides to steal his breath. Luke let her move him up and down until she suddenly stopped, feeling his dead weight. She held his face between her long hands, staring at him curiously, yet somewhat distracted by herself. Chagrined, Luke rolled off her and she lay looking at the sky through the dense, quaking treetops. This land was unfamiliar to both of them, this dry and mountainous Northwestern country they were picking on their way to California's vineyards. But, as she lay watching the delicate leaves of the aspen trees above her, their long white bark standing so tall and slender, leaves shivering in their constant celebration of the wind, Jessie thought of Luke's body, light-skinned and lithe, trembling near hers. She turned her head from the sky and smiled down at him, marveling that his skin was so cool and smooth.

Gathering his small roots in her hands, she guided them between her legs, where she held them, outside her body, with her thighs. After rocking him gently she felt him rise up and delve deeply in her; his arms clenched around her as if he climbed up her body. Now they both climbed and Jessie imagined she was moving up wooden rungs like those she once nailed to a tree as a child. In rhythm they moved up the tree, together breathing in the thin, high air near the top. Jessie was like some tree-born animal, knowing the bark to hold, arms and legs clasped around Luke, the trunk, scaling him until he was left far below. She waited, teasing and looking down from some high branch, calling his name as she laughed, jouncing branches and his body. His eyes beneath hers reflected the sky, but they were clouded and heavy with effort. He called her name, telling her to go on without him, that he was older and had gone high enough. She would fell him and he might fall, his hardness becoming earth, soft and uprooted. But she only played for a while quietly before coming back down to him, cajoling and frantic for herself. And he climbed up, her energy in him, pulling himself high until he was shivering against her, shaking and making sounds heard only in the light, high air. Challenging him to fall, Jessie let go the tree; his body swayed alone, poised in the wind before he, too, fell, leaving his head behind him, lost somewhere. Their bodies slapped together once more before they each felt the earth taking them, closing around their damp, yielding skins. It buried them so their bodies took root, dying into the earth with one long, trembling breath.

All season long Jessie kept up with Luke, picking alongside him, though her belly was so low and swollen she could not reach the vines growing closest to the ground. Luke began picking behind her, to get the vegetables she did not reach. They worked steadily, without words, but at the end of the day they met in the nearby woods to rest together chastely like kin, she coiled around her own belly and he around her.

One evening after picking a full day's load of corn, Jessie lay in the woods by a field and, with the help of the gang's midwife, gave birth to a baby boy. "Here's our judge, honey," Luke said, holding the baby gently and laughing, "What you say, chile?" He laid his ear to the tiny, squinted face; the baby's fists boxed Luke's ears. "He say, Jessie wins!" Luke leaned over and laid his hand on her flat belly as she nursed their child.

During the next years Jessie picked alongside her husband, unless her belly swelled low; then he would move behind her to retrieve what she picked over. Several seasons apart Jessie gave birth to two more sons. Then there were no more children. With three small boys, Jessie had no time to meet Luke at the end of their rows and wander off into the woods. She would rush to finish her row, stop to nurse a child, see the oldest child's constant demands, and then rush back to begin another row, leaving the boys in the shade of nearby trees. Once or twice, when they worked Northwestern fields, Jessie would remember the aspen and she joined Luke in the stand of delicate, swaying trees; they made frantic love, for the children were howling from the fields. At night the migrant camp was so crowded Luke rarely touched his wife and took to drinking with the other men. Jessie sat with the women, cooing to children, chatting and doing the necessary chores for the next day.

One night while their gang picked orange groves in south Florida, Luke disappeared after a terrible drinking spell. Jessie knew he was gone for good, and at first was too numb to mourn him. The saving distraction was her three sons, growing straight and tall as saplings, all picking alongside her in the fields, so small and low to the ground they could retrieve any vegetables she missed. In each of her children Jessie smelled the fruit season in which she bore him: Nate, the youngest, like that sticky fragrance of ripe peaches, frightfully soft to the touch, yet she wanted to gobble playfully great bites of her baby's peach skin, this luscious pink sweetmeat; her second son, Leon, smelled sour and green like a vine's first hard tomatoes, and her oldest child, Virgil, had the sorrowful smell of late adolescence that struck Jessie like the hidden acidity of berries, modest black currants in self-imposed privacy that burst forth from every branch, their liquor startling and bittersweet, staining all who touched. Fruit and her children were forever linked in her mind not only by smell but by their indentured future. Before Luke's desertion there might have been another life besides this undulant and endless stretch of fields, another smell for her boys—even coal dust or machine oil or mill floss—but her sons would learn to forget their father and with that loss would forsake any life but a migrant's. Jessie would not forget well enough.

Luke was always in the back of her mind, behind that beckoning tree at the end of her row, just one more row and she would come to him, to rest in the shade. About a week after Luke disappeared Jessie straightened at the end of her row and looked ahead only to see three bobbing black heads earnestly bent over her plants, picking ahead of her toward a future of fields. Jessie's face fell; she looked around desperately for trees to shelter her. But the soil was too sandy for trees and suddenly someone called out to her as crew boss for advice. Wiping her face, Jessie stooped to the next row. Suddenly she felt the corn stalk reach up to pick her, its green blades etching her face like razors, the cornsilk web catching her eyelashes; she did not know whether the blackness seeping into her skull was rich loamsoil or her own despair. Without warning, Jessie sat down in the middle of her row and wept. Her boys hovered around their mother. Jessie's blurred vision warped her sons' swarthy and spent faces into three mirrors, each revealing a side of herself that was more disturbing than any self-scrutiny, because they reflected only her resignation. Shaking her head and sobbing so hard her boys thought she might suffocate, Jessie kept reaching for them, then roughly pushing them away, "No!

Leave me be. Go play, son! Git from these fields; they'll ruin ye like a killin frost! Run from them!"

They stayed with her, fussing over their mother like sisters as they awkwardly smoothed her hair, shook her shoulders, and grabbed her flailing hands, but she did not stop weeping. Finally they carried her to their pickup, explaining to the others that she had taken a fever.

When Jessie awoke there was no familiar face, nor setting, nor sound, simply the rustle of darkness: a tree branch scraping the screen window, grating crickets, and from somewhere near her head a hoarse whisper, whether woman or animal Jessie could not discern. From her knees up, Jessie saw that she was naked, but across her belly and thighs were phosphorescent zigzags like lightning striking along her limbs. Suddenly out of the darkness emerged a blacker shape, its skin oily as if bruised to a high sheen. The woman spoke in rhythmic, jingle-like chants.

"The Spirit must have water," she said and helped Jessie drink from a swollen gourd. Jessie drank, then fell back against the pallet on the floor, surrounding herself with the silence that lay inside her; Jessie hoarded its deep dark as she would an unborn child.

When Jessie woke again, she knew much time had passed, for her body was so weak she could not lift herself up from the pallet. For the first time since yielding to this darkness, Jessie thought of her sons, her migrant gang, her husband. The thought of Luke started a great hunger in her, but it was hunger that fed on itself, on her own body; suddenly Jessie called out for food, for fruit, calling her sons by name until her voice gave out and she fell back weakly. In answer, Jessie saw a flame scratch against the darkness as a woman laid the match atop many thin candles, wicks singeing before taking the fire. On a makeshift altar were nine candles, black and pink, arranged in the pattern of the letter S like a moving serpent. The Mambo woman sprinkled holy water over what seemed like a straw mat, but as she stretched it out, laying it reverently over her shoulders, Jessie recognized the grooved leather mosaic of a diamondback rattler. The snakeskin shimmied across her shoulders, a fragile, crinkling noise as the woman swayed back and forth, head thrust upward, eyes closed.

On a low table near her pallet Jessie saw a surrounding disorder of odd-shaped bowls, tin plates, a dented milk bucket, a pitiful bird-like shape (Jessie thought it looked amazingly like a wizened chicken with all its feathers stuck in backward), and—here Jessie caught her breath, sickened by the confusion of smells: cheap lavender toilet water, orange blossoms, the humid sweetness of honeysuckle smothering her as if she were in a cave; ginger, garlic, and sarsaparilla root made her eyes tear, then the nauseous mixture of cider vinegar and strong coffee. After days without food, the onslaught of smells was enough to send Jessie sprawling back into unconsciousness, but suddenly she was struck with a smell too rank to escape—the pungent odor of fresh dung and the gamey scent of freshly slaughtered animals. Warm blood stiffened the air; Jessie recognized it not so much by smell as by the air's aftertaste lingering in her mouth like raw, salty innard-bile, or the darkest yellow piss.

Arms flailing, Jessie tried to make her body respond to her terror, but it lay lifeless, though she could feel something within her rushing, moving away from this dark shack and the Mambo woman now reeling and spinning on one foot in dizzy abandon. "The Spirit must see sacrifice . . ." the woman's words seemed thrown off by the whirling gravity of her body. A high, whirring song hummed off her; Jessie heard the tuneless and inhuman noise, but not through her ears.

The woman's pitch vibrated as if she had struck a tuning fork against Jessie's jawbone and the cold, shivering steel sounded up into the hollows of Jessie's skull. Teeth on edge, hands covering her ears, Jessie sat cross-legged, mesmerized by the spinning siren. The woman's breaths came in rhythmic heaves.

"Kindly spirit, hunh!" the woman was suddenly still and upright, body quivering slightly like a twanging knife thrown deep into the wooden floor. "Big good angel, hunh! Loa, and my Mambo, whose spirit name is Damballa, answer me! O Great One, she comes to you with her heart bowed down and her shoulders droppin and her spirits broke . . . hunh! I pray you, take off this curse. Yes, for her man's spirit done tampered with her life's breath, hunh! This spirit's backbit and withered her soul till no hair grows and fingernails fall off and bones crumble. Her mind grows dark, sights fail, and seed dries up so her blood don't see flesh. She's athirst after righteousness, hunh! She's hungerin for stones. Ain't no moon or night gives her peace. Ain't no man or child hold her to earth, hunh!" The woman's last words were weary, except for her panting breaths, hunh, hunh, and the shushing hiss, yes, yesss.

Jessie dared not move, but watched the woman as she snuffed out each of the candles with a wet forefinger. Once again cast into darkness, Jessie felt the woman's cool palm against her brow, a brief touch that felt for fever and, for the first time in three days, found none.

"Yes," the woman said firmly, "his spirit, your man's spirit, sees this sacrifice. Woman, you are worthy. Ask him to take you . . ." and she gave Jessie a bitter, moist cake, three drinks of a sweet syrup, then covered her in snakeskin and sleep.

Jessie moved now without the anchor of her body. Hovering above a quiet, naked woman that she only vaguely recognized as herself, Jessie felt little pity or sorrow in leaving her earthly shape. The only sense of loss she experienced was in seeing the dirt road stretching ahead of her, empty of all except a crawling plant life that grew, inching along beside her like a lush, alien companion.

It seemed she had walked for generations carrying many of her in one, when at last she came to a bright river. Sun and shimmering sound rose off the swift waters like steam and the air around her was cool, quickened. It seemed the river spoke to Jessie until she saw the voices came from the opposite shore. In the distance, encamped in radiant disarray, was a circle of shapes—wandering specters passing a thousand days together before moving on. Jessie strained to hear their words and saw them metamorphose into the shapes of their stories. These spirit storytellers summoned up earth's characters the way humans told ghost tales; they spoke hungrily, compassionately, the sound of their mortal longings like a lament or lullaby.

They did not hear her calls, nor recognize Jessie as separate from her companion of creeping ivy. But for an instant she saw Luke, illuminated and tall, before he changed into a white-barked shade tree, delicate yellow leaves adorning him, shivering. Then he became a specter and joined the wanderers on their pilgrimage in worlds Jessie could not yet imagine; but she knew they journeyed to find forgiveness. She yearned to follow them in her spirit form but was confined by the intimate ivy that twined and rooted her to the alluvial banks of the river—this resplendent river that had not granted her crossing.

"Drink this, Ma," it was her oldest son, Virgil, pleading with her. When Jessie opened her eyes, she was blinded by unexpected sunlight as she lay, not in the humid swamp shack, but in the back of her pickup. Peering over the metal siding, Jessie saw her migrant gang, gathered together, talking excitedly, pointing to her as if she were still unconscious. The well water was tart, a thin and clear gruel compared to the black syrup she had suckled on for so many days. Her youngest son, Nate, sat in the pickup eyeing her soberly, so calm and separate it made Jessie laugh.

"What you see, little one?" She ruffled his spiky hair, but still he did not smile.

"We didn't know if you'd come back to us," Virgil said. "The Mambo woman said you bout gone. . . ."

"I did wander a mite too far," Jessie smiled and reached for Nate, holding him tightly so that he cried out.

"Leon's gone to fetch more water. Last time ol farmer Martin said no more trips to his well. We been here too long, he says. Pickin's over, Ma, and we best be gone."

Jessie closed her eyes but her son kept on—the season was short, had to get to Georgia, these swamp people were suspicious. "Hush up, son!" Jessie finally interrupted. "We'll be gone soon enough."

That night when the town's minister and sheriff accompanied the orange farmer to the migrants' camp, their gruff pity of the past few days had changed to stern intent.

"If the woman ain't well, jist leave her with the minister here," the sheriff said to Virgil, who was considered crew boss in his mother's sickness. "Reverend Staunton will put her and the little boy up. She'll follow y'all when . . ."

"Reckon I'll follow right now," Jessie sat up, gripping the pickup sides for support. Her face was sallow, splotched with sweat, but she had enough presence to command everyone's attention. "Much obliged, Reverent," she nodded curtly to the minister, a small and dark-skinned man who seemed riveted on Nate sitting next to Jessie. Reverend

Staunton returned her nod, but instead of retreating, he came over to her, eyes still on her son Nate.

"Leave the boy. Settle him here. My wife and me, we'll root him down. . . ."

Jessie ignored the small, intense minister and pushed Nate behind her. The child peered out at the Reverend, returning the man's stare with more curiosity than Jessie had ever seen in him. It was not the minister's face, but his hands that absorbed the boy's attention.

"Look, Ma," Nate whispered behind her back. "You can see clear through his skin!"

Jessie watched Reverend Staunton's hands as they clenched the truck's metal siding. Pale to the point of transparency, one could make out the mapping of his blood veins—raised purple welts crisscrossing white hands whose only color was the dull pinkish hint of bone. His hands seemed flayed and raw; Jessie thought perhaps the hands belonged to a healer. But were they forgiving hands, she wondered, or did they feel down to the bone, all-perceiving and pitiless?

"Come here, boy," Reverend Staunton suddenly said and Nate let himself be lifted down from the truck. He stood as tall as the Reverend's shoulders, peering out from beneath a wide, skinless hand at his mother. "Root him here with me, woman. I will raise him as my own son."

"He'll save that boy sure, Miz Walsh," the sheriff piped up. "Don't you want to keep your chile from this Godfor-saken wanderin life?"

"The boy will save me," Reverend Staunton said softly and took Jessie's hand. "You have other sons to root ye. But I have nothing. You can visit the boy ever year when you come to pick these orange fields. Anytime you don't think he's happy, take him on with your gang. But give me this time to root him, to hold him down to earth so he won't fly off, rootless, like you just done."

Jessie blanched at the mention of her recent journey. How had this minister known of the hoodoo woman? Had he sent her? Surely not. Perhaps it was the woman who sent this man, but for a cure? "I'll think on it," Jessie dismissed the gang of men and lay back down in her pickup.

All that evening she listened to the gang discuss their next job, heard Virgil's voice command their attention. Beside her in the truck lay Nate, not yet ten, yet picking alongside her. She held him to her side, a shape almost as long as her body, yet he seemed weightless in her arms. He breathed steadily but with a heaviness that told her he slept the dreamless sleep of all wanderers.

The next morning was the first day Jessie had been up since Luke left her. There was great commotion in the camp, the women cooking grits and bold coffee, the men loading the trucks, her sons skittering across the fields as they announced the approach of the sheriff and the Reverend.

Jessie dressed Nate in his only set of clothes, overalls passed down from his brothers, already inching up his ankles and frayed across his narrow, tight bottom.

"Root him here a spell, preacher," Jessie said to Reverend Staunton and watched her son stare again at the man's large, raw hands.

"I'm obliged to ye, ma'am," the man stammered and waited as Jessie hugged her child.

Nate seemed more numb than curious and though Jessie had explained to him that she would come back soon, he had showed few signs of understanding and even less of fright at their leave-taking. Perhaps, Jessie thought, it was she who was numb, beyond all grief after Luke's desertion. But it cheered her to see Nate walking easily with the small man, intent on the hand that held his, not turning back, except absently when his brother called out, "Little one! You grow tall and straight, hear? And when we come back again, we'll pick ye like the ripest sweetness ever seen!"

Jessie did not call back to her son; she watched them walk until it seemed the shapes of the hanging kudzu swallowed them up in a lush, grotesque embrace.

GOD'S SPIES

Whether the Reverend and Mrs. Staunton asked to keep
Nate Walsh out of faith or as a charitable chore, the Reverend never explained, except to say, "Wanderers are God's
angels or devils come to test us. God protects beggars, strangers, and supplicants. Can we go against the Lord's chosen?"
But even as a child Nate sensed the Stauntons' caring for
him was dependent on the extremity of his gratitude. He
was not at first grateful. His mother had told him that these
people would change him so that he would no longer be
shunned as a migrant. They would lend him the narrow stillness of settled folk that admits no wandering, body or spirit.
But soon Nate felt more rootless and anonymous than ever
before; it seemed that the Stauntons borrowed something
from him, that it was he who held them to earth.

Even so, Nate liked this intimate back country of swamps
and rain forests. The Stauntons' prim clapboard was overgrown by palmetto, its spiked fans like green accordion
curtains across Nate's window. Everywhere were palm trees
strangled by pale, spidery moss and the backyard bordered a
hotsprings, the azure color of water-colors. It all struck Nate

like the picture-book paradises in family Bibles that he had pored over. And now here was such a country; colors had a vibrant pulse and the humid air ached with sweetness. Now Nate was not looking at the countryside from the rain-splashed windows of his mother's pickup, but from his own window; and the vision seemed all his own.

The Stauntons gave Nate a room in the back of the house that had been built on as a greenhouse. Every hour of the day it was suffused with light, great geometric angles of light that overlapped, leaving not a shadow in the room except Nate's own. The floorboards of Nate's room slanted upward and away from the rest of the upright structure, as if Nate's room kept its distance, determined during the common hurricanes or typhoons to be the first separated and flung skyward.

Mrs. Staunton had long ago given up her greenhouse and instead took to long hours of piano practice. She rarely had reason to come into Nate's room. But every morning her music stole over Nate, dissonant spirituals that woke him with the sound of lamentations. Mrs. Staunton's voice was wavering and slightly sharp, but she sang lyrics with so much assurance that Nate soon began hearing harmonies. His harmonies were pure and high, but he kept them to himself. And every afternoon when the swamps expanded with heat, thick slime-surfaces shuddering against the sun's merciless curiosity, when every nook and cranny of the Stauntons' own rooms were illuminated by the humid light, Reverend Staunton would come to tuck Nate in for his nap, before he and his wife retired upstairs for their all-consuming sleep and prayers.

Nate lay beneath a bulky quilt while the Reverend's rapt voice bound him in a circle of Biblical fire—the burning bush, fiery furnace, a pillar of fire he must follow through the wilderness, hellfire's lake, tongues of Pentecostal fire, the burning Babylon, ashes and burnt offerings—on and on until Nate seemed not to sleep but to faint from the heat. Nate was very still during the Reverend's sermons, allowing the shrill man to do battle and wander within his silences. All the while the boy watched the play of light around the room; sometimes it seemed that brilliant light took on shimmering shapes to embody the dry and arid stories the Reverend was unleashing. Other times the light seemed to come from within Nate himself, beginning in the secret hollow of his breast bone and radiating first down to his belly and then rushing up to suffuse his skull so that Nate imagined that bony cave illuminated, all its mysterious passages open; and if there was any darkness now, it was outside him. For inside Nate was dry and light and revealed.

But Reverend Staunton did not see the boy's metamorphosis. He always ended his stories with a look of defeat to see Nate's blank, bleached face, his monotonal voice answering, "Yessir. I heared," and Nate's eyes were so distracted Staunton knew the boy was unmoved.

As soon as the Reverend was gone Nate fled from his quilt's burning bondage. He kept a respectful quiet, but all the while performed Lazarus-like miracles, his imagination fired by the light within him. Sometimes the light took on voices that moved through Nate. Stamping his feet, whooshing wind through pursed lips, and murmuring scriptures like powerful spells, Nate scattered the ashes of Babylon across his pinewood floor, where they immediately took on the shapes of grateful armies encamped around him as if it were the blackest of nights and he, a fire to warm them. Other afternoons, tired of flesh and blood, these kin conjured in his own image, Nate called upon the Biblical beasts—Behemoth, the first work of God, bones of bronze and limbs like iron; then Jonah's greedy Leviathan, willing to swallow one up in the darkest night of the soul. Amidst his heavenly menagerie, the monsters never disturbed Nate as greatly as the halo-enshrouded serpent, Beelzebub's first incarnation. How to banish him without exiling his own chimeric servants? Every time Nate proclaimed, "Git thee behind me!" his bestiary dissipated into darkness, a forsaken phantasmagoria. Then his inner light fled and Nate became aware of the swamp sun, whose light was yellow, diluted.

One afternoon in the midst of listening to the beast's complaint and revelation—hoots, honks, and wheezes like a wind-filled bagpipe that Nate easily interpreted—the boy felt another presence in the room. He whirled around to find Reverend Staunton in the doorway, his face clenched in amazement.

Staunton's voice was almost a whisper. "There is no Spirit here, boy. The Devil done his work and gone on." Staunton gestured to the lush countryside. "Spirit needs the desert of our Lord to survive, to humble the body and make strong the soul."

"But it's kinda . . ." Nate felt a part of himself expand to escape his body as if his spirit, like water, evaporated, yearning toward the sky. "It's kinda pretty here. And I seen pictures like this. I seen Bibles say this be paradise."

"You seen but you ain't listened. You ain't heard how we was drove *out* from paradise. We was sent to wander in wilderness and desert." The Reverend paused, then sat down heavily in a chair near Nate.

"But ain't this like them pictures?"

"All this . . ." the Reverend spread his arms to encompass the gathering twilight which even now was sharp and bright, "this green world is no Canaan, for we have not wandered in the wilderness to enter promised land. The Old Testament prophet says, 'In the desert land, waterless, dry, and pathless, I appeared before Thee, that I might see Thy virtue and Thy glory.'" Staunton looked out Nate's window and whispered, "Bright world, you keep me from prophecy, from the desert of my Lord's righteousness."

Nate circled the room as if any minute he might bolt out the door. For a few more minutes Reverend Staunton talked on, but his voice was so low Nate could not hear him. Suddenly the man reached for Nate and easily caught him. He peered into the boy's light eyes with that same curious expectation Nate had seen the first time they met in the migrant camp.

"Chile, you see worlds in your wanderings . . . worlds not so cursed with beauty. Worlds dry and delivering us from evil."

Nate said nothing, until Reverend Staunton shook him. "Sir?"

"Ain't you seen them worlds?"

"No sir."

"You seen signs," the Reverend nodded but looked past Nate as if carrying on a conversation with the squabbling birds. "Yes, you been visited, you seen visions like no one else."

"No sir," Nate shivered a little. "Nobody visits us."

"I knowed it when I heard tell how you interpreted tongues your ma spoke in her spirit wanderings. Knowed it when I come to curse that Mambo woman and find your ma's body there empty as a cocoon. Lord showed me to watch your ma, to foller her back to the migrant camp and I'd see a sign." The Reverend eyed Nate. "Was you I found. You been anointed by God. Don't you remember?"

Nate remembered the all-consuming calm that had held him those days of his mother's mourning. He heard her feverish wanderings and understood her words. It was only when his older brothers asked Nate to interpret Jessie's ravings that Nate had realized he alone heard. It was then they knew to bring her to the Mambo woman. After Jessie's recovery Nate's brothers withdrew from him; and when Jessie told Nate she was leaving him behind with this Reverend, Nate had accepted it as her judgment against him—his interpretation of her despair had been a violation. Because of his trespass, his sin of knowing, Nate understood that Jessie and his brothers left him behind. "I don't recollect nothun," Nate finally said to Staunton.

"And then I seen other signs of your prophecy here in my house, like Eli done seen the call of his child Samuel to judgment and prophecy," the Reverend continued almost to himself. "These visions and voices you hear done anointed you. But me, I'm still wandering and listening."

Nate tried to stop Staunton's voice in his head; perhaps all these words, too, were not meant for him, but for the Lord. Perhaps he did wrong not to stop his ears or silence the man. Nate slowly raised his small fist, taking aim with his eyes narrowed to slits. "Hush!" he commanded and his fist came down in a high arc to hit the bony crown of Reverend Staunton's head. The man seemed not to have felt the blow, but remained motionless, his whole body in an attitude of extreme attention.

"I was chose to hear you answer the call, 'Here am I, Lord,' to give yourself up a prophet to your people," Reverend Staunton opened his eyes; they glistened, a lighter color of gray. He stretched out his hand to Nate, but the boy hung back. "I don't need you near me now," Staunton said and clenched himself with both hands. "I done found you, Nate, in you found wilderness."

Every day after that Reverend Staunton entered Nate's room for his afternoon storytelling with the words, "If you're going to be a prophet, best study signs and miracles." But one afternoon Reverend Staunton did not come to do his prophetic battle. The boy waited in silence, forsaking his own daily visions. When Staunton had not come by evening, Nate cautiously climbed the stairs, listening for the sound of the Reverend's sleep-racked breathing. Nate opened the door to their stifling room and saw the Stauntons resting as he had only seen dead people do, laid out in pious attitudes of eternal abandon. Mrs. Staunton's face was folded into a hundred wrinkles, all crisscrossed at the corners of her crooked smile. Slightly open, her eyes rolled upward to expose a filmy, twitching whiteness, the look of a blind woman listening to the bustling charity about her. The Reverend was austere, eyes righteously closed on this world. Stretched open across his chest was the frayed family Bible, leaves as yellowed as Staunton's skin. There was the clammy, sweet scent of old people's sweat and stale rose sachet, a smell Nate recognized not from their hugs, but from playtimes he spent enveloped in the piles of dirty clothes at the bottom of the laundry chute. Stealthily Nate would slide down the chute, landing with a soft flurry of shirt sleeves, stiff trousers, and flannel nightclothes. Here he nested like a small bird, clothing himself in their smells, covering his own stringent scent, until he was one of them.

Smiling, Nate took a deep breath of their familiar smells and stepped farther into their room. Both Reverend Staunton and his Mrs. were covered up to their necks in a gay patchwork quilt on which a Haitian servant had pieced a vainglorious aviary of peacocks, nightingales, and hawks that metamorphosed around the quilt's more colorful borders into double-headed, fabulous bird-creatures: griffins, basilisks, and feathered dragons, all made of bright rags, their wings stitched in silver and turquoise threads.

It was this Haitian quilt Nate remembered most, for he

was sure one of those mischievous birds, and not he, made the singsong noise startling the Reverend from his sleep. Eyelids flapping open, he started up in bed, eyes fixed not on the betrayal of birds or the frightened child by the open door, but on his wife. Squinting, his black topknot ruffled like a bird of prey, he watched his wife for some sign of death. She was more sickly than he. But when he laid his ear to her heart he breathed a long sigh that struck Nate by its unexpected expression of triumph; he was not deserted, nor had his wife winged her way toward a heavenly home before him. In their long sleep, this competition for heaven, it was again a stalemate. The Reverend settled back into his sleep, as earthbound and impatient as those caged, quilted birds.

From then on Nate had every afternoon to himself to share with his visionary family. Now freed from Staunton's interruptions, Nate's beasts and prophets took on more commanding voices. One afternoon when Nate heard a shriek, he did not recognize it as human or separate from his unearthly visitors until he heard rampaging footsteps upstairs. A voice kept calling his name. Quickly now, Nate ran into the sour-smelling vestibule. No one. Passing the Reverend's study, he peered into the cold, clean kitchen, empty except for the full-bodied smells of coffee and jam preserves, strawberry and apple and oily paraffin simmering, brooding on the stove for days. In the parlor Nate listened with his eyes, unable to blink as he roamed the downstairs rooms, scrupulously avoiding the bedroom upstairs. In the parlor sat stern, high-backed chairs gathered like polite, hungry guests around the dining table; in the hallway stretched the black, upward sweep of the staircase and the scattered throw rugs, their woolen braids coiled in the corners like a knot of snakes waiting. Suddenly a rail-thin arm clutched Nate, dragging him up the dread staircase by the seat of his pants; his small hipbones bruised against the wooden banister.

A demon had him. Its shrill voice demanded, "Where's Reverend and Missus?" shaking him so hard Nate's teeth made clopping sounds like horses' hooves. "Chile? Answer me!" Nate just gaped, staring at the Stauntons' empty, newly made bed. The demon slapped him and was gone, banging the screen door off its hinges.

It was only later Nate heard about the accident. The same demon reappeared late that night, in the form of a grieved, but more composed neighbor. She fixed the child some supper, staring at him while he ate. At his last bite, the neighbor took on her demonic stare and the strident voice screamed, "Ingrate chile! Now you got two more shadows to talk bout and stow in that back room where you keep them imagined folk you always convulsin with. Two more saints. The Reverend and Missus has gone to their reward. They was taken quickly and together. Reverend did drive too slow," here the demon's face metamorphosed into the familiar, almost kindly face of the neighbor woman, as she broke down. She sobbed harshly on Nate's shoulder. "They stalled at them crossroads out by the sawmill . . ." The woman hushed, and the demon took hold of Nate's shoulders, hissing, "Now, child, don't you listen to no foolish talk bout them jist waitin for that train, hear? You honor Reverend and Missus' memory."

The demon took Nate home with her to a squat cabin the child shared with eleven other children. Now Nate had to crowd his beasts and Biblical prophets into his mind. The only prophet the neighbor woman allowed Nate to give voice and vision was Reverend Staunton. But even as he mourned the Stauntons, Nate mourned the loss of his afternoon Old Testament communions more. Lost and wandering inside Nate's head, his forsaken companions quarreled and cried out for Nate's attention. His head ached with shouts and commands that clapped against his skull. Voices without worldly shape longed for the limitless hold of Nate's spirit. Gathering the force of wind, the voices moved against Nate to sculpt his skull from the inside out until only the thinnest last layering of bone separated them from escape. With great gasps of spirit the arid and dark wind moved over Nate; its force desiccated his body, and his bones broke down into their original elements: dust and sand. His earthly shape was now a desert wilderness over which Spirit brooded like wind.

Nate was quiet now, outside and in. Lost in a soundlessness deeper than death, Nate's mind and body were swept clean —ruined barricades against the dark, arid spirit that left him deserted.

"Figure he's gone stark deaf and dumb?" the many children in the cabin asked their mother.

Nate saw their tiny mouths flap open, shaping sounds that whooshed over him. He tried to return their small winds. The children looked at his blank face, his eyes as startlingly blue as a mirage.

"Reverend and Missus might as well taken this dead chile with them on their journey," their mother said and let her children play with Nate as if he were her gift to them.

At first Nate felt a craven responsibility to tell these people of their danger now that he had set free such Spirit. Its prophetic winds would hollow them out, too. But they showed no signs of hearing, of recognizing their fate and extreme frailty. All of them went about their daily chores, oblivious to Nate's knowing stillness, the desert of his Lord's affection.

Jessie Walsh and her older sons fell back from Nate when they came to reclaim him. No one had summoned them; it was orange-picking season and this year, as in the past several years, Jessie had passed through, making a point to visit Nate, even if she had no job picking in this back country. Each time she had come calling on him Nate had greeted her with less and less affection so that now Jessie wondered if Nate's silence was simply the logical extreme of settled life. She was as foreign to him now as his roots were alien to her.

The neighbor woman watched Jessie's arms fall slack at her side, their embrace undone by Nate's muteness, his severe distraction. "Your chile's been saved," the neighbor explained, her voice terse, but her face showed some shame.

Jessie looked closer at her son and saw suddenly that his face was so full of hollows that the blades of jaw and cheekbone struck the skin like long scars. His eyes seemed to rupture from his head; lashless, they were a bruised color. "What you done to him? He looks half starved!"

"Ain't done nothun no Christian woman wouldn't done," the neighbor was outraged. "Treat him like my own, even though his folks left him."

"We didn't jist leave him for nothun!"

"I said *his* folks . . . the Stauntons, God rest 'em. . . ."

"Yes'm," Jessie's voice was menacing, "I heared how they done rested themselves. Word's all over town."

"When first this boy came, why, he weren't nothun but sorrow. Reverend Staunton seen that, took it on hissself and saved your boy."

"Reckon that Reverend saved hisself!" Jessie said and, motioning for her oldest son to lead Nate away, she slammed out of the cabin.

For the next several weeks as they traveled with the crops, Jessie watched Nate. At first she thought his muteness, this almost idiot lull in him, was a punishment she had inflicted

by leaving him to settled life. But her despair soon gave way
to a realization that something else stalked the boy, something that had nothing to do with her, perhaps not even with
the Stauntons. Jessie watched Nate now more impersonally;
it was then that she understood her son was wandering, pur-
suing his inward course as if to lose whatever had hold of
him. Now he seemed too weary to run farther away. She
imagined that inwardly Nate was somewhere along the road
she had first discovered in her own wanderings. He stood at
a place where many paths converged and summoned courage to turn around and face what pursued him. Perhaps it
was as simple and intimate as his own shadow; Nate needed
but to turn around and be reconciled to the part of himself
he could not exile. Perhaps her son didn't know that at the
end of the dirt road ran the river—that clean, forgiving river
where he might find other wanderers. She tried to tell him
stories, both of earth and of spirit. But he remained unmoved.

Now for the first time in years Jessie dreamed; and all her
dreams were set in that familiar Florida back country, the
country she picked by day and hoped to escape at night. At
first Jessie told herself she dreamed to understand Nate, but
finally she admitted that she dreamed for herself, to find her
own spirit. A memory kept moving over her: she lay in the
back of her pickup truck, the faces of her sons like the pale
moon in various stages of eclipse around her. One face
leaned near hers and as she felt words rush out of her with
every harsh breath, the calm, moon-like face shone more
brilliantly, returning her words to her with sweet breaths
like breezes so that she lost nothing; her fever was exhaled to
be returned to her in cool, private words she did not recognize as interpretations of her own ravings. The memory of

that sweet-faced moon gleamed over her, a face she now recognized as Nate's.

Often during these damp nights Jessie was woken by screams and immediately left her bed in the back of her pickup to go into her sons' tent and comfort Nate, to return to him the constancy and cool breaths of their spiritual kinship. But she always found Nate deeply asleep and then Jessie knew the screams had been her own. Bending over Nate, Jessie wept and was so fearful of violating her son with her sorrow that her tears were all she allowed to touch him.

The first sound Nate heard since the Stauntons' death was that of a woman's weeping. Shallow, driven breaths, her weeping struck Nate as more beautiful than any sound he could remember. He lay still, afraid she might quit crying if he stirred. Perhaps it was his long muteness, but Nate had no memory that this breaking sound was how the body relinquished its sorrow. Compared to the deafening winds and voices of Nate's wilderness, this woman's weeping seemed like humid music, a playful abandon, a fool's complicity with her body's bountiful noise-makers. Her sounds, so airy and yet punctuated with a guttural snuffling, evoked a companion grumble in Nate's own body. And suddenly his belly laughs struck Jessie like cool winds.

"Chile, what in the world . . . ?" Jessie grabbed him up and Nate felt her neck slick with a stringent wetness that he did not recognize as tears.

"Please, I don't mind," Nate said, but his throat seemed rusted from its long silence and Jessie did not understand him. She kept rocking him, holding Nate so tightly she imagined her hugs, squeezing air in and out, were all that kept him alive.

Nate stared at the night world around him, his dim eyes
squinted against the stars' pale radiance. They were in a
migrant camp, tent flaps moved easily in the breeze and
small fires were strewn around like crude reflections of the
constellations. Everywhere was stillness and movement—the
density of sleep and the thrashing dreamers, the women
nursing new babies and the motionless men on watch, their
bodies as lean a silhouette as the nearby orchard trees. Occasionally a man might be shrouded in smoke, his cigarette a
spiraling pinpoint of light like the moving center of himself,
his soul. Nate felt Jessie drying her face and his with the
palms of her hands. He looked up at her, and suddenly it
seemed the whole world changed and was luminous with
early-morning light.

"Ma," Nate said, his voice clear, "ain't this place pretty?
Ain't there prophets here in this wilderness?"

Jessie hesitated a moment, looking around at the awaken-
ing camp. "Reckon if it's wanderin them prophets do, son,
they's all here." When she turned back to Nate she expected
any expression but the one he wore—a weary smile, self-
treasonous because it seemed as if the boy were unaware of
the split in his face: eyes squinted with pain, but mouth
stretched wide in sublimely indifferent smile. Jessie knew it
was not Nate's smile, yet after its first appearance the expression never left her son's face.

As the migrant families moved across the country with the
ripening crops, Jessie kept one eye always on Nate. He was
picking alongside his older brothers now and his quietness
was not so evident; for all the migrants moved in a soundless
world, under a gravity so intense they must walk slowly,
speak little, show no luxury of expression. The migrants
never questioned accepting this gravity; it was a matter of

necessity. Necessity had moved them so much that soon nothing else could move them.

In much the same way, the migrants accepted Nate, his strange smile and ways. But Jessie never ceased to be startled by the change in her son. Now it seemed a chore for Nate to meet his mother's eyes, not because he wasn't curious or pleased but because his attention seemed diverted by an urgent inner life, one that left him utterly exhausted. Jessie knew that whatever stalked her son was demanding battle. Nate's eyes did not show his fatigue; they wore a look of constant and virgin astonishment such as one might see in a newborn. Yet her son's weariness was quite evident. Jessie wondered now that she had not recognized it before—the extremity of his fatigue matched the extremity of his smile. Spent from searching his inner worlds, Nate simply had no energy left to work his face.

At last Jessie felt her love for Nate mixed with mourning. Sometimes while picking she stood up and called for the water carrier. Dribbling cold spring water over her wrists, face, and neck, Jessie's eyes instinctively rested on Nate. Then an extreme of love she had only felt for Luke surged over her, leaving her breathless, her belly tightened with the same tearing cramps that signaled labor. She yielded to a sense of loss akin to that a woman feels on delivering herself of a stillborn; and that was the love possessing Jessie—the love of the lost, the unknown, the stillborn who in their desertion denied that they had ever been inside her. But still she carried them, her deserters.

Jessie watched her sons picking in the fields. Nate bobbed easily from his picking bag to the green-covered ground. "Flesh born of flesh," Jessie said quietly and drank from her cool water dipper. "And spirit born of Spirit." She had carried children, perhaps would carry them still, but Nate would never be hers. Now she let him go, freed him from her expectations, from the bondage of her blood. Across the fields, she saw him straighten and look around, not at her, but at something just behind him. And it seemed she no longer knew him; he was simply another person whom she must love as if he were her own. He moved quickly down the row, oblivious to her meditation on him. Jessie knew his movements were dictated by the gravity of his gift, the burden of the life he carried inside, the children of his spirit, stillborn to all but himself.

"Nate," Jessie gently shook her head, "I'll never have another child like ye. You're my terrible blessin, my punished, pure-born boy."

SETTLED FOLK

Her newly settled existence in Jordan County, Georgia, Jessie now thought of as an afterlife—"Not heaven sholy," she told her sons, "but a new earth." How deeply this new earth would root her and her sons, Jessie often wondered. Over the past months the Walshes had worked every off hour cleaning, repairing, and fitting the broken shape of Lloyd's cabin to themselves. Slowly the cabin accepted them, opened its rooms to human sounds and fixtures where for so long it had received only stealthy, crawling creatures—the rats, spiders, and weasels that left its wood gnawed, its ceiling web-hung, and its dirt floors strewn with animal dung that looked like odd footprints. Virgil had tackled the roof, laying rows of grainy shingles that defied rain or wind; Leon wielded his saw, and his carpentry was so well crafted the house seemed to draw a sharp, inward breath of pride and straighten up, girded by ribs of pine-hewn rafters. The hollow, dim inside of the cabin fell to Jessie and Nate. From her long hours of weaving oak-bark baskets for field picking, it was no trouble for Jessie to make lattice bottoms for Leon's carved straight chairs. Painting required the same stoop and sway as had

Jessie's picking work and she fell into the patient rhythm of slapping paint on the walls.

Nate helped his mother whitewash the cabin's rotted walls. He did not paint as placidly as he had picked, and at first Jessie was troubled by his frenetic energy. Not content with a single brush, Nate made wide rollers from baling wire and an old carpet that left its bristles in the fresh paint.

"Looks like a porcupine done throwed its tail quills into that wall," Jessie laughed.

Nate ignored her and sloshed his roller in the paint can, dribbling whitewash over the dirt floor to work in the cabin's back room. At the end of the day his walls glistened unevenly, white swatches of wall radiating color as phosphorescent as shafts of sunlight. But other areas seemed only tinged with the pale paint as the cabin's dark stains bled through. Surveying the job, Jessie shook her head and moved her tin of paint into the room. "Chile, you think cause I ain't never had no room to my own that it don't matter to me? Looks like you done throwed the paint on with a bucket like pitchin slops!"

Nate turned around, the familiar smile stretching across his face in an extreme of determination Jessie had learned to dread. "This be *my* room."

Jessie's jaw dropped and she stared at her son, "Nate Walsh! I can still whup the tar out of ye like I never done when you was a chile!"

"You sleep in town," Nate said and his smile trembled. "You aimin to anyway."

Jessie was upon him before she could think, slapping his face back and forth with her hand. Nate's face dripped white paint and Jessie noticed her fist still clenched the paintbrush. Paint was splattered over everything. Then she was laughing, a shrill, loon-like laughter. "Nate," she said, trying to control herself, reaching for him, his white face silly as a clown's, but expressionless, "I never meant to . . ."

"Room's yours."

"No, you take it, chile," Jessie touched his shoulder. "You and your brothers. Nate, you been settled before and know how to be inside your own walls. I'd go stir crazy."

"It ain't jist for me!" Nate suddenly cried. "Ma, I got to have room for . . ." As if someone slashed his face open, Nate's smile divided him.

"For who?"

"It ain't for me," Nate said and clambered out the window, walking quickly across the fields to the nearby pine woods.

For a long while Jessie stared after him. Now she became aware of her own shadow. Falling across the pale walls, it creased in the middle to flatten out and follow other shades along the earthen floor. Her shadow was not solid, but everywhere riddled with light that streamed through it like luminous veins. Her reflection was so lean and wavering about the edges that Jessie thought a wind could sweep this cabin clean of her. Staring at her weightless silhouette, Jessie suddenly felt as unsubstantial as her shadow. Holding the walls, she made her way, pressing palm after palm along the wet whiteness of the wood until she came to the corner of the room where no light followed and her shadow again merged with her body. Its slight weight was enough to hold her down to earth as she slid weakly to the dirt floor. For a few moments Jessie gave way to tremors that racked her body, but she did not have the strength to weep. Instead she clenched herself, the long muscles in her arms like knotted ropes to gird her. What had she almost lost? Jessie wondered. It had not been like that time with the Mambo woman when her spirit abandoned her feverish body as easily as exhaled sighs. It was more terrible and somehow damning, this feeling of life inside her shadow rather than herself, this knowledge that she was simply a reflection thrown by light from outside, perhaps from another person.

A lifetime of moving with the seasons had not made her feel as weightless as did this settling down. Perhaps the gravity of the migrant world had forced her to stoop so she was part of the earth. But now it seemed she stood still long enough to feel the great losses of her life. What did she have of herself? Jessie wondered. What had she lost all those years of wandering, of sowing her spirit aimlessly about, that could never be restored her by shelter or settled space or human roots?

And what right did she have to settle here? Jessie wondered. Suddenly she stood up and began moving her belongings from this back room to the center of the cabin. Nate had first seen that she had no claim here, Jessie thought. Nate knew she did not take up her rightful space, that this wide room would overwhelm and swallow her up—a whirlpool of air centered in her vacuum. But Nate, Jessie thought, his spirit had always carried on a hundred lives that might fill up the room like rays of light. Nate could claim this room and cabin like settled folks; his spirit could usurp all other presences. *It's for my sake Nate wants this room*, Jessie thought. She looked out the window for signs of him. In the overgrown pasture nothing moved, no wind stirred the trees, and yet Jessie felt suddenly cool as if all humidity evaporated and her body was dry, bleached as white and brittle as this room. It was Nate's room now, Jessie decided, it was the shape of his spirit.

Slowly Jessie moved within the two-room cabin, carrying her belongings from the back room out to the main room, where Virgil's and Leon's clothes and few possessions were piled in a corner. In another corner Jessie deposited her things, but she dragged her mattress outside to the front porch. "Leastways it don't sag so I sleep sideways," Jessie mused and plucked long splinters from the mattress. Back inside she arranged Nate's room and put his bedroll on Nettie Sloan's old bedsprings. At last the house was settled—Virgil and Leon in the main room and Nate in the back of the cabin, his windows facing south toward the longest hours of the sun; now, Jessie thought, all that intruded on Nate was light.

On the front porch, Jessie's bed barely fit between the wall and wayward steps. She would sleep here the summer and by fall maybe move into town. "Now, jist don't knuckle under with me here," Jessie advised the front porch and sat down heavily on her mattress. There was a brief protest, a settling of wood, and Jessie slept until mid-morning when Lloyd Sloan came by to take her to the diner.

Jessie's diner work had lent her not a single acquaintance. Her silent and at best monosyllabic serving of the townsfolk and their vigilance against her made Jessie feel invisible. Jake had instructed her not to talk or let anyone know her past. "They git wind of migrant in my kitchen, they'll be feeling lice and scabies of a sudden and never darken this door."

Her first days in the diner, the more curious, time-consuming customers had asked Jessie the ritual questions.

"No, I wasn't borned here," Jessie answered, and when prodded said, "I'm not from these parts."

"Where was you borned?"

"I don't rightly recollect," Jessie finally said and saw the blank, deeply offended faces fall away from her.

Though Jake told Jessie that his diner had a regular

clientele, Jessie saw no consistent customers except Sheriff Lloyd's deputies, a few night watchmen and shopkeepers; all barely took notice of her except to demand seconds. Jessie figured other customers had been warned off the place. If it had not been for Lloyd's visits several times a day, Jessie would have been desolate. The first thing she discovered about settled life and work was its loneliness. Her migrant days had left her with an abiding sense of solitude against a backdrop of strong fellowship, but now she felt starved for some community even as her solitude was broken by the demands of customers who saw her as inseparable from coffee, food, and silence. It made Jessie want to startle this town with her presence, instead of taking her place in its pecking order. But still she held back from going to church, the center of all community; she hesitated out of shyness and a sense of her own spirit's poverty, rather than out of sin, as some of the church people suspected.

All summer and fall Jessie worked quietly behind the diner counter, serving fewer and fewer customers. "Soon's we git this harvest in, I'm goin back to that diner and rid her of your gal," Jake told Lloyd, not unaware that Jessie's sons listened from the fields. "My bidness jist slacked off somethin fierce!" Jake paused and took Lloyd's elbow, saying low, "Listen, Lloyd, I know you got your reasons . . . hell, when my wife died I'd see a woman and . . . well, you know the hankerin. But this Jessie Walsh can't even hold herself down. You seen how she sleeps on that porch like some trash paradin herself. She can't hold down my customers, neither."

"You'll have to tell her to leave," Lloyd said quietly and called her sons to come help with the tractor. "Jist go on back to your kitchen now. Me and my boys will finish this here harvest."

"Damn right I will!" Jake yelled and swung up onto the

tractor seat. "Soon's winter sets in I will, I swear. You tell her that!" and he roared off down the field, pulling a flatbed of fresh corn.

But winter changed everything. Farmers took odd jobs in shops, the mill hands worked graveyard shifts, the townswomen were freed from their schoolchildren, and church circles congregated in town to do charity for the shut-ins or backslid who hibernated until better weather. And Jessie Walsh had begun to talk and to make doughnuts. Every morning very early a night watchman or sheriff or overworked merchant, even a church woman who had spent all night struggling with a sickly sinner's soul—all could be startled awake by Jessie's strong coffee and watch her run from doughnut press to the tub of splattering grease, where she fished for the light brown sweetcakes, expertly throwing them onto the cooling grill. If a man was in a hurry to get to work, if a woman was somewhat hesitant about exchanging words with a woman known to have been around so much nothing mattered to her, both could snatch a hot doughnut and be done. But most of Jessie's early customers waited, watching the new glaze machine Jake had bought with his harvest profits. Thin syrup pooled in the narrow pan, and as the machine clanked over, the pan moved back and forth like a long arm over the doughnut rack, glaze trickling down in a miniature white waterfall. The townspeople had never seen anything like it and their fascination with the glaze and doughnut machine soon extended to Jessie Walsh. Folks realized they had never seen anything like her, either. Here was a woman who had traveled their known world and way beyond, who had lived a hundred lives to their own. Sometimes, if she was too busy to think, a customer might lead Jessie into a story that fell from her effortlessly, in rhythm to her work, more startling than her coffee, but never bitter.

Soon Jessie was known as a storyteller. She leaned over
her counter, one long arm outstretched, balancing hot plates
stacked from her wrist to the crook in her elbow, three fingers looped through the handles of steaming coffee cups,
while with the other hand she gripped the tin tea kettle,
waving it around dangerously as she told of her travels.

"Is there any place you ain't been, Jessie Walsh?" her
customers teased her, wide-eyed.

Jessie smiled and let them endure her reverie, then she
explained, "Shaw, I seen places ain't in this world, I remember things and folks only half-happened before I moved on."

"Then you're lyin!"

"No sir!"

"Well, you ain't exactly tellin us straight," they protested
and Jessie smiled, distractedly running a hand through her
hair.

"Oh, hellfire, don't care nothun bout that." Leaning over
closer, her elbow on the counter, she confided, "Folks are
changelin things. You got to make them hold still a bit whilst
you see and listen real hard. But the minute you let them go,
they's off and different. You got to fix 'em that one time they
linger. Then it don't matter how they go, ifn they die or git
strange or you pass on away from there forever, cause you
still safe-keep them right here," she pointed to her forehead,
"anytime you call them back, they come."

"You got hold of me, Jessie Walsh?"

"Oh, you know I do!" She waved her coffee pot in the air,
laughing. "You want seconds?"

The swell of her hands in the air, the rich and urgent
voice, the bend, stoop, and sway of her body—whether Jessie touched someone or not, she did hold him. But now she
found herself holding more than the interest of her customers; she held herself. There was a heaviness within her

now, its movement and presence not unlike that of an unborn child, and Jessie knew herself rooted by her stories.

Now Jessie felt full and weighted enough to take up space in her own home. "It's winter," she told Nate. "And, chile, I thank ye for fillin up my room here. But I reckon I can move in now without gittin lost."

To her great surprise, Nate protested and at last moved out of the house completely. Virgil fixed up one of the outbuildings and Nate took up residence there, appearing only for meals and sometimes late at night when it seemed he was suddenly frightened. Jessie repainted her room a pale green and had Virgil build her bookshelves, though she owned only a Bible. The remaining space she took up with odd-shaped rocks, colored matchbooks she collected from her counter's forgetful customers, and an accumulation of cheap bric-a-brac bought with the raise on her diner salary.

No one, except a few wives, protested the diner's long winter hours. These women said Jessie's wondrous talk could kill a man quicker than a bear; a bear just hugged you to death without beguiling you into weakness. But Jessie did both. She ate a man up in her great belly laugh, swallowing and keeping him whole inside while she still whooped, wild and guttural. The man inside might be almost grateful if it weren't so disquieting and warm. To be remembered by Jessie in her tales was to be shaped by the hands that were never still and too knowing. She seemed to feel whomever she laid her eyes on deeply as if she had hold of one's very bones, her thumb or forefinger tightly pressed, the nerves in those fingertips listening to some swift and secret blood pulse.

No one, except a few husbands, listened much to the women's complaints about Jessie Walsh. But in midwinter, when folks passed on their way to the all-day Sunday revival to see Jessie waiting on a full counter, there were loud calls from wives and deacons alike. It was the Lord's day of rest and it should be Jessie's, too. Himself an ordained deacon and member of the budget committee, Jake struck a bargain: next Sunday Jessie was in the choir loft, singing alto in that full, harmonious voice. The Sunday after that she was leading the choir; the first soprano had discovered Jessie's talent for teaching shape-note singing. In her travels Jessie had learned not only the strict harmonies of hymn books, but the driving rhythms and dissonance of the five-toned spirituals heard only rarely in this county, when the summer revivalists passed through.

Like those traveling revivalists, Jessie was now trusted to know about heaven and hell simply because she had seen more of this world. But unlike the zealous evangelist who searched his own sorry, wayward past—a history as intimate with sin as the years after his call were with salvation—Jessie never seemed to tell stories about herself. The preacher's dramas had the same three characters speaking in two tongues: the Devil tempting in sweet, wheedling whispers beneath the Lord's unworldly weeping; or the Devil's raving against the Father's knowing joy. All voice in between was that prodigal, mute wilderness of man.

"Ifn Jessie was jist still," some people began complaining about her stories and, accordingly, stayed away from the diner. "Ifn she'd jist keep her stories straight." But Jessie was blessed with the gift of speaking so many tongues and there was no one to stand up and interpret her. At least a minister's stories, no matter what the underworld detours, always arrived at the predicted moral end. The wide, unkempt way became narrow and divided as judgment itself. But Jessie wandered without a tidy end, lacking admonishments; and if there was justice in her tales, the listener was usually left feeling an uneasy compassion for both lost and found. These townspeople began to suspect: perhaps this woman took no moral stand because she had no beliefs. Where had she come from? The sheriff said she and her boys were his distant but not blood kin from Arkansas. Hap Bailey's boys said differently, that she was a squatting migrant. Rumor said betweenness was in her blood, that she had traveled with Negroes and was accepted as one of them. Whatever her past, some folks suspected she was privy to their hearts because of her own shrewd, unsparing separateness. Did she take sides behind that selfless narration? Had she chosen against them long ago, taking her bearings not from the sunlit world they labored in, but from the dark and quick insinuation of the spirit? Perhaps her thickness with them, like that rich mingling in her blood, was not kinship but recognition. For everyone knew the Devil still stalked one like a shadow, feigning sympathy, speaking in many voices, bestowing kindnesses, all the while hoarding your soul. And wasn't it just the Devil's sly design to enter this world through the ear and mouth of a woman? Yes, a few townspeople now whispered among themselves, the first sin was listening.

TOWN

After Lloyd Sloan's wife left him and his seven-year-old son, Lloyd carried on his intimacy with Jessie Walsh in broad daylight. He was one of her early-morning customers, sitting several hours before dawn while she made coffee and doughnuts for him and his prisoners to eat on the road as they drove out to farm Sloan's land. By now Lloyd had managed to buy back over half of his property with the shrewd profits he made on his good crops, though there were some townfolks who objected to the Bailey farm project. They said Lloyd should decide whether he was a sheriff or farmer, and certainly not get paid for both, especially from the town's scant tax revenues. But Lloyd's and Bailey's supporters countered that the prisoners' work saved money and the excess food went to help out the poor. This winter Lloyd again put his prisoners to work, constructing houses for a new mill company. Their income went directly to Hap Bailey, who, in turn, paid off the county authorities for their silence, and then applied the balance to Lloyd's shrinking debt to buy back his old land. The crops and construction work had been good enough to leave a tidy profit to Bailey.

Some men, unable to make a living in these hard times, struck a bargain with Lloyd and landed in jail on some minor charge: three of Jessie's hot meals a day, work, and, if he had a family, enough credit to keep them from starving.

Upstairs in the jailhouse, Ira Sloan waited for his father to return with the inevitable foil-wrapped diner plate. But now, instead of sharing a silent supper with Lloyd, there was Jessie Walsh. Ira's chore was to set the table for three, using his mother's best dishes and tarnished silverware. Nettie Sloan took little with her. Nor had she sent word to gather her possessions and send them to wherever she had gone. For a while Sheriff Sloan tried to find his wife, and a deputy in another county traced her as far as the bus station in Atlanta. But where she traveled from there was anyone's guess. Some people hinted that Nettie had gone only as far as the Yellow River. No bodies were found washed ashore but the suspicious still argued that the river's deep gullies were dammed up by trees and the cottonmouth water moccasins in this territory were fabled to devour a grown man in minutes, leaving no recognizable rings, bits of bone, or clothing. Sheriff Sloan told his small son that his mother had gone to visit relatives and stayed on.

More and more, Ira Sloan resembled his father, though sometimes his unruly silences and slow walk brought to mind the image of Nettie. He had spent this last year between the rowdy schoolroom, where he suspiciously watched the young schoolteacher, and the jailhouse, where he fretted restlessly during his father's rambling talks; finally he fled to the dark comfort of the back cells, where, wide-eyed, he settled near the bars and listened to the white prisoners—the squeaky-throated jokes of traveling salesmen, fidgeting and selling from their primly made bunks; or the slurred, slow talk of the faceless factory drunks who, worn out from the aching boredom of the mill, had been spotted by a foreman and given a day's drinking pay and been assured a night in jail before they had to rejoin the line. Only surrounded by men who paid him little mind did Ira ease his wariness and listen to the men's tired, familiar games, their jibes, sorrows, and curses. As for paying heed to his father, Ira had learned to listen and not to listen. Sometimes late at night, when his father forgot to put him to bed, Ira would slip down the back stairs into the annex of forbidden cells, where he overheard stories from deep black voices.

One evening, just after sundown and supper, Ira crept down the stairs and into the cell annex. The men had settled into the idle hierarchy of their bunks, smoking and silent, vaguely aware of the comfortable, soft crying of doves that scudded like tiny white ghosts along the cornstalks Lloyd had vainly planted back of his jailhouse. Ira waited for the men to begin their stories, but suddenly, over the song of tree frogs and doves came a guttural keening. Like the wails women make over their dead, the voice rose up in high lament, then fell back into the intimate monotones of a mammy's lullaby; once or twice the song found words, LuLaLuLaLoooo . . . , a rhythm that urgently slapped against Ira's ears. "Jist some drunken siren," a man whispered to him and sent the boy away. But Ira lingered out of sight.

"No," he heard another man say, "she's come to beg her man's nature duty." There was a stirring in the darkness, a tinny protest of bedsprings and moaning, then the wet, pungent smell of fish. But Ira knew the voice was coming from outside, stealing through the windows as easily as the cool night breeze one waited for all day. Ira thought the woman was a banshee, not to be caught and never silenced by a man's pleas. Every time after that when Ira heard the wind he remembered this woman and wondered if she were a black spirit and, if so, did women maybe change to become wind when they left their men, when they left earth and their sons? For no one, not even a jail nor a grave, could hold a woman as terrible and fanciful as the wind.

Lately, Ira's father had been so distracted that he let his son stay late in the cells. "Look like mebbe he's taken more to thievin and the like," Lloyd joked wryly with his men, most of whom shrugged indifferently or busied themselves with small, useless chores. "That's why he always buried things in the backyard as a chile . . . fixin to learn to steal and hide, I reckon."

These long nights in the jailhouse, Ira learned quickly. He screwed up his eyes in imitation of the men and swiftly comprehended when cheating was to be allowed. If the men were in good moods, Ira stuffed his pockets with oddities won from checkers and poker. It was never money—those pawed trinkets, lady pictures, rare bottle tops, penknives, even private letters, lost and loved, and now despised—but strange, unprofitable bounty. Ira hoarded it all until he could understand. Until then, he walked around sullenly, hands jammed in his pockets. His pants made grown-up noises, jingling like a man's money.

It was through the prisoners' insinuations and hushed stories that Ira first understood the reason his father was so distracted and why the diner's cook stayed for supper after bringing the foil-wrapped food. Ira began to watch Jessie Walsh with the same squinted eyes he had learned from the prisoners' playing poker.

Every evening Jessie completed Lloyd's and Ira's supper table with wild flowers and matted ferns arranged in a porcelain vase. On Saturdays she and Ira spent the late afternoon preparing for Sunday-morning service: first the ritual bath, then the go-to-church clothes ironed and starched so stiff Ira felt they stood at attention while he slumped in his pew; then there was the wondrous feast Jessie laid out for Saturday suppers, the one evening the diner let her off for more than a supper break. Late that night, after Ira was in bed, Jessie would return to her cabin and begin the ironing and starching of her own sons' church clothes.

The first Saturday afternoon that Jessie Walsh had appeared, a sweet-smelling satchel in her arms, Ira hid in one of the jail cells downstairs. But the criminals surrendered him up to her. Jaw firmly set, Jessie carried him kicking up the stairs. The kitchen was a swirling cloud of steam and somewhere in the middle was a large tub into which Jessie plunged him, clothes and all. "Might as well wash them overalls, too," she drowned him with a bucket of boiling water. "Lissen, honey, overalls ain't skin; you can take them off a time or two and your blood and innards don't all spill out!" Underwater, she stripped him, wringing the denim out over his head; the hot water was now a steaming, stained blue. A scratchy sponge hit him full face, soap bubbling out of his nose and mouth. For what seemed like an eternity he was scrubbed, rubbed so hard he wondered if his skin was dyed blue, and finally dunked and held underwater without mercy. At last he was left, half dead, to soak in the metal tub, but that long-limbed woman still stooped over him as if any moment resuming her attack. She watched him strangely, "Without them overalls and with that thick hair plastered you look like a drowned dog, his fur all slick down to show such bony ribs you wonder why he ain't starved yet. How'd Lloyd git such a skinny chile?" For a moment Ira said nothing, only slunk deeper in the soapy water that protected his body from her eyes. "You're like the runt of the litter, son. You git teased at school?" she asked kindly.

"They call me . . ." he paused and took a deep breath, "call me 'swayback mule.'" When she did not laugh the boy looked up at her.

"Oh, they's jist jealous bout your small back, son. They know someday a woman's gonna call it her own holler and settle her hands there."

"Mebbe not," the child said and hunkered down in the tin tub.

"Mebbe so," she laughed and boxed him with the coarse yellow sponge. "Hollows and caves, bushes and valleys are all over a body. Look here, son. This crook in the neck that sits up on the shoulders, that's a cave restin high on a cliff. Big enough for jist one face to fit. You can hide or go splunkin!" Ira couldn't help but feel his own knobby shoulder bone and the inward slope of his neck where his veins stood out, throbbing.

"Sounds smotherin."

"And this bone ridge here, slam-dash down the back . . . that's your own mountains. Look ye, the Iry Sloan mountains, how you like that?" she tickled all the way down his spine, then scrubbed the small of his back.

"Women got mountains in front," Ira could not stop laughing.

"No, son . . . them's simple hills with a lonely holler between. But women got this same bone mountain down our backs, don't forgit, hear?" her sudden solemnity made him stop giggling. "Now, bout this swayback. Mules got it, men and women, too. This is called the small back, though it carries all the load that slides down your mountain ridge. This is called down in the valley, for bein low. And don't let man or woman tell ye this small back ain't the body's wildness.

Wildness ain't down here . . . root and thigh," he slapped her hand away, flushing. "Ain't here . . ." the flat of her hand thumped his breastbone. "Wildness is in this small back that's bent for bearin troubles. It's lean and worked clean to the bone, that's why I call this the valley of shadow and death. It don't git tetched, hands pass on through. Only sorrows settle here," she took a deep breath, the palm of her hand gently massaged his sloped, small back. His skin was the color of white sand in the sun, with that same rough texture on his legs, heels, and elbows; but every other part of his body was smooth, firm, and cool as the skin of a watermelon.

"Who give them body names, anyway?" The boy waited for her to return his smile, but she didn't.

"Voice cryin out in the wilderness."

"Say what?"

"Say ever valley be filled, chile, ever mountain and hill brung low, crooked come straight. Jist remember all backbones got this natural valley from bendin low and bein heavy-burdened," she ran a finger up his spine to the small cleft behind his neck. "Remember that when you git down in the back."

"You ever git down in the valley, Miz Jessie Walsh?"

She clucked her tongue and smiled at him, "Honey, you think I walk like a stoop-down nigger to look pretty? What you think I been pickin all my life—birds out of the sky? I been low, chile. . . ."

"Makes three of us," he suddenly dismissed her, standing up in the tub water, waiting for a towel. She handed him a wide, rough rag and he stepped from the tin basin, dribbling water over the floor as he padded to his porch.

"Not you, Iry. You're not low jist yet. It's your father who needs watchin."

"I don't mean him, neither. *She* was down in the valley."

Jessie was quiet for a long while, then nodded slowly. She had only once seen Nettie Sloan but she felt she knew that troubled woman well. Weren't these her gray eyes staring from this child's face?

"I say, *she* was down in the valley!" his eyes blinked back tears.

"Reckon she lived there, boy."

For the next four years Jessie divided her time between diner work, her own cabin and sons, and Lloyd Sloan's home. Every evening she brought leftovers from her supper menu and shared a quick meal with Lloyd and his son. Ira did the dishes eagerly, hastening the chore only because he was intent upon joining the men downstairs in their cells. After dinner was their time for checkers, stories, and confidences.

But one night, after Jessie had left for home and Ira had done his chores, his father called him into the parlor; Ira knew something was wrong because Lloyd was rolling his own cigarette; he never smoked unless greatly perturbed. Coarse slits of tobacco caught on his chin like curled beard stubble as Lloyd licked his ungummed papers and twirled the thin ends into tiny white corkscrews. Each drawn breath hollowed out Lloyd's cheeks and Ira wondered if his father's face would grow so inward and sunken when he was an old man.

"In here, Iry," an explosion of smoke from Lloyd's lips made his words all the more commanding. "Don't stand out there sulkin when I ask for ye."

"I'm late."

"You also got better things to do than hang around men twice your age and meanness. Sides, your friends downstairs got nothun but time to wait for ye to catch up. So, git on in here, boy!"

Grudgingly Ira obeyed his father, but stopped short of the parlor door. For an instant everything was the same as before—his mother in her straight chair by the window, a musty sweetness settled like dew over the bristling throw rugs, the dull, apprehensive darkness that hung in the air except for two shafts of lamplight. This glare illuminated a slow frenzy of dust, still swirling through the room like driven moths. "Ira," her voice came faintly like a breath of night wind.

"I tell ye, son, she's gone off and married again, after all. . . ," his father was saying, flicking his cigarette ashes against the chair's rockers that curved up into wooden wings.

"Shhh!" Ira hushed him. In the dark, in-between light of her parlor his mother seemed to rise up from the chair, moving more freely than she ever walked in life, as if her body were only a shadow and she wore it simply, like a cloak of dark, stately raiment. Ira stood very still, afraid she might fall into the unearthly gaps and haze of her parlor. Familiarly, she laid one hand on his head, resting there, before going past him, her face luminous, eyes blessing his world with hers.

"Married again after all this long wait. Iry, you hear?"

Turning from Lloyd to watch Nettie Sloan walk out of the room unhurriedly, Ira laughed, an edge to his voice. "No, she's jist now gone."

"She found some fool feller out in Utah, for God's sake. Probably a miner, or Mormon with ten wives," Lloyd shook his head, "and me here waitin on her . . ."

"Waitin?"

"Well, son," Lloyd looked up sharply, sucking smoke through his front teeth. "You'll want to git to know Jessie

Walsh better. She's fixin to move in with us. You and me and mebbe more soon," Lloyd grinned. "I say, son . . . hear me? Your new ma."

"My mother is dead." Ira stared behind him, a glint of wonder still in his eyes.

Lloyd snorted and stood up, flicking the hot ash off his cigarette with his forefinger, then grinding out the cool stub in the palm of his hand. "She ain't dead," Lloyd said and strode past Ira. "Way I heared tell about your ma, son, it's been *us* dead all these years!" and Lloyd was out the door.

Ira laughed softly and crossed the room to the window seat. Almost mischievously he reached for the tobacco pouch and paper squares; he rolled three squat cylinders, scattering weedy brown slits all over his shirt. Then he moved her abandoned straight chair near the window and stared outside. A cigarette hung from his mouth, smoke spiraling upward, stinging his gray eyes to tears that splashed down, making a sizzling sound on the cigarette paper.

Ira forgave his father the kind lie, for he knew his mother was dead. Ira looked up to see the sky's dazed white clouds hung low, swollen with evening rain. Now, he thought, this sky belonged to Nettie Sloan. Wasn't she in heaven, contentedly rolling her own cigarettes, and wasn't her smoke, like his, filling a wide sky with clouds?

II

When Lloyd Sloan made Jessie Walsh his wife, he also kept her migrant sons, saying he always made room for bloodhounds as long as they treed, hunted, and kept from under-

foot like his own dogs. Ira expected these huge, shy stepbrothers to sleep under the house with the hounds; instead,
they fit their stooped bodies and tiny suitcases into Ira's own
room. Ira slept in the porch swing during summers, on the
parlor sofa's soft pulp in winter. After much loud quarreling,
Lloyd Sloan adopted Jessie's sons, giving them his legal
name and rights to his will. Even before traveling the ambi-
tious distance from Lloyd's and Nettie's first run-down cabin
to this sheriff's two-story brick jailhouse, Jessie's sons had
bettered themselves. Virgil worked in the silk-hosiery factory as a knitter; the middle son, Leon, found work with
Bailey's chicken business; and Nate was hired by Mr.
Quince, the town's undertaker, who also owned a tombstone
factory. Nate's few years of schooling and vast memory of
scripture made his carved poetic epitaphs a wonder to
mourners accustomed to standard tombstone texts.

It was Nate that Ira shirked more than his other stepbrothers, for while the boy was twice as old as he, Nate had
seized on Ira with the absorbing devotion of a servant. From
the beginning Ira found Nate's willful selflessness more
maddening than his other stepbrothers' neglect. When the
Walsh boys squatted in Ira's room, it was only Nate who
offered up his bed, unwilling to let Ira be dispossessed to the
porch. Yet it was Nate upon whom Ira vented his indigna-
tion. When the older boys exchanged privacies, it was Nate
who allowed Ira to listen, only to be railed against. It
seemed that every distance Ira put between himself and his
new family was violated by the tireless figure of Nate Walsh
trespassing and taking blame.

Jessie had watched Nate's change with growing excitement. As he grew less wary and inward, she allowed herself
the luxury of expectation—at last her son would come back
to her, be restored to her through this settled life and the

intercession of Ira Sloan. When Jessie first met Ira she held back from his anguish, if not his need. But quickly the boy claimed her attention, perhaps even more than Lloyd. For here was someone who felt her lightest touch, whose response to her, even if it was outrage, was still an instinctive opening of his deepest resources. Jessie knew that nothing of her was lost on Ira Sloan; she felt herself carrying on yet another life, not of her bone and blood, not even of her stories, but within the depthless imagination of this child. Jessie wondered if Nate were drawn to the boy because Nate, too, felt alive within Ira.

These first days of living together in Lloyd's town house were good ones for Jessie. It was enough for her, these two families, though Lloyd still spoke of sons. "After all, it's legal," he said. "He'll have my name."

"Ain't no law against bringing Sloans into this world," Lloyd kissed her gently. "Lord knows, it's been a long time without them."

And soon Jessie found herself carrying Lloyd's child. She had never seen a man so grateful. But just as Lloyd drew nearer her, she saw Ira become inward and disinterested. Now it was to Nate that Ira turned his rapt attention. Jessie could almost mark the split second Ira forsook her because she felt lifted off the ground, again weightless. If it had not been for the sharp movement of the child within her, Jessie knew her spirit would have gone into mourning and wandered as it did during every loss.

For the first time in her life Jessie withdrew from everyone close to her, even herself, for she did not go in search of her own sorrow. Instead, she shaped herself around the child within. Her whole body ached with the stirrings of this new child. She imagined it a creature without face or dreams, a shape of darkness, using her skin, but skin that it would someday shed as naturally and remorselessly as any animal renounces its old self for a new life.

"You were right that first morning," Jessie said to Lloyd as he settled against her to sleep, his arms barely encircling her. Sometimes he slept with his ear to her high belly, listening.

"Right?"

"Sons leave ye."

"Yes, honey, but this one's right close," and he thumped her belly gently, tickling her until she was forced to laugh; and her laughter made her suddenly feel separate and hollow.

Jessie's withdrawal was hardly noticed by Nate or Ira. Their attention was riveted on one another—Nate in an all-consuming need to tap the deep wellsprings of Ira's belief, so strong because it arose from the boy's intense doubt, and Ira in a denial more painful because here was a brother to his solitude. From the beginning Ira reminded Nate of Reverend Staunton. Nate perceived that Ira's spirit, like Staunton's, was both stern and hungry, capable of great extremes of faith and despair.

"You know I been called," Nate confided in Ira one afternoon when he found Ira sitting by the Yellow River.

"You been touched, that's all," Ira said and skipped stones across the still, pale water.

"Ever fear for your soul, Iry? Ever think bout losin your life to find it?"

"Ain't you noticed?" Ira turned to him in anger. "I done lost it since the day you and your family squatted in my place."

"When you lose your life, Iry, others give it back to ye. The Lord sees to that."

"*You* ain't seen to that!" Ira suddenly shouted. He clamped his arms to his side and shivered violently. "Give up my life? Don't you see you and your kind done taken it until I ain't nothun?"

"Yes, but that's how a body must be for the Lord to take him," Nate said with satisfaction, only to see the boy grimace absurdly, then break into tears. The sight of this hump-backed sobbing boy made Nate recoil, but when Nate closed his eyes he could come closer because the sound of Ira's weeping seemed so beautiful that Nate did not want to silence it. Nate thought Ira's sorrow was simply the Spirit overwhelming the body with its dark sweetness. Listening to the sounds of this boy's repentance was to Nate like hearing the unearthly music of rapture; its rhythmic rise and fall lent Nate a sense that his own sure sorrow was in harmony with something outside himself. "I can save ye, boy," Nate opened his eyes and as he reached for Ira, Nate felt the first stirrings of pity. "I know how it be when you feel like nothun. Because I been called a prophet."

"You ain't been called!" Ira shouted, ashamedly rubbing his fists in his eyes. "It's you do the callin."

"Iry, I can give ye all I never did give anyone but . . ." Nate hesitated, then added in a muted voice, "but my followers."

Ira stared at his stepbrother and for a moment Nate thought Ira was on the verge of more tears. But it was laughter that broke over Ira's face. "Follow you?" and suddenly Ira stopped laughing. "There ain't no chosen, Nate. We don't need your old-time prophets no more."

Nate gripped Ira's arm. Ira watched his hands, huge and chiseled like a stonemason's with the same sensitivity, power, and perhaps violence. Nate's face betrayed a pallor— Ira thought his brow too high, lips too wide and chapped, ears flayed back from his face, a nose flat as his cheekbones, jaw round and smooth as a child's. There was nothing in that face that was distinct, recognizable, Ira thought; it was as meaningless as one of those waiting slabs of marble Nate carved. But suddenly Ira was frightened by his stepbrother's eyes. An unclouded, searing blue like the summer sky during drought, Nate's eyes were not fixed on Ira, but turned inward and abstracted. Without another word Nate released his hold on Ira, but when the boy whirled around to run from the woods, Nate suddenly lunged for him and, with one wide hand clasped over Ira's face, lifted him off his feet and hurled him in a high arc into the river. Bare back slapping the water, Ira lost his breath in a startled scream cut short by the river's hard surface and the hand that slammed against his face until his head hit stone and river-bottom sand.

"Nate! My God, Nate!" Virgil and Jessie came running to see Nate holding Ira's head down as the boy tried to break water. Jessie pushed Nate into Virgil's arms and saw Ira's face surge up, his mouth streaming breathless bubbles, whorls of light. Gasping, Ira fell back in a faint, but Jessie caught him and dragged him up on the bank.

His breathing was loud, irregular, and Jessie quickly checked to see if his head was gashed and found a soft dent in the back of his skull. "See to the boy," Jessie ordered Virgil to fetch Doc Varnon and carry Ira to the house. "I'll be right there."

"Ma . . . ," Virgil began, eyeing his brother as he held him.

"No. Leave me be with Nate. You see to Iry and find Lloyd . . . quick!"

Virgil lingered, then hastily left, carrying Ira.

Jessie went to Nate and took him by the shoulders, turning him around to face her. She expected any expression but his habitual smile. "Why in God's name you slappin that chile around, Nate? Ain't he been hurt enough?"

"He ain't been hurt like his soul needs," Nate said, the smile twisting his face. "Not like I suffered for him, for all of them."

Jessie hesitated, then caught her son's chin between her fingers. "You listen good! Ain't no one forgivin ye for this but yourself. Ifn I loved ye less, I'd slap you like you done that chile, wipe that sinful smile off your face, and make you beg the boy's forgiveness. . . ."

"I ain't beggin from nobody," Nate shook himself free and strode away. "Not Iry and never you. It's you should beg pardon, beg the Lord's mercy."

"*My* Lord gives it!" Jessie shouted after her son, flailing her arms in the air. "Never ye." And Jessie sat down heavily on the ground, holding her swollen belly with both hands. She could almost hear the sudden tearing in her belly. "Oh, Lord," Jessie breathed and struggled to stand, feeling the warm river break out of her body. She painfully made her way toward the house. "Lord, don't give me no more pure-born chillun, no more punishin angels."

She made it to her room and eased onto the bed. "Have mercy," she said over and over in rhythm to her pains and suddenly there was the midwife's calm voice singing back to her.

"Mercy and hot water, honey, that's all we need," the midwife said and quieted Jessie with a soft bit of knotted bedsheets.

Nate waited in the hallway with a satchel under his arm. He listened both to his mother's tight screams and to Ira's whimpering as Doc Varnon explored the pulp of the boy's nose.

"Quit cryin, it ain't broke," Doc said. "But it ain't gonna be so pretty from now on neither."

"Why's that?" Lloyd's voice was distracted as he, too, listened to the noises in Jessie's next room.

"Nate jist knocked it caterwonkous, that's all," Doc laughed. "Here now, jist hold that ice compress against it whilst I take some stitches in that knucklehead."

Nate heard Ira suddenly draw a breath and the room was still except for Doc's grunts each time he pulled the thread tight.

Lloyd Sloan took this opportunity to leave Ira and go to Jessie's room. But Nate stopped him in the hallway.

"Sir."

"Not now, boy," Lloyd pushed past his stepson but Nate pushed back.

"I got somethin to say."

"You done said it!" Lloyd snapped. "And them that's heared is pained and laid out ever whichaway." Still Nate did not step aside. Lloyd raised the back of his hand. "Ifn it's punishment you want, I can dole it out good as ye!"

"I'm leavin here."

Lloyd snorted, "That your punishment?" Then Lloyd caught himself, "Is this what you told your ma to bring on her early labor?"

"She don't know."

"You waitin round to tell her?" Lloyd paused and listened to the harsh breathing that echoed from Jessie's room. Suddenly he grabbed Nate by the shoulders, "Ifn my chile's stillborn, I'll kill ye, stepson or no!"

"I'll live out the old cabin where you first settled us," Nate said calmly and Lloyd dropped his hold.

"Go on then, boy. You never needed my word to move on."

"But Ma, she . . ."

"Your ma's carryin so many chillun, she won't miss ye," and Lloyd swept past his stepson. As Lloyd gingerly opened the door and stepped just inside Jessie's room, Nate caught sight of his mother—a writhing whiteness, whether sheets or flesh Nate did not let himself see; and his glance would have fled her if Jessie's eyes did not reach out for him. Widened with pain, her eyes rested on her son. "Nate," she said, the word clenched by the bedsheet bit between her teeth. "Never ye mind, son."

Nate suddenly felt all other voices, all children of his spirit, flee his body as if in birth and in his emptiness was revealed what was most humble in him—pity. Effortlessly Nate moved toward her, though his body stayed behind, a clumsy shape in the doorway. Cool lips brushing against her feverish face like the faint rustle of wings, Nate blessed her.

"My pure-born boy," Jessie whispered, a wan smile wavering as she gave way to a final separating spasm.

"No, honey, it's a girl chile," the midwife held a slippery creature up to Lloyd, who came toward the bed, face drawn; then the midwife turned to show it to Nate, but he was gone, the door still open behind him.

Nate walked down the hall to Ira's room. "I come to beg your forgiveness," Nate said, not looking at the boy.

Ira was silent for a moment while Doc Varnon pulled the thread through his ragged skin, then the boy cried, "You ain't got it!"

Startled, Nate looked at Ira and the sight of his battered face, disfigured by pain, made Nate feel hollow, unprotected. "But I'm gone down before ye . . ."

"Reckon mebbe this boy's gone down first," Doc Varnon laughed.

A voice that Nate did not recognize, that was so resonant and commanding it changed Varnon's and Ira's faces, came from Nate, " 'Why doth this man speak blasphemies?' " and Nate knew his visions had come back to protect him with the punishing force of wind. " 'Who can forgive sins but God only?' " Nate left the room, but even as he ran he felt his body break asunder, a dark and arid nothingness that nevertheless fled toward light.

III

When Jessie delivered herself of a girl, Lloyd brooded about a day before he was completely caught up by his child. "Hell, honey, another time it'll be a son. This little girl's already a ravin beauty," and when he felt the soft cleft in her head, his jaw slackened in awe. Ira watched his father make ridiculous clown faces and coo like a mourning dove, holding high the miniature, screw-eyed daughter, her skin shriveled, dark, loose like prunes, as if Jessie had yielded strange, old fruit. In sullen dismay Ira eyed his new half-sister, refusing to make faces when he played with her; yet, for all Ira's dispassion, it was to him the baby seemed to turn during the first weeks of her colic. After sleeplessness, lullabies, and diligent feedings, the baby had changed hands, from Jessie to Lloyd, to the older brothers, so often that Virgil joked they should name her "Hot Potato," for that was the passing game they played. One night, close to tears, Jessie told Lloyd to call on Ira to comfort the child's colic.

"You're the only one she ain't wore out yet," Lloyd woke Ira and handed him the squalling infant. That night Ira did not succeed in silencing his new half-sister, but the next night he managed to feed her a formula Doc Varnon hoped might work better than Jessie's breast feeding. She almost slept the rest of the night.

From then on, it was Ira who woke at the first shrill blasts from those seemingly operatic lungs, who warmed the bottle and scalded his wrist testing the milk. It was Ira who padded around the parlor in circles, never singing, not making a sound, except to clap his palm monotonously against the thin back until the crying stopped, completed with a burp so loud it made Ira think of sows snorting. Whether he came to feel anything deeper than tolerance for the baby was a moot question because before the child was old enough to exchange affectionate play or demand a curiosity to equal her own wide-eyed self-absorption, Jessie was pregnant again.

Whining, fussing, spitting, crawling, yowling—the second of Ira's dark-skinned sisters struck him as uglier than the first. But this child had no colic and spent most of her first months surrounded by a doting family—shapes she saw as inseparable from herself. By the time a third baby girl howled her way into Lloyd Sloan's small house, Ira made no attempts to join the circle of family, constantly fascinated at what Ira saw as more of the same. The only difference was that each daughter demanded more space, emotionally and physically, so Ira spent more time away from home, playing and stealing through the back country where he made his own territory.

In summer, he sunned midstream in erratics jutting from the river's cataracts as spangled white water in spates chilled him. In fall, he holed up in a backyard bramble-hollow whose thorns were dried and forbidding, a natural fortress; in winter, he lay deep in the warm straw of the henhouse and, chided by the chicks' throaty squabble, Ira giggled at a bantam hiking his claws into a hen's backfeathers as he rose briefly off the ground, beating the air. But in the spring, Ira hid farther from his house in a splintered slash-pine forest that fire had made barren, except for the breeding of wood ticks. Once, his little sisters had toddled after him and he led them on a thicket chase that landed them all in a tin tub where they fought Jessie's quick tweezers, scalding water, matches, and turpentine as she picked off three heads full of bloated mites.

Despite the crawling-tick season, the cool winter, or the summer's rainfall, Ira would steal away to these close strongholds and watch his house. He squinted against the sharp afternoon sun setting behind slanting horizons of roof-tops. And when Ira could hold his eyes wide open against the veiled sky, when shadows engulfed the house and jail beneath it in greedy, soft oblivion, then he left off his vigil and came home for supper.

Inside his familiar second-story home, Ira's three sisters spied on him, waiting in the dead ends of hallways or behind his sofa bed to find him naked, or studying, or just staring at walls; whatever he did in his privacies had peculiar meaning to them. They whispered stories to one another when they knew he might overhear. Awed and possessive, the girls thought Ira was the most handsome boy in town. When first he heard them confide this to a neighbor, he was startled— not because they thought him well blessed, but because he had not noticed until this instant that his sisters looked dif-ferent. They were blooming, but as if backwards, growing ripe, lush, and intimate as the country that grew them. Ira kept this stern wonder to himself. Soon his sisters' whispers became shrill and insistent and their high-pitched sounds vibrated in his ears even when they were silent; it was the suggestion of their voices that disturbed him, lingering in his most awkward dreams. Later, the girls fell strangely quiet around their half-brother. They began comparing their own roundness or the meager, flat faces of their elder half-brothers to Ira's fine, hawk-like features; the eldest girl always burst into shuddering tears over such comparisons. Confused, and like two skinny mirrors, the littler sisters mawked her hurt, whimpering after Ira. Firmly, he explained to them: They and their migrant brothers were not his real kin; they were as common as those ticks that caught onto any flesh. After this revelation his sisters could not sleep unless Ira first went to their bedsides and carefully arranged them in their quilts like small, irksome animals, then swore he had lied about their blood. After this ritual they fell off quickly; but he found himself often lingering, caught by the frills of their girlish intrusion on his home and their intimate scent, the same as his own childhood—smells of damp, sleeping heads tart with cleansing and sweet with sweat and talcum.

These years with his second family did not pass quickly. Each day since Jessie had moved in with his father, each night her oldest sons loitered between town and their women, slouching on porches or over counters as they would never dare in their stepfather's home; each year a baby girl had claimed a corner of his house like a loud, indignant squatter—Ira marked them and was himself scarred. His anger moved like a sharp, cutting hand, cleaving his mind like soft, impressionable clay. The blunt memories of these times hardened, but only to hide a changeableness, the way familiar ground covers quicksand.

It was always in summer that Ira felt the most raw and ungiving. In that heavy, wet heat nothing found forgiveness. Under a stark light the land and woods and his house seemed barren, cruelly exposed. The whole structure paled; ripped porch screens swung crookedly on their hinges. Below the second-story weight of Lloyd Sloan's new family the jailhouse sagged, its back porch perched on pine stilts

that every year sunk deeper into the unsteady silt left by the
Yellow River. These doldrum days that becalmed even the
insistent buzz of tree frogs and crickets, Ira fled himself and
his house. Bare feet slapping slanted porch steps, then mud,
Ira ran to the river. It was his own backyard miracle; while
all other bodies of water borrowed the violent blood color of
this country's clay, the Yellow River had no weather or earth
in its veins. Its name was its color—a luminous topaz flowing
beneath trees' stooped shadows. After stirring rains the
waters might cloud and glare dully, a dead light adrift over
the sallow surface; but more often the river was scintillant,
laving the eyes in light, the body in cold embrace.

In the humid morning air Ira made his river run, stripping
his nightshirt and diving headlong into the swift water. Lifting high, the current bent him double, then moved him in
the weightless ecstasy of water. It was only when he swam
upriver that he remembered his body like the dry earth and
was recalled to land, a loath deliverance.

Every morning as he walked back from the river to his
house, Ira did not listen to the sounds that came at him from
every room. In his ears still rushed the shushing river. But
after a few moments a hoarse curse or thwack from the bathroom as his two stepbrothers swatted one another with
towels always alerted Ira to the family around him. In the
bathroom one older brother was shaving; he cursed the dull
straight-edge in that slow and intimate way he had with his
mother and small half-sisters.

When Ira walked past his stepbrothers in the bathroom,
they fell quiet. "Mornin," they each said in their turn and
then shyly went back to washing.

"Mornin," Ira hurried past the door; *it's always the same,
their quiet with me, their grins that go away when I come
near. Always the same sounds inside this house, the squallin*

*sisters bein petted and fed, the callin of Jessie after Pa. But
me, I ain't the same. Not with them here. And I don't make
no noise.*

Nor could Ira feel safe or intimate with the jailed men
downstairs, those prisoners who once welcomed him into
their games and rituals. He was fifteen, too old to learn any
more from their counterfeit exchanges. Ira did well in
school, but he stayed apart, watching others skitter back and
forth across the unreasoning threshold of adolescence. It was
not that Ira was reluctant to cross over like others of his age.
Sometimes he longed to like his brothers enough to exchange
manly games of bathroom chivalry and coarseness. But
somehow he was made to wait, even while his body changed,
his voice dropped, and his face gathered its dark, fine stubble around a jawbone so like his father's that folks said Ira
was Lloyd's spitting image. Restlessly, Ira waited not only
for his own changes, but for those around him to change.
Perhaps he and his family would all meet on the other side
of their private boundaries? Then his own past would unite
with his future, after all in between—his father's silences,
Jessie's spasms of care or jealousy, Nate's lingering demands,
his stepbrothers' and half-sisters' shy exclusion—had passed.
Perhaps his second chance would come when this new family fit him more closely, the way a body accepts new skin for
its own growth. Then, Ira thought, he would love them as he
did himself.

IV

Hap Bailey knew his townspeople. Though quick to judge
others like themselves, they still would not be coaxed or

hurried into condemning a man like Sheriff Lloyd Sloan. And Hap knew better than to go the ruinous back roads of gossip and scandal—a maze that might well turn against the man who began such stories. Instead, he simply listened and made suggestions to the town's most inventive storytellers—a few languid visits to store porches, a stop at the minister's study, a trip to the catalog store every sale time, visits to shut-ins (the town's most revered observers), and Hap's job was done. He only had to wait and keep careful track of the stories.

Within a year it was common knowledge that Lloyd Sloan had beat his first wife shamelessly, some said senselessly; that Nettie was never barren and had given birth to several migrant children on her journey west; that she was befriended by an Indian tribe on a reservation and there she learned all the spells and cures for her madness; that Jessie Walsh was a mulatto whose mother was a Haitian voodoo witch and her recent resignation from the diner job was because of Lloyd's incessant jealousy; that Ira Sloan was caught stealing but never punished by his sheriff father; that the sheriff was using free jail labor to work his land back from Bailey; that his marriage to Jessie was thwarted because she bore him no sons, and that her own sons who had followed her from the migrant fields now married the town's most industrious and buxom women for the simple purpose of breeding. Hap Bailey could hardly have done better to rile up a strong judgment, for the town's conscience was a destination arrived at only through imagination.

Bailey's chicken business, though at first floundering from the town's ridicule, was now proving more profitable than anyone predicted. Though Lloyd had worked back most of his land, Hap Bailey still eyed the old Sloan territory for expansion of his chicken coops. With Hap's help a youngster, newly graduated from a south Georgia school with a degree in criminology, appeared just in time to register his name for the county elections. The young man spoke passionately; he deplored Lloyd's coddling and abuse of criminals in the field labor.

"Yessir," the townspeople responded, "Sheriff Lloyd's past his time for doin good. It's doom and change he's not reckoned with."

That fall when the politicians wound up their well-timed tales of woe and promise, Sheriff Lloyd was not in his usual pre-election haunts. Instead, Lloyd made no pretense of running a campaign against this young criminologist whose photo startled even his admirers, staring out from the inky rhetoric of a political poster, his mouth unsettled, looking like a printer's smear, and his tiny, bright eyes as clean and unfeeling as two black bullet holes bored unevenly under his brow. Sometimes the opponent spoke reverentially of Sheriff Lloyd, but he also raised his voice in ringing admonitions about the underside of crime, the minds of murderers, and his perfect solutions: understanding, vigilance, and a lie detector. Not once did Lloyd Sloan give a speech or say anything in his defense except to remark to his prisoners, his voice soft and scathing as he warned them like children, "Now, we got only ears, you see; but that young buzzard, he's got wires like blood veins hookin right into your heart. Ever time your heart takes a skip, or beats from nerves or dryness, even private thoughts, why, then he catches your body lyin. That's all the fool knows to lissen to, that's all he thinks wrongs us." A few of Sheriff Lloyd's criminals agreed with him, but they could not vote. Lloyd did not speak to any other supporters.

When Hap Bailey came by the jailhouse, a nervous smile on his face, Lloyd said nothing. He took an envelope from his desk and gave it to Hap, who did not open it. "It's all there," Lloyd dismissed him and went to get himself a cup of coffee, "my last payment on that land. You best check to make sure I figured it right." Hap put the envelope back down on the desk.

"I given you a year to consider, Lloyd. Now, consider agin. Lease me back some Sloan land!"

Lloyd leaned way back on his heels and shook his head, a grin splitting open his face.

"My sons need that land for some more chicken coops and yards; Sloan land's right next to Bailey; we supposed to set up another bidness halfway cross the county?" Hap demanded.

Lloyd only sipped his coffee, staring at Hap over its brim.

"Leastways my sons gonna make use of what they got. Who's gonna work your land?"

"You sholy got a rotten memory," Lloyd said and with his hands gestured to his back cells. "Was your suggestion got me field hands stead of jailbirds."

"Who's gonna work your land?" Hap repeated and suddenly he was smiling. "Ira aims to git shut of ye and your dirt-farmin soon as he can. And, ifn I know this town, they gittin shut of their sheriff come election. So, Lloyd Sloan, who's gonna work all that old land? Now, my sons'll pay you rent and keep it in use and . . ."

"That chicken mess of yourn scratchin the dirt to ruin!"

"Listen," Hap came over and poured himself a cup of coffee, "I can see to it that you stay on as deputy, ifn ye lease me jist five acres. I can do that much for ye."

"The time you do for me is the time I know to run!" Lloyd said and strode out of his office.

All the rest of that summer and into the early fall, Lloyd campaigned for sheriff. But for every evening he visited with the men in the diner or town hall, the young opponent was close behind him, quick to point out that while their sheriff spoke of justice and duty during the night speeches, he spent his days hauling public prisoners out to his private land, not only to farm—for at least the crops could save on buying food for the criminals—but also to help Sheriff Lloyd build himself a new house. Lloyd answered this accusation by saying that if he lost the election he would need another place to live. Surely this young opponent did not want to share his new home and office with a man he called criminal.

By November Lloyd's new house that he built on his property was only half finished. After the election he was invited to remain in his home upstairs from the jail in case the town's new young sheriff needed his help. Though he was sworn in as deputy sheriff, Lloyd received no salary, except for the commission he made every time the new sheriff busted a still or drunken funeral wake, every time he arrested a thief or a speeder. Once there had been a small salary set aside for the deputies, but now, with the new sheriff's drive to raise enough money for the town to buy a lie detector, there was nothing left for extras or charity. Lloyd worked on his house by himself, occasionally getting help from old hands the mill was laying off again. His son helped on weekends, for he had a summer job helping Bailey's sons clean up chicken coops. The money he saved would go for schooling. Jessie arranged to get an old, deaf woman to do light housework and she went back to work at the diner. Again the diner changed its hours, and often Lloyd would wait in his parlor, looking out the window all night long watching the diner lights. Inside he could see Jessie moving slowly, her hands more quiet. In the early morning she took a break to bring her husband fresh doughnuts. Over her strong coffee they talked until dawn.

The day that was to break this fall's heat spell was as blisteringly hot as any summer dog day. Ira was up early in the morning for a swim before he would have to go to work at Bailey's business. All the way back from the river Ira did figures in his head: the money he had saved from summer, the money he could count on if he borrowed against his father's will, the money he had gotten from a school scholarship. By the time he reached his porch's screen door, his clothes weighted him down so that he bent over, still distractedly figuring his money.

Inside, Jessie stood very still, one arm braced against his bed table, but Ira did not notice her. The minute he leaned to pull his pants down Jessie made a small, startled noise. He stood up hastily, pulling up his trousers. "No," he waved her away crossly, "nothun for breakfast, Jessie," he stripped off the damp shirt.

"Them dry clothes been waitin on ye," Jessie pointed to his dresser, "laid them out myself."

"Obliged," Ira waited for her to leave.

"Leastways, can I git ye some coffee?"

"Too hot!"

"Iced, then?" there was something frantic about her voice. "I'll jist ice it a bit . . ."

"I don't lack nothun, and I'm very late!"

"Sholy," Jessie nodded, shifting uneasily; she pretended to study the sky. "Rain, I reckon."

"Mebbe," he looked at her for the first time, curiously, then he shrugged and began stripping his belt through the dungaree loopholes. "Well, best be gittin out of these wet things."

"Your father says I should tell ye . . ." her voice trailed off and she flushed darkly. "Damn this heat!" but she said it softly, soothingly, as if imploring him. For a moment Ira searched her face, the shivering set of her jaw, the eyes lighted.

"Git out!"

"No, son."

"Git the hell . . ."

"Lloyd says . . . says you'll be needin . . . Oh, she was ever subject to be poorly and . . . dammit, honey! I seen she runs deep with ye . . . but . . ." her hands flew toward him as he struggled to catch his breath. "Iry, Iry . . . don't be pity and shut-mouthed! Ifn ye take comfort from Jessie, like my own chile, I swear I'll . . ." she took a step toward him, then stopped, her jaw falling slack, shivering, "let me . . ."

"No!" screaming, he furiously but methodically began tearing his pants off; the wet, clinging skin came off slowly so that he tugged and pulled more desperately, all the while his eyes fixed on Jessie.

"Iry . . ." then she stopped, her whole body easing until she stood calmly, almost slouching, eyeing him with great gentleness and pity. "Chile, hush!"

But still he stripped until his pants caught around the bony crook in his knees and he stood bolt upright, arms hung at his sides, eyes dazed and blinking; he shook his head and for a moment seemed about to break into laughter. But even while he moved his head to find his bearings, his legs came toward her, haltingly, step after step. If not for the catch of clothes around his ankles he would have already been upon her. But Jessie had turned away. She swung her face around first, then her body followed clumsily, as if unwarned to flee. But she did not turn hastily enough for Ira to miss seeing her underbite fall, bringing down with it the whole shelter of her face. Her brow, like rafters, was low and bent; she looked primitive, as if in one moment he had undone the higher evolution of a face—a face that had survived even worn fits of happiness.

"Never mind, Jessie," she had turned into Lloyd Sloan, who stood right behind her in the kitchen doorway. Gently, he put his arms around her shoulders, and looked at his son. Helplessly, Ira was still shuffling toward them, his face vacant and separate from the steadily working legs. "Son! I'll see you here, when you git off them wet clothes." Lloyd took his wife inside the kitchen, speaking only low and simple sounds. Jessie was also wordless, laughing without mirth.

Late that afternoon Lloyd and Jessie found Ira as they had left him, standing by the porch swing, still half-dressed. Ira slouched almost lazily, but his face was set, grim. Only when his father came very near was he startled from his reverie. Lloyd waited, watching his son as if to catch his thoughts. "Your mother weren't never mean."

"She ain't my mother!"

"I said, *your* mother weren't never mean. She couldn't do no hurt . . ."

"Not to you anyway." Ira halted seeing his father's quick, twisting expression. Lloyd looked down, then came to the porch swing and fell into it, wearily rocking himself, his eyes on Ira. "What in the world you studyin at?" Lloyd did not answer. His jaw fell slack again as he took in Ira's rigid body, the muscles in his arms and chest tight from years of swimming, the small, clenched hands, the wrinkles etched around his eyes from squinting, and finally the troubled, deep-set gray eyes; it was as if Lloyd recognized for the first time his own image; the pale resemblance frightened him because of its possessive and overripe determination. Lloyd thought at any moment, if his son did not unlock his knees or fists, if his face didn't abandon the animal outrage it clenched like small prey; if Ira's heart didn't break wide or skip a beat, long enough to give way to sorrow—then he would be split asunder by his own fury. Lloyd was very still, feeling himself split into a thousand pieces. One of him was across the room, broken and unbent, another of him was in the house laughing with the seriousness of a child at play, and yet another part of him was lodged like a painful splinter somewhere behind his eyes where the memory of Nettie blinded him.

"She's buried here!" Lloyd stood up so quickly he had to grab the porch swing for support. "Your ma's buried right here!" He held his head with his hands. "Even before this, even before . . . she ain't jist new dead. She died when your labor tetched her, when she come in, droppin a son so strange you wonder how she carried him so long, you wonder ifn she jist didn't find him in the field someday and that's why the ground was so barren that year!"

Ira made an ugly sound with his breath, snorting and turning away, but he saw his father's hand move across his face and eyes, the same way he wiped away spittle or sweat. Ira kept still, angry and shy in the face of his father's grief. For a long while there was no speaking except the breathing of both—unsteady, loud gasps as if against heavy weights. Jessie stood apart from Lloyd, but at the slightest sign from him she would come near.

"They's shippin her back home, son. She asked it. Jessie and me, we'll see to her," Lloyd stopped and took a deep breath. "And you know, Iry, that's not what I meant to tell you. With your ma passed on now, I mean to give . . ."

"Don't want nothun from you!"

Lloyd grimaced and turned to Jessie, who touched him gently on the back. "He's goin to leave me," Lloyd whispered to his wife so Ira would not hear.

Jessie shook her head vehemently and faced Ira. "Chile, there's some things you should hear . . . now. Now your ma's gone it won't mean nothun against her memory; but it sholy might help your memory so you'll not wrong your father."

"Yes, son, there are stories . . ."

"I don't believe Jessie's stories!"

"You believe your ma's own words, what she did that made her go?" Lloyd demanded and saw his son hesitate. It was enough time for Lloyd to tell him about the night Nettie had been seen running barefooted through the piney woods to that cabin Lloyd first built for her; now it belonged to Jessie Walsh and her sons. When they came home they found Nettie Sloan huddled in a corner of what had been her room. "The room you was born in, son," Lloyd added with difficulty. "See, that was where she began dyin, son. You and me, we didn't know it, but she was leavin us then; she was long gone for years before she left us."

"Gone for you, mebbe! But not me, I remember . . ." Ira halted, in tears.

"No, Lloyd," Jessie said quietly. "His ma was there for him. Iry's right. Nettie was with him until . . ." Suddenly Jessie stopped, then turned to Ira. "When she left, you was no baby; don't you recollect some things happened?"

"No," Ira began dressing hurriedly.

"You don't remember nothun that happened between you and your ma before she left us for good?"

"No," but Ira had paused as if remembering something, then he angrily waved his hand to dismiss it.

"Nettie asked Jessie to care for ye . . . her own words, son."

Ira hastily pulled on his wet shirt and went for the screen door. "No."

"Ifn ye leave, son, without lettin me give ye some truth, some story your ma would want me to tell . . . now that she's at peace . . ."

"God damn you, shut up!" Ira was down three steps before his father spun him around, his face clenched with rage.

"You'll have none of her, jist like you never had none of

me!" He shook Ira with all his might and threw him back against the porch swing. "I never had no son!" he yelled. "You're jist like her!"

"No!" Ira said, running toward his father.

"Leave me like her! Leave me be!" Lloyd's mouth went red and slack, yet still opened and closed as if his blood were words. Ira's fist slashed back and forth, catching Lloyd's jaw until the lips formed no words, no shape, except quick, hot swelling. Even then, Ira's fist made the mouth work on, jawbones grinding against each other.

"I . . . told . . . you . . . to . . . stop! I told you!" Ira gasped, his hand falling limp at his side. Standing very still, he sobbed, dry-eyed, his chest heaving up and down.

His father was quiet, too. Only his eyes moved, burning Ira like licks of fire and ice. Then, in a slow, pained movement, Lloyd's lips split open with the gritted effort of a smile; he held it only a moment before his face again set, clenched and grim and ghastly. "No," Lloyd said, "your mother's love had no meanness." He watched his son run out, the screen door slamming behind him. Lloyd waited until he heard the far-off splashing river. Brusquely he went inside, staunching the blood with a fresh tobacco plug.

That night Lloyd spent alone, having borrowed back his old jail office from the young sheriff, who was pleased to show off the filing shelves and lie detector. But Lloyd quickly banished him across the street, telling him to fetch coffee all around for the weary, unfamiliar men who were indifferent, if not respectful of Lloyd's solitude. The coffee, the sight of their old sheriff quieted and sobered the men enough for Lloyd to spend the night listening to the sounds his son made upstairs. The cracks and scrapes were carried through the bent, yielding ceiling.

By very early morning everything was silent enough for

Lloyd to climb the back stairs to his kitchen; there he made his own thick, sweet coffee and managed to get down one of his daughter's hardtack potato rolls. Then Lloyd washed his face, careful not to get the soap in his raw, grazed bruises. He went straight to his own bedroom, passing by the porch and the parlor without looking in. Nor did he stop off at his three daughters' rooms. Lloyd went to his bed, easing his short, intent body under the quilt as if it were a great woman. Jessie did not stir, did not speak, only lay awake listening for the long time it took for Lloyd's regular breathing. When it came—brief, hushed winds that carried his privacies, his sorrows and smells to her—she got up, replacing the covers under her husband's bruised chin.

Now in the dark, in-between light before dawn, Jessie groped for the bureau, banging her shins against the credenza, glass bric-a-brac tinkling like wind chimes. Her whole body wearily felt for the deep armchair and instead tripped over the low hassock. She remained upright by wedging her slim hips between her daughters' parlor clutter of sewing machine and the cool metal clothes mannequin. It seemed to Jessie that her parlor was again full of other presences—Nettie, Lloyd, Ira, her own daughters, even their dress model, this shapely steel woman. Of all the spirits in her parlor, Jessie knew she was the only one who still cast no shadow, but was weightless and confined to always wander, to haunt her own life as most settled folks did their afterlife. Perhaps that was why she now moved unsurely through her rooms, touching the lemon-wood bureau, hard chairs, a finger running through the dust of the musical credenza. *Iry's now the migrant*, she was neither pleased nor sad, *but he still lives here more than me.*

PART III

CHOSEN KIN

In 1954 when Ira Sloan returned from his six years of schooling he was recognized as the last full-blooded son to carry
his family face and name. In his hometown, weatherbeaten
and silent since the hosiery mill closed down and moved to
Atlanta, Ira found his older kinfolks fast dwindling, childless
and untended except for the church's shut-in visits. In bare,
closed clapboard houses the few scattered Sloans were dying
quietly without hesitation or struggle, each passing on in
dignity and a steadfast shyness that marked all survivors of
the high-spirited family. Although he had sworn during
school that his new pharmaceutical degree was necessary
and welcome to both town and kin, his family elders needed
none of Ira's comforts. Patiently, he sought to reason with
them. But when he called at the tidy, dim houses where the
smell of death was as familiar as the stale breath of sleep, he
was gravely surprised. Rising up from the depths of sunken
sofa cushions like dusty ghosts or sitting in stern-backed
chairs like skeletons of his childhood memories, Ira's folk

greeted him and his satchel of sample syrups or pills with polite suspicion; this wariness took the form of warm, trembling embraces held overlong to avoid those first reproachful words.

"Law, where you been so long, boy?" Great Uncle Matt's widow chided.

"Forgit your way home, Iry?" her sister added.

"No'm, Aunt Lucine, Mrs. Ebbins, I didn't forgit. . . ." Ira laughed a little.

"Jist took the long way round comin back," the staunch women nodded, eyes narrow, vaguely smiling as they looked past him to some more familiar knickknack or portrait on their ancient bureaus. Perhaps one might begin a story but stop midstream when she saw the private fidgeting of Ira's fingers, his eyes listening only to her helpless, sharp breaths; when she coughed it felt like her wide hipbones were knives crossed at right angles to cut deep into her belly and down into the black-veined hollows of her great thighs. The old woman's story would end with a blunt dismissal.

"We farin right well, son. But you, why, you look a bit peaked, like your mama's side. Where you been all this time to look so sickly? Iry, need to stay with us? Will Lloyd Sloan let you back his house?" And before the questions buried him, their pity overcame his outrage, Ira made his goodbyes without leaving them any medicines.

From those first days on Ira did not darken the door of their obstinate houses again. For their part, the old Sloans lingered, separate and alert. But every so often Ira heard word of another distant cousin or aunt who had left off his vigilant life to accept the grave's narrow heaven.

Though these last of Ira's first, spent family left him too much alone, there was the second brood of Sloans whom he could not get away from. They settled over old family terri-

tory on the outskirts of town, breeding like a tireless swarm
of locusts. These were Jessie's Sloans, the Biblical begets of
those oldest two sons who had trailed after their mother's
marriage like following fruit in season. Ira refused any close
kindness from his sprawling second family, these two stepbrothers and their fertile wives. He had nothing in common
with their slow, hapless discourse of spirit, crops, kinship,
and rain. They hinged together like doors that open only
from the inside. But in his heart he begrudged them every
breath they took, every inch of the land they squatted on.
Over the years these second Sloans had worked their borrowed earth as deeply, mercilessly, as they did their women—
breeding down to their lowest common origin of clay, yet
unable to make anything of themselves or their farming. The
women still yielded, but the country was exhausted. Now
the Sloan family face resembled this barrenness, the flat
sameness of features, like a field empty and worn with sowing only one seed over and over again. Ira laid the blame for
this not on his father, but on Jessie; it was an excess in her
blood, a clotting thickness in a woman whose curse was
cleansed only by forever passing off children, baleful, dull,
and inviolate like a crop of stones. And like these stones—
humble and everywhere underfoot—her offspring seemed
always to set themselves in Ira's path. Grudgingly, he
answered their inquiries and offers when he first returned
home.

"Consider this your home, ifn ye need, Iry," his eldest
stepbrother's wife smiled, rubbing her red hands together,
bits of pie dough dropping to the linoleum, where three or
four dogs fought over the crusts.

"Much obliged, Lena, but . . ."

"Well, leastways let us feed ye some!" Lena laughed and
called her brood of squint-eyed children to the supper table.

"This is your . . ." she paused, perplexed, and ran a white, flour-powdered hand through her dark hair. "What are ye anyway, Iry? What kinda kin?"

Ira shrugged and looked down awkwardly, fingers twisting a bit of paper napkin.

"Oh, chillun, jist call him Uncle Iry."

"Uncle Iry, he been starvin, or always been so beanpole skinny?" one of the children asked between mouthfuls, his eyes running up and down Ira as if watching a ball bounce.

"Takes after his pa, I reckon," Virgil said, giving his curious son a look, his eyes pointing toward the corn. "Pass it to Iry, he's off his feed." The table laughed, expecting Ira to guffaw the loudest.

After supper he stayed to help Lena with the dishes and look at his stepbrother's guns, snakeskins, antlers, and new baby boy. But Ira left so soon afterward they knew he was not one of them. They said they forgave him his separateness and unleashed him from any family yoke as effortlessly as forgetting someone's debt once he's out the door.

After leaving Lena's and Virgil's ruined farm, Ira had meant to finally go to town, to his old home above the jailhouse, where Jessie and Lloyd Sloan now watched over their own three daughters. Virgil had said that Jessie's oldest girl was wise and buxom, but not quite old enough to marry, though there were enough insolent suitors in her stable. He said the other girls, bearing only a slight resemblance to Lloyd Sloan, were still cat-fighting over who had grown enough to fit into Ira's abandoned clothes.

Though Ira felt an unexpected pleasure in seeing his homeland again, he still could not bring himself to go to Lloyd Sloan's tonight. On foot, hiking through the back country he knew like his own body, Ira still tried to fool himself that he was headed in a homeward direction, though his feet knew he was veering off into the woods that would take him to the outskirts of town and Quince's factory and mortuary. All the years of Ira's absence he had written no one but Nate, and him only when it became apparent that he would return home in humiliation unless someone lent him money to finish school. Ira's first letter to Nate had been business-like, each paragraph a promise of future benevolence; but if Nate could not see his way to investing in Ira, then the letter made clear that Ira never did think too much of Nate's offers of brotherhood. By return mail Ira had received twice the amount of his requested loan. There was not a word from Nate, simply the return address embossed in official script: "Quince Bros., Inc." Uneasily, Ira had returned the extra money with a note, "I don't need you embezzling from Quince!" But still no letter from Nate, except every year after that Ira received the familiar envelope with another loan in it. At first Ira accepted the money, but after several years he had enough saved from odd jobs to return the annual envelope, unopened. Ira was convinced that Nate had told his family that he begged for money.

Now, walking through the back woods toward Quince's, it struck Ira that his aunts and stepbrothers had seemed unprepared for him; perhaps it was he who rose up like a ghost in front of his ancient aunts and perhaps Virgil's children knew so little of him because he was a stranger, unheralded by family histories and expectations. But surely Nate would not be so startled to see him home?

Ira climbed the back steps of Quince's, figuring that Nate's room would be that high, lighted window, a room that seemed an afterthought to Quince's mortuary and residence. As he expected, the door was unlatched; who would rob the dead? Ira thought, and managed a smile. Then he remembered Nate's habitual harrowing grin and Ira's face fell. Since Nate had left Lloyd Sloan's house Ira had rarely seen his stepbrother. Ira remembered that the last time he and Nate spent any time together his stepbrother had all but broken his nose. This thought made Ira stop just outside Nate's door. All the years separating that single blow from this moment now filled Ira with abiding satisfaction, as he turned the doorknob to see Nate bent over a desk, his shock of black hair bristling around his narrow face as if the electricity in his lamp moved up through his body. *He ain't changed*, Ira thought, and felt that his travels and schooling now lent him a vision beyond these townspeople and his family, beyond even the far-reaching grasp of Nate Walsh. Whatever had been broken in Ira when he left here, now seemed healed; and Ira felt separate, for the first time free from any hold.

Proudly, and with the force of his sudden indifference, Ira entered the room, stepped into the bright circle thrown by Nate's desk lamp. But Nate did not look up. There was in him such an attitude of attentiveness—head cocked to listen, eyes open but downcast and empty, mouth slightly open, limp hands palms upward on the bookkeeping ledger, and his body so flaccid it seemed to fall off his bones as if flensed, held to him simply by the light bondage of his work clothes. *He's been round the dead so long he's beginnin to look like one*, Ira thought and made himself smile. Even from this distance he could see the thick vein in Nate's neck throbbing. But just as Ira was going to call out, Nate's posture changed. His body arched intensely as if awaiting a blow, not cowering but willing it; his fingers clenched into fists, his eyes gathered light that made the lamp's electric glow seem to blink, then grow dark, and his lips stretched into a rigid smile.

Ira did not recognize this smile; no more a habit, a sign of fatigue, his smile was now an ecstatic grimace. This triumphant expression Ira had seen on faces of the dying and it had left him desolate, unconvinced, as he watched the body will itself into an outward expression of faith, when the spirit was held in the face's death grip—eyes rolled upward into luminous white worlds, jaw in a paroxysm of clenched joy, and brow arched, so pale and round one longed to lay hands on that forehead, expecting fever but feeling the unwrinkled, cool skin sculpted as stone. Others took this seizure of faith as a sign, a visible blessing on the body, but Ira thought it more a sign of spiritual anguish, for the body hoarded spirit at the very moment when it should surrender.

"Why you here?" It was Nate's voice, calm and dry.

Startled, Ira looked at Nate and was relieved to see his stepbrother had not been watching him, but was again bent over his yellow ledger, upon which were scrawled columns of numbers, precisely matched like mathematical armies moving in formation against some invisible foe.

"Well," Ira shifted nervously, then drew a breath. "I come back to practice my trade."

"Why you here?" Nate said again, without emphasis, except to tap his pencil against his paper, leaving several leaden slashes in the ledger.

"Here with ye?"

"Yes."

For the first time Ira noticed that there were wide dents darkening the skin beneath Nate's eyes. "It's late to be workin so hard," Ira said, his voice gently commiserative.

"Reckon it's never too late when the books don't balance."

"Thank ye, Nate," Ira heard himself rush on, "I come here to say that. When my books didn't balance, was you made up the difference."

"Anyone woulda done the same."

"Not my pa," Ira said softly.

"Especially your pa." For the first time Nate looked up; his face lost its smile and he seemed kindly. "You see him yet?"

"No, figured I'd come here first."

"Much obliged," Nate nodded. "Now you best git on home."

Ira hesitated, "Did you git my letters?"

"Got my own letters . . . returned."

"Well, how come you never wrote nothun? Mebbe I woulda taken the money ifn ye spared me a few words."

Suddenly Nate dropped his pencil and eyed Ira, his voice harsh, "Lissen, I ain't got nothun to spare!"

Ira backed off, and muttered, "Sorry to trouble ye," as he turned to go.

"No," Nate halted him. "It's me makin the trouble." Nate said no more, simply stared down at his hands. At last he began, "Iry, when you asked me to give you money I sent it. . . ."

"Yes, and I'm obliged."

"That weren't nothun to me!"

"Was to me," Ira laughed.

"But words and other gifts of spirit," Nate halted, then laughed harshly. "I don't got overmuch to give."

For a moment Ira watched Nate, trying to discern his stepbrother's meaning. The recent image of Nate's rapt, listening face overpowered by his faith still worked on Ira. "Why, Nate, you can call down the Spirit like the old-time prophets. I seen it. I jist now seen it."

"Ifn we believed already, we wouldn't need no prophets," Nate said, his voice so fatigued it sounded sorrowful.

Ira fell silent in the face of Nate's despair. He had never seen this about his stepbrother, never imagined this powerful, puzzling brother had ever doubted himself or his God for one moment. This doubt struck Ira as deeply as if it were his own longing and he felt some love akin to pity for Nate. Then as if to protect Nate from himself, Ira said, "Remember once you told me you was called. Sholy it's so if even I believe it . . . now."

"You don't believe it," Nate said. "That's why I can tell ye, because you'll believe I ain't got nothun to give. You was the first to see that."

Ira shook his head, "Well, then, all this other . . . this call and giving spirit . . . ain't important to ye," Ira laughed. "You know you're jist as poor as the rest of us."

At this Nate flinched a little, "They think I been chosen."

Ira hesitated, "They?"

"I wished you woulda been my follower when I first asked ye," Nate suddenly said, his voice urgent. "You keep me from prophecy."

"From what?"

"From them," Nate's face was drawn and Ira saw sweat beading on his brow. He had the instinct to wipe it off and Ira wondered how he'd let Nate draw him in so deep, what his stepbrother had done to make him lose his first sense of indifference. Perhaps this ability about Nate to discover one's most subterranean wellsprings of doubt or attention was what led others to him, as if Nate was encircled by an energy that bound all those who doubted too deeply. For it was doubt that now drew Ira nearer Nate so that he stood illuminated by the darkness that seized his stepbrother.

"Who follows ye, Nate?" Ira asked gently, rapt.

"Them that's also chosen," Nate said quietly. "Unbelievers."

"Your followers don't believe?"

"Mebbe the Lord chooses unbelievers as His prophets."

"That don't make good sense," Ira burst out and could not help but laugh.

Nate did not look up, "Makes all the sense in the world. Unbelievers got to see, but not for themselves. They want prophets, signs, and miracles before they believe," Nate's voice wavered. "My followers, that's what I ain't got to give them. I ain't so sure no more, Iry! I don't hear no voices, don't see no familiar signs . . . ain't never healed nobody . . ."

"You jist don't got the know-how," Ira said, not unkindly.

"Then why do I got followers?" Violently Nate made long, leaden lines down his paper. "Oh, that ain't for you to answer." He waved Ira away and began intently scribbling his numbers.

"Mebbe I'm the only one can answer."

Nate laughed and shook his head. "You been called, too? Mebbe the whole damn world's been called, huh? We all babblin here below and answerin for the Lord and He can't git a word in edgewise!"

"I'm the only one can answer because, Nate, I know how it feels to want to heal folks," Ira rushed on, seizing the moment, but surprised at his own zeal. "See, when I watched my ma go dead inside, or mebbe jist wander so far away from herself she got lost, couldn't hear us callin . . . then I knowed there was somethin I could learn to give folks sick and lost like her. Why you think I studied all these years? I ain't never heard no heavenly call, but I listened to her lost and ailin and I aim to keep on hearin so's I can heal. Why, I got medicines to . . ."

"You got even less than me, boy!" Nate jumped up and moved toward him menacingly. "You got a cure for lost souls? You ever seen the body break into nothun when Spirit humbles it? You ever . . . ?"

"Ifn it's Spirit that goes breakin a body, then I reckon I should foller you around and git me started in my bidness!"

Abruptly Nate turned and started laughing, a high and harsh laughter that every once in a while made a noise like retching. "You think you been chosen, too," Nate wheezed and held himself.

Ira straightened and made to leave. Summoning all his dignity, he said, "There ain't no prophets. I told you that once and you bout broke me to pieces for it. Now you know it's true!" and Ira suddenly realized that Nate was weeping, but dry-eyed like a drunk's retching when his belly is hollow.

"I ain't got no will left," Nate's words came in heaving breaths.

Slowly Ira felt the anger flow out of him as he went to his stepbrother and laid a hand on his bent head. "Shhhh, now, Nate . . . ," Ira said and after a long while when Nate was quiet, hiccoughing like a small child, Ira added, "There's jist those of us waitin on God. Waitin on him for healin . . ." Ira's voice was hushed. "Like my pa told me when my ma was ailin, that she was jist waitin. . . ."

"I only got to wait for one sign," Nate looked up and disengaged himself from Ira.

"Well, I ain't gonna devil ye no more, Nate," Ira sighed. "You got devils enough."

"Iry?"

"Say what?"

"You talkin bout your pa . . . he ain't got too much longer to wait."

"On me?"

"He don't know nothun bout ye."

"Didn't you tell him where I was, doin what all these years . . . didn't you tell him how I borrowed from ye?"

"No, Iry, I jist told them I didn't hear nothun from ye so they come over the years not to expect you back."

"But all along . . . ," Ira began, then halted, confused.

"All along it come to be like you was dead to them," Nate said quietly.

"But I thought you woulda said somethin . . . anythin!"

"I pitied them, Iry. Now you tell them yourself."

"I will . . . but I don't know much to say after all their unknowin these years."

"They ain't the only ones unknowin," Nate said and his smile was back as his eyes ran over the strict columns of numbers, moving his rigid armies toward some solution, some act of will that might make them balance.

"Thank ye, then, Nate," Ira said, but Nate's eyes did not follow him. Ira gathered himself and again felt separateness closing around him as he left the well-lit room for the cool night walk home.

Ira arrived at his home after midnight, and without disturbing the family he went to the back porch to settle in the splintered swing. The night's heat lay with him like another body or like a memory of a child's feverish dreams. He lay still, rocking idly and listening to the swing's creaking chains. *If I don't sleep*, he thought, *I might hie down yonder to Yellow River. Been long time gone.* He heard his river had been flooding all summer, the cottonmouths thick in some inlets; but before he decided whether to risk swimming or not, he heard the soft, sibilant rattle of screens and felt rain drizzling into the back porch, drenching him like a hot-springs. Cursing, Ira moved to a straight-backed chair in the corner, letting his sweat cool him. Here, bent over himself so tightly that his heart beat against his bare thighs, he realized why he was doomed to come back home. This was not his own doing. His home, his family, his blood and face conspired against him.

Here, conspiracy was in the very air; one breathed in and

was dazed, by this weather's weight, its primitive heat. But the conspiracy was more than the heat, his family's hold, or the spirit world's shadows; something else worried Ira, something unacceptable like an old belly scar or an ill-cut conviction that, even after hardening, has a tight, untouched feel. He worried that some force in him over which he had no control already condemned him—be it his blood or some hurt done him when he was too young to be himself or some weakness he would not suspect until one day his mind might go away and, like his mother, he would wander inside his solitude, lost and lonely for that self his body betrayed. Perhaps the conspiracy was simply the insinuating yet intimate dread that he was too close to this country and its fate. Just as there seemed no break in the weather, there promised no other future in his breeding. Jessie, his half-kin, even his failing past family, everyone accepted this: things would get no better nor no worse.

This acceptance was in the low gutteral brood of voices, just as surrender was in the easy smile and steadfast, sullen movements that marked anyone born here. Pride was in their acceptance of this country's weight, the slow futility of its burden. Families guarded their resignation as if it were a family trust, willed generation after generation, until it took on the value of instinct or wisdom.

Still, from somewhere came belief; it was contrary, yet as instinctive as rain, with the same rise and fall. Belief was in the voices. Talk began weary with itself, slow and complaining, but then it rose up, ending on a high, vulnerable note, as if in prayer, question, or surprise for still hoping differently. Though Ira had been vigilant against his own voice, though he had better schooling and knew a precise, blunt language of medicine, he had never lost his native accent, nor the lilt of its loose endings that lent his most profane swearing this sound of incredulous faith.

"Damned ifn it ain't Iry!" Startled, Ira jumped from his chair and stood for a moment in the shadowed porch corner. For years he had heard her voice only in his nightmares; it was then cold and guttural like the coarse call of a cat in heat. Old Black Misery, he called her all these years; but now her voice was warm, its twanging accent not like the mosquito whine he remembered, but like the rhythmic shush of water over rocks as she ran on, hugging him so close he could hardly breathe. "Lord, I thought you was a spirit trompled down in that corner, son! Lloyd!" Her voice flooded every room in the house. "Lloyd! Look who's home!" But Lloyd Sloan did not join her on the porch. Ira waited a few minutes and then followed Jessie, who tilted her head and frowned suddenly. "He's been askin after you all these long years, Iry. Where you gone that you couldn't tell us? We didn't know you from a dead man, boy!" Ira said nothing, but walked past her into the bright kitchen. She sternly grabbed his arm to halt him. "You fixin to root down here? Cause ifn you ain't, jist pass on through this door the way you come!"

Ira shook himself free and glared at her. "Why don't he come out here hisself and say that?"

"He's hurtin. Don't trouble him ifn ye come home for somethin sides settlin in as his son."

Ira looked down at the linoleum floor, pursing his lips.

"But now . . ." Suddenly, in a different tone as if struggling with a part of herself still vigilant and tirelessly watching him through dull, leaden eyes, Jessie said, "You here might help some."

"Reckon I'll be puttin down roots here so deep you'll weary of my face." He watched her through a wide smile; she seemed taken aback. "Got me schoolin proper now."

"What you gonna do with it?"

"You already said it: help. I know remedies and cures you never thought possible." Jessie was silent, perplexed. "In plain words, Jessie, I am a pharmacist, or I will be when I git a shop, supply medicines, and start gatherin practice."

"You . . . yarb doctor?" she roared, throwing her head back. "Hell, chile, I coulda learned ye them remedies. And what strange roots is this you gots to travel so far before plantin them here at home?"

Ira stared, bewildered by her ignorance. "What's Doc Varnon say?"

Jessie frowned, irritated.

"Well, Pa called in that fool, didn't he?"

"Old sluggard says, 'Don't worry over Lloyd. His quick flustration, it'll pass,'" Jessie sucked on her teeth then said, more quietly, "Only thing passed was Doc hisself. Dead as a dodo and now Lloyd . . ."

"He ain't seen no doctor since . . . ?"

"I make do, Iry. Ain't nobody else know to heal him."

Ira scowled and laughed.

"That's right, boy! You grin like a possum now, but where was you when your pa got chilled! You was dead to us then! I swear Lloyd was so sick he'd had to git better to die!" Jessie calmed herself and straightened, looking at her stepson with a fierce smile. "Now, I ain't very high learned, Ira Sloan, but I know . . ." She stopped abruptly, biting her lip.

"What you know?"

"Never mind," she said. "But ifn I was in this country yet when you'uns had Nettie down with that cowsick, bet I . . ."

"You were," Ira said flatly, turning to retrieve his black satchel from the corner of the porch. "You were here," he shoved past her. "Where you got my father holed up?"

CHORES AND RITUALS

Ira found Lloyd Sloan in the high, iron-spoked bed that had been Nettie's, this same duck-feather mattress and patch quilt that Ira once sat cross-legged on, braiding bits of yarn or clover, all the while staring at his mother's white, thick face. Her dreams and breathing had moved the whole bed and set the coiled springs to singing; now Lloyd's rasping cough made it wince out metallic whines. Ira held back a moment. His father was so terribly thin that without the second skin of his flannel nightshirt, his flinty, gut-lashed skeleton might collapse into an awkward and angular heap of bones. But his father's face was much the same, lips stretched in that aching grin, jaw unhinged, but firm. Only his eyes had changed; where once they had been the rich black of loamsoil, the color was now a weak, shallow brown. Beneath each eye ran deep ruts, as if he had done battle with some power—a half-human demon or night animal who, meaning to claw out his eyes, had instead gouged these thin white scars, shaped like the crescents of a swelling moon.

"Go near, Iry," Jessie gave him a slight shove toward the

bed. "Lloyd's so wearied seein visitors that his sight's failin now."

"Sloans been visitin him?" Ira was surprised, for ever since Lloyd married Jessie, his side of the family had not set foot in this house.

"Yes, my sons come round regular."

"I say, any *his* folks been out?"

"No."

"What visitors, then?" Ira demanded as he moved closer to his father's sickbed.

Jessie shook herself and poured a glass of water from her husband's pitcher. She drank deeply for a minute, then turned back to her anxious stepson.

"Seems that other kinda kin come callin at night. They lay down on Lloyd to steal his breath like an old suckin cat, cause he can't pull in enough air, and what does whooshes right back out with mutterin."

"Think he sees me?"

"Don't yet," she came forward and touched Ira lightly on the neck, thinking, *No, he ain't never been out of his valley. He's livin there sholy like his ma. But he's Lloyd's boy, too; he carry it all over. That still won't save him. He's got Nettie's starvin eyes, got the Devil in his eyes lookin out on this world but hungerin for the other. Only Ira don't know his hunger from meanness, nor bein alone from bein left.* Jessie felt Ira's body tremble, arching under her hand as if unable to bear her slightest weight. *He won't never let no woman lay on him, stretch herself clean out flat from mouth over belly to toe. Restin over him like dead that's floated up by river water. This Iry won't float no body now. He's afeared he'll sink deeper. Well, Jessie ain't beggin.* She leaned instead against the door jamb, feeling shaken, weary of this boy's urgent vengeance and his father's slow renunciation of

all she had struggled to give freely, without shame or outrage. *The both them begrudge me air I breathe. They won't
tote no weight that's got my name or body. When I die,
Lord! You best give this woman wings, ain't nobody liftin
me up. They'll drop me in the ground so fast, they won't git
their hands dirty.*

For a long while she watched Ira's back, saying nothing,
but finally she spoke, and the quiet in her voice surprised
even her. "Iry, be kind. Listen . . . listen to me! I'm talkin
bout his night visitors, his dreams. You're one. Oh, not you,
but what's lodged in him of you, like a sore splinter he's
tryin to work out. He like to kilt hisself watchin out for
spirits these nights. Like I say, we took ye for daid." She
paused and thought a moment. "Well, come day he ain't got
eyesight left. Not for me. And now, not for ye . . . not for any
flesh."

Ira ignored her and bent low over the bed, whispering.

Suddenly Lloyd opened his eyes, the thin moons beneath
quivering and swelling like two milk teats heavy-laden with
sleep, forgetfulness, perhaps long suffering. Was Jessie talking sense? Ira wondered suddenly. Perhaps the visions fed
off his father's second eyes. Every night, did these inward
eyes suckle familiar spirits; did they ease his grief, drinking
it in—these shadows that needed only the taste of blood to
become flesh? And each morning, was the spirit sated, flee-
ing back into the eyes' narrow caverns, the hollows of bone
or these moons underneath his eyes?

Ira watched his father's cold, dark eyes and saw a sudden
flicker, not meant for him, but like a spark that ignited his
whole body—warm skin and bones catching fire like dry
tinder; the body's temperature flared up, blood swiftly boiling through fallen veins, tempering the taut muscles of
hands and legs, and finally burning a hole through the skull,
an opening bored wide and deep enough for one simple

blind shaft of light to illuminate his labyrinth of sleep. Sleep lay inside this hollow cave, this skull where he had been lost all night, feeling his way by memory, brittle fingers tracing the loud, sweating walls that sheltered his brain. Then there were two holes, two eyes through which daylight shone into his mind.

But even as Ira watched his father come round, slipping from the shadow of his dreams, he wondered, where did the spark come from? Nate would name it his "spirit." He'd say it did not just call on him at nights; it lived in him, ravenous, feeding off some source. Ira knew he would spend his whole life searching for this power, this beginning. Even now he felt the hunger in himself and his instinct was to root it out, find it with his new tools, the knowledge these past school years lent him. He would discover it first in himself, but he might begin to find it just beneath him, hiding in his father's frail body.

Did your spirit haunt you only as visible as a stalking shadow, or did it dwell in regions mysterious, yet common-place? Ira remembered suddenly Jessie's body names from those first few baths in this house—valleys, ridges, caves, and hollers—did Jessie know herself? Did it hide in the spleen, the simple, throbbing heart, or the back of the head where the brain laid its maze passages of balance and memory? Where, Ira thought furiously, where did this soul, this secret sharer of all thoughts, acts, and words, exist? Could anyone find it, without help, stumbling over it in the simplest act like lovemaking, staring at another, or sleep? Did it speak, still and quiet, so that you might lay an ear and catch its pulse, the swift, intimate rush of the spirit, like beating blood?

"Git gone!" Lloyd's muttering startled his son.

"Papa . . . ," Ira said quietly, but his father made no answer, except a low, throaty mumble that became a cough. Only his eyes showed any signs of recognition. Warily Lloyd Sloan watched his son lay several bottled medicines on the bedtable. When Ira roughly peered beneath the old man's eyelids, Lloyd thought his lids were permanently flapped upward into his head; he would be denied the blind solace of blinking. When Ira listened to his pulse, Lloyd threw off his hand; coughing violently he felt a familiar movement in his chest as his anger hollowed out another cave inside, moist warmth radiating out to numb his heart. At last silent, chest heaving, Lloyd's jaw hung loose and he smiled up at Ira a moment before he turned and spit blood on the bedsheets.

Inside the black bag, Ira had stashed his parchment degree with all its symbols and signatures, as impressive and meaningless to Jessie as had been her eldest daughter's French exercise books. During the short and silent exchange between father and son—Ira holding his wrist, touching his eyelids, his neck and forehead, bending his tall body way down, pressing his ear against the heart, listening not to the rhythmic murmur but to the cough that gathered itself, creaking inside the wide, fallen chest—Lloyd seemed pleased to see his son. But as he eyed Ira's hawkish face, the gray, troubled eyes, the jaw that clenched and unclenched without tobacco, Lloyd felt himself grow more and more distant, as if he were falling into the hollows of himself, his tired skin sloughing off his bones, all sinking into the center of his body where the cavernous coughs swallowed him up, making greedy, sucking noises like a drainpipe. Now, while his son carried on a whispered conversation with Jessie, Lloyd saw his second wife's arms hanging still at her side, making fists every time she spoke; Lloyd turned on his side and stared out the window.

It was just dawn. Lloyd remembered many things about this time of morning, though he hadn't been up before dawn in several years, though he hadn't been up at all this spring and summer. He recalled the distant past, forgetting first the present. Here was the image of Nettie as a child. She was walking back from the fishing hole, her long, wide plaid skirts catching on the briars of every blackberry bush she passed. Toting an armload of books, she stumbled, intent on the cloudless sky. He remembered waiting at the end of a long row of tobacco, picking suckers off his overalls, beating the dust from his stained hat, and catching a quick look at his own thin, tanned face in the pickup's mirror as he took long draughts of liquor from a flask, waiting for the school-teacher to pass on her way home from school. They would nod to one another. But Lloyd Sloan never spoke to Nettie in his old work clothes. They kept silent, though seeing one another in passing twice a day, until Sunday afternoon, when their embraces were like a clean rain after drought.

Now, every time Lloyd coughed it seemed to bring up more memories from some festering cavity deep inside; these memories tasted of tobacco and bitter rumination. Lately, he was never surprised when, metamorphosed from the bulky ridge of the heavy comforters he threw off during his night fever, Nettie's body molded next to his and held him before rising up and moving slowly into the kitchen. Clanging buckets, a slamming screen door—"My sign to get up," Lloyd would mutter; but nobody, least of all the swarthy, rail-thin woman next to him, understood that there were fields to be broken up and cows to be milked, and soon a small son's hunger to fend off.

Other times during the day, most often in the late evening, Lloyd woke from his fitful oblivion, her cold hands against his forehead. Looking up into the sunken, high-boned face, her eyes unexpectedly dead, but the jaw slack, shivering, Lloyd saw his midwife. She was shaking him, cool fingers running up and down his face, chest, and belly, pleading, pulling him up from this bed he kept falling through every day as if it were a well; and he could hear his body splashing above him as he plummeted deeper down into the fever, the hot and wet earth. As the midwife worked over him Lloyd would say, "Tryin to git me borned, eh?" He stretched his lips in his haphazard way of smiling. But Jessie never answered him. He told his second wife many secrets but she never heard. Once in a while he found her watching him from the distance of their bedroom, she seated in a rocker, her hands sculpting the air as she wove a white-oak strip, making those same scooped bark baskets she once wielded, balanced on her hipbone, in the migrant fields. This didn't surprise Lloyd, either, though Jessie had been away from picking for many years. To Lloyd the natural order of his life was right to be reversed; the past was beginning all over again. And now, here was his son Ira, looking not much thicker than when he disappeared years ago. Sitting at the foot of his bed, his son stared at him. Was it shrewdness or suffering that marked his face? Lloyd wondered and squinted as if a bright light burned just outside the circle of his vision.

When Ira had first walked into the room, Lloyd knew himself finally dead and resurrected. "Backwards to be born again," Lloyd said to his son and midwife, laughing, spitting up blood. Lloyd was startled when he saw his son and Jessie jump back from the bedside. "So you'uns ain't deaf, eh? Decided to listen to an old man finally?" Lloyd tried to lift himself up on his elbow; Jessie was close by, adding her weight to his. "Now you go on, son. Let your mother and me git some rest." He looked at Jessie with soft, but lucid eyes.

"That film . . . ," Ira went on, his voice tinged with preci-
sion. "Lackluster, opaque, cloudy . . . peripheral vision . . .
hardened lens . . ." He whirled around and demanded of
Jessie, "You think to have this lens removed?" but before she
could respond Ira turned back to his father, "Gray pallor,
looks like he's hypervent. Here, get him out of that old
nightshirt and . . ."

Lloyd raised himself and with one hand slapped the air
near Ira's nose. "Git gone!" he yelled hoarsely. "I hear you. I
hear you talkin through your new hat."

Ira grimaced, but made an effort to change his face into a
smile that was as resigned as it was familiar. "You rest some,
Papa." Ira nodded to Jessie to come away with him to the
next room.

"No, leave her be," his father said, falling back onto the
sweat-stained pillow. "Seems like I ain't seen her in as long a
while as I ain't seen you, Iry. I been busy gettin borned
backwards," he lay looking at Jessie and she nodded.

"Thank ye, Iry," she said, her eyes hungry. "Now he'll be
back for a time like his son."

Ira knew his father's ailment; it was emphysema in the
last, racked stages. Had Doc Varnon seen this before he
died? Ira wondered. Had that suffering fool seen anything
ever since he'd first found forgetfulness, that dry and amber
blindness he nursed on? Perhaps Jessie did right in not seeing another doctor? There was only one, Dr. Rayburn two
counties over, in the holler called Hag's Creek, and he was
mountain people, a suspicious, surly lot, Ira thought, not to
be trusted with their charms and potions. Ira thought about
calling him anyway, but resisted the idea. Hadn't he just
finished more years in medicine than most doctors around
here would ever see?

Sitting on the porch swing now, running a hand through his damp, sour-smelling hair, Ira tried to quiet the uneasy fascination he felt toward his father's illness. He could not rest for the thought of finding a way to help his father fight this sickness; perhaps he had at last heard his call—that glimpsed spirit flickering in a man's eyes.

That night Ira dreamed he heard whining voices, far off but intimate, as if he had caught himself uttering an unknown tongue. He tried to wake himself, but was trapped inside his dense skull. Was this the dread sleep that nightly gouged out his father's eyes, leaving him blind by daylight? Ira managed to lift his eyelids halfway open. It seemed there was a light on somewhere, a yellow bulb burning fitfully like a dying fire, his dreams casting shadows across the wet white linen sheet—this veil wrapped around his body so tightly his legs and arms were dead, stinging; they hung down off the porch swing, fingernails scraping against the wood floor as he swung back and forth, stirred by his terrible breathing. Again Ira struggled to wake, to sit up, but the shadows lay fettered with him like familiars, their weightless, dark bodies falling heavily against his breast. All these close, chattering shadows, their faces and tongues flickering across the slits in his eyes, their mouths against his, stealing, sucking his hot, sweet wind, until he heaved, arching his back and screaming as he struggled up to the surface of his sleep.

"Shucks!" A strange voice came from the kitchen a second behind the sound of shattered glass. "You gone and busted this last jar of goofer dust; got to fetch more tonight." Ira was up from his porch swing, eyes swollen shut, mouth gritty, his skin clammy and itching where mosquitoes had stolen blood, raising red welts on legs and thighs. Who was in the kitchen? The noises of cabinets shutting and bottles clinking made him first fear the slam-bang tantrums of a meddlesome, much ignored ghost.

Carefully, Ira went to the kitchen door and hid behind it. Relieved, he stifled a laugh. Here was Jessie's angular, shambling shape. She stood in the darkness, muttering, as she gathered bottles from the herb cupboard. *Mebbe she's had bad dreams, too.* Ira remembered Jessie's saying that nightmares made the body hunger and thirst. You had to jump up from bed and feast your spirit so the dreams were sated and never come begging again.

I'll scare her silly! Jessie'll jump up and yowl like a cat in heat! Jist scratch her back and she'll shed three skins gittin loose! But something made Ira hang back behind the door. Idly, he watched her dark body move around the kitchen, stealthily like a cat but without her usual grace. Jessie was skitterish, her motions unsure and halting; only her stoop up and down from the lower cabinets was fluid. Though she was fifty-three, Ira could not help fixing on her high, small breasts, her round and sturdy buttocks, her long legs.

But suddenly a memory struck him: on one of his childhood walks he came across an old black woman digging in the dirt. It was not ordinary red clay. This soil beneath her scratching nails was the rich earth of a newly filled-in grave. He had seen the granny woman in the cemetery before, but usually in the colored burial ground behind the cross-and-carry fence. Here she was scrambling like a daddy-longlegs spider over a fresh grave with a pink marble statue that could only belong to a good family. Mumbling to herself, she filled jars full of the deep loamsoil, only looking up once, irritated at this child's wide stare. "You want some goofer dust, too? Little cracker like you got notions to do devilment? Hah!" and she threw a fistful at him, shooing him home with curses and strange, chanting songs.

Goofer dust? Off whose grave? Ira meant to demand of Jessie, but again he held back, feeling suddenly weak. She took bottle after bottle off the counter, putting them in her basket, counting each as she went; her soft laughing broke her own spell as she picked up her basket apothecary and carefully walked down the hall to Lloyd's sickroom.

With a sudden sense of outrage, Ira followed, walking very quietly so she would not hear. He stood just outside the door and peered inside, waiting for his eyes to absorb and be freed from the darkness. The outline of Jessie's body was framed in the window, moonlight falling like pale splinters broken off from the darkness as if by force. She knelt, head bent low. Ira barely heard the humble prayer as her finger-nails clicked off the rosary beads, droning a Catholic Latin litany. Ira thought to leave this beggarly ritual; but his eyes suddenly fixed on his mother's ancient bedtable, upon which Nettie once rolled her endless cigarettes. The last time he saw this scratched redwood piece was in the attic. Now, here it was by his father's sickbed. It had not been in the room this afternoon.

A framed photograph was set in the middle of it, but Ira could not see the picture for the surrounding clutter. Very quiet, like a frightened child, Ira pressed against the wall. Jessie never looked up from her prayer and in the dim light what Ira had assumed was a prayer shawl now looked more like a crinkled animal skin. Ira edged toward her and saw that what shimmied across her shoulders was a snakeskin, its orange-and-black mosaic as translucent as a butterfly wing.

For almost an hour Jessie clicked her rosary beads, until Ira thought he would faint from his rigid, stiff-legged position. Suddenly Jessie fixed on Lloyd, flapping her mouth at him, wordlessly. Ira watched intently, eyes narrowed. The woman was deep in her trance, and the voice that rushed from her now and then was not her own, but impersonal and more commanding. Her words rushed out like a river's rapids, sounds swirling and splashing loudly against one another. But, Ira thought suddenly, so much of this woman was not heard, the way a river, its moving body of water, is most silent as it flows out from the shore and its shallows. Now, Ira listened as if to find the part of her that was so deep, the current so swift, that it seemed still. And then he heard her cool, ecstatic voice.

"Yes, chillun," the voice filled every corner of the room, "I tell you now, this sickness is a call. When the Lord gits lonely He swoops nearer His earth, and whispers . . . shhhhh, He whispers so low. That's this sweet wind. But we don't lissen. Then He weeps over our deafness and that's the rain. But we don't pay no mind unless floods ruin our crops. Even when the Lord groans, O mighty Spirit! Groanin and gnashin His teeth, like thunder and lightnin, we don't hear His call. It's only when He tetches us . . . ah, chile, His love and your affliction! The Lord tetches a body, He don't mean mebbe! Sholy it's like holdin a baby with all love's power and not knowin you're huggin too tight, hurtin your chile. That chile wails like cryin in the black wilderness for pity. The Lord lissens and lets you go so quick your body falls back sickly and sore, lonely for His tetch and afeared that when He holds you agin it'll be your death! That's the embrace ye long and shrink back from, chillun. The Lord's always willin to hold His own chile, but we can't bear bein tetched too long. So sickness of body is the only time we lissen to the Lord's call, cause we let Him come so near He like to swoop us away to glory! But we shy away, sholy we shy far away, fallin back from His hands, almost broken by them. And ain't it jist so, chillun? Ain't it? After all, this Lord made mountains not meanin to. He was jist strokin the world's dark flanks, but the great weight of His fingers raised up welts, blue veins like mountains and splinters like piney woods, and rivers runnin like blood from this world's being tetched by powerful love. Yes, chile . . . lissen to His call, His hurt and blessin."

Until the first light fell across the sickroom, Ira listened on. Or maybe he had dreamed and slept. For suddenly he heard voices—one strident and one underbreath.

"Rest a spell side me, I say." Ira almost jumped six feet in the air when he heard his father's gravelly, dazed voice. "I say . . . cows don't need you strokin nigh as much as me," his voice was barely more than exhaled air, yet Ira understood every word. "Linger near awhile longer . . ." and then he laughed, red spittle dotting his chin, coughing; but his eyes were open wide and he turned his head as if watching something rise up from the bed and walk slowly through the room, out the window. "Never did see a woman so well fixed as ye. Walk, why you jist rockin along, like a natural cradle rockin me, gittin me borned backwards." Lloyd half sat up in bed, his bones creaking like rotted wood. "Nettie! Wait on me!" he cried.

"Shhhhhhhhh . . ." Jessie's voice was now her own, more weary than Ira could ever have imagined it. "She linger too long and be shut out her own grave, Lloyd." Her voice was blank, almost a monotone, as she continued, "She'll be back tonight to lay with ye sholy. You live for that leastways, honey. But you linger till then with Jessie . . ." and her voice broke, ragged and hoarse.

Ira was up, coming over to her; he knew he would comfort his stepmother, though the feel of that snakeskin around her shoulders already made him shiver. But she suddenly whirled on him. Weariness had been only in her voice, for her body stretched itself up full and towered above him. Streaked with oily paint, and jagged silver lightning strokes down her neck and arm, Jessie had four eyes, two on her cheeks, painted a brilliant, bloodshot red. Her arms were knotted, fists hanging from each taut wrist.

She did not see him, though she stared in his eyes. She saw only what moved them all, and in a voice that split the room wide open, she screamed out, "O Lord, ifn you take his body, don't be stealin his spirit! Leave me some sign, let him call by my name. . . ." She halted and turned back to beseech Lloyd. But he lay looking out the window, watching for dawn, grinning, his jaw chewing his tongue, his mouth occasionally spitting blood. Jessie cried out, glaring at the window, "I ask ye for all this, Lord . . . for she has dragged me in the dust and destroyed my good name, broken my heart and caused me to curse that day I was born!" And without looking at Lloyd again, she walked straight to the door, almost knocking Ira to the ground.

He knew she was gone, how long or where, he could only suspect. Now he moved to his father's bed and sat down heavily. He stretched, his feet touching the iron grillwork at the bottom of the bed. For the first time since returning, Ira felt he was home; this knowledge deeply comforted him. His father did not notice his weight or stir, just kept staring out the window. The morning air was already steaming, but a breeze off the backyard river moved through the room with the threat of rain. Ira slept then, resting easier than he had since the day he was born.

"Son."

"Sir."

"I'm gone."

"No, jist a bit peaked," Ira tried to grin, cleaning the filmy sleep from his eyes with one knuckle. He raised himself up on one elbow, and saw the same film forming over his father's dark eyes. There were no scars or moons beneath those eyes now. The skin was already falling back from his face, effortlessly, until his jaw and cheeks seemed as smooth and cool as baby skin. The mouth moved again, not up and down, but sideways like an animal's.

"Find five dollars on my bureau there, son." Ira nodded, but did not get up from the bed. He tried not to think of what else his father was willing him. But Lloyd said nothing more for a long time. Finally he whispered, "Five silver dollars, son. Use it on some of them grave flowers you fetch . . . for her upkeep," Lloyd reached out and held his son around the waist. Ira felt the old man gather himself together, laying his skeletal head against his son's backbone, nestling for sleep. His voice came again, muffled by Ira's dense nightshirt. "I mean, son, flowers fresh-cut . . . kind that last more'n a day." Ira lay very still, rigid, feeling his father's scant breaths against his back. "Every year now to this day, you lay flowers over her, hear? Jessie'll give you the money special . . . in silver . . . I've saved . . ." He fell off, coughing, and Ira felt the wetness against his shirt.

"Pa?" Ira asked, not moving, but terribly frightened. "Pa?"

"She knows the rest," Lloyd managed between gasps.

"What's she know? Tell me, Papa . . . tell Ira!" He tried now to move, but his father clenched his arms around him tighter.

"We obliged to that woman, son." Ira wanted to ask, *Which one?* but was afraid of either answer, so he lay back, still. After a while his father asked, very quietly, his voice calm and easy, "Son, are you sleepin good?"

"Yessir." His father held him a moment longer, shushing him like a child, rocking them both in the bed. Ira felt the

hot morning wind against his face and smelled the brooding
rain. Soon he sat up in bed, gently disentangling himself
from his father's rail-thin arms and the swarthy face that lay
very quiet against his back.

Ira sat up, not needing to look back at Lloyd Sloan's body,
for its shape was imprinted on his back. On the bureau he
found the tarnished silver dollars and a piece of paper with
his mother's name on it in a huge scrawl. Pocketing the
money, Ira went over to the altar—in the daylight it looked
harmless, a child's gaudy clutter—and took the photograph
without glancing at the face he'd known was there.

Walking along the hall slowly so as not to disturb his half-
sisters, Ira went into the small chamber where his stepmother had slept since Lloyd's sickness. It was empty, bed
not slept in. *Today's Sunday*, Ira remembered vaguely, *she
might be down at the church leading the choir in their
worship songs. But she might be somewheres else, too, I
reckon. Well, I ain't meetin her, not there!*

Now it seemed like his whole body was moving in slow
motion, as if underwater; Ira carefully placed the photograph on the mahogany bureau and for a long time eyed the
portrait. Here were a startlingly slender woman and a young-
blooded man, posed in clean, loud Sunday clothes. Both
grinned like cats, he staring at you with bold, joyful hunger.
She, too, looked straight out, eyes holding yours, vigilant but
deeply obligated, sated. He was clenching her to his side,
roguishly leaning against the running board of a dented car
that trailed tin cans and gay crepe paper from the bumper.
And she hugged him, too, her smile instinctive, wonderful.

Ira Sloan felt very old. Looking at the expectant faces of
Lloyd and Nettie, it was as if he saw his own children, made
bold by their hunger for his blessing.

Ira turned the photograph face down and rummaged a

few moments in the chest of drawers, but there was no will hidden here, simply cotton undergarments and little bouquets of stale lavender. *He left you nothing, nothing,* a cold voice that Ira did not recognize said suddenly. *Listen, fool . . . nothing, nothing, nothing!* and Ira ran out of the room, pursued by the thin, cruel voice. *Hear? Nothing!* Ira ran the few miles out of town to fetch Mr. Quince, the undertaker, thinking, *Now that woman's the only one my father belongs to. I belong to no one. Nothing belongs to me.*

II

"So be it," Jessie said. "Soon as it storms, Lloyd'll be gone." Breathing deeply, she eased her worn, sweating body down against the cool mud. Feverish air shimmered over the family cemetery, boring a thousand needles into her scalp. "I'm heat-stroke," she said, stunned, her nerves gone dead, stinging, like those of a sleepwalker. Through slit eyes she watched the glazed monuments like so many rows of squat granite ghosts marching toward her. "Stones are memory," she said in the voice that had been coming from her belly ever since she let herself be taken last night. This voice was cold, austere, but it was familiar—a generous tongue she summoned from her past without realizing she knew the language. But Jessie knew the voice would speak only a few more times; she must listen with all her soul. Sitting up straight in the high weeds that covered this grave, Jessie waited. Humidity beaded on her skin, sweat running down her arms and the small of her back; now the snakeskin was moist, smelling like mineral oil and mineral silt, but she did not move.

It was just dawn, early enough to see heat lightning glower and flicker against the dark, new sky. No thunder yet. Birds and crickets chattered and Jessie felt colonies of chiggers burrowing into her naked legs and ankles, breeding in the pores of her skin. But she did not scratch. Perfectly still, she waited until the wind's voice squalled, gusting up, hot breezes rustling the goldenrod's silk tassels, scattering the trembling gnats, rattling corn husks, their sibilant, hollow hushes telling Jessie everything. And then a dry, hard rain that lasted only a few minutes; the only sign it had fallen was the steam rising off the weeds.

"So be it," Jessie stood up, knees buckling. She held on to the gravestone for balance against her fainting spell. But the dizziness passed and she said, in her own voice again—urgent, full, and rhythmic—"Now you got him in the next life, jist like you had him all his days on this sore earth! He was beggin your pardon like a chile but you shunned him. Ifn you're still revengin your sorrows on Lloyd, I say . . . Nettie, quit! Leave be! He was always yourn but prone to wander this life as next. Ifn you haunt a body, haunt Iry. He craves your watchin." Jessie sat down heavily and leaned against the hot, grainy headstone.

Nettie Sloan
1902–1948
Beloved, go with God

the grave marker read. Lloyd had asked Mr. Quince to do the carving himself on his finest pink marble; perhaps he had known the whole town would turn out for his wife's funeral, though she was dead to them for years. Jessie had never seen so many flowers, their rank luxuriance and the heat spell had almost made her gag as she stood watching behind the great mass of townspeople surrounding, possessing their ex-sheriff and his young, brooding son. Jessie had not been to this family cemetery or Nettie's grave since that day six years ago; and by the look of Nettie's overgrown, neglected grave, her son and husband had not visited her here, either, though Lloyd had made her promise to lay fresh-cut flowers on his grave and see to it that Ira had the special silver money, every year on the anniversary of his mother's death, to bless her grave. Did Lloyd believe that his wife existed here in this grave only when joined by him? Jessie wondered. *Mebbe he knew she weren't restin in this dug shallow earth,* Jessie decided. *But she's here now, waitin on him to lay down side her and git some good sleep.*

"Yes, I'll be sittin a spell, honey, jist you and me. He's comin along," Jessie said suddenly and laughed out loud. The two painted eyes on her cheeks streamed red and the jagged yellow lightning on her arms ran in rivulets that left traces of color like open veins. "Well, at last I see my own blood—it's yaller, like all cowards," and she tried to laugh, but was bent double with dry sobs, her arms flailing the dirt, raising clods of dusty red as she hammered the grave with both fists. "Damn woman spirit! Ifn I had your flesh before my eyes, I'd cut you deep! Gash them fatty white arms! Reckon you'd smell hot and faintish like your ghost that walks through my house. Oh, I seeked high and low for ye, yes ma'am! You been livin there sure as me. And I'm only a coward cause I can't find your flesh to run a knife up against. But ifn I found ye, Nettie Sloan, you'd be kilt good and daid this time, like you done kilt him . . . too soon, before he knew me good, before he seen what he's cheatin," Jessie straightened up, her voice low, menacing. "I'd cut you in two! Let the blood flow and then I'd cut my arm—my blood would be no different! Hear me talkin, sister?"

The crickets and shivery corn husks answered, and Jessie fell back, exhausted. Heat was a thick second skin against her body. Sweltering, she threw off the ancient rattlesnake skin that smelled of rot, wishing that she could shed this heavy air as well. She lay flat, head propped up on the stone, watching her own breasts heave up and down. Now, in the eye of her heart she saw their bedroom. A slim shadow moved around the room, complacent, his deathbed chores as rigid and scrupulous as any Jessie had ever witnessed in all her years of midwifing and conjuring and worship. She watched the undertaker, Mr. Quince, reach deep in his linen pants pocket and take out two silver dollars. Bending over the body that had slid as if down an incline to the bottom of the bed, he laid the shiny coins against Lloyd's transparent eyelids. Then the undertaker gently pulled back the covers, grimacing slightly at the heap of bones. Stripping Lloyd of his foul nightshirt and the mattress of its yellowed bedding, Mr. Quince walked slowly outside, hanging up the linen as a sign to all passing, *He's gone. Covered by red earth now.*

Now Jessie knew the undertaker was washing his body, lathering Lloyd's cold skin with green lye soap. This was the only deathbed chore Jessie missed doing herself; but this vigorous scrubbing was never for kin, only for hands unfamiliar with the body's hollows and bends; a stranger's fingers did not linger over the flesh, so convinced were they that the spirit had departed. If she had been allowed to do this death washing, Jessie would have bathed him like a child, memorizing for the last time the frail and, to an outsider, awkward privacies of his body. Perhaps the spirit took its time in leaving, she thought. Perhaps Lloyd would enjoy this cool early-morning bath, even more so because he was in no hurry; maybe there was nowhere to go right off and he was just lingering, at last lucid and full of some truth it had taken a life and long dying to earn. *Quick, I'll go wash him down. Mebbe he's still there, waitin to git clean.*

She stood up and was about to run the two miles down the river to her house, but a force like a fist slapped against her backbone, humbling her. She fell on her face in the mud. Wind stirring again. Crickets hushed. But there was no more demand, though Jessie searched the clouds and tops of trees for a conflagration or sign. Silence. She yielded, but in her mind she was running toward the house, slipping along the riverbank, arriving just in time to see the yellow linen flapping on the clothesline and, inside, Mr. Quince bent over Lloyd's body, laying a saucer of salt on his abdomen. *Keeps the belly from bloatin,* Jessie remembered. Now, shushing her presence, Mr. Quince brewed a weak tea from the bark of the wahoo bush and soaked a sheet in it. He laid the sheet across Lloyd's face, but Jessie's presence said, *No! Leave him see me!* Mr. Quince cocked his head, listened, then shrugged and removed the sheet.

Now the townspeople were arriving, drawn by the britches and bedclothes hanging outside the dead's house. A young couple took this early-morning stint at the death watch. And in between bitefuls of the elaborate bag lunch brought by neighbors, they kissed, knowing Lloyd Sloan did not begrudge them. He lay, scrubbed, jaw slack—Jessie would ask Mr. Quince to stitch it tight in that stretched grin he always wore when pleased or pondering.

Jessie heard her name called suddenly, but it would be only the neighbors asking where she had gone so long. She should be home cooking for her callers. And where was Ira? Jessie knew he was no more in the house than she was. Had he gone away, traipsed off again for six more years? *Every death sends that chile runnin;* Jessie's thoughts abandoned Lloyd's death ritual for the few moments it took her to wonder if she would be pleased to find Ira gone again. "Lord, no! Ifn he goes, he'll come back one day sayin what's mine is rightfully his. I aim to settle this! We'll jist wait and hear what Lloyd left . . ." But she broke off, feeling a sudden certainty that she should not expect a thing from her husband, not the way Lloyd had carried on about Nettie and his son these past months in his high fevers.

"And me, where I been runnin?" Jessie asked the mud beneath her. Then she let out a long, high laugh. "Hell, Nettie . . . he's done gone from us both. Wanderin somewhere still beggin pardon. Lord knows who from now, since he got yourn long time ago." Jessie knew she spoke truth, though it was her own voice and not that conjured certainty that dwelled in her belly. She rose up and took a stick, marking the grave next to Nettie's. "This is where he sleeps when he needs rest from beggin pardon and blessin. He got mine last night. Mebbe he's seekin Iry's now. Yes ma'am, we all seekin Iry's now."

Jessie remembered last night, feeling Ira's presence as he pressed his narrow body into the wall. But she had not obliged Ira with reasons or arguments, because her inner voice would not be neglected, and Lloyd was finally dying. Jessie had known this by the way his bones slid downhill in the bed, by the way his numb fingers played with the comforter's stray yarn, twining it around his hands as if he were an old woman knitting, counting each stitch, exact, yet fidgeting to be done. Also there was the dense, sweet smell of crushed pumpkins—a sure sign that he would be gone by morning. So Jessie had let Ira stay on in the room, and soon she lost awareness of him as the voice took her, demanding.

But now there was no voice, only crickets and the lilting hush of the nearby Yellow River. Again the watery sounds reminded her of voices and Jessie stared intently, listening to the unseen river, remembering that first vision lent her by Luke's desertion and her own despair. In that swamp country her spirit had wandered as Lloyd's and Nettie's did now, not seeking blood and flesh—gifts of this life—but to join their spirit-kin, those radiant specters that Jessie had first seen as wandering storytellers.

Suddenly Jessie straightened, her attention rapt at the unfolding of her first vision—now she saw the wanderers on the last lap of their pilgrimage. No stories now, no shapes of mortal longings, only a living silence and light that flowed like a river over their souls. The light blinded Jessie and she stood illuminated to the pilgrims who revealed: forgiveness flows like this river.

"Forgiveness flows like the river," Jessie repeated in her deep voice. She spoke now not to her vision but to Nettie and Lloyd, whose spirits seemed to join her, resting moments beneath the warming ground before they would depart for their journey. Jessie knelt on their graves, one sunken and overgrown by wildflowers, the other unbroken dirt upon which she had drawn the place of her husband's burial with her finger in the moist morning earth. She bowed her head and finally stood, striding away through the woods.

The Yellow River was cool, luminous, and carried her floating body swiftly downstream to her stepson's house where Lloyd's empty body was laid out.

III

Nothing, nothing, nothing! the voice still pursued Ira as he trudged slowly back to town from the mortuary. Mr. Quince had offered him a ride home, but Ira refused, hoping the long hike might exhaust the cruel inner voice that had possessed him since his father's death this morning. But as he approached the outskirts of town, the voice followed him, more insinuating than a shadow, because it kept no distance. *What are you comin back to? Nothing!* Ira climbed the stairs, taking no note of the church women in the kitchen whose voices sounded so thin next to his inner voice as if he overheard whispered conversations.

"Iry, we're so sorry, boy."

"Iry, we come to help."

"Are you hungry?"

"He's shut from his sufferin, son. Don't grieve long over him." And when Ira turned to enter his father's death room, someone said, "Wait!" but he had come in to find Jessie washing Lloyd's face with her tears, using her nappy hair like a rag.

Solemn, his presence still surprisingly felt, Lloyd Sloan lay on the high bed. As his eyes moved over his father's small body, Ira felt calmed. But then he saw his father's hands, gnarled and waxen, clenched around one another in a grip Ira could feel around his own throat. *He's nothing!* the voice mocked and Ira held his head, then said wearily, "It's mornin, Jessie. We best git him laid away."

"Yes," she straightened up and watched him, he thought, like an animal that is both prey and predator. "Lord, but it's hot!" her voice broke but she went on, "Best bury him early on whilst there's still shade."

Nothing. Nothing. Nothing, the voice's shrieks blurred Ira's vision as he followed the pallbearers up the hill to the graveyard. Lloyd's earthen pit was deep and rust-colored, red mudpuddles pooling in the bottom. The coffin made a resounding thud, muted by the damp mud walls. *He is noth-*

ing. He gave you nothing. He left you. Nothing. Nothing is left. You. Nothing, nothing, nothing! Ira closed his eyes but could not shut out the voice; it bored through his eyelids, piercing stabs of light swirling dizzily; a rail-thin arm grabbed his shoulder as he fell down, down into the earthen pit, head thudding like his father's coffin, his screams swallowed up by the sliding mud walls.

He was dying, but not like his father. His vision was unmocked by survivors standing over his grave, each with his likeness planted so shallowly in his face, each smiling down like a grave robber, having stolen him away in death as they had in his lifetime. No, Ira lay alone, breath ebbing from him quietly in a rhythm as slow and natural as sleep. He was in his childhood room. Only accidentally, in the bureau mirror, did he catch sight of his face, years older— features softened, falling into furrows like loose plant flesh wasting on a vine. It was his own face now; Ira saw that he had inherited his own face at death; he had earned it. It was as much Ira's own and rightly to be buried with him as his earthly remains: those trinkets, spare change, random tokens strewn about on the bureau top, that someone indifferently slipped into slit pockets of his mourning suit, as if in burial of necessities for the beyond. No mourner bothered changing his face. Someone simply closed his eyes for the price of two quarters—these, kept back from Ira's pocket change and laid against his sockets with the finality of sleep, the heaviness of silver. Yes, Ira thought, to die alone was to be great and simple and unchanged.

Ira made it through his father's funeral without crying and, supported by Jessie's bony arm, without fainting, though all around him the cold voice of blackness bore through his body, possessing him with the vision of his own death. Later that afternoon it was the reading of Lloyd Sloan's will that pained him to the bone, unleashing the deep, shuddering anguish Ira had waited for since the moment he felt his father's breath stop and the body embracing his grow cool.

"'And to my son, Ira Sloan, I leave nothing; he'd have none of me and mine,'" the lawyer read with a monotonous drawl.

Nothing. Nothing. Nothing! the strident voice sang out triumphantly.

"That can't be," Jessie shook her head, stunned. "No, Iry, he were beggin pardon. I know that can't be truth!"

"'I hereby bequeath my land and savings to my wife Jessie Walsh Sloan, to her kin and our daughters, to be divided as she sees fit,'" the lawyer droned on, peering over the top of his bifocals as Jessie flew toward her stepson.

"Iry, he were beggin pardon!" she laid her ashen cheek against his unshaven face. He heard her jawbones clenching, cracking inside his own skull. "Beggin from you and from your ma." Suddenly she straightened, eyes swollen wide with sorrow. Astonished, she stared at him. "From me . . . Lord, he were beggin from me! Oh," she broke down, but her sobs were angry, fists flailing against his chest. "What can I do for ye, Ira? Let *me* beg his pardon! Take your share, son. Let me . . ."

"Leave me be," Ira said quietly. "That's all forgiveness I'll take from ye." He took her arms from around his neck, but with a firm gentleness he had never felt before, Ira held her as she wept. "Jist leave me be."

PART IV

STORYTELLERS

"Lord, it's so blazin hot this morning, stumps and stones'll be crawling off in the shade!" Hammering the knife with the heel of her hand, she gashed open the coffee can. "Hear that wind woosh out!" The woman's tongue pushed against her two gold buck teeth, working them loose in her gums as she sawed around the tin can's ragged rim.

"G'wan, Bernice. You ain't seen doodly squt!" the other chided, running a dark shammy over her fountain counter. "Now . . . when we was chillun I swear one dog day Old Hannah sun come spyin so close to earth she singe off them stringy gold curls . . . burnt nigh bald! And I seen the iceman totin a cake froze cold and big as a mountain; before he git near my mama's door, ice sweat done drownded him."

"Keep them lies to yourself, Nelda Moseley! Ifn grannies don't keep false toofs in their mouths, they drools to death!"

"Do, Jesus!" Nelda eyed her younger cousin with an imperious shake of her head, kinky braids alternating with long, bald scars to make a pattern like furrows plowed in rich black loamsoil. Bernice stretched her face sideways, ignoring the old woman's glare. She gave her knife one last lick and the can teetered, coffee grounds spilling onto the floor. "Fool! Git a broom!" Bernice obeyed, sweeping the slanted wood floor, swaying mildly. She paused, grinning, using her sleeve like a rag across her brow; the cuff came away with yesterday's stain deepened, the stiff yellow of starch and sweat. "G'wan! Keep sweepin us up some wind, Bernice. Raise a dust storm and conjure us out from this dog-day drought!"

"Reckon on rain, cousin?" Bernice snickered. "Been spittin and cussin at the moon again last night?"

"Don't take no goosebone prophet to reckon signs!"

"Jist take ignorant and foolishment. . . ."

"Young'un, don't gimme no word for word! Usn gonna have a storm blow us right smack dab in the middle of next week. Lissen! Critters, crops, folks . . . all feels rain's comin. This mornin I seen hawgs closely seekin the sky, seen sundog circle Old Hannah; I done stepped on three snails and spied a hound gone mad, chawin grass. I heared m'skeeters swarmin like suggins and tree frogs and katydids whinin loud as whippoorwills," Nelda narrowed her black eyes, spitting on the floor where her cousin had just swept. "And . . . runned up by that lightnin-bug church them Pennecost peckerwoods got and spied Ira's stepbrother, Nate Walsh Sloan, hanging two snakes, dead and belly-up, on his granny's back fence. They was measly chicken snakes, but Nate told me solemn he sniffed snake snarled in his tater vines— their skin smells hot like cowcumbers—and next thing, hanh! Up jumps them no-meanness serpents and tackle him down!" Satisfied, she breathed deeply, her two fists lifting up and rearranging her small, knobby bosom with the dignified effort of an ancient woman holding up the weight of a man's world, as if she carried it not on her back, but cradled in the hollow of her breast-bone, where two empty burdens lay heavily on one heart. "And ever fool know when Nate Sloan conjure rain, Old Noah hisself ain't dry!"

Bernice shrugged and made a clucking sound with her teeth. "I'd ruther git rain than any Sloan's squallin."

"Spect both, Bernice. Old Maker gonna scrub him heaven's floors an the spill-over gonna wash this world down. But, mind . . . it's Mr. Iry Sloan gonna weep rivers, gonna thunder and storm when he come for work *this* mornin."

"Say what?"

"Say, Iry Sloan be suckin sorrow."

"Aw, quit woofin, Cousin Nelda. When did you git close enough to know this buckra's bidness?" Bernice flounced around the counter and sat on a frayed red stool, leaning on her broom handle.

"I mammied him. Reckon I knows him so good, he gots my very resemblance," the old woman laughed, tapping one forefinger to her chin, humming. She turned her back to Bernice and began greasing the skillet, swirling pasty yellow lard round and round with an old toothbrush.

"You speakin truth, he do look like a gila monster! Hah! But he don't tell you nothun now, Mammy."

At this, Nelda whirled, cutting her eyes to the storefront window where a pickup rattled by, spluttering gravel against the glass.

"Hush!" Nelda grabbed her cousin's ear. "Humble down an' mind when I tells you!" At this she held the slippery skillet up as if to hide their whispers. "Iry Sloan be low cause it's his weakness come callin today!"

"Jessie?"

"Say the name, she the same," both burst out laughing.

"This sholy be a day for squallin!" Bernice bent over the counter and shook herself with laughter, her chin knocking against the wood. "Iry Sloan ain't neighbored with his stepma since she done healed Jarmy Coggins from his yaller janders!"

"Even Doc Varnon, ifn he seen fit to drink well water and live longer, . . . even he'd never spect the yaller janders in no nigger. And Mr. Iry, Mr. Iry big-brain sass-gut Sloan, he declare it was wind on the stummick! Hah! But I helped Miz Jessie hunt in the woods and we come back with black haw bark for brewin powerful tea. That Jarmy did sweat wonderful with Jessie's yarb liquor."

"Bet it was somethin to see," Bernice commented, trying not to smile.

"I were there, li'l bit, reckon I do the tellin!"

"G'wan, woman."

"Tea . . . and then Jessie fried her some fishworms in lard and balled the gunk up, stuck it down that nigger's throat like these big, hard pills Iry Sloan try to make folks swaller ever last time a body comes in for my coffee and salmon cakes. Lord, Mr. Iry don't give comfort like his stepma do. . . ." Nelda scooped out a spoonful of gray batter and let it sizzle in the grease until it was crisp and dark, smelling of salt and sweet fish. "You, Bernice . . . ifn you ever git ailin, don't go on more to Auntie Hat; she done lost her power. You git Jessie for your yarb doctor. She got hair hang off her haid jist like a white woman, but she knows niggers like her own skin."

"You old monkey!" Bernice laughed. "Best stop cookin up them slimy, crooked lies. God don't eat okry."

"I knows what I knows but never shows. Mebbe when you gits sickly, you ask this Iry Sloan to study up a cure." She threw her hands around the store, gesturing contemptuously to the few back shelves stocked with rows and rows of vitamins, cold and sinus pills, cramp, cough, and gas-pain potions, and other non-prescription medicines which Ira tried to sell along with his groceries and dime-store bric-a-brac.

Nelda at last nodded her head and gave her cousin a mean-
ingful look. "See them potions and brews he got squirreled
away in them back cupboards? That ain't right! Law, he
ain't no doctor. What's he doin with all them medicines? I
tell you what . . . he's makin you gag on them rabbit drop-
pins he call pills. He's makin you swaller them poison syrups
he call pain-killin, and all along he's sayin his prayer: 'Lord,
open heaven for Hagar's chillun; I send you one nigger
fast!' "

"Any more prayers, Aunt Nelda?" Ira Sloan said quietly,
letting the screen door flap shut behind him several times. He
eyed the two women, who were suddenly intent on the
stove, the cupboards, the clean floor.

"Nossuh, Iry," Nelda cut her eyes at Bernice, who made
not one sign of a smile except to push her gold teeth farther
out of her mouth. "But I learned you better'n to sneak up on
folks?"

"You got any more advice?"

Nelda shook her head furiously, frowning. She watched
Ira intently, bearing up under his dark look without the
slightest chagrin. Finally, after several long minutes during
which Bernice fluttered around, flaking the wet deerskin
against the already spotless counter, Ira smiled, yielding to
Nelda's outraged affection. "Well, then . . . any coffee?" His
smile stretched in that same sudden delight that so became
Lloyd Sloan, but Ira's was fleeting and he threw it off with
an inward shiver, a shy reproach as if he'd caught himself
grinning like a child.

"You rassle!" Nelda refused to smile, still eyeing Ira; but
he saw her brows fidgeting and simply waited for the deep-
throated, almost grumbling laughter that always startled
him, coming up from such a frail woman who, with each
belly laugh, seemed to shrivel, yellow skin drawing up.

"I declare, Aunt Nelda," he sat down on a stool and

watched the old woman curiously as she broke down laughing. "Don't rupture yourself making fun of me."

"You're late, Mistuh Sloan," Bernice said, swinging around the counter, with a calculated carelessness about how she poured the coffee.

"So's the rain. I don't need you remindin me."

"Ain't said nothun."

"Never do, Bernice." He watched her severely. "When did you start sloppin coffee like servin up hawgs? Only time I seen waitressin like that was watchin Jessie Walsh jabber, spillin hot coffee on any fool that sit still round her."

Bernice said nothing. She glared at Nelda to see whether the old woman would mammy Ira enough to let him get away with that, but Nelda busied herself with the salmon cakes, fuming. Bernice poured herself some coffee and waited silently. She watched her old cousin's back, and once, when Nelda turned around to adjust her apron, the two women exchanged looks.

"Eat up, skinny chile," Nelda served him up a plate piled with crispy salmon cakes. "What kinda man is this Iry that ain't no bigger'n a minute! Chile, you don't eat, you don't throw no shadder or leave no tracks! Sop it up with some of this cold buttermilk."

Ira stared at the platter, "Too hot."

"Well, Mistuh, ifn it ain't too blazin hot to be hangin mercy over a stove *cookin* them larapin fish cakes, ain't too hot to git them down that skinny gullet!"

"For the umpteenth-jillionth time, Auntie Nelda, I tell you I ain't hungry in this heat."

Some folks sees their duty and don't flinch. Some usn put out for Iry Sloan . . ." she paused and took a breath, not looking at him, "like the lady goin walk allway to town this mornin to do her duty by you."

"You niggers always know when misery's come due!" Ira stood up abruptly, his elbow knocking over the coffee cup.

"Looks like Bernice ain't the only sloppy . . ." Nelda began, hands on her hips, scowling at her soggy but still precisely stacked salmon cakes.

"Don't be plowin so deep, old woman," Bernice retorted and turned to Ira. "See why you got no customers with this big hot-wind woman blowin a body to kingdom come!"

Nelda swatted her cousin with the shammy. "You! Little buck-toof nigger! I'm gonna stomp your guts out! Jist as contrary and sneedlin as the Devil. You a fool for convulsin with her, Iry!"

"Don't nobody talk to nobody, then!" Ira said, stalking into the back storeroom and stripping his shirt; he flickered on his fan that hung low from the ceiling, sucking in all its own air so that below its grinding wings Ira felt the promise of a violent wind, always moments away. Pulling on a fresh, starched work jacket, Ira calmed himself and for a long while stood watching hopefully out his window. No sign of callers. "Reckon I'll take any customer comes through that door," Ira sighed. "Even niggers. Even . . . hell, I knowed Jessie'd make me wait on her."

Ever since his father's death last summer, word had gone around that Ira Sloan wanted to be left alone, even though he had recently moved back into the town's second-story jailhouse abandoned by Jessie and her daughters now that Lloyd Sloan's new farmhouse was finished up by her sons. Before returning to his childhood home, Ira had lived in a neighboring county doing odd jobs and saving money to open his own pharmacy. When the mortgage on a run-down shack in the woods near his hometown came due and its owners let it go, Ira had promptly laid down half his savings to buy the property.

He did not know whether the town laughed or yawned when word went out that this old ruin was now his Yellow River Market, a store set way off the main road, perched atop the county's steepest hill in a splintered piney-woods forest. Aside from its discouraging location, the market could not decide whether it sold groceries or medicines, but hopefully offered both to an underfed and suspicious town-folk.

In the past month Ira sank the last of his savings into renovating his store; but his repairs did nothing more for this single-room pine saltbox, with its rickety porch and be-grimed fieldstone chimney, than confirm the appearance of sincere neglect. For the whole structure still slumped and lurched. On the outside the Yellow River Market looked rusty, burnt; this worm-eaten wood had weathered the elements so well it threw off fresh paint as if it were the vain splatterings of brightly colored rains. Here and there one found signs of new paint left like ruddy or yellowed high-water marks. But inside there was no attempt made to cover its original stain, the poor man's everlasting mixture of var-nish and animal blood which dried into a bruised moldering the color of brick cellars.

Now a kind of distraction came over Ira when he thought of any further mending of his market's broken skeleton. For the many times he had paid to have the clapboard siding jacked up and evened; for the hours he had clung to the slanted roof, nails in his mouth and slate shingles slung over his back, scrambling madly like a spider spinning a wide web; for all his relentless self-improvement, the store was just that much more obstinate about preserving its right to fall apart at any time, and with less excuse than a spider's shelter against the wind.

It was Ira Sloan himself who collapsed, inwardly. Now

from behind the shelter of his few but well-stocked shelves he watched his two black cooks as they moved, silently, within the narrow territory of their makeshift kitchen, managing never to touch shoulders or elbows as if out of infinite politeness. Mid-stoop and sway, they seemed to lean crazily on the thick air, heads cocked to catch the gruff voices that drifted in from the front porch. Every day since he opened his store several old farmers had settled on his front porch, deserting their acres of corn, peaches, and peanuts planted in the phase of the moon that had promised a hot, wet summer. Not one of these old men, the town's weathervanes and storytellers, had seen this drought predicted in the sky's signs. In dismay they met daily on Ira's porch, to commiserate and compare sorrows. These clannish curmudgeons were Ira's first and only customers, though they had bought no more than one box of kitchen matches, pipe cleaners, and several plugs of chewing tobacco.

"I say, ifn you folks ain't buyin, git gone!" Ira shouted out from his storeroom and saw the men nod in pantomimed pleasantry. Whenever Ira spoke, the men were suddenly deaf.

"No, didn't reckon on this drought," one man continued. "I did see the moon holdin her water, untipped, splinter no bigger than my thumbnail . . . but, law, that don't explain this stingy weather."

Ira shook his head, dismissing the old men, but he watched their bobbing, bald, and downy noggins. He listened to the men as they whittled, littering his porch with their sharp-smelling shavings, as if talking with knife and wood.

"This old slubbedeguillion shack'll run riot over that Iry Sloan," one man was saying, punctuating his prophecies with splurts of tobacco juice against the steps. "Jist like it done ever other fool fiddles with it!" A few nods, more silence, and then the eldest cleared his throat and began his long jawing.

"Old geese," Ira muttered loudly, "Gaggle of geezers!" But no one on the porch heard him. The eldest cracked his cane against the steps to illustrate some fine point in his narrative and all heads nodded. Ira snorted and went back into his storeroom to unload some produce crates, leaving the men to carry on, undisturbed, with their fiercely personal visions of this shack's history. All morning they had argued over the town's creation and agreed on nothing. But when it came to this shack, this complacent, stubborn eyesore the town had tolerated for almost a century, each man gave his own quirky gesture of assent when the eldest pronounced,

"One thing surely, this place first had an unhappy owner. Always did, always will. Mighty miserable, I tell you . . ." and with that, they began tracing the different stories, threading in and out of one another's words as if practicing harmony a cappella, voices often high-pitched and dissonant, but always accompanied by great gusts of spirit.

II

There was no more common image in the town's memory than this storefront shack. Being so familiar, it was ignored; but those few times townfolk thought of it as any more than a natural catastrophe—the perversity of a God who spared the unregenerate in man and his shelters—they lapsed into reverence, that humorless honor with which a village dotes over its own deformity or monument to a lost war. And perhaps that's what it was, for every generation had its tale of a determined man defeated by the shack's homely vigilance.

Some storytellers traced the original owner to the Blue
Ridge Mountains and their first Scotch-Irish settlers; but a
few seers swore he was a renegade Cherokee from the Great
Smokies.

One ungodly winter the blue mountains shivered deep
down to their bony ridges. With great shouts Earth shattered
along ancient scars, splitting open solitary hollers where
men had lived humbly for ten thousand years. Like tall ice
slivers stabbing the sky, all mountains froze hard and silent.
Now the only sound was wind forever lost and lonely for her
steep haunts. "Shhhhhh . . . ," she consoles herself. "Shhhhh,"
her echo sternly hushes. And from far below come cries of
uprooted men, sounding in the heavens like that plaintive
mewing of the newborn. All winter long the mountain people tumbled down from their narrow innocence. Families
and all their possessions, mules, children, flapping chickens,
sometimes even a loose, creaking shack came sliding down
the cold mountains, careering so dizzily they couldn't mark
the way home.

At last the falling families and their few surviving shacks
settled here in the fertile north Georgia piedmont. Strong
proof of this story is the extreme squatness of the natives and
their shelters, as if both were dropped to earth from a great
height. After its fall the shack that would become Ira's Yellow River Market enjoyed its first respite from the cruelty of
human expectations. It metamorphosed with the seasons,
letting spring floods adorn it in bright, bloody clay, allowing
rats and weasels free run of the single room. In summer the
house basked as a glowering sun raised blisters and warps in
the clapboard siding; and in winter's damp the wooden walls
drew up, front porch buckling like a man tucking his legs
under his settled belly. Left to its own excesses, this old ruin
soon fell into a profound and grateful slump.

But folks did not let the shack alone. Every generation

there was a stern young man to violate its solitude. Before it was Ira's store, the shack was many more things: first, a tobacco shed, wooden slats torn off to let the wind blow recklessly, drying the pungent green leaves until crisp, profitable; then, during the mid-and-late-eighteen-hundreds' gold rush in Cherokee and Lumpkin counties, it served the booming town as a makeshift bank, robbed repeatedly by prospectors too lazy or too wise to dig in the ground. After a brick bank was built the shack became the town's tavern, lending itself to the drunken lurch and stagger with an ease that came of long habit. With no upstairs it could not also be the whorehouse and was soon put out of business by competition from a nearby wet county.

Finally, the shack was made respectable again. A stranger appeared on the town's main street one day, carrying no mining equipment; but his mule was burdened until she was swayback with books—well-thumbed tomes of poetry and a Bible so wide and deep it threatened to tumble out of the saddlebag. Declaring himself a circuit minister led here by signs and wonders and word of lost sinners, the man felled an acre of timber around the shack. These roughly hewn planks he balanced on cinder blocks for pews and at the back of the place he built bookshelves reaching to the ceiling. He called this place his temporary church, but it was temporary only in his eyes.

After his first sermon entitled "Redeemed, How I Love to Proclaim It!" he asked for a special love offering to be used in building a new church. "Sinful town like this needs a worship place ain't so sloven and contrary!" the minister cajoled his congregation. "Build me a better church and I'll build ye better men." His continual harping on the subject of a new church often sent folks home on Sundays with the vow never to return.

"Hell, that preacher's a gold digger, only he's diggin right deep in my pockets!" But the next Sunday that same man was back warming a bench, shuddering and sweating wonderfully, singing out his husky "Amens!" with the most fervent deacons. It was his sermons on forgiveness that brought the gold miners to church and sent them back out into the fields as dirt-farmers, forgiving, if not forgetting, the wasted memory of the earth's rich yield.

"Mercy, brothers and sisters," the minister often wept after preaching all morning, words still moving inside him as he battled his own ecstasy; all around, women wailed and men hollered.

Mercy is man's spirit-bread
   and water
Have mercy, Lord!
His mercy is not mild. It
washes away sins of this
   world.
Listen!
In the days of Noah
God wept mighty rivers over
man's transgressin
God cried deep blue oceans
over man's lustin
God sobbed terrible tidal
   waves
over man's corruption.
I say, our Lord broke down!
Forty days and nights His
tears flooded this bone-dry
   world.
He blotted out ever livin
   thing upon the face of earth.

But, brothers and sisters,
was mercy washes us white
as snow. Was mercy made
God hide Noah from his
   cryin
storm, He said,
'Noah, build me an ark!
Hide the beasts and little
chillun away from my
runnin-over grief.
Sail high and far on my
sorrow, like sun-bird hawks
and soul-bird doves.
Sail on, little chillun!
Till I wash me this world
clean as newborn
Till I forgit what pained
me in my man.'
And Noah's tiny ark sailed
high on his sorrow.

The minister breathed in short gasps, hands clenched, head thrown back, shaking. He closed his eyes, his breath came in sobs. A deacon shouted: "Let the church say Amen!"

"Amen. Amen. Amen!" With one surging voice the brothers and sisters bore him high with hallelujahs, with their shuddering shouts, flailing limbs, and loud rejoicings. But a little while later, when the minister called his deacons forward to collect the building-fund offering, he saw his brethren fall quiet, faces spent and closed. If the mercy he so earnestly hungered after had been anything but money, they would have blessed him a hundredfold; as it was, he might as well ask for stones.

Though Ira Sloan was only eight when Jessie began taking him, his stepbrothers, and half-sisters to church, he well remembered the minister's preaching. Every Sunday, before worship services, he gathered all the children in the front benches and, in the guise of Biblical storytelling, confided in a low, tremulous singsong his own visions. To a child the ancient minister embodied all the bold and driven prophets who so peopled his sermons with outrage and sudden revelation.

His brittle fingers and tufts of hair like a sparrow's nest perched atop his huge head's balding knob, that voice echoing from the pit of one's own hollow belly—all this lent him the very "likeness of glory" with which he conjured up images of his God. Whether he was Jonah in the fish or Daniel in the lion's mouth, or rough-hewn Ezekiel, eyes singed with visions of Yahweh borne to heaven by beasts, the minister possessed his children's imagination as no other man.

Ira and his little half-sisters listened with their eyes tightly closed, believing. But his older stepbrothers had no

patience with the minister's demands for a new church
building or long-winded stories. Especially Nate, in whom
Ira had once thought to confide his sudden belief that here
surely was a prophet.

"Mebbe he's been called," Ira suggested.

"No," Nate said emphatically. "He's an old unholy fool."

"Leastways he's got followers," Ira always ended his ar-
gument, satisfied at Nate's chagrin.

Soon Nate quit attending the church altogether, instead
wandering by himself in the nearby piney woods. "You got
your own church out there with them songbirds and wild
kudzu?" Jessie at first chided him. "Come on, son, church
needs ye," she laughed. "And Lord knows I need your singin
in one ear to drown out Lloyd's bellerin in the other. Come
on with us, now."

But Nate steadfastly refused the minister's church as if
resisting a sin. "That fallen-down church jist ain't big
enough for two prophets," Ira said and took Jessie's outstretched hand to walk with his second family to the church
shack.

The minister could not relinquish his vision of a new
church building, though he no longer harangued his congregation for offerings; instead, he confided in their children the
secret behind his mission. For a long time this ramshackle
church had been haunted, he whispered, not by human spirits, but by extinct animals who mistook it for an ark. They
had missed it once and in afterlife were determined not to be
left behind again. Every night the minister beheld a procession of mighty beasts. At the stroke of midnight all animals'
apparitions dashed in through the church's closed door, ran
around its single room chasing one another's spiked tails,
and finally plunged headlong into the wide stone fireplace to
vanish up the chimney in billowing puffs of yellow smoke.

The minister's children were awestruck by his nightly bestiary.

"Behold, chillun . . . ," he began in a voice trembling, as if stunned by his own memory. "Behold the beastly procession into my ark! The clock strikes midnight down in the town. Nine, ten, eleven . . . and, Lord, what a wailin of wind, a mighty gnashin of teeth and moan of tongues. Up in the rafters a swoopin and flappin of wings, then a siren's shriek cryin out, 'Your blood, the blood of your lives will I require; at the hand of every beast I will require it; and beware, thou man of little faith, for I come like a thief, like a night animal!'"

The children were hushed and rapt at the minister's wide black eyes, but soon their attention was riveted on his hands; for he whittled as he spoke. Between the minister's fingers the sharp-smelling plug of pinewood took on shapes: here was the hunchbacked, serpentine lindworm; here the woolly mammoth, pine tusks thrusting upward, scooped and honed sharp as the knife blade; and on very special Sundays, here was the pale, delicate unicorn with burned knotholes for eyes between which one horn spiraled, twisting out like a corkscrew. The minister said he whittled from memory, saving each beast from extinction, from the nothingness of night and sleep.

"Now you'uns come here by me and I'll whittle ye a dinosaur bird this sky ain't never seen. I'm sandin her neck down real smooth. She'll give no splinters when ye stroke her. See, I'll jist cut me some slats in her side and slip in balsam wings. Look! Way up she goes, flyin high at the end of your hand. Here, Iry Sloan, this flyin dragon's yours. Come . . . she won't bite ye!" Sometimes, if the children were very still, the minister made a tiny, hollow ark that always resembled his slapdash church shack. Another Sunday Ira listened so earnestly he was given an ark of his own to float in the river, his bath, or red mudpuddles. Secretly Ira believed that, no matter how unsightly, his roughly hewn ark was haunted by the minister's resplendent beasts.

But if the children fidgeted during the minister's stories his whittling hands grew rigid and seemed twisted together like knotted tree roots. Flinging his ivory-handled switch-blade into a wooden pew, he took up a vicious curved hunting knife. Only his hands talked, hacking the pine plug into a coarse and sinister wooden doll, etching little notches like scars against the belly, leaving the face blank wood—no mouth, no eyes, no way to breathe. "This be how it feels when my Lord gits hold of ye! He's always got you'uns in His hands, whittlin away sins till nigh perfect. Ifn ye don't listen, He holds a little too tight. Hahnh! Evil chillun! You'uns be deader than this plug of wood. My Lord, have mercy!" Some folks called it voodoo, these caricatures of their children that the minister carved; but it made them sit up and listen, and whatever charm worked, that miracle was perhaps worth the child's nightmares about creatures no one had ever heard of in these parts.

Mercy at last came to the minister and his terrified children in the form of what grown-ups call a "bolt from the blue." But Ira and his friends knew better. When the minister stood up from his children's sermon, brushing the curly pine shavings from his pants, emptying his shoes of their sawdust, the children knew what flung his eyelids open like rattling shades and who stole his breath, knocking him backward, hands flailing in front of his face to fend off this violent stampede. The children saw him trampled to death right in front of the church by creatures only he and they saw: the pterodactyl's scaly wings slapped his face back and forth a hundred times; and the unicorn and woolly mammoth took turns goring him until blood rushed from his mouth and ears. Looking up, the children saw a siren screaming, "Your blood, the blood of your life will I require; at the hand of every beast I will require it!" and with a shout their minister was finally extinct, too. Ira himself saw the telltale yellow smoke lingering in the fireplace, and ran in terror from the church, hiccoughing all the way home. Though Jessie assured him the minister's fatal hemorrhage was natural and quick, that all his rattling and convulsing was long after he'd gone to heaven, Ira rid himself of his treasured ark that same night. Unable to burn what he had so often touched lovingly, he hurled it down the Yellow River, where it disappeared in shaded, swirling currents.

The minister's funeral was that next Sunday morning. This was the last time—before Ira bought it a decade later for his Yellow River Market—that the old shack was used as the town's church. The townsfolk maintained they did not abandon it because of the children's silly stories about haunting beasts, but for the simple reason that their minister's memory deserved honor. They erected a new church in his name and on the property he willed his congregation. That last day the townspeople filed one by one past their minister's open coffin. He had carved it himself, hiding it in the cellar until this longed-for day when he would be laid gently inside its oaken belly as if it were a canoe or elongated cradle. Passing by, curiously eyeing the old man's sated but radiant face, Ira was startled to see all the minister's carved beasts lying in the coffin beside him—intricate sculptures like those treasures ancient peoples buried for the next world. *So this is the real ark,* Ira thought suddenly, *he's saved them beasts forever. They don't need hauntin when he's took them to heaven alongside him.* From then on, every time Ira passed the deserted shack that had seen so many earthly salvations and refused them all in favor of some unseen blessing, he felt a secret longing, a hunger akin to worship. Despite its increasingly run-down demeanor, Ira still believed in the shack's mysterious powers to transform, if not itself, its owners. Until the day years later when he bought the place, Ira trusted this instinct.

III

Now, standing in the back room unloading a crate of bruised oranges, listening for the first sullen words his two cooks threw off to one another as a prelude to all apologies, Ira Sloan gave up his old trust. He suddenly recognized himself in this solitary, ruined store; no matter what was done to him or by him, he, like this stern shack, would never change. He was someone to whom nothing would ever happen, for it was his instinct to resist. Inwardly, Ira felt the truth of it even more, for he saw his inner countenance: it was blank as the wooden faces of that minister's pinewood dolls.

"Hell, right bout now I'd sell this old slubbedeguillion to the first soul got two bits!" Ira broke out, ripping slats off another crate. The smell of moldering oranges, a pungent rot, hit him full face. Straightening, Ira heard the cackle and drone of the old men on the porch and he felt the urge to walk out and confess they prophesied rightly: he was just another in this shack's long line of unhappy, failed owners. He came into the store's front room and poured himself coffee.

"Jessie ain't comin," he said to Aunt Nelda.

"She comin alright! I seen her truck stalled awhile back down by the river. She's comin, even if it be on foot!" For no discernible reason Ira let loose the grin that ached around his jaw. Astonished, Aunt Nelda muttered to Bernice, "This boy never knowed his own mind." Bernice was intent on the window, peering into a humid gray haze. Suddenly she threw up her hands and ran to the screen door.

"Sweet Jesus! Here come the rain! Hear that platter-plash!" She wiped her dark, damp face and threw the shammy on the counter. When she pulled open the heavy screen door, she let out a long whoop. A sweet, humid whirl-wind blew in through the door, gusting recklessly around the room, lifting cartons and bottles from their shelves like a hurricane. Ira watched the screen door slam back and forth with the rushing wind. In his mind the wind was the stampeding ghosts of that minister's extinct animals. They could only be precursors of wondrous things, signs of change and miracles. Perhaps they would bring him customers, believers in his medicines, the healing he could give. He would not tell simple stories of animals and arks, but he would give balm just the same. Ira felt the wind as a blessing; but with it he expected great transforma-tions to begin.

"Bless my soul! I ain't seen such lightnin and thunder since the mornin stars sung together!" One of the farmers was up and running for the road, so excited he left his knife standing straight up in the porch floor.

"It could rain forty days and forty nights, and my crop'd still be thirsty." Another walked off at a leisurely pace.

But the third remained seated, suspiciously eyeing the sky and his retreating cronies. "Now, I jist didn't figure this holy storm," he contemplated the heavy clouds. "Sholy, I saw snails and spiders crawlin round like they's lost, and last night, why, I thought the glowworms did shine out brighter and the sunset was bloody, but . . ."

"*I* seen the signs!" Aunt Nelda called out to him. "Next time you need to know bout the weather, come ask me!"

With great dignity the farmer stood up from his stairstep seat, cocking his head curiously toward the store, then shrugging as he left for home and his grateful crops. "Old man's gone deaf agin, Aunt Nelda," Ira laughed, and the frail yellow woman clucked her tongue.

"Fool cracker! Jist wait till them farmers see what kinda rain this is," knowingly she laid a finger to her nose and sniffed. "Old Noah hisself gonna seem dry! I know my signs," and she went to close the inner door against sheets of gusting rain.

"No!" Ira called out, smiling. "Leave her be open. We gonna have callers."

"Even Jessie ain't gonna slog through this storm," Aunt Nelda said, "and we best be gone, too. You gonna have a flood come pouring right through this front door!"

"Yes ma'am," Ira nodded, "and we got plenty of room for the whole town in here to hide."

Aunt Nelda stared at him, pop-eyed, her arms askew. "What do you think you gots here, Iry Sloan?" she demanded. "High ground? This ole slubbedeguillion don't even hold water, how it gonna hold folks?"

"She'll hold, all right," Ira said and strained his head to see outside. "She'll hold us all."

"Fool and fool again! Bernice, git yer wraps. We be gone."

"No! We're right safe," Ira laughed and pointed outside. "We're safe and dry inside this old ark. And look ye who's first inside from the flood!" The two women turned and saw a great, slick black shape like a strange beast sidling and slipping in the mud as it made its way toward the porch. Bernice let out a frightened shriek, but Nelda peered into the fog.

"Looks like an old black cat, dead and drownded and all swoll up," she muttered, eyes narrowed.

The beast clambered up to the porch, shook itself furiously, and with one claw opened the screen door. A deep, roaring laugh, three hoots and a holler, and a spirited voice sang out, "Rain! Rain like a cow pissin on flat rock!" She threw off her slick rubber rain clothes, shedding them like serpent's skin. Ira recognized Lloyd Sloan's rain gear lying on a black heap on the floor. "Rain! Rain like the Devil whuppin his wife, she's cryin up a storm!" Jessie smiled and turned to the two black cooks, who were bent double, joining her high, hooting laughter. But when she turned to Ira, her wet, swarthy face was pale. "Mornin, Iry Sloan," she said, her jaw shivering slightly.

Ira nodded to her gravely, but for all the world he could not throw off his smile.

"Git her some breakfast and git gone," Ira called out to Nelda and Bernice, who hung over the counter, watching in amazement as Jessie peeled off layer after layer of the slick black rain gear.

"How you know to dress for this bad rain?" Nelda demanded.

"I seen signs," Jessie smiled and the two women nodded respectfully to one another. "Thanks kindly," Jessie made room for her serving of salmon cakes and coffee.

"We gonna be out your neck of the woods this evenin," Bernice said. "Nelda and me carryin supper for the menfolks whilst they pitch that revival tent."

After a moment's hesitation Jessie said, "Mebbe I'll see you'uns there."

"Hope you didn't come all the way out here on this miserable day jist to git me over that revival tonight, Jessie," Ira laughed as he retreated to his back room, flapping the air with a wet deerskin rag; then, knotting and pulling it straight through his fingers, he smiled widely, handling the shammy snake as if he were one of those backwoods men who appeared every summer—those believers who took up serpents, teasing copperheads, running bony fingers over the scaled, oily skin of diamondbacks. "You know I can't stand them summer meetings. All you righteous folk screechin to high heaven."

"Ain't nobody draggin ye," Jessie said simply. She nodded to the two black women, who were pantomiming their goodbyes and promises, grabbing their wraps and out the door, calling back to Ira, "Afternoon, you," Bernice said and stuck out her false gold tooth.

Jessie sat thoughtfully, looking after the women through the storefront window. Rainwater ran down the glass, meandering, making vague writings and many little rivers; she stared into them as if deciphering hieroglyphics. The heavy rain began leaking through Ira's sieve-like roof, pinging into tin bowls, buckets, jars, and washtubs like so many spittoons that the cooks had set around the store. Shivering, Jessie sipped her coffee.

"You cold?" Ira asked from the distance of his back storeroom.

"Oh, wind done shaked my back down," Jessie laughed; a long shudder shot through her, running from head to foot like electricity, grounding her to the floorboards. "You cold?"

"No," but as if to betray his word a clattering stream of rain suddenly leaked through his roof, splashing down the back of his collar. He, too, shivered.

"Reckon you is now!" She laughed, clenching herself against the gusts of wind that swept in through the screen door. As Ira watched his stepmother look around his store he felt suddenly shamed—the sunken, stripped linoleum, the sagging half-full shelves, the rafters askance and awkward, and finally that front window; it seemed a huge painting done by the elements, no more transparent than canvas, with rivulets of red mud splashed haphazardly about and gray, begrimed drops of humidity as if the window itself sweated, while all inside was dismal, cold. Ira watched Jessie for her reaction to his shack; in her posture, face, or her hands he could find no signs of rebuke, yet he felt chastised. He stood in his back room's dingy doorway, feeling as small, coarse, and unyielding as the shack itself; his damp work shirt hung heavy and yellow and his face was unshaven, pale—to all the world a failing man. And it was this woman, more than any other misadventure in his life, that always unearthed his inner failings; they lay like subterranean faults that scarred the surface, radiating out from a despair, live and limitless. Old Earth-shaker, Ira once had called Jessie; and in her presence he was as defenseless as his shack was against the elements. But he did not have this shack's inward strength like a backbone that held firm no matter how hard the fall. He had only its vigilance. Since beginning business, Ira held out against the town's suspicions and indifference; but Jessie had only to appear for him to capitulate, agree with the next person who called him a fool, a failure. She had only to speak for her low, rumbling voice to break him open; she laughed now and his skeleton unhinged, spine splintering as he collapsed inward, his spirit buried deep in the rubble of his own bones.

"How's bidness?" she asked and he was ruined.

"I don't suffer for nothun."

"Oh," Jessie looked at him intently and held out a steaming cup of coffee. "Mighty hard startin up bidness in these parts. I know."

Ira was surprised to find himself crossing the store to his counter in one easy motion. "Do, do you?"

"Folks here was jist as close against me as they are ye." He said nothing, but took the coffee. "You, chile, suppose your pa left me a gold mine? That land he loved is jist mean an' stingy, tight as a tick when it come to givin back the blood it stole. My chaps, they work it, but that don't even feed chickens and hawgs. What you think I been doin this long year alone? How fend for my gals and me?" Ira admitted that he had not once thought of it. Because he was left nothing, he assumed she had everything. "We been scratchin bottom, Iry."

"That's a sorry story," he said. "Ifn I knowed, you coulda come worked here."

"Thank ye. Then we could starve together," she laughed shortly and from her pocket took out five silver dollars, wearily stacking them on the counter. "Well, that's what I come for," she stood up. "Much obliged for that coffee."

The familiar sight of his father's silver dollars moved Ira, made him remember his promise—grave flowers for Nettie and Lloyd. Lloyd's last gift to a wife to whom he never gave flowers all his life. "Well . . . what?"

Ira made a sign for Jessie to sit down again.

"Pardon?"

"What you been doin all this time?"

Jessie settled herself on her stool. "Waitin, I reckon. Waitin to begin agin." She fixed him with her leaden, large eyes that now seemed a deeper shade, almost blue-black.

Since Lloyd Sloan's death, she said, things had gone from bad to miserable and were only now looking better. All year Jessie had worked her old diner job, waitressing all night, dragging home to her three daughters just in time to watch them down her coffee and fresh doughnuts before running off to school. Before their high quarreling was out of earshot, Jessie fell asleep, a fitful and dreamless nap before noon. But all afternoon she poured over the frayed chapters of a correspondence course for her beautician's license. During Lloyd's lifetime she had studied these great, wordless books illustrating snarls, tangles, curls, clips, ratting, and even konking kinky hair, with a kind of distracted excitement; those days the idea of being a beautician always lingered just out of sight, "down the road a long piece," as she rued to her daughters and an amused husband.

"I'll be a kept man," Lloyd had teased her when she sent off her third lesson. After his death she took up the course again, but as her waitressing went on and her daughters' complaints rose to a shrill pitch, Jessie's once eager task was no more than another necessity. She studied doggedly now, though this work was less humiliating than nights spent cooking and listening to any fool who had a dime for coffee. She never fell asleep over her books, but sometimes she found herself bolt upright hearing her daughters slip in and out of the kitchen, breathlessly stealing peeks at her as she sat, eyes glazed over, brittle fingers bent backward, convulsed around a comb or imaginary curl. Midwinter she numbly sent off her last course work and received a fancy certificate in the mail. But before they licensed her she must come to Rome, Georgia, with her own live model, to be tested before the state board. For the first time since Lloyd's death Jessie was elated—choir members heard a familiar flat and piercing soprano sail past them, raised to the rafters; sullen night watchmen heard a startling "Thank ye kindly," after doling out the nightly dime, when before there had been an imperceptible grunt to match their own; her daughters heard her talking in the intimate whispers she usually saved for Lloyd's guardian ghost; and everyone heard Jessie's hopeful request: "Be my live model for them state boards? I'll do ye up real natural and nice. You jist won't recognize yourself!"

"That's what I'm afeared of."

"Thank ye jist the same, Jessie Walsh. Reckon I'll make do."

"Hah! Lawd, no, honey! Look at them hands. Turnips and onions are the only heads them hands are fit to yank up and wash down. Where you git the notion that hands been pickin over dirt clods all your life belong to beautifyin?"

"Quit this frivlous idee, Jessie," a kindlier woman pleaded. "With Lloyd gone and them gals growed you should settle into somethin sensible, quiet-like. You'uns thick-settled herebouts now, so don't remind folks you're still stranger somehow; this town likes simple. We ain't no rich folks cravin servants, primpin us up. Ifn ye ain't half-nigger, you should never be askin to work like one."

Jessie was stunned at the suspicion her request had brought to the surface; it was as if she had confidently leaned over a river's looking glass to seek her own reflected smile and was startled by some lurking water creature that slinked away, stirring the murky depths into a swirling darkness. What was it she saw flicker across these familiar faces, hastily hidden by a politeness more inscrutable than mud? Now that Lloyd was gone, what stale, storied air did these townsfolk breathe again, if only for the moment it took Jessie to sense it? She knew it was bitter air by its telltale smell, like the ferment a sick person exhales in his slow fever. Now when she approached neighbors asking her simple favor the air thickened around her; slowly her blood congealed, though her heart still thundered, hanging on one sharp breath that bruised her ribs like a stone. One day she was face to face with an old friend, a diner customer from her early days. He smiled but his crooked grin seemed wicked, his eyes spiteful. Jessie shunned him, passing him on the street with a pursed mouth; but two steps beyond him her mind registered his dismay and the collapse of his wide, gap-toothed smile. That moment she felt herself sinking, staring up at the familiar and innocent face through a dark, convulsive underworld, and in shame slinking away from the illuminating light of his eyes.

"Jist cause these turntale folks breathe begrudgment don't mean I got to waller on the river bottom without air!" Jessie pronounced one morning to her daughters. They greeted this cryptic comment as yet another example of their mother's increasing strangeness. They resembled her not at all, but were separate in spirit and instinct like hawks in an eagle's nest. Jessie had nurtured them with this knowledge from the moment she saw her girls staring out at her from the Sloans' rapier-boned face, their eyes expectant, hungry, and the family's long jaw so unhinged by words or grins that it stayed sternly clamped shut. "I ain't beggin now," Jessie continued, eyeing her eldest daughter. "I'm askin polite-like for volunteers. You, Sylvie!"

"Mamma, what you talking bout?" Sylvie demanded, a slight edge to her voice. She was the smartest girl in her senior class and spoke in the soft, lilting accents of any north Georgia native, not the lively, wide-open singsong of her mother's hillbilly drone. When Jessie mispronounced a word, Sylvia pedantically drilled her in the correct way until her mother snapped, "Jist how you know that's *the* correct way, chile? I been all over and ever place thinks they got the only words. Know what? It ain't never the same nowhere twice!"

"Where you been, Mamma?" her daughter retorted. "Ever heard this?" She let loose a stream of curved and guttural gibberish that seemed like she was in a delirium, having trouble swallowing. Startled and subdued, Jessie wondered if her daughter had learned the secret of some animal's talk to eavesdrop on birds, raccoons, or even unseen spirits. "That's French from Europe, across the sea."

Jessie was less impressed. "What good's that kinda talk when you have to go all round the world before a body sees ye ain't a babblin idiot?"

"It's still good," her daughter cried out, "because you can't understand it!"

"What I'm askin of my three gals," Jessie watched them over their coffee, speaking carefully so as not to rile her eldest, "is to do yourself and me proud. Now, Sylvie . . . I used to pin-curl that honey hair ever night. I can do it in my sleep now."

Sylvie shot her mother a baleful glance. "Last time you gave me a permanent wave I hung upside down from a tree like a possum for three days to make those pickaninny knots shake free! Kinks didn't come out for three years!"

Jessie ignored her, eyeing her second child. "Della, now, I cut your bangs straight as a shingle . . ."

"And left stubs sticking out from my forehead like a bristle rug!"

"Callie, little one," Jessie wheedled, "you look a might bit shaggy round the neck. Let me jist git my scissors and snip . . ."

"No! No!" the three burst out in one outraged voice. Sylvie stood up from the table. "In the olden days they used to have daughters for sacrificial victims!" she shouted. Aghast, Jessie stared at her daughters before finally letting out a long whoop and holler.

"Ohhhhhh, pity! Pity my poor little lambs! Give your mean mamma a knife and I'll carry you'uns yonder up the mountain and give ye up to God!" Jessie laughed herself silly, then stopped, deadpan. "But before you'uns go . . . let me pretty ye up some!" She was after them, chasing them out the door, tousling their precisely teased and lacquered hair, pinching small bottoms; she caught the youngest girl in her arms and kissed her smack on those pursed, indignant lips, sucking in her child's sweet, sputtering winds.

After that morning she said nothing more about any beautician's job. She did not abandon the desire, simply shifted it from one shoulder to another. Jessie continued to make ends meet by her waitressing work. These long nights she passed in silence, moving hunchbacked as if every evening she suddenly aged ten years; at midnight after the sullen graveyard shift had lumbered off to their work, Jessie took a half-hour break. It was not time to run across the street to her home. Her daughters were asleep; why disturb them with her loneliness or envy? So Jessie took some strong coffee outside, crossed the street stealthily, and went around back of her house to the porch Ira had called his territory during all his childhood. She lay in the porch swing, musing and remembering people and distant fields—stories that were so far gone she wondered if she hadn't made them up. During the course of these inner ramblings over old or imaginary landscapes, Jessie studied the night sky, this dense blackness pulsing like her own blood, the myriad constellations like great cobwebs spun from the underbelly of the sky's black-widow spider; shooting stars, like dewdrops caught in her wide web and dying, burned brightest in the heavens. How vulnerable once beneath these stars when she, a small child, first had raised her face to the dark heavens! Fire and ice and eyes falling down on her, flinging her to her knees, gravity like a cold hand bending her head in worship. "Awe-stroked," Jessie later named that night: a child paralyzed by wonder.

Now, when Jessie looked at the stars, there was none of the dread with which a child greets those dizzying thoughts of the infinite, simply a great pleasure. Gravity was no more than cold hands stroking her feverish face, massaging deep in her worn temples, clasping her head all around. When she lay looking at the sky the stars did not weigh her down, they lifted her up.

Jessie told Ira that this midnight break to study the stars was what had saved her sanity during the past year; already in the habit of study by day, Jessie could now take in the stars more fully, remembering how her migrant kin had lived with these heavenly bodies, easily but with the reverence one saves for his tribe's elders—the wise ones who guide them as surely as the stars. Migrants hoarded their grandmothers and grandfathers, carrying them from camp to camp like precious possessions; for inside their frail, knobby skulls were preserved the name of every child born or buried by some roadside, the face of every boss or sheriff or vigilante, the images of goodness that rose up here and there like a mirage, the songs and cures and dreams. At night, when the farmhands lay in their blankets, backbones stretched straight over the pocked ground, they watched the migrant stars and listened to their old folks recite stories: for stars were wanderers, too, they said. Constellations and planets and endless galaxies also traveled as unrelentingly as we do on this earth. They follow the seasons like us, carrying their stories with them. Stars are always meddling with the earth like we do, coaxing, punishing, and soothing. You watch as you wander and you listen to their movements. Here will come old Sirius, at its zenith signaling dog days, flood, or drought; and watch for Taurus's triangle, the Hyades horns bent to plow up spring's thawed ground; and in fall here are those three wild Injuns hunting their Great Bear, when they find him with their starry arrows the blood from his wounds streams down to earth, turning leaves this burnt and rusty color. In winter we honor a giant among hunters, Orion, his dazzling bejeweled belt pointing to a festoon of blue stars, the Pleiades, who remind us of all our women, all sisters, lovers, and mothers who mourn their lost men. Here, too, in the cold winter depths of heaven swims Cetus, the sea whale bound for the chained Andromeda; Algol, the winking blue star that is Medusa's glint-grieving eye; Pegasus, great square offspring of this snake-haired sorcerer's dying blood and Neptune's teeming waters; and Cygnus, the swan, diving down to search the earth for the body of his beloved but foolhardy friend whose sun chariot left the whole world bruised, barren, and burnt to the bone many years ago.

Jessie recognized the constellations now as she had in other times, and these stars and stories replenished her midway through the work shift so that she might return to the diner and her counter's row of silent men, a few women, all bent over like migrants during the day.

If Jessie had moved as slowly as a daddy-longlegs to begin her evening's work, after midnight she was moving as if frantically pursued by a child's spider hunt. Polishing silverware, scouring the iron skillets, mopping the warped linoleum, filling salt and sugar shakers—all this she did at lightning speed; her customers felt a wind come off her as she ran up and down behind the counter's gangway. They paid her little mind; the six-to-two shift were as far away from quitting time as possible and wanted only two things from this whirlwind waitress: silent companionship and strong coffee. She gave both. These faceless customers from the textile factories and fields around town would meet with surprise or perhaps indifference news of Jessie's past popularity. She was very polite, but now gave off a vigilant sorrow these men knew all too well. They never imagined she held their town's history, ribald and reverential, behind those leaden, serpent's eyes. Those who would remember many nights spent under Jessie's spell were now dead or

kept home from her storytelling by a squint-eyed box of
shadows and its mechanically comforting static. "Ifn I got to
listen to cacklin shadows, might as well sit me down before a
roarin fire in my own chimley!" Jessie said, after having first
seen this newfangled gadget in a neighbor's home.

One evening she had taken time off from work to drop by
some homemade pies for a woman who was dying of leu-
kemia. Expecting to hear that urgent hush which so con-
sumes a sickroom it seems the house is holding its breath,
Jessie was startled by inhumanly high giggles and growls
like a death rattle. Gathered in the bedroom was the whole
clan—cousins and callers sprawled around in rockers, on the
bureau bench, on chairs, hassocks, and window seats, and a
knot of young bodies thrown over the foot of the bed, wedging the woman's wasted body against her headboard like a
flat feather pillow. All stared at a noisy box, faces bathed in
its blinking blue light.

"Evenin, Miz Payson, I brung ye . . ."

"Shhhhhhh!" the congregation hushed with one voice.

Mrs. Payson gave Jessie a pained smile and nodded.
"Thanks kindly, Miz Walsh," she whispered. Jessie eased
herself between the radiator and a stout, scowling cousin.
She smiled a lot, returning Mrs. Payson's nods and brittle
handshakes; they carried on pantomimed pleasantries
against the machine's whirring whines and whispers. Self-
important, this box's voices struck Jessie, but the black
images were like women laughing. Jessie looked around at
the spellbound faces in the room, but could see no sorrow,
only blank, distracted dread. But as she leaned away from
the radiator's hard ribs she suddenly found the sorrow. It
was a smell lying close to the ground, almost obscured by
dust, talcum, and lemon wax. Like the smell of the Yellow
River during a drought, you had only to lean and breathe
deeply to catch the sharp, mineral stench of algae, silt, and

salty cottonmouth snakeskin—these only survivors of dry spells, that lived on in the dead river bottom. Mrs. Payson lay in her sickbed and all around her were strewn survivors smelling like cottonmouths waiting on death. Rapacious as serpents, Mrs. Payson's kin lacked only that creature's subtle patience.

Jessie straightened to go, clenching the woman's hands. She tried to grin but her underbite shivered and fell into a slack, gaping stare. Mrs. Payson's hand lay quietly on the bed like a deaf woman's fingers, tired of talking. Her smile slid off her face, disappearing into a crease in the pillow. But her eyes possessed Jessie's, wandering all over her face with that critical intimacy, an attention to detail, that most women reserve for their mirrors. Jessie was very still, listening. "Is it a live model you need, Miz Walsh?" Mrs. Payson said very loudly and all the faces around her clenched. "Hear? Shut that thing off!" Someone flicked a switch and there was quiet except for the sickroom sharply holding its breath. "Git me that picture yonder." A cousin obediently gave Mrs. Payson a small photograph of herself as she must have looked ten years earlier—a plump, ruddy, and dimpled young woman. Mrs. Payson handed the picture to Jessie. "Ain't askin miracles. Jist do me up right." No one moved or spoke. Jessie made no pretense, she nodded simply, studying the photograph. "And Jessie," Mrs. Payson said sternly, "no smiles. Hear? Don't let them stitch no smiles on me."

"I hear," Jessie promised.

IV

Jessie told Ira that she soon had realized it was not such a strange switch in jobs. A month after her visit to Mrs. Payson the diner's manager had installed a television over the counter; after a week of its maniacal laughter and that sermon-like voice that chanted local news that every fool with an ear to the ground already knew, and preposterous stories of this world's destruction that made Jessie shudder as she did at Biblical descriptions of Judgment Day, and a fast-talking weatherman who was always pointing out at you with a stick, drawing chalk maps as if clouds or thunder could be held by these zigzag boundaries—Jessie gave notice. Or, rather, she walked out of the diner one midnight break, studied the stars, and decided it was time for her to move on.

"You gals git your own breakfast," was how she informed her daughters she no longer had her job. "Jist consider it a new kinda diet like them you'uns always on; only this is called go hungry. It's terrible simple." For the next month they lived off Jessie's savings—what little money she had put away for her future beautician's work—and when that ran out and the rent came due Jessie rounded up her girls and moved back out to the half-finished Sloan place Lloyd willed them. Jessie's sons helped her fix it up and put in a small garden. They managed until summer, when the girls were faced with the prospect of ruining their hands in the garden or doing light housework for some ladies in town. Looking at their mother's notched and coarse hands, as large as any dirt-farmer's, the girls chose to make beds and do other women's laundry.

But in early June one of the Payson boys called on Jessie. "It's time for ye, Miz Walsh," he said and quietly counted out twenty ten-dollar bills into her hand. "Ma left it to ye. Now best come do like ye promised."

For a moment Jessie balked. "I don't got my license, see?

Sides, I don't know nothun bout unstitchin smiles. Jist hair and fingernails."

"She weren't smilin anyway when she went," he said simply and put on his hat. He drove her to town and Quince's Mortuary.

"Reckon folks won't mind much . . . you practicin here," Mr. Quince had said when Jessie offered to work without salary on trial.

In her dark practice room Jessie worked diligently, often so lonely and frightened at first that she talked to Mrs. Payson in a half-soundless, half-animated manner. The whole town turned out for the funeral, though many hardly knew the Paysons; it was Jessie's handiwork they came to judge, and after the burial three elderly women shyly approached Jessie with an odd request.

"I'm not talkin bout anytime soon, understand. I plan on lingerin some . . . but when I go, you be there, Miz Walsh. I rest easy knowin that." Money was pressed in Jessie's hand, and within a month she had ten women, some ancient and tottering, some still spry, but all lined up for future beautification. Still Jessie had no volunteer for a model to pass her state boards.

One breakfast, she grabbed her eldest daughter by the arm, sat her down with a thump, and took the scissors to her hair. Each squalling daughter had her time in that kitchen chair until Jessie felt she had practiced enough; then she loaded them all in her pickup truck. The wind dried their short, layered hair as they drove down to Rome. She presented her daughters with their hair, but not their eyes, dry and shining. If the board was not satisfied, she said, they could just watch the three girls go through it all over again. But a man with wire-rim glasses took one careful, compassionate look, signed Jessie's license, and saw the three out-

raged but cowed daughters out the door before he burst into
laughter.

"At least it grows back," he whispered to Sylvie, and to
her mother said, "Good luck, lady. But you can't go round
hog-swagglin customers like ye done them poor gals!"

"Listen, I got customers lined up for years comin!" Jessie
retorted and started her motor. "Ifn I can jist wait that long,"
she muttered underbreath.

Jessie did wait, doing funerals meanwhile for a pittance
from bereaved families and finally a part-time salary from
Mr. Quince. It was hardly enough to live on. But her sons
had finally finished building a small one-room house close to
town that was to be her beauty salon when she had live
customers. Sylvie had already lettered the window sign in
delicate pastels, each word ending with a frill that was de-
cidedly foreign; it read, "Chez Jessie," and underneath for
those who were suspicious, "Cut and Curl." On either side of
the sign were two Breck advertisements, the women staring
out a simpering invitation, their hair an impossible smooth-
ness for any native of this humid weather, black or white.
On the door Jessie's other daughters pasted silhouettes cut
from black construction paper, the ladies' hairdos piled into
curls whose edges were jagged, pointy. "Jessie Walsh Sloan,
beautician," was pasted under the posted beauty license. Inside the quiet little shop was a candy dish with one hundred
hand-printed cards, proclaiming discounts to the first one
hundred ladies to cross this threshold. Jessie had bought two
stand-up hair dryers in a Rome auction and her sons had put
in two deep sinks for washing hair. There were shelves and
shelves of bottles in every shade of amber, brown, pink, and
blonde. Framed on the walls were magazine women model-
ing hairdos, permanents, and tints. Even when her beauty
parlor was finished Jessie sat three days a week with no

customers but her daughters; they pretended resignation at each cut or curl, but were secretly pleased at these myriad visions of themselves. Jessie waited for the town's women.

She kept her mortuary job on weekends and waited patiently for another month. Her reasoning was shrewd if laborious; for if beauty made little difference in the women's lives here on earth, the afterlife was quite another prospect—that of going out in style to meet one's Maker with at least as much talent and looks as He had given in the beginning. This dread of not looking any more beautiful in their coffins than in their sickbeds made women feel unholy terror. The burial insurance that many had scrimped for ever since marriage, even those five- and ten-cents-a-week policies, did not guarantee good cosmetic care; and no matter how grisly or violent one's end, she could not count on a closed casket against the curious. Soon Jessie's services were taken more and more seriously.

Some of the younger women, many of whom had just attended a funeral of an elderly kin, came round to call on Jessie—just to chat, they insisted, but stayed to look through some magazines, to listen to Jessie's stories, and finally to give one quick nod. No sooner was that head bent in assent than it was thrown backward and into a deep sink, strong, lean fingers massaging a head that hadn't been touched like this since childhood or courtship. Smells of pine and peppermint in cold rivulets around the crown of the head and then another scalp massage, only this time less vigorous, more languid, as if those fingers were memorizing every mound and dent, every bony ridge, giving it particular meaning and dignity. Then a bristled towel wound tight as a turban, smooth combing, snipping scissors so deft and fast there was no time to protest, then the waves, the curls, the pungent-smelling permanents that squeaked with each crimped roller. Blasts of hot, swirling air, eyes closed, almost drunk with the warmth of one's own sweat and exotic lotions. Finally the cool, kind brushing of a scalp that felt clean even beneath the skull. Now look: a strange woman stares out from the mirror, her hair so silky and tightly curled like a halo around her face; suddenly the image is lost in sweet, misting lacquer like perfumed humidity. This is the smell that hangs over you for days after the curl is gone.

After the young women came the old. "No sense in waitin till I'm dead and gone," they explained nervously at the doorstep. "Leastways now I can *see* what I look like beautified." They found Jessie's permanent waves lasted so long they were "fit for heaven . . . or the other place as well!"

Jessie gave comfort to their unspoken fears. "Listen, honey," she said, "you come in here to me, saggin and wore out on Wednesday for a set and rinse, or needin to lie a mite bout your age—a tint mebbe. And say you don't last to see your next appointment! Well, now, I'll take ye on that same weekend sholy. Jessie ain't gonna let you'uns go traipsin off into eternity lookin anyways else but as ifn ye jist come out from my parlor. Lord! Like you done prepared yourself the way all pretty and enterin that kingdom, everlastin and primped better than angels theirselves!" Now business was picking up. It was not yet a habit with her younger customers, but the old women came religiously for their close perms, silver tints, and blunt cuts. They swore by Jessie Walsh, saying she made all the difference in the world, and in that world to come.

V

Ira was staring at Jessie without changing his attitude, his polite but dubious elbow-on-the-counter posture as if humoring her long story.

"I see I'm takin your time with my troubles," Jessie said without anger, her voice flat. "I didn't come for myself . . ." She hesitated, then let her forefinger light on the stack of silver dollars.

Ira scooped up the dollars in his hand. The sight of these heavy coins summoned up a memory of the first time he had laid out the silver for Lloyd's and Nettie's grave flowers; he had bought roses, pale yellow roses as delicate to the touch as cool moss, and when Ira laid them across the rounded earth, they were shafts of the warmest daylight cleaving down through the cold, dark graves. "Thank ye kindly for comin, Jessie," Ira said. "You been good to remember them."

Jessie stepped back from the counter as if to respect the territory Ira now laid open between them; for so many years it was a battleground, but now his words gentled it like those natural elements that wear down land until it is smooth, passable.

"I didn't come for myself, Iry," Jessie said hesitantly, wanting to prolong this moment with her stepson.

"I know," Ira's voice was awkward, hushed. "You come for me."

For a long time Jessie could not say a word, only drink her coffee and consider whether she would now say what she had come for. At last, almost angrily she said, "It's true, Iry. Now that I seen you agin, see how lost we been . . . I been . . . without ye, without Lloyd. Now I know I come for you alone, because mebbe you're more mine than any flesh and blood . . . and spirit."

Startled, Ira shook his head, "You come for Nate, didn't ye? It's Nate on your mind."

"It's all of you'uns on me!" Jessie blurted out, her voice pleading. "Nettie, Lloyd, and now Nate . . . and it's you, Iry, most of all. I come to ye because there's more of me in you and I got to talk to someone like myself."

"You done good at that already," Ira said, but he was taken aback by her intensity.

"I trust ye, Iry," Jessie continued. "Always knew that any chile loved someone loyal like you did your ma, that was a body to trust your soul to."

"What you talkin bout?"

"Nate trusts ye, too."

"Nate don't trust nobody, especially hisself," Ira said.

Jessie eyed him with relief, "Oh, then you done heared about my boy."

"No. Only what my cooks say bout him conjurin rain and the like. They always talk superstition. Don't pay niggers no mind."

"I pay ever man and woman mind, Iry," Jessie said. "I lissen long and hard when they tell me Nate's done worked miracles."

Ira laughed, but there was some wonder in his voice. "So that's where all my bidness goes. Reckon they done hear his healin call."

"You know better, son," Jessie insisted. "It's Nate needs healin." She eyed her stepson until he stopped laughing. "You seen my boy lately?"

"No. You?"

"All the time," she paused, "but he don't never come home. I see him like misery at work. Iry, I need your help. My boy listens to ye. There's somethin terrible workin on him. I heared he's got hisself some kind of followers, nobody I know, or ifn they is, Nate's told them to keep still. But some of the migrants I got camped on my back forty tell me Nate's got some kind of church round him."

"And what you want me to do . . . join his church?"

Taken aback, Jessie leaned across the counter and laid her hand on his arm, never taking her eyes from his face. "Iry Sloan! I'm askin ye for all the world to do what you come home for."

"Say what?"

"To heal, wasn't it, chile? That's why you come back?" She saw Ira recoil, as if from a blow. "You said once that ifn there'd been a man like ye all them years ago when your ma was ailin, she'd be well and a live woman today. Because you'd know enough to . . ."

"She'd be gone jist the same, wouldn't she?" Ira looked panicked, and stooped behind his counter.

He had carried the truth of his mother's desertion—sickness or not, Jessie or not, son and husband or not—since his childhood; but it had lain hidden among a child's self-seeking memories that valued only what was most strongly felt, not understood. Ira wondered, had he saved anything from his childhood that was really true about his mother, that did not reflect her in his own image? Was she lost now? No, Ira struggled to remember the gifts of spirit his mother must have offered him, at least once. He had thought she was giving him something for his own; but she was simply lending the truth of herself to preserve, to forgive? "She would leave again," Ira continued slowly, thoughtfully. "Jessie," he suddenly asked, "you know why she left?"

She hesitated a moment, "Mebbe so, but, Iry, I was askin about Nate . . ."

"Tell me," Ira insisted, then after a long silence he added, "Ifn you tell me bout my ma, I'll sholy help ye with Nate."

Jessie considered, then said, "No, Iry, you don't got to do nothun for me or Nate. I'll tell ye because it's your right to know," she paused. "But don't you remember nothun, chile? And I ain't exactly the one should tell ye . . ."

"I know she left after you come to town," Ira said so seriously he took no notice of her discomfort. "But it wasn't only because of ye. There was something else, not *someone* else . . . but somethin I've forgotten to remember all this time . . ." He broke off, shaking his head as if to rattle the memories, hoping that the one to spill out might be what he needed.

Jessie watched her stepson and shifted uneasily. "Mebbe it's come back to ye."

"Mebbe," Ira frowned, waiting on her.

After a long moment during which Jessie seemed to fall into herself, shoulders collapsing, she suddenly said in exasperation, "All right, Iry Sloan! Fetch me more coffee." He was quickly behind the counter to pour the thick black brew into his largest mug when she said, "It'll come back to ye."

Both stared down at their coffee for a few moments. Suddenly Ira smiled mischievously and bent down, taking out a liquor bottle. He poured a generous helping into each coffee cup. "Keep us from catchin cold," he said.

Jessie smiled, but crossed her arms and ignored the drink, watching Ira take a long swallow. When he looked at her again, his eyes were clearer, less gray than hazel, as if the strong liquor had burned a fog off them, revealing familiar earthen colors—streaks of green, brown, and orange. "You know half us Sloans don't drink," Jessie said.

"*We* do."

"Who's we?"

"Pa, me . . ." Ira smiled widely and nodded to her. "And Jessie Walsh Sloan."

"Yessir," she laughed and took up her cup, "first medicine I ever knowed." She drank hers down slowly. Ira joined her, then poured two more cups full, this time without coffee. Then he sat back, waiting on her. "You'll be wantin stories now," she said, looking more sober after two drinks than he had ever seen her.

"Yes, please."

She said nothing for a long time and when she finally began, her voice had that singsong rhythm as if far off, separate from her. But Ira knew she watched him closely; at the slightest sign from him—a smell of fear or a suddenly held breath—this woman would fall silent or, worse still, wind up her words in a more merciful fiction. Ira resolved to obscure his face and hands as much as necessary by tending to their drinks, stooping below his counter to hide and coming up with a smoothed face and another bottle of liquor, to make him forget and remember himself.

"I first met your pa when he was drinkin hard," her voice was soft.

"Were you drinkin with him?"

"There was women drinkin, too . . . but not like you think. And yes, I was drinkin. But only between times."

"Between what?"

She eyed him curiously. "Between the woman's labor pains. I was midwife . . ."

"For my mother?" he exclaimed, "*you* was the one brought me into this world?"

She laughed out loud. "Mercy no, child!" she laughed until she caught her breath. "I didn't meet your ma for years after I met Lloyd . . . and his son."

"When did you meet me?"

"First things first. I was sayin that Lloyd Sloan was fallin-over drunk when I met him. He was sheriff come to move us migrants down the road . . . what town called 'anywhere but here.' He come on us one night when I was midwifin a woman in the back of a pickup truck. I knowed why he come, but I paid him no mind. Damned ifn I was gonna let any fool move that baby down the road before it got borned!"

"But he didn't send you away," Ira said quietly.

"No. No, he practically begged us to stay put. Strangest thing, too. Lloyd were dead drunk but I jist looked him once in the face and knew there was as much misery in him as in this screamin woman I was workin over. Only the woman was gonna shed her misery any moment when it came cryin out from her belly; and for a long time after that birth she could believe it was only the chile give her pain. But your pa, he knowed he'd be carryin his misery from here on out."

"So you midwifed him, too," Ira said quietly and bent down behind his counter.

"Yes, ifn ye mean I helped deliver Lloyd from some of his sorrow," she paused, eyeing the top of Ira's head. "But ifn ye mean I stopped him from carryin the misery called Nettie Sloan, no! He carried her till the day he died."

Ira straightened up and set the liquor bottle on his counter. He struggled to keep his face very still, but it was taut and pale.

"When I first met ye, Iry, you carried Nettie Sloan, too. Then you wore this same tight look that's on your face now," Jessie stopped suddenly and took a long drink. "This what you want to hear, son?"

"Yes," Ira nodded slowly.

"All right," she watched as he poured each of them a drink, this time mixing his with coffee. "You look like Lloyd now, but then you were her spittin image, leastways no one doubted you belonged to Nettie."

"How did I belong?"

"Heart and soul, chile!" Jessie laughed. "I seen it was you that latched on to her. But some folks said it was she kept ye prisoner in that house. They said the jail was both downstairs and upstairs, where you and your ma was holed up."

"Who said that?"

"Church women mostly. They was in the habit of carryin

Nettie Sloan around with them, too; only they always got her off their chests right quick . . . ever time anyone asked, I reckon."

"Yes," Ira said sourly, "I do remember those women comin around all day, fussin over me, always tiptoein cept when it came to closing Ma's door. Wham bang! they slammed it shut, and give each other looks like prayin, 'Lord, ifn you don't see fit to take her away, leastways spare us the sight of her.' Like death was the only polite, decent thing left my ma. No, we didn't never thank them ladies for their trouble!"

"Mebbe they got their thanks in other ways?" Jessie's voice was pleasant, but she watched Ira carefully. For a moment Ira seemed perplexed, cocking his head, listening as Jessie went on to tell a story about the peculiar, even amusing acts of vandalism that had once made Lloyd Sloan and his deputies the laughingstock of the entire county. Impatiently, Ira heard her out.

Mrs. Merkins returned home late one afternoon to find her kitchen clock's crystal smashed and the compost can dumped out on top of a dining-room rosewood table, neatly set with her finest silver and china. Next day her neighbor came shrieking out of her outhouse, tripping over her own drawers, down around her knees. Someone had hung a furious hornets' nest from the rafters of her two-seater outhouse, and as soon as she eased herself into it, the gray mud-mess toppled into her hair, hordes of hornets clinging around her neck; her wrists buzzed with a live brown-yellow bracelet and her ears were pierced by stinging earrings. The next two weeks she spent either in a tub of cold water or on feather pillows. Nothing happened for a few more days; but one morning Mrs. Burke and her widowed sister arrived at their garden, armed with a rake for the massacre of tomato slugs, with pruning shears, and some mail-order praying mantises for the beetles; they found what looked like a tangled, lush battleground, as if those rows of stalwart corn stalks had declared war on the opposing rows of squatting beefsteak-tomato plants, and all vegetation in between was trampled underfoot. Timid radishes, ground-clinging cabbages, wilted lettuce, frantic cucumber and melon runners slithered away or climbed up to safety among the pole beans, potatoes, onions, red beets, and carrots with their heads hidden deep in trenches. Mrs. Burke, who had raised her hoe as if against an unseen enemy, remarked with certain amazement that their garden resembled one giant tossed salad. But her sister's face was drawn and frightened as she walked gingerly among the fallen, sinewy plant flesh strewn across the field; naked and uprooted, its brown veins seemed to have spilled human blood, staining the earth this deep, startling red.

"Weren't no animal." The sister grimly beckoned Mrs. Burke to come closer. "Look here!" Every cucumber on every vine had a huge bite eaten out of it; ripe watermelon, cantaloupe, and squash were all split wide open as if from a kick; corn was husked, fresh milky kernels picked out painstakingly in patterns like a gap-toothed yellow smile; tomatoes were splattered against the side of the outhouse; every spindly string bean and pea pod was pinched off, littering the ground in green tatters and pebbles. The only plants untouched were the roses and the sparse, fan-like to-bacco leaves, flapping lazily in the early-morning breeze.

"Now, I can't say for sure your ma did these things," Jessie was saying when she saw Ira taken aback, but just for a split second, after which he smiled—not at all his usual smile, but a mischievous, crooked child's grin.

"Mebbe it weren't Nettie a'tall."

"Mebbe not," Jessie smiled now, too. Ira said nothing more, but hoped perhaps she could follow his thoughts. For he remembered it all now, or at least most of it: climbing out the second-story window, sliding down the drainpipe, and landing with a soft thump in the high weeds that lay against his house. He moved stealthily along the jailhouse wall, fingers chapped and grainy as he counted each brick until he knew he was almost at the corner of the house. A quick look up the street, across to the diner, down the street, and then a dash for the woods. From there it was simple to carry out his myriad missions. You followed the Yellow River around three bends and there was Mrs. Merkins' house. The other virtuous women lived close by. None of them were ever home in the afternoon; they were out doing good. Meanwhile he blessed their own homes: a broom handle shattered a clock's crystal; a simple heave-ho and rank garbage was set for supper, a rake reached up into the barn's rafters for that angry hornets' nest. Let them see good works so simple a child could do them. But the garden was the most difficult because at one time, when Ira was very little, he had talked to dirt, trees, and crawling things. But now his feet, fingers, and fists talked.

"Mebbe it were done for her," Ira said simply and sipped his coffee. His face was almost serene. "I remember how we laughed when I told her!"

"Yes, I seen how you'uns laughed together," Jessie said. He was surprised to hear her voice so strong and mutinous.

"Oh, Jessie . . . you probably laughed, too, when you suspected it was me."

"Yes, in the beginnin I laughed . . ."

"Well, don't be cross, then. My mother and me, we didn't hurt nobody."

"Nobody but yourselves."

"What?"

"That all you remember, Iry?"

"Yes," he said cautiously.

Jessie hesitated, then shrugged. She volunteered nothing more, and for the first time since they began talking, she would not meet his eyes. Bewildered, Ira waited on her, but when she suddenly turned and eyed the gray rain splattering against his window, Ira knew she would be gone unless he helped her stay. Yet he remained silent, for a memory was gathering in the back of his mind; but it was obscured, as if the ground fog outside had seeped into the back of his head. Suddenly he dreaded its clearing—that lucidity like a lift in the fog that reveals one is terribly lost.

"Jessie, how'd you know it was me did them chores?" he finally demanded, at the same time steeling himself against his memory. "Now they seem mean and strange, but as a child it felt perfectly natural. Made good sense someway."

"You did right by your ma's world, Iry," Jessie nodded slowly. They had both set aside their cups and were staring at one another intently. "But nobody lasted long in Nettie's world, not even Nettie. Was *ye* claimed her longest, son." Jessie looked down at her hands a moment; when next she spoke, her hands, but not her voice, trembled. "Nettie's world was terrible, but pure-born, too. I reckon there weren't no shades or shadows in Nettie's mind, jist light—strong and blindin when it tetched ye, like lightnin slashes, so nothing ever looked bright agin. After Nettie, other folks' light looked yaller and thin, like from behind clouds."

"How you know that?" Ira demanded, flinching.

"I never seen Nettie till the night before she run off, but then I felt that light and fever off her, like you and Lloyd did. Before I'd only seen it reflected on you'uns' faces . . . pale and stunned and wide-eyed like deer been caught dead-still in a car's headlights. Iry, you always had that look when you come out of the house them afternoons, bent on your ma's no-good chores. But one afternoon I seen ye comin back home totin frames and color weddin pictures and baby pictures all sticking out from under your little jacket. Lord, chile, you looked like the Devil stealin souls!" Jessie paused and laughed to herself; she still kept her head down.

Ira stared at the top of her head as if he hadn't heard a single word. He closed his eyes tightly, pinching the bony ridge along his nose as if his fingers could clench the pain of sudden memory, holding its writhing images in the hollow at each corner of his eyes, just out of sight. But he was remembering; he remembered. Pain split his skull open at his eyes, a hundred slithering cracks that circled the bone cave, and through each crack in his skull came a searing light— memories were illuminated, no longer shimmering chimeras, but flesh and bone.

"Right then I figured, ifn this chile's a devil, it's cause he's been goin home to pure hell! I followed ye there, Iry," she stopped and caught her breath. "Yes, I hung my griddle apron on the closest nail and slammed out of that diner, crossed the street, and run up them back stairs before you come round the corner, janglin them filched pictures and whistlin. Was it a secret whistle that told Nettie to look for ye?" Jessie stopped and for the first time raised her head to find Ira staring off in the distance, eyes dazed, their color changing from hazel to gray again, but a shining, luminous gray like quartz crystals. "Ah, chile . . . ," Jessie breathed and bit her lip, "it's come back to ye."

Nettie Sloan lay back deep in her quilts and feather coverlets, all soiled with ashes, black coffee, tobacco, and sweat. She did not recognize her son's peaked, curious face until he laid its cool, blade-like bones against her cheek. With great ceremony Ira then made ready for the presentation of this

day's gifts; he closed the damask curtains, propped his
mother up beneath great, dented pillows, locked the door
against the church women's bustling charity, and finally
peered beneath the bed, half expecting to find some troll-like
do-gooder assigned to this vital, albeit underhanded mission.
There was nothing under the bed but billowing dust every-
time Ira checked, but this dust had the suspicious look of
having been disturbed. Smiling broadly, Ira set each picture
on display: a photo of Miss Eugenia Crebbs beaming out at
her camera-bug sweetheart; an old-time snapshot in an oval
frame of Mr. and Mrs. Sol Eberhart, their sallow, elongated
faces set in tight-lipped smiles, Mrs. Eberhart's crooked grin
as if telling her husband jokes out of the side of her mouth
and he giggling into the stern white wings of his collar. On
the dresser Ira put matching pictures of the Burke sisters as
children. Even then the eldest had her no-nonsense and
brisk kindliness as she clenched a beach bucket and miniature shovel; her sister's face was obscured by a flurry of sand
as she dug with both hands. Behind them a wan, startled
mother looked down at their sand castle encroaching on her
bare toes. On the other side table Ira leaned a picture that
had, until recently, hung in the church fellowship hall. It
showed rows and rows of adolescent gap-toothed girls, the
Junior Choir, caught in the middle of a performance of
Handel's *Messiah*. There was one little boy in the back, his
head ducked down, mouth pursed fish-like as he struggled to
sing baritone without the telltale crack in his boyish voice.

Balancing herself on her elbows, Nettie Sloan sat up to
survey her newly decorated bedroom and the bright, false
faces of her visitors. Everywhere she looked was a laughing
face, infinitely mocking; and here, close to hers, was a small
face so consumed with a smile that it split the child's face,
lips a wide, bloody wound; she saw her son was scarred by

this brave, terrible smile that hurt if held too long. Even now his chin quivered, the smile falling slack, fatigued. *Don't,* she told him. *You don't have to smile that way, not for me, son.* But he beamed all the more broadly until his eyes were squinted shut. Then she saw he was sniggering, laughing at her like all the rest, staring out from the other side of a cool, implacable distance where everything was still, predictable, behind glass, caught forever by the camera, a box that stole one's soul. *You can take that smile off your face, Ira. Ease it off a little, like this.* With the back of her hand, the one with the thin gold band, she smoothed the smile away, as if it were an unsightly wrinkle in her child's brow. But he giggled, the scar across his face opened again, letting out his life's wind in laughing sounds—sweet, cooing gusts of breath. *No,* she said, slapping, staunching the air and blood that rushed from his mouth. Slapping and slapping until he wailed, hiccoughing. She saw the only way to close that wound in his face was to hold him tight, saving his breath; his sobs exploded against her bosom, rocking them both. And suddenly she was standing up, carrying him high on her wide shoulders, his feet balancing in the hollow of her hipbones like stirrups as she walked back and forth across the room, pounding her son on his back, shushing him with an old lullaby,

> Baby sails the silver sea
> Searching for the moon.

Soon he was snuffling softly, his small mouth blowing against the wet dent in her shoulder. Patting him, she still carried her son easily, though he was half her length and once in a while would slip from his bony perch, bare feet scraping against the floor. Nettie laughed and heaved him

higher, calling him her bag of feed, her Indian papoose and
hobo knapsack that she'd carry with her on her next wandering. Finally Ira was quiet. She sat down in her chair by the
window, balanced him on her knees, and began rolling a
cigarette. She made the usual thick cigarette for herself and
another long, thin one for her son. For a long while they said
nothing, each obscured from the other by spiraling clouds of
blue smoke.

But when she saw her son again, through the mist, he was
smiling and behind him a congregation of townsfolk
smirked, all with the same expectations that Nettie had
fought to stave off for years. Suddenly she grabbed Ira, shaking him so hard his teeth chattered. "Ira," she said, "Ira!"

"Ma'am?"

"What you want you don't always have to steal. Hear?
Hear?" She slapped his face back and forth. "I never raised a
son to steal . . ." Frantically, he scrambled down from her lap
as she slapped at the air near his head, only hitting him once
more, a resounding smack on the ear that sent him howling,
running out of the room, right past a thin, dark shadow that
was in the doorway. When he looked at her, eyes blurred
and swollen, he thought it was just another church woman,
and before he was caught up in her fussing, hateful arms he
was out the screen door and running to the river.

"You never raised no son a'tall, Nettie Sloan," Jessie
emerged from the other room. She had sent the church
women home long ago.

"No," Nettie did not turn around but began rolling another cigarette. "I expect you'll see to that now, Jessie
Walsh." Jessie said nothing and when Nettie at last turned
around, her eyes had this same gray and luminous lucidity
that was in Ira's eyes now as he listened.

"Her eyes were brimful of tears, Iry," Jessie was saying,

"Tears was spillin over and dousin out that cigarette she kept hangin from her mouth. And then she snuffed it out. 'I'll take this ash tray, ifn ye please, Miz Walsh. And them three print dresses, my books, and my skillets . . .' and then she fixed on me good and said, 'You know what I'm doin. Jist help me along with my bags.' When I made no move to help her pack she stood up and come over, took both my hands, leanin hard on me, and says, 'In God's name, Miz Walsh, won't you do right by me, and them?' So I helped her pack her pitiful few things and promised I'd ask some my migrant folk to come by for her at dawn next day. Meanwhile, I went back to the diner to fix you'uns up a strawberry-rhubarb pie, thinkin to tell Lloyd about Nettie when he came to pick up supper. When I told him, he jist laughed and said it was some notion she probably forgot the minute it was out of her haid. But, Iry, she was gone the next mornin. And it were never me told them migrants to come by for her. But she was gone jist the same! And when Sheriff Lloyd went after her, out to the migrant camp, they'd all moved on."

"Did they take her with them?"

"Damned ifn I know, Iry. But she was gone and we never heared a word till that note come two years later sayin she was marryin some miner out in Utah. But how she got way out in that wasteland or how she come to know migrants good enough for them to carry her with them . . ." Jessie paused, shaking her head.

"She knew ye," Ira said, but not unkindly. "She knew me and my father and half this town. I reckon she knew migrants."

"Yes, son, for Nettie we was all passin through." Jessie said nothing more for a long while. "Well, I best be gone," she stood up but seemed to wait on Ira. "Got to get to work before nightfall."

Ira nodded absently. He fiddled with his shelves, his back to her. Finally, when she was at the door, he said, voice muted, "I'm obliged, Jessie," and when she waved her hand and quickly put on her rain gear, Ira added, "It's you do all the healin here."

Jessie paused, waiting for him to continue, but Ira quickly occupied himself with clearing their coffee cups and cleaning his counter. With an air of disappointment Jessie turned to leave, "Evenin, Iry."

"I ain't forgot bout your boy Nate," Ira said. "I jist think you can help him more'n me. You're better at that."

"Ifn I was better, you think I'd trouble ye?" Jessie eyed him sorrowfully. "I reckon I did come for myself, then. Figured mebbe you'd care to help *me* ifn you couldn't see your way to Nate," she paused, then asked, "Come home for supper, Iry? We'll have us some catfish fresh-caught. Then after that we can go to that revival meetin they fixed up on my back forty. Then ifn my Nate does come like they said, you can leastways help me know what to do with him. Iry?"

"Well, Jessie, I got this chore that . . ."

"I'll not look for ye!" She was out the door, almost running, before he could tell her it was his graveyard chore that kept him from her. But he did not call after Jessie and sensed some relief to see her trudge down the steep, lush hillside. But when she disappeared around the bend Ira suddenly felt terribly isolated. Then a great weariness possessed him and he sat down heavily on his porch steps, leaning his head against a wooden pillar; its creak and sway reverberated through his skull. The clouds hung so low, his hilltop store was above them, shrouded and lost to all in a swirling, wet whiteness. Ira squinted against the rain, seeing no farther than the fog.

Suddenly Ira felt the porch pillar near him jerk upward as

the porch roof collapsed beneath the hurricane-like rains. Diving for the mud, Ira felt his wooden stairs bend and break under his weight. It was only another second before the whole porch collapsed. There, twanging eerily in the wind, sheaves of his corrugated tin roof shimmered down like shook foil. Porch and steps knelt beneath this burden, but the pillars poked up through the fallen tin like several crooked spines, fossilized mid-air.

"Sweet Jesus, that's one powerful rain!" After the first nauseous wave of horror Ira surrendered to his own desperate laughter as whirlwinds blew in through the door, gusting recklessly around the room, hurling bottles of cramp, cough, and gas-pain potions and dime-store bric-a-brac from their shelves like a hurricane. "Misery come due," Ira said and stopped laughing. Would his store hold? Without waiting to see Ira made his way over the porch debris and hurriedly stowed all his medicines, his framed degree, his few syringes and shiny instruments stolen from school labs. The groceries he left for marauding animals and their hungry looting after the storm. Already the store sagged under a foot of water. *High ground, ha! She won't last the night!*

He stamped around the store, his feet's rolling thunder muted by turgid water. His only gentle movement was in setting the medical supplies in his car's trunk. It seemed his car floated down the road as he drove, and he noted with a final surrender to laughter that the rains were heaviest upland; in the valleys the flood-level waters were contained by the Yellow River and its tributaries. Even the mill-town shanties he passed downhill from his store were intact; the farther down Ira drove, the less intense the storm, and at the bottom of his long hill he looked around to see the clouds clearing.

But he would not return tonight. There was a chore he

promised done, and nothing, not even mending his store's broken skeleton again, seemed as important as what he did now. Turning the car off familiar back roads, he came upon a slick asphalt highway stretching endlessly ahead. Ira picked up speed, passing the last familiar landmark without noticing. He knew only that he was traveling to the next county, to a shop that sold flowers. It might close before he got there, but it was the only place in three counties where he might find flowers fit to lay on his mother's and father's graves. His sworn chore: to find yellow roses, pale and warm and forgiving.

PART V

SIGNS

To judge from Quince's Mortuary, the way to heaven, which it zealously sought to align with its own pink marble steps and portico, was not straight and narrow but steep and wide. One couldn't walk into Quince's as he might another funeral home, a meek inheritor of this earth, but first must climb three dozen steps, each with scriptures carved on the high inset:

> *A man's steps are ordered by the Lord, how then can man understand his way?*
>
> *The foot tramples it, the feet of the poor, the steps of the needy.*

These were the inscriptions on the first and most effortless flights; but midway up and winded, one gripped another stern mourner in lieu of a banister, the stairs exhorting:

> *Thou wouldest number my steps, thou wouldest not keep watch over my sin.*

*Let the peoples renew their strength. Let us draw near
for judgment . . . whom victory meets at every step.*

Perhaps the somber architect willed these steps as a lesson in
spiritual ascension. His commandments in stone reminded
the flesh of its weakness, for every mourner was humbled.
Breathing through bared teeth, legs wobbling, handker-
chiefs drawn out from heaving bosoms, vest pockets, or the
heavy cuffs of wool sweaters—any dignity of entrance was
lost in a slavish sense of one's own mortality. Even piety, a
posture so like exhaustion in its rigid features and convulsing
eyes, was not preserved past the second flight.

The story was told of one dissolute old pallbearer giving
up the ghost and his end of the coffin, so that it shot out of
control like a hulking steel giant sledding down the steps.
Perhaps this was the origin of the town's maxim: "It is easier
for a sinner to enter heaven than a live man get up the
mortuary steps," or explained the often sullen and thug-like
strangers who served as pallbearers.

Townsfolk laid no blame on the present owner, Mr.
Ezekiel Quince; he was a cheerful and unprepossessing man,
not at all the sort one suspected of being a mortician, but
rather a mailman or modest civil servant. It was his great-
grandfather and great-grand-uncle who built this mausoleum,
as the silver plaque on the oak door informed each climber:

> *In 1863 Ezra and Amos Quince were the first civilian
> embalmers hired by President Jefferson Davis in the
> battle of Chickamauga during the Civil War.*

In 1858 when Ezra and Amos Quince were licensed to
practice their necessarily noble trade, Jordan County still
reeled beneath the wondrous weight of gold dust. Gold
hemmed the town round with railroads and hustled it and

herded its hillbillies into a sudden hospitality more naked than greedy. To the Quinces the gold rush intensified the daily sense of immortality that anyone in the business of death and bodily decrepitude never questions. It was rumored the capitol at Milledgeville might be moved northward, and consequently Amos planned to enter politics. They would be remembered, the Quince brothers assured one another; gold was the best embalmer. With these great expectations the Qunices commissioned Isham Fobb, well known for his courthouses in boomtown cities. Preoccupied with classical Greece, Isham Fobb borrowed its pillars and steps but none of its grace. His designs were much like a Roman's copy of a Greek statue: that beautiful face and fluid body reflecting the Grecian sense of immortality was, in Roman hands, never made more than human. The stone became coarse and tense; in the face was a brave barrenness betraying the Roman's poignant, physical sense of mortality. Surely with such influences Fobb's architecture belonged to a house of the dead.

In Jordan County there were some self-styled purists who refused these Roman parallels, saying Fobb's crude inspirations were a throwback to dim, primitive times; they placed Fobb somewhere soon after men wearied of dank caves but not after the ziggurats; and the only reason they allowed him that far was his slavish steps. Fobb's critics finally decided his architecture owed much to the Neanderthal period, when man for the first time had buried his dead, erecting narrow slabs—spirit-stones uniform in their grim watchfulness. Fobb's dazzling white pillars soon turned the rusty color of mud; the granite grew gray as a humid sky and the whole building seemed to brood, each pillar like some pagan god forever wrathful, heavy-browed, and earthbound.

Despite the criticism, or because of it, the Quince brothers never stinted in their mortuary's construction costs. Gold profiteering bought its sleek pink marble and granite slabs; slaves built it, step by step, and two years after its christening General William Tecumseh Sherman patroned it in his savage March to the Sea, leaving an army of dead that the Quinces might have called a windfall, had not all the corpses been gray-clad kin and they the first among them.

For several decades after the war their mortuary served as a boardinghouse for the soldiers' widows and orphans, and by the time Ezekiel Quince was born, it was a respectable landmark of the town's glorious past. Ezekiel Quince, tall, spry, and sweet-tempered, who even as a child remembered every date, incident, and anniversary as if mapped out in his mind, chose for himself the career of gentleman scholar; his passion was history—his own, his country's, or that of anyone who confided in him. The Quince family gently deflected him and he ended up with a mortician's license rather than a degree in genealogy. Townsfolk often called him Professor of the Family Tree, which flustered and privately pleased him. Personally, Ezekiel Quince greeted weary climbers at the top of his mortuary's steps. A consoling handshake and whispered confidences were his trademark and sometimes he half carried an elderly soul into the funeral chapel, apologizing profusely for his heat and prostration.

As if in further apologia, Quince's own additions to the mortuary—those back rooms where Jessie Walsh Sloan worked her cosmetic comforts, the barn-like tombstone factory in the backyard, and five acres littered with stone monuments—were haphazard and humble. Where the mortuary had steps, the tombstone factory had a gravel road, dirt floors, and an unhinged front door; and where the mortuary boasted pillars, Quince's backlot display of stone markers resembled a shabby army of squat stones, many slanting crazily against tree stumps and fences, supported only by matted crabgrass or blackberry brambles. The exhaustion and surrender of Quince's backyard seemed the merciful end to his ancestors' front porch and portico. It was in this backlot, amidst the earthly clutter of uncarved stone and wild growth, that folks gathered after the funerals; they wandered here a few unconscious moments, faces dazed and spent, like actors at the end of a play in which there was no epilogue, simply a swift curtain and dwindling human sounds: coughs, claps, and mute leave-taking. Perhaps Quince's mourners, like survivors in a tragic play, lingered backstage before returning to the world, as if freed from some inexorable plot—an ending that weights and shadows every action like the law of gravity. Death's gravity is then so close and unearthly there is that moment we do not feel it; at this instant we leave with our dead, long enough to accompany him on the first leg of his soul's journey. We travel farther than our imagination, past the cool beauty of black heavens. Our spirit might take us even farther, if not for the pull of this earth that calls us back. We return, not from fear but from pity. Earth, lonely for itself, longs for what is earthly in us; and before our last desertion we give ourselves up for burial, gratefully.

Ezekiel Quince's one vanity was in his marble sign, carved in Florentine style with stone flowers like scratches or vines throughout the lettering. It read "Quince's Monument Co." with a fancy arrow pointing to the far left where the barn stood, its mammoth wooden door hung open to reveal a cavernous view of the factory, as long as a tunnel and two stories high. One could barely make out the jagged mountains of marble and granite, gravel bags, sand, and lumber scaffolding, all guarded by stony angels and one meek lion lying down with a petrified lamb. Everywhere were smaller tombstones with inscriptions: "Our Baby" or "Died in Foreign Action," "Dearest Mother," "Beloved," or an outmoded "R.I.P."; some of the more elaborate monuments were etched with poems, scriptures, grievances, or the simple, private, and often inexplicable words of the dead. But most of the stones awaited specifics.

The dark, cool silence of the tombstone factory was occasionally broken by a whining diamond saw when Nate Walsh Sloan was at work, carving. But more often he was quiet as the factory itself. The only sound was the sudden scratching of gravel. Several yellow eyes shone out and the blackness took on shapes: languid, stretching wild cats that Quince let breed here, having found no earthly way to stop them. Draped over the white monuments like bunting, these mournful creatures served the same purpose as that grievous decoration—to scare away the irreverent. A thief or trickster who entered here felt scrambling cats tear at his legs, leap over his head, and swoop down like bats as they scurried to protect their litters. Screaming cats, then the kittens' strident mewing, and before the intruder dared another footstep, he was hushed by the gagging hiss of a wild mother. Anyone who had ever heard a death rattle was running for his life.

II

It was almost dark when Jessie reached Quince's. The thunderstorm had let up but the sky still glowered, clouds swelling so low their dark underbellies hung down to earth at the horizon, where heat lightning shimmered silently. Sweating and slipping inside her black slicker, Jessie trudged through the mud, fiddling with her keys to Quince's back rooms. Tonight there would be no company, no keening voices and breathed hymns through the parlor's old walls, no comforting murmur.

Tonight the buzzing diamond saw and languid cats not even bothering to guard their many litters told Jessie her son was working late in the tombstone factory.

"Evenin, Nate," she called out, making her way past the stones and litter toward the yellow light bulb burning in the back; as she came closer she could have closed her eyes and found Nate, for the thick storm of marble dust guided her to him. The whizzing saw kept Nate from hearing her entrance as he bent over a stone, bright sparks flying around his head like fireflies, sizzling the air, then blinking off into blackness when he finally heard her and shut off the saw. She touched his arm lightly, smiling. He nodded and shook himself from head to foot, splaying a fine white marble dust.

"Evenin," Jessie said. Nate wiped his face with a red flannel rag. He seemed somewhat irritated by her intrusion but the smile hung on his face unflinchingly. Jessie stared at him; the bright unfocused blue of his eyes reminded her of staring straight down into spring water and trying to fathom its source. "How you be, son?"

"Tolerable fine," he shrugged and turned back to his work, critical eyes going over the stone script. "Quince, he ain't around yet."

"No matter. I'm here to work on that Eula Cummings gal. Thought to find you here this morning when I come by. . . ." She paused a moment and at last he said, "Had things to tend to this morning."

"Well, I jist come in early to set Eula's hair this mornin . . . though sholy there won't be no crowd tonight at her funeral. Nate, mebbe you and me should go. . . ."

"And I got things to tend to tonight." The sound of his diamond saw dismissed her but she leaned over him and shouted, "You fixin to go to that revival?"

Nate did not answer and Jessie resigned herself to wait until he finished carving another line. Pretending to study his inscribing, she instead watched her son's face clenched in a furious concentration. There was something brutal in the way his eyes, his hands, and the noise of the saw worked together. Jessie broke off studying him and stared down at the pink marble stone. Suddenly she slapped him on the back. "Shut off that saw!" she yelled. "Off, I say!"

Nate glared at her, his eyes squinting against the bright sparks. Wearily he shut off the saw and straightened. "Ma," he said, almost pleading, "will you leave me be?"

"You pure-born boy," Jessie breathed, her eyes fixed on the tombstone. "Pure-born punishin angel boy . . ." She shook her head and pointed to the inscription.

Speckled shades of pink, gray, and charcoal, the stone bore Nate's broad, flowing script: "Eula Cummings 1935–1955" and beneath were the words from an old revival song:

This world is not my home
I'm just apassing through
If heaven's not my home
Then, Lord, what will I do?

"Ain't ye aimin to finish that song?" Jessie demanded.
"Why, no, guess you're begrudgin dead their due."
"Reckon even that was more'n she deserved."
"Ain't you heared bout that Eula?" Jessie asked quietly. "She's the one kilt herself."
"Well . . . she drownded, they say."

"Yellow River done baptized her, then," Nate said, but he did not smile.

"Shush up, Nate! We got to think kindly on her."

"Why?" Nate suddenly turned on Jessie, his face forlorn. "Why, Ma? When she never was kind to nobody. I know folks, so do you, that Eula Cummings kilt out of simple mean stinginess. Look at them sharecroppers all over her land . . . some of them spent their lives half dead under her!"

"We worked fields for folks like Eula Cummings, son," Jessie said. "That don't give us the right to damn them that's dead."

"You been away from the fields too long," Nate said scornfully and turned away from her. "You done settled in here like it's some heaven on earth and you jist don't remember how it is to be wanderin or lost."

"That ain't true," Jessie said softly.

"I remember, though. I didn't never forgit. And most people don't got the chance to forgit in the first place."

"Jist who we talkin bout, Nate Walsh? Ever time I talk to ye, seems like it ain't you but some crowd that I can't see. Lord, I swear the only thing I don't remember is the last time I got a pulse on ye. Ifn I been away from anythin too long, it's my son," and Jessie reached for him, but he backed off.

"That's too easy for ye," Nate said, nodding toward her outstretched arms. "You forgit and forgive so easy, like you jist fallin down before the very folks that wrong ye. I seen you do it all your life. But there ain't no judgment in fallin down before the Lord and beggin mercy, even ifn it's for other people—you still ain't facin judgment."

"I suppose *you're* facin judgment, Nate," Jessie said dryly.

"Leastways you see to it that some poor gal like Eula Cummings don't miss out bein on her knees before ye."

"She weren't no poor gal!" Nate cried. "You been far from the fields, you forgot and so you've forgiven. But me, I remember ever year I bent over, fallin on my face for mercy. . . ."

"You ain't picked enough to beg mercy, Nate. You been settled more than any of us."

"And I can't forgit because I still see folks like me, like the sharecroppers work the Cummings fields, like the migrants you got on your back property, like . . ."

"Your followers?" Jessie breathed and saw him flinch. "Yes, son, I ain't got so far from my own kind that they speak a foreign language. The migrants tell me you got some kind of church about ye." Jessie paused, her face fell into worn lines and angles as she sorrowfully asked, "Is it heavens on earth you're promisin them, Nate Walsh?"

"No," Nate said with sudden satisfaction, his smile securely hinged on his face. "It's jist the opposite."

"Then, son, I reckon a woman like Eula Cummings would be a fittin member of your congregation."

"Say what?"

"She was poor . . ." and when Nate made to protest, Jessie added, "poor in spirit. She never forgot or forgive. . . ."

"That's true," Nate nodded. "Especially her own hands."

"Especially her own self."

"What you talkin bout?" Nate demanded.

For a long while Jessie was silent, gauging her son's face, watching his smile waver, then reaffirm itself as he folded his arms across his broad chest. "Eula Cummings weren't no friend of mine," Jessie began, then smiled wryly. "Might say we didn't run in the same circles. But I can't lie, Eula was mean and miserly. She lived stingy and begrudged breath to anyone in the same room with her, even her poor ma. Eula jist mis- and half-treated her poor ma till Miz Cummings died for attention. But Eula, she suffered to death, too." Jessie paused and eyed Nate intently. "You know I worked over old Miz Cummings nigh on a year back . . . bout this same time?"

Nate shook his head, "No, I don't recollect carvin her stone."

"There weren't none," Jessie said. "Eula didn't ask it."

"You mean she saved her money," Nate commented, smiling.

"You gonna keep count of her sins?" Jessie said. "Cause you'll have to do some fast figurin to keep up with my story."

Nate smiled genuinely and gestured for his mother to continue.

"Yessir, one of my first beautifications was Ma Cummings. She were a pitiful little slip of a thing, worked like a nigger all her life, and used the earnins to spoil her gal Eula rotted. And to boot, Miz Cummings spared Eula any sorrow, even disallowed her to tend funerals. She'd advice Eula, 'Oh, I wouldn't go to that layin out ifn I was ye, honey. Jist convulsin and carryin on . . . nothun for a chile to see.' So that Eula never did learn to mourn others, and she a full-growed gal! Who'd spect the first funeral Eula would tend to was her own ma's!

"Yes, Miz Cummings passed of a sudden in the night, struck in the haid from cancer. Eula come in next mornin to do her usual early complainin and there's her ma, dead as a dodo! Well, Eula went right hysteric, sets in screamin like a hyena, and them eerie laughs ricocheted off the hills all down the holler. Postman finally toted her ma into town with his mail. Where was Eula? She plumb hightailed it to the nearest bootleg and near drunk herself stupid before we find her holed up in a hayloft, jist singin and moanin to the cows somethin pitiful. 'I ain't goin to no funeral!' she was wailin.

"Well, Mr. Quince come out her place and talked kindly to her bout the burial services, but she sit there on the sofa like a stone, and when he finished she says, 'Ma didn't leave nothun but hollow teeth . . . certain no burial insurance. You jist tend to it quick. I hear burnin's cheapest.' Mr. Quince told me he didn't know whether she was bein stingy or jist crazed, but he felt sorry over her state and told me, 'Don't linger over Miz Cummings. We'll put her away quiet, no funeral, like Miz Eula says.' Think on it, Nate! Eula wantin her ma burnt up like primitive days, like a human sacrifice. Laws a mercy, that's what she was her life long, I tells Quince; there's no need sacrificin her for eternity, too! That stirred me from the bottom. I went out to Eula Cummings' place and told her, 'I consider your ma a real challenge; you jist consider her my beautification practice.' Why, I didn't want Miz Cummings put away like some heathen! Burnt to a crisp and ashes scattered ever which a way. Eula says, 'What's this gonna put me out?' 'Lawsy, gal, I said nothun. It's my practice.' Then she up and says, 'Jist don't make too many mistakes, Miz Walsh. I don't want to have to see her ruint.' " Jessie laughed out loud suddenly, slapping her knee.

After a moment Nate laughed nervously. "Weren't her ma was ruint," he said and unexpectedly clapped his hands, laughing loudly. "Oh, weren't she a mean one!"

"Yessir, honey didn't melt in her mouth, that Eula," Jessie agreed, then hesitated, frowning. "Oh, but her ma was no bigger than a minute, lookin rickety and haggard when I laid her out. Face all gritted, too, like she's still feelin it all. Cancer of the haid, it snitches hair right out from the scalp, so Miz Cummings was bout bald, jist big tufts of hair in the back of her haid like mangy fur on a tomcat's been in a scrape, with big fistfuls all tore out. What hair I found I pincurled, but it was bristly with no wave. So I decided on a permanent, though I guess it didn't matter how long it lasted." Jessie laughed and ran on, "It was right hysterical at times to see. She'd trip me up cause when I'd be windin a bit of her hair real tight I'd catch her face twisted too, and I'd say, 'Oh, pardon me!'

"Now, it takes dead haids nigh on six hours to dry. When it come time to undo them pin curls they turned out real easy. Tight but tidy little waves in her thin hair. Still, I did worry over her havin no hair round the face. That bald trim round her face and tufts of hair in the middle of her haid, why, she looked like an old gentleman bald backwards!" Jessie stopped slyly, waiting for Nate to ask her to continue.

"Well?" he demanded, suddenly irritated.

She paused, somewhat bewildered by his tone; but then she decided to go on. "See, I felt a fool to find my beautification job so poor. Don't think me sacrilegious, Nate, but oh, it looked so pretty after I took Mr. Quince's pinkin shears to the back of Miz Cummings' haid, snipped off some soft curls, and used a smidgen of glue to stick them curls round her face—fluff round the face. And when Eula sees it before the funeral she marvels at the sight of her ma lookin so curly and quiet, like an old angel already in heaven."

"You reckon that's where she is?" Nate asked.

"Sholy nowheres else but in them mansions there," Jessie nodded firmly. "Well, Eula says, 'Oh, don't Ma look natural!' and starts in snufflin like a baby. Natural, hah! Miz Cummings never looked that easy when Eula had holt of her. 'Miz Walsh, you done yourself proud,' Eula says to me when she come round from her sobbin fit. I jist tells her it was that fluff around the face that made her ma so gentle and like an old angel stead of an old gentleman bald backwards. Eula looks at me strange and first I thought she was sly, cause when she talked it was all mixed up like that honey wasn't meltin in her mouth; but then I see she's gone off in her haid, woebegone and wailin over her ma. Got worse during the funeral. Was only me, Quince, and Eula payin respect to Miz Cummings, and Eula weren't like a real person with all her stranglin tears, so was jist me and Quince sayin last words over her ma. When we went to shut the coffin Eula sets in ravin like some hydrophobe, clawin and, at the grave, mad-dog diggin in the dirt. Pitifulest sight I ever did see." Jessie broke off, then sadly added, "Was that funeral kilt Eula. I knows it in my mind. There's some grief grows faster than any cancer and it eats you away. She give up her life to find her ma's forgiveness. So mebbe that river did baptize her, Nate, like ye said."

Nate gave her a dark look and shook his head. "Reckon she drowned."

"You, Nathaniel Walsh! Don't ye leave that song unfinished on Eula Cummings' gravestone! She may died a sinner in your mind, but you ain't no judge. The Lord don't let no one go to hell for grievin. Sorrow and seekin forgiveness ain't no sin."

"And what do you tell the folks she's sinned against, them people that starved and fell under her whilst she was off seekin her own forgiveness?" Nate demanded.

"Why, would it help them to know she's still sufferin, son . . . even now?"

"They know her soul's required in torment," Nate struggled with the words.

Jessie's face fell and she said in a hushed voice, "Mebbe, Nate, everyone is equal after they die. Now, wouldn't that be grace?"

"It ain't just."

"You'd never forgive the Lord's forgiveness, would ye?"

Nate said nothing, but looked down, his face rigid, listening, but not to her. His manner Jessie suddenly recognized as the most unendurable eagerness as he anticipated something terrible to tear him from his body, just for one moment, the twinkling of an eye. She had seen this look in those she loved as they leaned over her to lose themselves in her sickness or pain; she had watched it in her first lover as he bent over her, desirous and not shy, but as one surrenders himself to a beckoning abyss; and Jessie had seen this attitude in those mourners who, past any solace or tears, stood like soldiers with their knees locked and eyes dulled, but their bodies slightly swaying nearer and nearer to forgetting themselves until they were caught mid-fall, at the final moment when a workman began in earnest to heave fresh red earth over the coffin. It was this quality of perfect, all-divining attention, whose extreme end was a devastation like physical shock, that Jessie saw now in her son. "What is it, chile?" she gently shook him as one wakes a sleepwalker, watching the flecks in his eyes gather into bright clusters that blinked off like those sparks she had first seen as fireflies about his head.

Suddenly he returned her embrace, laying his head in the crook of her shoulder. "Ma," his voice was broken. "I ain't no prophet. Will the Lord forgive me that?"

"Forgive ye for waitin on Him, for bein lost and lissenin?" Jessie laughed softly. "I reckon that'll move God to mercy, son."

Nate now did something he hadn't done since childhood: stretching her hand out flat with his fingers, he laid her rough, cool palm over the crown of his head.

"Will *they* forgive ye, Nate? Your followers?"

He gently disengaged himself from her and sighed, "Yes'm

. . . you know their kind, poor and kin to disappointment. They'll take it like we used to pick fields: jist bend a little lower and move on to the next row."

"God moves 'em," Jessie said. "But you, son, what you movin to now?"

"I'll jist stay still," Nate said slowly. "Mebbe then I'll hear His voice."

"It don't take hearin voices to know when you got a call-in . . . when He's callin."

"God always gives some sign," Nate said.

"He give us the dead. Ain't that enough of a sign for ye?" Jessie nodded toward the marble stone.

Nate went to his workbench and picked up his diamond saw. Surely, and with great care, he carved the last two lines to the revival song on Eula Cummings' gravestone. When he straightened to show Jessie his handiwork she laid her hand on his back.

"Don't all this talk bout prophets and passin on make you hungry?" she suddenly asked. "I never got a better appetite than when I'm thinkin of them gone where they ain't got my fresh-caught catfish or strawberry-rhubarb pie. Reckon even Lloyd's up there in heaven complainin bout the food. Come home, Nate, and I'll fix ye supper."

"Much obliged . . . only . . ."

"Only you got followers waitin on ye?" Jessie frowned. "Son, let them wait."

"That revival tonight . . ." Nate broke off.

"Ifn ye want to go, Nate, I'll go with ye. I lent them revival folks my back property, but I usually don't give 'em a chance at me. Sides, honey, I can see sufferin ever day of my life."

"I'd be obliged to take supper with ye ifn you give me a lift over the tent afterwards," Nate said slowly.

Jessie smiled, "We'll go, boy. But we'll go with our bellies full, not so hollow as our souls." She laughed and took his arm to walk with him to the door. Jessie began humming a few bars of the old revival hymn, but Nate interrupted her.

"You reckon she found it? That Eula Cummings?"

"Heaven?"

"No, forgiveness."

"It flows like the river," Jessie said and took his hand so she would not stumble in the growing darkness. "Now walk me up to the back door, son."

They made their way through the stone debris and scattered tools of Quince's backlot and Jessie began humming again. Nate finally joined her on the chorus, "This world is not my home, I'm just apassing through, if heaven's not my home, then, Lord, what will I do?" Jessie's voice wavered between alto and melody; Nate's high and syncopated harmony wound between and through her sweet notes, adding dissonance. Struggling for breath, the two leaped over some fallen monuments and took up another verse, those last words Nate had inscribed on Eula's stone: "Those mansions wait for me on heaven's golden shore, and I ain't going to stay in this world anymore!"

"Well, Nate," Jessie said at the steps to Quince's back rooms. "I best see to Eula and you can finish up the fancy carvin on her stone. I'll look for ye at home soon."

She heard his voice as he left her to return to the factory shed, and she imagined the clarity of his song made even the stern pillars of the mortuary seem not stone, but luminous shafts of moonlight. She listened to her son making his way through Quince's backlot that was littered with marble flowers and statues leaning like saplings. And Jessie thought Nate now moved through a makeshift fantastical garden growing in the dark, as he found his way, singing.

III

When Nate finished carving Eula Cummings' tombstone he stood up to survey his work and was pleased. Glancing toward Quince's back rooms, Nate wondered if Jessie might still be there, and, if so, she should see how well the stone had come out. Lights were on in several of Quince's small chapels, but when Nate let himself in by the back door he saw Jessie's workroom was empty.

"She's gone home." Mr. Quince caught Nate as he was about to leave. "Boy, do you have a minute?"

"Them balanced books is on my desk, Mr. Quince."

"No, it ain't bidness." Quince took Nate's arm in the familiar way he had of asking favors. "I ain't never had to drum up mourners . . . ," Quince began, then sighed, "No use explainin, except to say that there's this couple heared you singin awhile back and asked me ifn you'd sing for their friend jist passed on."

"Jessie's waitin supper on me," Nate said and hurried down the hallway.

"I'm sorry to ask you, Nate," Quince spoke softly. "It's jist that there ain't nobody else to ask. I mean, if there was a few more people come to this woman's funeral, mebbe at least enough for a trio or a good quartet, but . . ."

"One song," Nate said and let himself be led into a deep, dim room.

Even with the merciful, wavering candlelight Nate knew he would see her well. Eula Cummings lay in the simplest coffin made—some might say the cheapest, Nate thought. But it was not the light that made Nate wonder if it were a different woman, nor was it the gentle veil of Jessie's handiwork—it was the way the old man and woman sitting in straight-back chairs near the coffin looked at Eula Cummings. Nate recognized the old couple, a brother and sister who had often attended his own meetings with the other Cummings sharecroppers.

Awkwardly, he nodded to them, and they returned his greeting silently. "Are there others comin?" Nate asked. "Because I'll wait."

The old gentleman's voice was very soft. "You know there ain't." He leaned over to his sister, who took his hand and gestured toward Nate. "My sister wants you to sing, boy," the man said. "Miz Cummings liked to hear singin."

Nate nodded and drew a sharp breath, then lifted his voice.

> Oh, Love that will not let me go,
> I rest my weary soul in thee. . . .

Nate's tenor was dissonant and disturbing, like an eerie descant to a missing melody. After a few more lines his voice no longer sounded incomplete, but separate and so pure that any harmony or accompaniment would corrupt the cool clarity of tone. Both old people listened as if Nate's song was another language unknown before this moment. Through his graceful translation, the couple seemed to understand at once his inner voice. Nate's song swept over them like a bracing wind; they leaned into his song as they had all their lives leaned on the constant wind that blew down the hollers and over the flat, unfertile lands of this high piedmont, so that when Nate suddenly faltered they both fell slightly forward, frightened at the unsupporting silence. But Nate began singing again, his voice full of sweet persuasion.

> I give thee back the life I owe
> That in thine ocean depths its flow

May richer, fuller be.
Oh, Love that will not let me go . . .

Suddenly a movement caught Nate's eye as the brother leaned slightly into his sister, whose head was bent low. Cupping her hand in his, the brother lightly spoke into her palm, his fingers dancing against the delicate, rounded ear that clasped each feeling word, hushing it as it struck her skin. Never before during all the sermons he'd given his small group had Nate noticed the old woman's deafness and her brother's interpreting. Now Nate thought perhaps these two had discovered that words led a separate life, for the old people held all sound inside, in silence distilling the spirit's sweet urgency.

Nate began singing more earnestly than before, his voice high and vibrant. "Oh, Love that will not let me go . . ." and he saw the old man's swift, silent translation into his deaf and dumb sister's hands. Nate imagined those sculpting hands held prophecies and secrets of the silent spirit world that Nate could see only in silhouette. For in the old brother's hands Nate saw his song take the shadow-shape of a bird, its wide wings fluttering as it built a nest in the woman's cupped hand. Gathering twigs, wildflowers, unwanted dust, and blades of grass, the bird made a high nesting place for its offspring, those messenger birds who would carry his song on to the highest heavens. Nate fell quiet at the end of the second verse, forgetting the chorus. Here the silhouette bird seemed to settle into its nest to silently wait for its children to grow wings.

But Nate was taken aback to see how the old couple now watched him, waiting. Hands knitted, fingers fraying his silken shirt cuffs in a rustling cadence, the old man shook his head tersely when his sister leaned against him. Her face was stricken and confused as he folded her dejected hand, covering it with his own. The sister did not understand why the song ended midstream. Again she nudged her brother, trying to free her hand from its cage, but he held her voice in his fist. Silenced, she desperately opened her useless mouth—a shivering oval forced out sounds in the mute's strangled tongue of croaks and guttural slurs.

She don't hear herself. Nate was glad deafness spared her. *She don't know her words are harsh and ugly, terrible to hear. Mebbe she believes she's singin wonderful sounds,* and suddenly Nate stopped, realizing, *But that's how we must sound to God, even our songs like ugly, imperfect imitations of words we've never heard, only guessed at their sound, like deaf mutes who can't even hear themselves, but still sing praises.*

"Shhh, sister!" her brother said. "Be still!"

Why, she ain't nothun but stillness! Nate thought and saw the old sister's bright countenance clench in shame as she bowed her head, silenced by her brother's eyes. Nate saw the old man drop hold of her hands. Suddenly the woman's hands beckoned the air to coax its music as if she played an invisible stringed instrument, making songs heard only in the high, pure world above human sound. *Like an old angel with fiddle or harp,* Nate smiled inwardly, watching her, *or mebbe a flute, a woodwind because of the way her mouth blows in and out, followin her fingers as they play, simple as breathin. Mebbe our soul is like this sister's invisible instrument in the air, like a wind instrument, our soul; it fills this body with breath and song and words, because that's all we got to give, and when the breath stops, why, then we can be still and know.*

Be still, suddenly Nate's blood seemed to pump to this two-word tempo. *Be still,* a hollow sound said, not an inner voice

but a shivering whisper like wind. *Be still.* The sound nour-
ished itself on Nate's held breath, rushing inside his head
until the sound bored a wide hole in his skull; then Nate
heard nothing but sound seeping inside his head, filling his
eyes with a cold blackness.

Where did it come from, this searing but chill sound that
filled his skull the way spring water fills a drinking gourd?
Without melody or color, the sound was transparent, consist-
ing only of movement: the soundless hush of drawn breaths,
the rapturous whispers of silk against the skin like rustling
wings—these were the only accompaniment to the vision
that emptied Nate's head of all except an austere and steadfast quiet. He only heard the pressure of a presence—a pressure like underwater silence. But where did it come from,
Nate wondered, this silence entering his body through the
skull and flowing downward through his bloodstream?
Nate's heartbeat slowed in reverence as if recognizing its
older rhythm. *Be still*, his blood sang, *and know.*

After a long while Nate opened his eyes. The room was a
blur of dark, contemplative colors, daubed with two white
faces that waited on him in infinite and humble stillness.
The woman's face was uplifted and her brother watched
Nate with a gentleness he usually reserved for his sister.
Don't they hear? Nate wondered. *Sholy she's heared me. She
ain't nothun but knowin stillness.*

But as he looked closer he saw they waited for him to
continue his song. Her hands lay limp, sorrowful, in her lap
and her brother's hands now seemed gnarled, knotted, as if
he had nothing to give her.

"Listen," Nate said. "Don't you hear?" and when he saw
the old man's bewilderment, Nate thought suddenly, *No,
they ain't heared . . . it's my call.* And without another
glance at them Nate fell to his knees and thanked the Lord

for this sign, this knowing stillness that he alone had heard and now must teach others who every day played their soul's wind instrument.

Yes, Nate prayed, *I been called. I been still. Now I know. And these signs shall follow me.* As Nate strode from the room he did not see the old man reach for his sister's flying hands to take up the song Nate had left unfinished.

Nate Walsh Sloan arrived at the back-woods cabin only an hour later than expected. When the door was opened the light illuminated a small circle of his followers: the Outpouring of the Latter Day Rain Church. "I been blessed," Nate said, almost weeping. "I heered that still small voice. . . ."

"Sing glory!"

"Hallelujah!"

A chorus of ringing praise echoed around him and someone took Nate's arm. "Let's show our thanks that we been chose to hear," a voice said and the small troupe streamed out of the shack, following Nate across the fields toward the brilliant lights of the revival tent.

THE MEETING

NOW IS THE TIME FOR
SIGNS, WONDERS, AND MIRACLES

read the wooden sign that pointed the cars and families on foot to the revival tent pitched by the Yellow River. Chameleon-like, the tent weathered this country's rainstorms by taking on its colors: canvas awash with rust-red soil and spirals of grass or pine-gum stains. By its familiar stale breaths the people recognized this tent as they would some old relative at a summer reunion. Streaming into the tent to fill the rows of straight chairs with bright sound, the crowd raised up a sawdust storm that reeked of rain and compost. Crisscrossing the tent's peaks were wire strands of yellow bulbs; painted with a thin coat of citronella, the lights oiled the air with a stringent lemon fragrance. Children watched their own shadows like long fingers interlocking across the tent's low ceiling; and women sang out welcomes to one another, their greetings lyrics to the piano's sharp, rhythmic prelude. Lingering just outside the tent flaps, many men smoked and at the last minute flicked their cigarettes out into the river to move down the aisle one step ahead of a marching, dark-robed choir.

The tent was full to overflowing. All faces were white, the blacks having held their own revival and foot-washing last month. There were many large families, look-alikes positioned in stairsteps from largest to small, the patriarch overlooking his clan, arms slung behind a wiry child's head as if in embrace or warning. Hushed, the congregation waited, a few children still creaking in their chairs or flapping the stick fans donated every year by Quince's Mortuary. The once crisp fans were now frayed and scrawled upon; the scene, a country church set in an oasis of palm trees and palmettos, was washed away by sweaty hands and tears until the sketch was so impressionistic and abstract most mistook it for a picture of the mortuary itself: palm trees were pillars and palmettos were those sharp steps.

Finally the preacher and his stewards arrived, stationing themselves at the tent's back flaps and at the front filling the choir's urgent need for tenors. The preacher, Brother Emmet Underhill from Savannah, was lanky and tall with a mutable face. He seemed startled, finding himself surrounded by people, and he searched the crowd as if for someone in particular. A woman raised the crowd to its feet with her hands, cued the pianist with her eyes, and with one voice the tent swelled into song.

> Lord! Send the Old Time Spirit
> That Pentecostal Spirit
> Thy sluice gates of Mercy on
> Us pour open wide . . .

They sang a swift two-four beat, the women's and children's high soprano hurtling up through the harmonies of the bass and old people's alto while a few men attempted the tenor part, unsurely hitting notes that carried no known melody, only a brave dissonance.

> Lord! Send the Old Time Spirit
> That Pentecostal Spirit
> Let sinners be forgiven and
> Thy name glorified!

"Jist screech owls, screechin to high heavens!" Ira Sloan muttered to himself as he hesitated outside the back tent flaps. A few deacons beckoned him inside but it was the singing that swept Ira into the tent, where he was lost in deep, ecstatic song from a multitude of voices, overflowing the tent sides, flooding across the back country to become a mournful melody, an echo more intimate to Ira or any native of this piedmont than the constant shushing sounds of the sea. Ira found a seat and braced himself against the sound by leaning on the chair in front of him.

Ira cursed himself for coming, but at the same time instinctively returned a townswoman's beaming welcome with a polite nod. Chagrined, he looked down to avoid any more greetings. *Leastways be good for bidness,* he told himself, then thought, *ifn I had a bidness left.* The image of his Yellow River Market flooded, broken by the storm that here in the valley had simply quenched the crops' thirst to give this crowd of farmers a night for rejoicing, made Ira feel like breaking the several hands now extended him; but to his surprise his own hands flew out to clasp the gnarled fingers of other men, the lithe, strong hands of a woman. They all seemed to recognize him, but Ira saw not one familiar face.

"Lawsy, it's Lloyd Sloan's son," an old man nudged his wife and she turned, her face breaking open.

"The spittin image," she breathed and pumped Ira's arm. "Like Lloyd's done come back to us."

"I been back a long time," Ira said and reached for a hymn book to avoid any more handshakes.

"We jist missed ye, son," the woman said and her face was so earnest that Ira found himself near smiling. He fumbled with his hymn book, though he knew the song well. But when he found his place, the organ was winding down and all music fell into flat murmurings from those in back, just finishing.

For the life of him, Ira could not figure out why he had come tonight. Driving home from the graveyard where he laid flowers on Lloyd's and Nettie's graves, Ira surprised himself by turning down a back road, driving at breakneck speed, and coming upon the brightly lit tent. Before he caught his breath he was slamming the car door and stalking up to the open flap, where he was able, just for an instant, to linger and demand of himself, *What am I doin here?* before that flood of voices bodily pulled him inside the tent like a singing undertow.

As the preacher called the crowd to prayer, Ira looked around, hoping to see Jessie or Nate, but he could not find them. It struck him that they might not come and he wondered if he could slip out the back unnoticed before the prayer ended. But when he turned to leave he saw a small knot of migrants who stood in the back of the tent though there were several empty chairs near Ira. With more curiosity than disdain, Ira eyed the migrants. These must be the gang Jessie let camp on her property every year, he thought, before her eldest settled sons moved them on down the road. Only one of the migrants returned Ira's stare, a sun-blackened fellow who, after a moment's hesitation, nodded, half-smiling. Surprised, Ira found himself returning the greeting, thinking that perhaps this man knew him from one of Jessie's convoluted stories of kin, both imagined and blood. Ira was struck with a certain pity to see how pleased this token of recognition made the migrant. But as if exhausted after so simple an exchange, the man's face fell slack and his eyes wandered evenly over the bent heads as if surveying a drought-stricken field.

"Come, Lord, to revive the hearts of the humble. . . ." Ira heard the preacher raise the pitch of his prayer, his voice easily carrying outside the tent. Without hearing the man's words, Ira listened to his voice, those familiar tones running deep and changeable with drastic inflections, now intimate and cooing, now flaring up into shouts—all punctuated by great sighs and gasps, as if preachers learned to breathe through a great bellows in the belly. By easing his air in and out, the preacher controlled his spirit, though the effort shook his body and once or twice snapped his spine. Without this rhythmic wheeze and repetition of "Glory!" or "Say Amen!" the preacher might never release the terrible wind inside, and would fall to the ground along with the many other worshippers who now kneeled in grateful, stammering oblivion. "Let the words of my mouth and the meditation of my heart be acceptable in Thy sight, O Lord, my strength and my redeemer. Amen!" the preacher sang out and the crowd's chorus of "Amen" struck Ira like a great wind. "The Spirit is movin here tonight," the preacher's voice was suddenly hushed. With a wide white rag he wiped his forehead and took his place near the altar.

The crowd, too, was hushed—those on their knees found their chairs again, children forgot to pick up their fans and leaned their heads against a father's shoulder, and everywhere people settled deeper into themselves, listening.

A woman stood up from the choir, smiled tentatively to

the pianist as she passed her on the way to the pulpit. With
no more introduction than a drawn breath, she sang:

> Oh! Had I the wings of the morning
> I'd fly away to Canaan's shore
> Bright angels should convey me home
> To the new Jerusalem . . .

She digressed into a deep, incantatory harmony that shivered on a withheld note; then she swallowed a moan, muted
it inside her throat, rolled it along her tongue, and spit it out,
letting it quiver up high as if air seared her lungs.

> Oh! Had I the wings of the morning
> I'd fly away . . .

The song went on forever, over many valleys, mountains,
and desert wildernesses, crying out until at last, hoarse and
weary, she gave up with one tremulous note that Ira thought
shimmered in the air like heat lightning.

At the end of her song, Ira had no desire to leave the tent.
There was in the crowd an inward and absolute attention
that Ira would not be the one to break. But suddenly from
the back of the tent came commotion: scuffling feet and a
muffled command.

"And these signs . . . ," a voice rang out, "these signs shall
follow them that believe!"

Ira turned to see the migrants shoved roughly aside as a
small group of people flowed into the aisle toward the altar.

"Brethren! I call you to prayer!" the preacher stepped to
the pulpit, gently moving the singer away. Behind him half
the choir fled their loft and the pianist struck up a hymn, its
soft rhythm distractingly familiar. "Every head bowed and

eye closed . . . ," the preacher commanded, but few obeyed. Most eyes were riveted on the moving assembly that now formed a circle in the front of the tent.

In the center of the group Nate Walsh Sloan stood on a wooden box. Around him his followers began a mournful, swaying song that the crowd instinctively fell into.

"Come, dear Lord . . ." the preacher's voice was desperate and his was the only head bowed as he gripped the podium, crying, "Revive the hearts of the humble!"

But his voice was drowned by the moving circle beneath him and suddenly the strident up-and-down, steel-string strum and twang of a guitar was punctuated with stomps and kicks against the wooden box that Nate stood upon. A woman ran her bare knuckles over a washboard, sharp bone against the shivering tin, but it was enough rhythm to move the crowd more deeply into the chant begun by the circle.

> Glory! Glory!
> Hallelujah
> Since I laid my burdens down
> Glory! Glory!

The whole tent took up the words and the preacher looked up from his pulpit, his eyes wide and bright; quickly he left the tent. But the pianist stayed, her hands flying over the keys in time to the crowd's movement.

"Be still," one voice rang out from the center of the circle. "Be still, I say!" Nate Walsh Sloan stood atop his wooden box, his face rigid, intensely pale, every expression and movement held in abeyance as if to give more power to his voice. " 'Canst thou draw out Leviathan with an hook?' " Nate exclaimed as he stepped down from the box and bent to unlatch the wire door. " 'Will he make many supplications

unto thee? Will he speak soft words unto thee?'" Slowly, in
one graceful motion, Nate felt inside the box, one stream of
sweat trickling down his cheek. "'Will he make a covenant
with thee? Wilt thou play with him as with a bird?'" Nate
stood up and all fell silent, except the dry, nervous rattle as
the thick coils of snake wound around Nate's arm. "'Lay
thine hand upon him, remember the battle, do no more,'" he
breathed, his voice trembling.

Nate's face fell into flat planes and his jaw hung open in
surrender to the feel of this serpent as it constricted, moving
up his arm like climbing a slender tree, winding, its head
almost touching its own delicate, skeletal rattle that whispered in hoarse and urgent hisses. The snake's head was
dented, dark nostrils like pinpricks, and its unblinking eyes
were gem-like, a hard, glassy obsidian. Tail and tongue
quivering, feeling for the moist sound of the boy's voice, the
satinback rattlesnake moved slowly, knotting its lengths
around his shoulder. Chanting fervently, Nate bent stiff-
backed to feel inside the wooden crate again. "'Who can
open the doors of his face? His teeth are terrible round
about. His scales are his pride; one is so near another that no
air can come between them. His eyes are like the eyelids of
the morning. In his neck remaineth strength, and sorrow is
turned into joy before him. When he raiseth himself, the
mighty are afraid; by reason of breakings they purify themselves. . . .'"

In Nate's hands was a snarl of snakes, all twisting in slow
motion, their slick, glistening skins braided together to make
one many-colored beast—a Leviathan, his tentacles circled
in high yellow bands, red and black rings, diamondback
mosaics, all studded with scales, coruscant layers like shimmering transparencies of mica. Suddenly the beast separated
into two coral snakes, a timber rattler, and a cottonmouth

water moccasin. Several unsteady hands reached out to take the snakes from Nate. Slithering through his open fingers, one coral snake glided into the hands of another man, whose face contorted into a mask of horror and detachment as if he were watching this snake twine around someone else's fingers, its iron lips narrowly open near another's eye, the fragile, forked tongue quiver in the warm air against a neighbor's ear. Each side of the snake's lower jaw moved separately, revealing tiny, hooked teeth on the bottom and two grooved fangs, the hollows of which held veins of poison.

Then Nate allowed the other snakes to slide over and coil around other believers, but he kept the lithe copperhead, its pale hourglass pattern of rust and earthen colors tightening around his wrist. Slowly the snake straightened itself, hanging down from his fingertips, then recoiled and slid upward, listening along the length of Nate's belly and breast to his vibrating heartbeat. With the large copperhead draped across his chest, Nate raised both his hands and began preaching, his voice soft and child-like, yet stronger than the moans and whimpers and praises of the other worshippers as they passed the snakes from hand to hand.

" 'He maketh a path to shine after him; upon earth there is not his like who is made without fear. He beholdeth all high things; he is king over all the children of pride.' Yes, dear sisters and brothers in the spirit, this snake is the descendant of Leviathan. This snake is God's first-loved creation, his spirit-creature," and then Nate began to tell this story:

Even in the beginning the snake was God's most spiritual creature; perhaps he was a fallen angel, for it is said that all living things, except the wise serpent, bowed down in awe and reverence when first they beheld the still-shining creations of man and woman. Their skins were sleek, dark as potter's clay, and glistening from God's sculpting touch. The

woman, more angular and thin, was made of bone; the man's
flesh was rounded out, cool as the evening earth. But, humbled by their own beauty and innocent of all need, they
forbade the animals' homage and asked that the creatures
join with them in worshipping the Creator. To reward this
grace, God sent His angels down to exalt and rejoice in the
humans; all angels came for the celebration, all but the en-
vious serpent, who refused to worship man. For this dis-
obedience God expelled the serpent from among His companions, His first circle.

In his earthly exile, the serpent was not as we know him, a
low thing of the dust and brambles, stealthy and shunning
all intimacy; then he walked in comeliness, his lithe limbs
barely touching the ground as he explored the new paradise.
Though it was lush, resplendent with every beast and land
imaginable, it was not the world he longed for—that realm
so suffused with God's presence, the air shimmered like
lightning and His night's feeling dark was infinite, still as the
soul. The serpent saw earth's sunlight as shade and its black
sky's silence was broken by white-hot stars, curiously crack-
ling. As he wandered through this earthly garden, oblivious
to the caress of fern or forest, the salty sting of the sea smell,
or the kindly animal eyes that watched him pass, he was
shrouded in his eternal longings. The serpent remembered
his ancestors, God's first creations—Leviathan, the sea-
serpent, or Behemoth, that great beast that it is written will
devour the world; they had satisfied the Creator for so many
millions of years, before man or woman.

Perhaps it was the forsaken serpent's way of redeeming
himself, his lost world, when he offered to be God's messenger. "From my long exile, I am familiar with earth," he
argued plaintively, "I know human speech and habits; yet
they do not know me, for I have never worshipped them as

do other creatures, and they did not name me." Perhaps God entrusted the serpent with such a grave task because He knew if He came to earth, His glory would so obscure the message, the humans would accept it unthinkingly. Perhaps, too, He had missed the serpent's companionship and counsel. So He sent this spirit-creature, his first-beloved creation, with this message:

In the garden are two trees; wondrous and benevolent, they bear strange fruit. Here is the Tree of Life, its fruit will grant you immortality, that eternity I always had in mind for you, so that you might be always with Me, even unto the ends of this earth. This is why I have created you, to dwell within Me and I in you, forever. But here is the Tree of Death, the tree of the knowledge of good and evil. Do not eat of it, for that day you will surely know death and will forever confer its fruit upon your children. Choose which you will eat in remembrance of Me.

Why did the serpent, wise and wishing forgiveness, not deliver this message? Perhaps because when the serpent returned to God's shining realm, he was blinded by the dazzling light and the deep stillness. For upon returning with his message to earth's sudden green shade, her caves and dark valleys, the fiery firmament, even Eve's delicate, wandering songs in the cool mornings—this bountiful, bright world cast its spell over the serpent. Deep in love, he embraced the earth's round body, but jealously. If God forgave him as reward for delivering His message, the serpent would forever have to share this paradise with man and woman. When Eve came upon him encircling the wide world, biting his own tail, possessive and protective of his beloved earth, the serpent beguiled her with his broken speech.

In mortality, he said, is knowledge. Eat of this Tree and you will know more than your Creator, for even He is not intimate with death. In mortality you will find those companionable shades, Good and Evil; forever they will vie for your soul and you will be blessed with many gods, tongues, and fates, soon forgetting the simple oneness you know here. Eat then, be separate, and see how all light casts shadows. And Eve did eat with Adam from this unholy Tree. But the wily serpent slithered over to the Tree of Life, feasting on its luscious, ripe fruit—a taste of sweet melons and strawberries and tart apples; its juice was cool, honeyed, and quenched the serpent's eternal thirst, like spring water. As soon as the snake did eat of this Tree, he felt his body tremble, skin crinkling into a dry chrysalid that sloughed off as he ran, the golden second skin catching on trees and brambles. But he felt no pain, only a freedom of movement and a chaste nakedness. Shining through the tears in his old skin and wonderful to behold, the serpent saw his new body, flushed and untouched as a newborn's. "On your belly you shall go, and dust you shall eat all the days of your life!" This curse was all the serpent heard before his mouth grew thick with earth and sharp scales pierced his soft belly. The ground seemed to slide beneath him, pulling him along lengthwise, and his embrace of this earth was never again broken.

As the serpent moved he saw bits and tatters of his old skin, that heavenly body now shed. Glimpsing his lost, angelic form, the serpent cried out in his shame and triumph, "But I am immortal! Forever will I haunt this earth with the remembrance of my first purity, the righteousness and beauty before man when I was God's own Leviathan, his strength and servant, and His messenger who waits on Him still, and on His new creatures."

"Yes, sisters and brothers, this snake is God's messenger," Nate finished by pulling the copperhead off his shoulder and holding its head directly in front of his face. Quivering, its tongue felt for the boy's warm words, moving in and out of the snake's narrow mouth as if secreting the message inside. "He is everywhere in this world. Lightning is a celestial rain serpent, rivers snake their luminous lengths to the sea that holds this world in watery embrace; some people even used to think their ancestors came back to this world as snakes, guardians to carry God's messages. We must send the message, 'We accept!' I say, brethren and believers here tonight, don't we accept that fruit the serpent stole from us? When we take up serpents we command it to give back our birthright, to carry back to God this message, 'Yes, I believe I was made of the earth's elements, dust and clay and God's fire, made not to return to earth in spirit. But my body has eaten of the Tree of Death and knows the shadows and valleys far from God's light. Yet will I return to thee, O Lord, my fate and my preserver!' " Nate held the snake close to his lips and very quietly kissed that iron mouth, its tongue slithering out to hear the boy's warm, humid breath. Then Nate wrapped the limp snake around his head like a brightly colored crown. Transfixed, he threw back his head. "He will carry the message," and the snake's head bobbed up and down, tongue listening to the air.

"Ahnazanahanna . . . zalahzana . . . thalanazzna!" a man shrieked in tongues as tremors shuddered up and down his body, playing him like a reed instrument.

"Yes, work it through, brother!"

"Naanaazahahnaza . . . !" The man's face was a convulsive, bruised color, mouth screwed up in a painful pout before his tongue began wobbling around his teeth, slobbering out sounds.

"Glory!"

"Sing Hallelujah!"

People pressed in from all sides. Nate held out his hands, and they let more snakes slither up both his arms, coil around his ankles and hands until all snakes but one were wound around his body. Nate stepped forward, his eye on the woman in front of him who now held the great rattlesnake. *Yes, and the snake still hears,* Nate thought sadly, seeing the serpent's tongue catch the air around it, its body listening to the woman's shuddering woes and longings, her blood shouting out with each heartbeat, a surrender of secrets. The woman's face grew tender, musing, as if she held a child in her hand. "Shhhh," she whispered something to the snake and it swallowed, tasting her words. Nate thought the woman beheld another world, for her face was so radiant, and yet stricken, as if she alone sensed the beauty of this world or the divine sorrow at its heart.

"Sister," he said to her, holding out his hands, his lips quivering. She let go of the snake and it slithered effortlessly into Nate's waiting fingers; a lighter weight than he expected, the snake hung down from his hands like a living rope.

Calm. A swift, senseless calm; numb shivers started at his feet and raced up to shatter inside his skull. Was this the anointing? Nate wondered. All noise was muted as the snake moved up his arms and shoulders, then coiled, constricting around his face like long, cold hands clamped against the hollow of his temples, holding him in this harsh and wondering calm, like that hush accompanying a stillborn child. This calm tightened his head and screwed it down to his backbone, then drove his spine like a stake in the earth; his feet were the fragile, dead nerve shoots shoved deep in the ground.

Now no one could see Nate's face, wrapped round with the rattler's leather ropes, but the boy's eyes were closed and he struggled not to scream. He thought the snake was boring a hole inside his head, entering as had that first blackness, but this time the dark hissed in his ears, infinitely mocking.

Ira Sloan had finally pushed his way through the crowd to his kinsman, near enough to touch Nate; but Ira held back in horror. Swaying again, the crowd abandoned itself to a surging song praising Nate. Many people fell to the floor, tongues again gagging out gibberish. Only Ira saw Nate's neck slick with sweat or tears, his fingers clenching and unclenching, his legs begin to buckle as he tried to stumble forward, one arm completely coiled round with the coral snake's red, yellow, and black bracelets as he blindly grasped empty air.

"My God!" Ira breathed. "God help him . . ." and he felt himself move forward, then fall back again as the crowd circled Nate. A burly man almost toppled Nate as he fell forward, but the man caught himself just at the last moment, steadied by a neighbor. At first Ira thought the man falling with fits, but then he saw it was Jessie and the migrant Ira had first seen in the back of the revival tent, pushing people out of the way as they came toward Ira. Jessie shook him violently, unable to speak, but her mouth opened and closed, shaping words. "Iry!" Jessie made the one word, but the rest she said with her eyes—lidless, black, they beseeched him; like snake eyes, Ira thought and shivered inwardly. He reached out for her, to steady her, but she was already in motion toward Nate, who, at the sound of her voice, was stumbling forward, shuffling as a snake caught around his pants cuff. The angry copperhead struck so quickly Ira was not sure it had even moved, but the boy cried out, blood spurting from the wide artery in his wrist.

Jessie caught him as he bent over in pain and held him at the shoulders as the hissing snakes coiled and uncoiled at his foot, his face, his arm. Deftly, Jessie rested the bulk of his body against her shoulder and worked with both hands to tear the fangs from his wrist. Holding the serpent by its head, fingers clenched just behind its open jaw, Jessie raised the snake its full length and slammed it against the nearby pulpit. The resounding slap of its snapped spine echoed through the whole tent like a whiplash. Nate sobbed with pain, a muffled whimper barely audible through the snake's embrace of his round face. "Be still!" Jessie grabbed Nate by the back of his neck as she had the snake and slowly, painstakingly uncoiled the rattlesnake from his face, exposing Nate's eyes—white, pupils rolled back, unconscious; yet tears still gushed from those twitching, pale orbs. Already Nate's arm was swelling. Jessie grabbed the only tourniquet she could find, the dead snake, and knotted it around Nate's upper arm like a rope to cut off the streaming blood. "Ira Sloan?" she said firmly and Ira stepped so near her and the snake-encircled boy he felt warm blood splatter his face. Jessie gave him the snake from around Nate's head and Ira stood very still, hands outstretched as she unraveled the long coral snake and gently laid it in Ira's hand so that now he held a convulsing mass of snakeskin. "Run! Git them from here!"

"Wait . . . ," Ira warned her, daring not to move his head or hands to point at the last coral snake now uncoiling around Nate's ankle, darting toward Jessie's foot. It struck before Ira finished his one-word warning. Surprised and with an angry kick, Jessie tore its fangs from her bare ankle. Forgetting for a minute the snakes in his hands, Ira stared at her mud-splattered ankle, the blackened skin streaked with bright blood.

Someone slammed the wooden box down by Ira's own foot and he came back to his senses, dropping the snarl of snakes into their cage. Limping, Jessie dragged Nate to a corner and gently laid him on the floor. She made a better tourniquet from the hem of her long skirt and with this same gay, quilted material wrapped a bandage around his wrist.

"We don't believe in no doctors," someone ventured in a small voice.

"That's good, cause there ain't none around," someone else said.

Already some of the crowd had disappeared, a few of the migrants hovering still around Jessie. She shooed them away.

"You got anything for him, son, a potion?" Jessie's voice was shaking, and Ira saw her grind her heel into the dirt floor to staunch the pain and slow blood.

"No'm, I sholy don't. . . ." Ira knelt to cover her ankle with the palm of his hand, noticing the skin was callused and cold. The fang marks made bruised punctures in her ankle and it was already swollen twice its size.

When Ira looked up at Jessie's face he could see her eyes rolling back; she shook her head, biting her lip, but still gave way to unconsciousness. "Git away!" Ira demanded as a few people tried to help. Nearby, Nate's body began convulsing terribly and Ira left Jessie to some of the women while he and the migrant men worked to hold Nate down—a belt wedged between the boy's teeth, a man to weight down each arm, and Ira holding his jerking head—as Nate gave way to fit after fit from the powerful poisons in his blood. When there was a lull in his seizures and Nate lay spent, Ira felt his pulse and his sweat-dampened brow, surprised to see his stepbrother open his eyes.

"Good," Ira soothed as Nate tried to swallow some coffee fetched for him. "Now, try to be still inside." Ira watched Nate nod wearily, holding his arms rigid at his sides as if to clench any coming convulsions. "Good boy," Ira whispered and turned anxiously to see about Jessie.

Pure-born boy, I call him, Jessie thought from the depths of her coma; in her inward eye she watched them; Nate was lying so near she heard his troubled breathing like the child she had held close so many times; and this other child, born of her spirit, whose face was so like his father's, as Ira waited above her, weeping.

Jessie felt no pain or separation from her flesh and blood and beloved. She turned to Nate and in her mind laid cool hands across his cheeks, cleansing his fever. Then she held Nate's wrist until the swelling ceased and she heard his breaths come steadily. Reaching out, she blessed Ira, who was now gently shaking her by the shoulders, calling her name. *Iry,* she whispered from the dark depths of her cool, silent world; *chile, we both runnin to that river now. I stayed my spell, now I'll be on by. I got spirit-kin waitin on me, Lloyd and Nettie and someday more; we be wanderin still, seekin after forgiveness that flows, Lord, it's floodin over, like your river.*

EPILOGUE

Ira Sloan watched over his kinspeople all night. He and several of the migrants held Nate's writhing body, Ira knitting his hands together over Nate's skull as if this hold could keep the boy's chest, legs, and arms from their convulsive dance. But Jessie lay still in a circle of hunched and broad-backed women who begged each breath from her, their hands moving as if to bathe her body with the cool, rain-cleansed air.

All night it seemed to Ira that the women concentrated on a different part of Jessie—first her stricken ankle, massaging her limbs, then the belly, sunken and breathing shallowly, and on up her body, following the paralysis and the bruised swelling—until now they, too, cupped her head. Thin and dark, wrinkled as a newborn's, Jessie's face was not the one Ira knew. Still, he rested his eyes on her, and every moment he had free from Nate's fits, Ira helped the women ease his stepmother.

Sometime when the new light was not yet bright but spacious, Ira turned to find Jessie shrouded in the women's shawls and striped skirts—a gay, fanciful comforter that rose and fell over the valleys and hills in her quiet body.

"Rest her, Lord," a migrant said.

Nate's head now felt hollow in Ira's hands—*to lift up this skull and smash it against the ground, break it open like a water gourd and let spill the blood that was hers!*—but Ira felt his hold on Nate become all the more gentle and he bent over his stepbrother as the women began keening, one voice above them, soothing and rushing higher, singing a syncopated descant to the mournful lullaby.

> Out of my bondage, sorrow, and night
> Jesus, I come
> My Jesus, I come
> Out of the darkness into the light
> Jesus, I come to thee

"Oh, but listen," a woman touched Ira's bent head. "Nate, he's come through."

Ira stiffened and looked down at his stepbrother's blanched face. Nate blinked several times and tried to rub his fists in his eyes, but found that his hands were tied down. A look of desperation spread over Nate's face and the migrants motioned to one another to let him alone.

"Shhhh, boy, now you can move free."

But the look of panic did not leave Nate's face as he searched the people, only a few of whom he recognized as his own.

"Sing glory!" one of them said.

"By these signs," another cried. "Lord's called him with this killin cure!"

"He's come through!"

"Ain't she?" Ira beseeched them.

With a look of horror Nate searched the open space and his eyes at last settled on the circle that embraced the colorful shroud of his mother.

"Nate," Ira breathed and leaned down to support his stepbrother's shoulders. "She's gone." And he felt Nate's body shuddering against another fit.

"No!" Nate cried, his eyes flying upward.

"Shhhh, boy," Ira held him.

"No!"

It took all the migrants to keep Nate down, but it was not a fit that took him, for Nate struggled now not against his own body, but against those who held him. When they at last subdued him, Nate looked at Ira, his eyes searing. "It weren't her call," Nate said quietly. "I was knowin stillness; I served, but the Lord took her to glory." And the boy began weeping.

Ira straightened, "Call his kin."

"Ain't that ye?" one of the migrants said.

For a long while Ira stared at the ground, then nodded.

A man hesitantly touched him. "Your ma was mighty kind on usn," he said.

Ira looked at him for so long that the man shifted uneasily and dropped his eyes. "Well, we be movin on soon's as your other folks come to help with her layin out."

Ira grabbed the man, "You know her good?"

"Your ma?"

For a split second Ira paused, then nodded, his face pained and weary. "Yes . . . Jessie."

"She come round and told us stories ever night after supper," the migrant's face brightened. "Lord, but that woman must know more bout heaven, because she sholy knowed this earth all over!"

"Will you take me with ye?" Ira asked suddenly, still gripping the man's arm.

Stunned, the migrant slowly disengaged himself from Ira's grasp. He shook his head, perplexed, but could not help look Ira over, his lithe and lean body already stooped. "What about your kinfolks here?" the migrant nodded to Nate, who still wept, arms clenched about himself, a knot of followers hovering near.

"He's got family left . . . God help him," Ira said. "Please . . . let me follow you."

"You Jessie's son . . . ," the migrant began, and again Ira did not correct him, but waited. "Reckon you done picked your weight alongside her." The man turned and strode outside the tent, but Ira held back a moment, listening to the sounds of sorrow and singing around him. Then he saw the migrant beckon him from across the river to follow.

A NOTE ON THE TYPE

The text of this book was set in Caledonia, a typeface originally designed by W. A. Dwiggins. It belongs to the family of printing types called "modern faces" by printers—a term used to mark the change in style of type letters that occurred about 1800. Caledonia borders on the general design of Scotch Modern but is more freely drawn than this letter.